PRAISE FOR DEBORAH LEVISON

"*A Novel Crime* is a tongue-in-cheek tale of what happens when an aspiring author of bodice rippers decides to blackmail a famous author into writing her a bestseller. Humor and intrigue fly in this one as Marcy Jo Codburn, aka Summer Branigan, sets out to deceive and cajole her way into the big time. A fun, breezy read packed with drama and tabloid-worthy conniving."

—Gregg Hurwitz, *New York Times* and #1 internationally bestselling author of the *Orphan X* series

"Uproariously funny, exquisitely unputdownable, and ingeniously plotted with a heroine you'll be rooting for every step of her wildly hilarious journey, Deborah Levison's *A Novel Crime* is the perfect delicious escape!"

—May Cobb, bestselling author of *The Hunting Wives*

"Wickedly hilarious and utterly compelling, *A Novel Crime* is a delight. I was entranced and in stitches following the very endearing and imaginative heroine as she chases success while entangling herself in a heap of crimes. A refreshingly bold, highly addictive, and uproarious suspense that showcases Deborah Levison's phenomenal talent and warns us all how quickly we can cross the line from fantasy into a nightmare."

—Samantha M. Bailey, *USA Today* and #1 internationally bestselling author of *Hello, Juliet*

I0805908

"Levison nailed it in *A Novel Crime*. It's totally bingeworthy. Struggling romance writer Marcy Jo Codburn wants nothing more than to publish her novel and make her daughter proud, but how far is she willing to go to achieve bestseller status? When a fluke encounter with a celebrity author presents an opportunity to cut the line, Marcy casts her morals aside and seizes her chance. What follows is a mesmerizing downward spiral that ultimately leads to murder, every twist of which is delivered with tightrope tension and razor-sharp wit. Fans of Finlay Donovan and *Yellowface* will love this crime caper, and readers of all stripes won't soon forget Marcy's wild rise to the top."

—Tessa Wegert, author of *In the Bones*

"*A Novel Crime* is a fast, funny, utterly unputdownable romp through the wild world of publishing—where ambition meets chaos, and nothing goes according to plan. When Marcy Jo Codburn decides it's her turn to be famous, she launches a scheme involving a bestselling mentor, A-list celebrities, and a whole lot of trouble. Levison packs this novel with jaw-dropping twists, a mind-blowing plot, and an ending you'll be texting your friends about."

—Elise Hart Kipness, *USA Today* bestselling author of *Close Call*

"Wickedly funny, deliciously dark, and razor-sharp in its skewering of literary ambition, *A Novel Crime* is an absolute triumph. Deborah Levison spins a tale of envy, duplicity, and desperate reinvention that crackles with wit and menace. You'll laugh, you'll gasp, and you'll devour every page of this sly, twisted thrill ride. A dazzlingly original thriller that proves in publishing—as in life—there's nothing more dangerous than a writer with everything to lose. Levison turns literary envy into lethal entertainment. *A Novel Crime* is biting, brilliant, and impossible to put down."

—Steve Urszenyi, author of the Alex Martel series, including *Blood Oath*

"Deftly plotted with jaw-dropping twists and a deliciously dark turn that will leave you breathless. When aspiring author Marcy kicks down the door to her publishing future, there's no coming back. Deception, desperation, and duplicity combine for a thrill ride you won't soon forget."

—James L'Etoile, award-winning author of the Detective Emily Hunter series and the Detective Nathan Parker series

"*A Novel Crime* is a witty, engaging, beautifully paced nail-biter that channels a disarming narrative voice to deftly explore themes of artistic ambition, morality, female empowerment, and familial love. Deborah Levison has whipped up a true winner!"

—Elizabeth McCullough Keenan and Greg Wands, internationally bestselling authors of *Trust Issues*

"Aspiring to success (and the temptation to do whatever it takes to get there) is akin to breathing for an author. Stir in humor and creative twists and born is author Deborah Levison's *A Novel Crime*. It's a must-read for readers *and* writers, as both will delight in this cavalcade of crime, deception, and misbehavior."

—Luca DiMatteo, author of *Green Haven*

"*A Novel Crime* is veteran thriller author Deborah Levison's latest gift to readers. You won't be able to put this one down. From the first page to the last, Levison keeps her audience engaged and wanting more. A first-class work of fiction from a writer at the top of her game."

—Wendy Whitman, former Court TV executive, Nancy Grace producer, and author of the Deer Killer series

"*A Novel Crime* is cringey, gripping, and absolutely hilarious. Marcy has been working on the same novel for years. She put her ex-husband's creative work before her own. When her grown-up daughter starts to make life choices that Marcy believes will lead her on the same self-negating path, there's no more time to waste. If she's going to convince her daughter not to make the same mistakes she did, she must finish her novel and get it published. After witnessing her favorite bestselling author in a compromising position, the fun and frenzy begin. Marcy embodies Summer, her pen name and her charismatic alter ego who will do whatever it takes to become not just a published author but a bestselling one. Levison mixes humor and horror to make this a creepy psychological thriller you won't be able to turn away from."

—T. M. Dunn, author of *Her Father's Daughter*

"In *A Novel Crime*, the lines between right and wrong blur in a story that's as unpredictable as it is intriguing. With a cast of characters you won't soon forget, each chapter unfolds with unexpected twists that keep you guessing. At the heart of it all is a premise that's fresh and full of possibilities, offering just the right amount of suspense and mystery. Whether it's the charming characters or the surprising turns of the plot, *A Novel Crime* invites readers to dive in and discover something new with every page."

—Desmond P. Ryan, author of the series A Pint of Trouble

"Marcy has dreamed of being an author since she was a child. Not just any author, but a published, bestselling Pulitzer Prize–winning author with movie deals. Now that her husband has left her and her daughter is heading off to college, Marcy is desperate for success. Full of raw envy, humor, and jaw-dropping twists, *A Novel Crime* sends Marcy stumbling down a path of no return in pursuit of her illusive desire."

—Sharon Dukett, author of *The Shutdown List*

A NOVEL CRIME

OTHER TITLES BY DEBORAH LEVISON

A Nest of Snakes

The Crate: A Story of War, a Murder, and Justice

A NOVEL CRIME

Deborah Levison

THOMAS & MERCER

This is a work of fiction. Names, characters, organizations, places, events, and incidents are either products of the author's imagination or are used fictitiously. Otherwise, any resemblance to actual persons, living or dead, is purely coincidental.

Published by Thomas & Mercer, Seattle
www.apub.com

EU product safety contact:
Amazon Media EU S. à r.l.
38, avenue John F. Kennedy, L-1855 Luxembourg
amazonpublishing-gpsr@amazon.com

ISBN-13: 9781662532061 (paperback)
ISBN-13: 9781662532054 (digital)

Cover design and illustration by Kimberly Glyder

Printed in the United States of America

To my family, with love

PROLOGUE

Version Sixteen:

"What do you mean by this, good ser?" Lady Lisbeth asked huskily. Her breath caught in her throat.

"I mean to disrobe you." In between sensuous, slow kisses, Sir Devon slid her ruffled silk gown off her shoulders and reached behind her back to deftly unhook the corset. He pushed the whole contraption down to her waist and let his eyes sweep her alabaster breasts with their rosy pink peaks. "You are more beautiful than anything I've ever imagined."

Lady Lisbeth shivered with delicious tension.

"Now I want to touch you." His voice dropped to a growl. "Will you allow it, m'lady?"

"I will," Lady Lisbeth said ~~greedily~~ ~~uncertainly~~ demurely.

Sir Devon caressed her, and when at long last his long fingers finally surrounded the quivering rosettes, Lady Lisbeth gasped and threw her head back on her long swan neck. Never, ever, in her nineteen-year-old life had she felt sensations like these.

"Do you want to know what comes next, Lady Lisbeth?" Sir Devon looked deep into her violet eyes as his thumbs and forefingers worked their magic.

She moaned.

"I'm going to take off your chemise," he rasped. "May I, now?"

Lady Lisbeth gulped for air as if she were drowning, just like when she'd fallen off the drawbridge and into the scummy moat.

She wanted this knight, wanted his fiery touch, 'twas true; yet she felt a sudden choke hold of fear. She covered her pretty face with her hands. "I'm afraid, Sir Devon. I've ne'er been with a man before."

With a groan of impatience, Sir Devon willed himself to keep from ravaging the redheaded temptress. She was a colt to be tamed, gently yet firmly. Slowly, he reached out and slid the dress, and the white chemise beneath it, off Lady Lisbeth, and when she was completely ~~nude~~ naked, he pried her hands from her face so that she couldn't hide behind them. He then laid his feverish palms on her thighs, burning them with his imprint. "Open for me, m'lady," he told her, in his voice an unmistakable command.

Almost against her will, her thighs parted of their own accord, leaving her loins as vulnerable to his hungry gaze as a baby bird in its nest.

Like the arrows she'd ~~shot~~ loosed this morning in the woods beyond the castle grounds, his fingers found their target. Faster and faster they stroked her tender bud until at last Lady Lisbeth's back arched like a bow and she shuddered, gasping his name aloud in a tortured release.

Sir Devon smiled with satisfaction ~~and reached down to remove his breches~~

~~Sir Devon bit his swollen lip between his teeth and began to unbutton~~

~~Sir Devon growled and roughly tore his breches open~~

~~Sir Dev~~

Oh my God. Is there even consent here? Should Sir Devon be kinder? Plus, I completely forgot the rule about adverbs. I'll have to go back and take them out. And "to deftly unhook"—that's a split infinitive again. I keep doing that.

Ugh . . . this FRIGGING SUCKS.

CHAPTER ONE

This will be the year I sign with an agent and have my manuscript acquired by a top editor, at auction, with bids streaming in from every direction. I'll finally nail down that elusive contract of my dreams: a lucrative multibook deal with a gorgeous advance. I can't wait to join the ranks of a great publishing house, to be included in a stable of renowned authors, the ones whose work I read and admire, whose gushing blurbs will crowd my back cover. *A sweeping tale of deceit and desire! Most enthralling romance I've read in years! Meet your new obsession!* My announcement of the acquisition, in an eye-catching red, white, and blue notice, will get *all* the likes. By year's end the royalties will roll in, enough for me to buy a villa in Tuscany for my daughter and me. Well—that's the fantasy, anyway; I'd be happy just to pay off her college loans and set a good example of how to chase a dream.

All my life I've been *desperate* to write a good book. No, not just a good one—a fantastic one. A *New York Times* and *USA Today* bestselling, Amazon number one–rated Pulitzer Prize winner. I want it so bad I can taste it, the achingly sweet nectar of it. Every time I walk into a bookstore and confront that display of popular new releases, or the pennants fluttering from the ceiling to announce the CEO's monthly book club selection, or that entire table dedicated to you-know-who, the literati darling du jour whose embossed hardcovers are flying off the shelves . . . I can taste it. It's so *good.* I want to savor it endlessly on my tongue like a bottomless tub of white chocolate raspberry truffle–flavored Häagen-Dazs, which is better than *anything*.

Months ago I paid $200 for a webinar (the price dropped by half the next day) about positive visualization. The online host, a life coach named Ralph, taught us how picturing each facet of a desired outcome would allow us to realize our dream. I memorized his explanation of the cognitive behavior theory behind visualization: "By visualizing your dream in full sensory detail, your brain's neurotransmitters record the images as if they're happening today. Then your body, responding to the unconscious mind, will begin to manifest the new future event in the present moment." This sounded like something I could master, since I'm excellent at deluding myself.

I committed to Ralph's steps:

One, describe the desired outcome in detail. (Aforementioned Tuscan villa, and aforementioned daughter living debt-free.) Two, experience the emotions attached to achieving the desired outcome. (Elation. Ecstasy. Pride. Relief.) Three, actively take a step each day toward the desired outcome.

The third step is the hard part.

Every night since that Zoom session I lay in bed visualizing, using all my senses as instructed. In my mind I write that last tuition check and send it off . . . then turn to decorating and redecorating our charming Tuscan cottage. I can almost hear the birds twittering in the olive trees outside and smell the heavenly scent of bougainvillea right down to the last pink petal. Dream big, Ralph said, so I am. If this stuff really works, I'd better brush up on my Italian.

Heaven knows I've spent countless hours daydreaming about how it will feel to receive the first ARCs, advance reader copies, or get my first shipment of hardbacks delivered to my door by my regular FedEx driver, who will be *so* impressed. I'll ask him to video me brandishing a box cutter and slicing open the sealed cardboard flaps—ever so carefully, so as not to risk nicking a glossy dust jacket—to post on social media and relive over and over. My smile will be radiant.

And, oh, how it will feel to lift that first book baby into my arms. To cradle it, caress it, gaze at it in wonder, and know that its every fiber and tissue was conceived from my soul. Much like an actual daughter, I guess.

Don't get me wrong. It's not like I'm some dimwit with a pipe dream or wannabe who can't put a sentence together. I really *can* write. I've been telling myself that since first grade, when we six-year-olds had to fill a wide-ruled page about what it would be like if we woke up one morning with superpowers. My smudgy penciled paragraph—about having the sudden ability to wave my hands and make fruit trees grow at will, feeding all the starving people on the planet—made the rounds of the staff lunchroom, notwithstanding the fact that I'd pulled the idea right out of the Michael Jackson / Lionel Richie hit "We Are the World." My teacher, Mrs. Chiu, gave my story three gold stars. You don't get that kind of reaction unless you have true raw talent, right?

Ever since then I've been an author of one sort or another. In middle school I had a pen pal in Oklahoma who said my letters were hysterical. I've kept a diary. I even joined the yearbook staff in sophomore year of high school and wrote inventive captions for all the sports photos, like *"Swish!"* Okay, I didn't get a degree in creative writing or learn it formally. Dad, pragmatic and overbearing, had insisted I learn a trade rather than chase some "dead-end esoteric fantasy," as he put it, and my timid mother sided with him, as she'd always done. It didn't help that both my brothers became accountants. I guess I take after my mom.

My paying profession? Real estate. I had a handful of pretty good financial years, especially in my early twenties, when the market was hot and I was, too. Back then I rocked stilettos and power suits. Our daughter, Beatrice, hadn't been conceived yet, and Kevin's burgeoning career as an artist meant I had to put my novel on a back burner in order to pay the bills. Over the years I left behind the success that went with the heels. I also left behind my marriage, but that's another story.

Here's something exciting. These days I'm in charge of our office newsletter, so at least I get to flex my mighty writing muscles that way. My Realtor colleagues adore my work: the usual columns on new hires, industry trends, training resources, and company updates, of course, and I've expanded. I do a Seller Spotlight, and everyone's been clamoring for a turn to be featured. And there's my Milestones page, which last month featured four new babies and a one hundredth condo sale. In the rare quarter without births, deaths, or work anniversaries to fill the pages, I recommend local dining and take-out places ("Goa Goa on Main Street has amazing pork vindaloo, but if you have to *go-a you know where*, make sure you check for toilet paper first . . . they're always out." 🙂) or include fun recipes ("Ten 1950s JELL-O Desserts for Career Gals" and "Spamburger, Anyone? Yes, Please!"). Any leftover space gets filled with snazzy reminders ("Time for your flu shots, everyone!" and "Don't forget: June is our Picnic in the Park Month, so if you bring a dog, you're on Cleanup Doody" ha ha) plus inspirational quotes ("The only difference between ordinary and extraordinary is that little *extra*").

Real estate allows for flexible hours, when I try to hone my craft. I subscribe to a writerly YouTube channel. I try writing prompts. Maybe one day I'll enroll in a MasterClass with Margaret Atwood, but it's a little pricey.

I know what you're thinking, but despite how far-fetched my dream sounds, I don't have a quixotic view of the industry and what it takes to get published. I think about conflict and pacing. I try not to conceive a plot but rather a *situation*, as Stephen King suggests. I admit I have trouble with dialogue, but then again my genre, historical romance, is tough, since I wasn't exactly around to hear how medieval royals talked, so I have to make it all up.

There's a completed 166,000-word manuscript sitting in my bottom desk drawer. *A Knight to Remember: A Novel* by Summer Branigan. My name's not Summer Branigan, by the way. That's what I intend to use as my nom de plume, since my real one is sort of *meh*. It's actually Marcy. Marcy Jo Codburn. Boring, right? I might've considered keeping some form of my married name for Bea's sake, except that both "Summer Cod" and "Summer Burn" sound ridiculous. Branigan, it is.

Anyway, the manuscript. I finished it five years ago, back when Bea started her senior year of high school. But things didn't go as I'd hoped over the years . . . actually, things haven't gone anywhere at all. At the time I compiled a list of publishers who didn't require agented submissions. I found seven who were publishing historical romance in the USA, Canada, and the United Kingdom. I printed and bound the pages at my local Do It Depot and shipped one to each of the seven, of which six, over the course of these past five years, passed. The seventh went out of business. All the responses were cordial variations of "Thank you for thinking of us, but your manuscript is not right for us at this time." The most positive one said he'd never read so many synonyms for male genitalia.

I yearn for an agent. I composed a great query letter and refined it until it sparkled. Every week or so I reach out to a new agent with a personalized email. Out of literally dozens of agents, less than half responded, and I go into cardiac arrest every time one of those responses lands in my inbox. So far only one, Elizabeth R., requested to see the manuscript. Elizabeth R. didn't respond to the submission, despite my reaching out in a series of short, pithy notes—Hey Liz, just checking in to see how you're loving "A Knight to Remember," let me know! 🙂—as well as a handwritten card, which included the knight piece from a toy chess set. I'm embarrassed to say that just before Thanksgiving, as she was leaving her Union Square office, I presented her with a homemade medieval apple tart sourced from historically accurate online recipes. Clearly Elizabeth R. had no idea who I was, nor did she remember having requested my manuscript, nor did she express any interest in having me resend it. Apparently, though, she was fine with accepting the proffered tart. I watched forlornly as Elizabeth R. disappeared down the steps to the L train, beribboned box in hand, never to be heard from again.

My gloom lasted a month. You'd think that for all the rejection, not to mention the small fortune I'd spent on printing, binding, and shipping all those freakishly heavy boxes, I'd call it quits for good. I almost did.

Yes, I stuck that original manuscript out of sight in a drawer. I said sayonara to my beloved characters, my knights, my ladies, my soothsayer, my foulmouthed chambermaid, even my cruel warlord. I put the extra ten just-in-case copies into a plastic bin in the corner of the basement, tucked behind Bea's purple glitter bicycle and field hockey equipment. I didn't attempt a single word of fiction except to write listings of homes for sale, many of which were in dire need of artfully fictitious description. My novel sat untouched.

Finally, one night last year, about four months after Kevin and I separated, I opened the old Word doc and started noodling. Not exactly a rewrite, but now I'm busily adding new pages, new chapters, in an attempt to salvage *A Knight to Remember*. In a gutsy move (gutsy for me, that is) I read the *Gen Z Guide to Publishing* and posted an excerpt of my novel on #LitAgentSeeker in the hopes an agent would fall in love with my work.

And then, in what had to be either divine providence or a huge coincidence, I spied a leaflet tacked to the bulletin board at the entrance of my public library, a squat, ivy-covered building gifted to my town in 1910. The flyer announced the launch of a new writers' circle. Precisely the kick in the pants I needed. I attended the first session that week.

And what do you know . . . I'd stumbled on my kindred spirits. What started as seven women and three men eventually whittled down to our core of four stalwarts: Liisa, Antonia (Toni for short), Mike, and me. We meet religiously every week to read and critique one another's work, then head out for drinks at O'Keefe's, the shabby-chic Irish pub around the corner from the library. Mike is a widower and a cop. A detective, actually, who works in the fraud division. You have to hand it to him; he's been churning out crime fiction stories in his spare time and has yet to be published, but he keeps chugging along week after week. Toni is much younger than us, with twin toddlers at home, and I suspect she uses our group as an escape hatch, which is fine. She has a flair for words—maybe when she's not chronically exhausted, she'll be able to devote more energy to her WIP, which stands for work in progress.

Liisa and I often close the pub. We're besties. Doesn't she have a great name? "Liisa" with a double *i*. It's Estonian. She's divorced, too, albeit amicably, and we both grew up in Connecticut. Her day job—she's a paralegal—keeps her super busy, and in terms of writing, we're in the exact same place: Liisa has a partially finished spy thriller manuscript she's been working on forever, which may or may not be based on her father's life, if you get my drift. She's just as frustrated as me with its progress.

We're at O'Keefe's now, and Brian, the owner, is looking pointedly at us as he finishes sweeping the scuffed wood floor.

"C'mon, ten more minutes," cajoles Liisa with a grin. "You know this is the high point of our week."

"Unless you count Tuesday at the grocery store," I say. "A guy knocked over an entire display of cat food, and I ended up restacking all the cans because I felt bad for the stock boy. So far that's been the high point of *my* week." Liisa and Brian exchange a grin.

I swallow a last mouthful of Long Island Iced Tea and frown at Brian. "Besides, do you really have anything better to do than listen to us complain about how miserably we're failing as writers?"

My question is rhetorical. Every Thursday night we watch a parade of young things flirting with Brian as he serves up their beer and cocktails with shaggy hair falling over his eyes and sleeves rolled up to reveal muscular forearms. There's probably some gorgeous coed waiting for him outside.

"You're not failing, these things just take time." Brian shoots us an adorable smile from behind his beard. "Don't get me wrong. I'm here to help you wallow."

Liisa is counting out cash from her wallet. "Oh, we know."

"Depression pays your rent," I add. I slide off my stool and anchor a generous tip under my empty glass.

"Thanks, ladies." Brian unties the apron to reveal a slim waist and long, straight legs clad in black jeans, legs that he crosses at the ankle as he leans on his bar. "And, hey, you never know. My mom was pretty desperate to succeed at something, so she started drawing pet portraits during the pandemic, and her business is still booming. And she's middle aged, too—if she can do it, you can."

Liisa and I wince. "On that note," she says, and propels me out the door.

Like I said, I am desperate. But never in a million did I think my desperation would lead to murder.

CHAPTER TWO

It's Sunday and I'm waiting for Liisa as I lace my worn sneakers. Wistfully I think of the new ones I found on clearance yesterday—the last pair, my size, woo-hoo!—but just as I was reaching toward the shelf, a woman swooped in and snatched them.

Once a week Liisa and I go for a morning jog on the trail, which means we start out at a brisk clip, slow down to a leisurely stroll by the halfway point, and end up sipping sugary iced mochaccinos at our favorite coffee shop for the next two hours.

She pulls into my driveway in a red sports car with vanity plates reading WAS HIS. We start from my house since the trail begins at the forested dead end of my lane. I'm in love with this old New England neighborhood—its small, quaint Capes and cluster of charming shops and restaurants surrounding town hall and a redbrick fire station.

When our property first came on the market, I glossed right over the listing, as I'd wanted a low-maintenance condo. But Kevin—who tended toward dark and brooding—had noticed the For Sale sign and was intrigued by the dark and brooding woods surrounding the house. Before we'd even made the turn onto Alpine Lane, Kevin insisted he wanted us to put in an offer. Neither of us had seen inside the home: a mid-century ranch sorely in need of a new roof and a paint job.

"Are you sure?" My voice reverberated with doubt.

Yes, he was. It would be an excellent investment, Kevin said, and asked why I had no faith in his judgment. I wanted to ask why he had no faith in *mine*. Every instinct I had as a Realtor told me he was "wrong, wrong, wrong" but I bit my tongue and agreed "location, location, location" instead. Like my mother before me, I wanted to please my husband, and so Kevin got his way.

Two days later we were the proud owners of a ramshackle fixer-upper. Or rather, Kevin was proud and I was ambivalent. The neighborhood was lovely, but we spent years arguing about repairs. Turned out, I was right; the place didn't triple or even double in value, despite its great location. We should have fixed things up significantly, and besides putting on the new roof and upgrading the old plumbing, I only ever did scattered DIY projects here and there. For all his artistic ability, Kevin never got around to beautifying our home. Whatever. I got the house in the settlement and Kevin went to live with his boyfriend.

I grab my Novel Idea water bottle and join Liisa on the road. It's May, and the forsythia and daffodils have been replaced by azaleas and lush rhododendrons blooming in riotous lavenders and pinks. It's also unseasonably warm. We step onto the trailhead, where the temperature cools several degrees under a web of tree branches.

"Guess what," Liisa says with a big-toothed grin. Classic Liisa: She's always bursting with news. "I wrote three pages yesterday."

"What?!" Without breaking stride, I reach out an arm for a congratulatory hug. Like me, Liisa's been suffering from a severe case of writer's block, so this is cause for celebration. "Tell me."

"Remember how I've been agonizing over the scene where Sasha disposes of the KGB agent's body? I couldn't figure out how he does it. The deserted warehouse is too cliché. I tried a butcher's shop, but it was very *Fried Green Tomatoes*, and a dry cleaner, but you know, traffic cams," she says, gathering her curly hair into a bunch. "Ready for this? Now it's the garbage dump."

"I'm pretty sure they have cameras at garbage dumps," I tell her gently.

Liisa stops in her tracks and stares at me. "No."

"To take pictures of your license plate. That way they can cite you if you dump stuff you're not supposed to. Like a body."

She swears softly, and we walk in silence for a while. "How about below O'Keefe's . . . maybe Sasha stows him inside a giant beer keg? I bet Brian would love that."

I laugh. "I already added a knight named Brian O'Keefe to my characters." We look knowingly at each other. Who doesn't have a crush on Brian?

Lime-green umbrellas have sprouted on the patio of Espresso Yourself, our local café, and almost all the tables are full on this springlike day. The umbrellas block enough sunlight that we can sit outside and still see our phone screens. It's our favorite guilty pleasure; we spend an hour or two each week dissecting the book news of the thousands of authors, editors, publishers, bloggers, and bookstagrammers we follow.

"Oh my goodness, look at this cover reveal," breathes Liisa, hunched over Facebook. "It's stunning. Exactly the kind of cover art I want one day—flowery and feminine, with lots of pastels."

"And yet you are writing a spy thriller . . . ?"

She sighs. "I know. My publisher will probably insist on something masculine in black and red . . . a smoking gun or a man in a trench coat." We both know she would be ecstatic with *any* artwork at this point. "Whereas yours will be the one with flowers. And a girl in a half-torn bodice."

"With wavy auburn hair blowing behind her as she descends the stairs of a turret." What can I say? It's my genre. "Here, look at Jen Emerson's post. A picture of her dachshunds—what a surprise, today's Sunday. She posts their pics on Sundays, Tuesdays, and Fridays. Nature shots on Mondays and Wednesdays. Book promos Saturday. Like clockwork."

"Do you think she could mix it up a bit? I bet Siegfried and Roy aren't even her dogs," Liisa says.

"The eighty–twenty rule," I point out. I press "love" and move on.

Liisa straightens. "Oh, wow! Julian Segal accepted my friend request. And listen to this . . . he is self-publishing his next work!" I lean over to read the comments as she types "Huge congrats" and adds a cake emoji, then deletes the cake and inserts a party popper instead. Men don't have the same emotional connection to cake as women.

"Did you know he started out as self-published? Random House bought his second book and it became a bestseller," Liisa says, trying to sound erudite even though she knows I know. We've discussed it a dozen times.

We switch to Instagram. There's so much news to catch up on. We spend the next half hour taking turns reading book reviews aloud, liking and following. "Look at the photos from Yvonne Manning's book launch last night. That Manhattan Book Club lady, Elianna Abrams, was there, and Sierra Eastman, of course." Quickly she swipes through the album.

"How stunning is Yvonne's dress? And the napkins and cupcakes that match the books?" I sigh. I want a beautiful book launch with cupcakes. Or vanilla milkshakes at a fifties-style diner, like at Sierra Eastman's celebration of her new Elvis biography, *All Shook Up*. Or a peach-themed brunch with all peach-colored decor and peach bellinis—perfect for Lilian Arnold's cozy mystery series set in Georgia.

I want a launch party so badly.

Liisa pushes her chair back. "Let's get going," she says. "Sasha obviously knows there are cameras at the dump. Somehow I have to make him drive in with a garbage truck so he can scope out the FBI agents before the Russian mob arrives." She lifts the lid from her paper cup and tilts it back to catch the last foamy drips of her mochaccino.

When she stands up, there's a smear of whipped cream on the tip of her nose. I reach over to wipe it away with a napkin—mommy habits die hard.

CHAPTER THREE

If Liisa can do it, so can I, I tell myself, sitting in front of my computer in the kitchen. Right now I have a little free time to work on a steamy scene before I begin tackling the monstrosity of a home project bubbling underfoot: organizing the basement. *Concentrate,* I tell myself, and squeeze out a few lines.

"Tonight we will serve the black wine," rasped Sir Devon, indicating the huge wooden barrels and crates of grapes stored in the cellar. "And you, wench, will pour it for the guests."

Lady Lisbeth lowered her lids with an obedient nod. If it meant being in closer proximity to the handsome knight, she'd gladly do his bidding. She couldn't help but sneak a sideways peek at him, inhaling sharply at the sight of his broad shoulders tapering down to—

My phone buzzes with a text. It's Kevin, wondering how far along I am in the basement cleanup and whether I came across a leather portfolio of sketches from his college days? If I haven't yet, I should look for it, as he wants to come pick it up.

I save my document and stand up reluctantly. He's right, I shouldn't put off this chore. Shoving my phone into my jeans, I descend the bare stairs and stub my toe on the corner of a mini fridge as I'm reaching to flick on the lights.

The task wouldn't be so overwhelming if I weren't so darn sentimental, as Kevin says. I don't question why he kept old drawings from college as I wade into the mess.

Besides a few pieces of furniture and accumulated odds and ends, the basement is crammed with everything I couldn't bring myself to part with: the remnants of Bea's entire childhood. Toys, clothes, children's books, arts and crafts projects, and sports equipment, stacked throughout the space in cardboard boxes and reusable grocery bags.

Bea's accumulated college work, along with the mini fridge and other dorm stuff she brought home a few days ago, has made it unmanageable. We agreed to go through it all together. In theory she's capable of doing it on her own, but this way I can spend time with her—time with her I missed these past four years. Soon she starts a summer research program that will keep her busy until she goes to grad school in the fall. For chemical engineering, of all things! I couldn't be prouder. She's already been accepted to a nearby college (in-state tuition, thank goodness) and will be staying in Connecticut.

She's still conked out after a late night. I text her: Call me when you're up 😜.

"How's my Bumble Bea?" I ask, smiling when she calls.

She yawns. "Whassup."

"It's after noon. I thought we were doing the basement?"

I hear the water go on in the bathroom. "I'll be down in a while. Just start without me."

"No problem," I say gamely. "Mwah." I blow her a kiss, but she's already disconnected.

I start. The first box I open, shoved into the farthest corner of the basement, contains old lab sets and textbooks. The one on top, *Chemistry for Kids*, is well worn.

Bea spent her entire childhood making concoctions: mixing flavors of soda, combining my shampoos and conditioners, and, in one memorable episode, trying the recipe from the page I'm looking at now: baking soda, dish soap, and vinegar, which sent foam fizzing over the counters and into every drawer, nook, and cranny. Our kitchen looked like an episode from *I Love Lucy* and took me hours to clean up.

As she got older and the formulas became more complicated, she spent hours and days memorizing the periodic table. I took her to every science center in New England. She learned about molecular structures and chemical reactions. She was determined to place first for her color-changing chemical clock in her middle school science fair, and determined to win the chemistry prize in high school. She won both. She seemed destined to pursue a career in chemistry, like a little freckle-faced Marie Curie; destined, I fantasize, for a Nobel Prize. It must have been that extra two weeks she spent idling in my womb before emerging full throttle.

Even though she shows more ability in science than art—neither Kevin nor I understand where that came from—Bea identifies as a "Daddy's girl" (at least that's what I overheard her tell her friends years ago at a sleepover). To his credit, Kevin supports her choices and doesn't try to steer her in a different direction. He pretty much cemented her career decision when he said, "It's like being an artist, but you are creating with chemicals instead of clay or paint," and her eyes lit up. It's not lost on me which parent she still emulates.

I open another box. Inside are the folded Halloween costumes I'd made for our family. I look up as Bea's staccato footsteps sound on the stairs. "You're just in time. Remember these?"

She crouches beside me as I dig through the costumes we wore year by year: a sweet pea onesie for baby Bea, with Kevin and me dressed as farmers; year two, Bea was Barney the Dinosaur, while Kevin and I were BJ and Baby Bop; then we were flowers, and she was a bumblebee at three, and so on. I hold the onesie to my face to see if it's held on to any scent.

"No way." She laughs, pulling out a furry brown getup. I recall the October night vividly because it was the last time she'd agreed to trick-or-treat with her parents: Bea in a Scooby-Doo costume, Kevin dressed up as Shaggy, and me as Velma. "And you pulled me around the block in my wagon, decorated to look like the Mystery Machine."

"And you called your candy Scooby Snacks."

Well, I'm certainly not getting rid of any costumes.

Bea is holding a faded picture from a ski trip to Vermont: a pint-sized Bea sandwiched between Kevin and me on the slopes. "I was proud of you when you finally made it all the way down the bunny hill without falling," she tells me wryly, and I think, *Really?* That's *what made you proud of me?*

I stand up to look at a trifold display board leaning against the wall. Her eighth-grade science fair, with a first-place blue ribbon prize stuck to the front. The papers are wavy from the humidity down here, but I remember as if it were yesterday how she sat at the kitchen table to illustrate color changes as a timekeeping mechanism. I close the flaps and notice Kevin's portfolio propped behind it.

Meanwhile Bea catches sight of the glittery tassels on her purple bicycle and, behind it, the bin containing my manuscripts along with stapled printouts of early chapters, dated before she was born. Long before. She lifts a sheaf of papers and flips through, frowning.

"Why do you still have these?" She tosses the pages back into the bin. "You're not going to do anything with them."

Bea's known forever about my dream of being an author. She heard me say a million times how much I want to be published. She knows I'm in a writers' group, but clearly she thinks it's a waste of time, that my dream will never come to fruition. It stings.

Her phone chimes with a notification. "Mom?"

"Let me guess. You're going out. To the party on the beach you've been talking about?"

"Actually, the beach can wait. There's a lecture on breakthroughs in cancer drugs at the community center. I'll be home later, okay?" She gives me a peck on the cheek and leaves, and I move on to the next box, and the next, and hours later my back is killing me, and I've succeeded in purging only a single garbage bag of dried-up magic markers, rancid makeup, old shoes, and mismatched socks. My progress in the basement is about as tedious as that of my manuscript. At least Kevin will be happy about the portfolio.

Upstairs, Bea has dumped a mountain of laundry by the washing machine, from the size of it the whole semester's worth, so I sort through and throw in a load of delicates. A girl needs clean underwear, doesn't she?

By the time I'm done it's almost dinnertime. There's plenty of lasagna left over from the tray I made yesterday, but after my stroll down memory lane I can't help feeling nostalgic. Bea used to love breakfast for dinner, so I pull out ingredients and start prepping. When Beatrice comes in, she surveys the bowls on the table heaped high with diced walnuts and chocolate chips and marshmallows, Nutella, sprinkles. I set a large platter of fresh pineapple-filled flapjacks in the center with a flourish.

"Grandma called that Pancakes Tropicana."

"I don't remember her ever making it for you," I say.

"She only ever made it when we were alone. Grandpa thought breakfast for dinner was silly," Bea says, heading upstairs to change. "Anyway, thanks, but I'm not really hungry. And also, I'm not a little kid anymore, Mom."

My shoulders sag.

I'm feeling more and more despondent as the hours pass. It's my usual Sunday-evening funk—three parts boredom and a dash of despair over my manuscript for flavor. It takes all my resolve to resist turning on Netflix to browse the selection of K-dramas.

Bea has gone to the beach for the bonfire, so I'm alone again, back in front of my computer, determined to crank out another paragraph. The pancakes are sealed in Tupperware, and the Tropicana toppings—fruit, nuts, and sprinkles—are stored away in their respective containers. I fixed myself a sandwich earlier, but now there's a Pepperidge Farm chocolate layer cake calling to me from the freezer, and even though I promised myself I wouldn't touch it, I tear open the cellophane and cut a generous slice. I don't even wait for the thing to defrost before scarfing it down.

I know I shouldn't take it personally. I'm sure Bea didn't mean to sound so dismissive of my writing. I just wish she'd take me more seriously. I always said, she's like sriracha—both sweet and spicy. I admire her spiciness, the spunk that seems absent from my own DNA.

Now that she's out with friends again, I'd be wise to use this quiet time for writing. I swallow another bite. I'm eating for two, I tell myself, mindful of my heroine—Lady Lisbeth is pregnant.

I stab the remaining forkful of cake on the plate; the icing is a little softer now. Creamier. Actually, I think, I'm eating for three, if you count Lady Lisbeth's unborn baby. I saw off another hunk.

If I were on a book tour, hurrying from one city to the next, one signing to the next, one interview to the next, I'd be busy and content. I wouldn't be tempted to snack, what with all the fabulous new clothes waiting to be worn at my appearances, not to mention the fabulous people lining up to discuss my book; and even if I were tempted to eat, I wouldn't have time!

But right now I do have time. Half the cake is gone and it's only seven o'clock, which means there's a good chance the other half won't survive the night. Empty hours alone are the worst. You'd think I'd be used to it by now.

Thankfully my Saturdays are filled with showings. I log on to MLS, Multiple Listing Service, to see what's moving in real estate. Even though the market is hot right now, I haven't sold anything in a while. I'm the listing agent for a neighborhood Cape, but the sellers aren't particularly motivated, and they've already turned down two offers, which means I should plan yet another open house. I'm also dabbling in commercial real estate. Right now my only commercial listing is a mostly vacant strip mall that could be redeveloped if only someone were interested in acquiring it. No one is. I need to step up my game. Going bankrupt is definitely not going to help my situation.

I turn back to the words on my screen. When I've read sections out loud to the writing group recently, their reactions have seemed lukewarm. I don't know why. Mike might not be the best judge, though, and Liisa would never hurt my feelings with harsh words, even when it's clear she doesn't like my work. And I often catch Toni yawning, but that happens regardless. Like I said, she's running on fumes. Her twins have been on opposite sleep schedules.

I remember many a sleepless night with infant Bea . . . even then, she calmed as soon as Kevin picked her up, fussed when I did.

Thinking of motherhood shifts my mind back to Lady Lisbeth. The book ends as a cliffhanger when Sir Devon discovers she's pregnant. Maybe I should continue it, though, through the birth of the baby. Wait . . . wait, what if someone in the castle stole it away from her? No, that would be awful, forget I even said that. But it would be such a tearjerker . . .

CHAPTER FOUR

Three days a week, we have a team meeting at the brokerage with Robert Verney, my manager. Bob the Broker, we call him. He's rotund and tense and his face is perpetually plum colored. A walking aneurysm.

He waddles in now with his paperwork and plops into his chair at the head of the conference table. "Let's rock and roll, folks," he greets us, which is how he usually greets us.

Around the table are several keen young agents fresh into the business and eager to one-up each other. On either side of me, they open their monogrammed bags self-importantly and announce their newest listings, under-contracts, showings, and sales.

"I have an offer on 44 Banbury for two point three," a prepubescent beside me says. She looks at Bob over her horn-rimmed glasses, which I'm pretty sure are purely decoration. "That's over asking." On my other side, a gangly young man in a bow tie announces that two of his properties sold in a day. As a group, we congratulate them both.

Across the table from me is my colleague Candace. Condescending Candace has been an agent for only a few years but thinks she is God's gift to real estate. She waits for our full attention before rattling off her recent successes.

When I'm the only one in the room who hasn't yet spoken, I clear my throat. "I'm planning some more open houses," I say, which is what I usually say.

Across from me, Candace clucks sympathetically, "You know what Tony Robbins says." And I do, because she's quoted him so often about the necessity of making changes to bring about change. There's an awkward silence. Candace never hesitates to dispense advice. She's a literal depository of helpful motivational quotes, a disproportionate number of which are directed at me.

"All right, then." Bob thumbs through his pile of papers. "This just came across my desk: a multifamily dwelling, fully upgraded. It could use someone experienced." His eyes slide around the table and meet mine briefly before moving on.

I'm experienced! I want it! I raise my hand to volunteer but before I can spit out a single word, Candace has already reached beside her. "I'll handle it," she tells Bob, snatching the listing and slipping it into her folder. She catches my eye, smug. *The early bird catches the worm,* I imagine her thinking.

That evening I pull into the library parking lot at the same time as Mike. We climb the dusty wooden staircase to the conference room and open our laptops. I tell him about my week: how I've put in super-long days at the office in an effort to accrue more real estate listings. He tells me about a cold case for which he uncovered a new lead. We chat about the book he is reading, a classic horror novel about an evil tree that comes to life. Weird, right?

Toni arrives next, also weird, because she's usually late, even an hour late sometimes. She's smiling and her braids are neat and she looks more rested than I've ever seen her. She tells us the twins, Bobby and Brady (clearly Antonia and her husband are millennials who don't watch retro television), slept ten hours straight, in sync. A miracle!

Then Liisa bursts in, looking as if she's trying to stifle an announcement that's sure to rock our worlds. *She probably wrote a whole chapter,* I think.

"I have news, everyone," she starts, pulling her laptop from her Vera Bradley and booting it up. "We're going on a field trip."

Not what I expected. Mike, Toni, and I exchange confused glances.

Liisa logs in and turns her computer around so we can see. It's a news article, featuring a full-page glamour shot of a woman reclining on a couch Cleopatra-style. I lean across the table to read the headline but Liisa saves me the trouble.

"Francesca Barber is coming to Connecticut," she squeals, an oddly girlish sound coming from her round face. "She's making an appearance in Hartford . . . one week from tonight!"

"That could be fun," Toni says.

"I'm game," Mike says.

I nod. It's all I can do at the moment. Of all the authors I follow, Francesca Barber is one of the most admirable. Mark Twain famously quipped, "There's no such thing as a new idea," but I'm pretty sure Francesca disproved him. She's just written her third mega blockbuster in as many years. Her previous two books, about a female astronaut who crash-lands on Jupiter and falls in love with an inhabitant, were adapted into movies that led the "Top Ten in the US Today" for weeks. Liisa and I gobbled up her books on preorder, devoured the movies as soon as they dropped, and, goddamn it, they were absolutely delicious.

It's no surprise, all things considered, that with the worldwide sales of the first two books and all the advance publicity, the third one hit the *New York Times* list on release and has already been optioned. Francesca's book tour, starting in Manhattan, will cover metropolitan cities across the country. I bet the tickets sold out immediately.

"How do we know there's—" I don't get to finish the thought.

"Availability? I booked four spots on Eventbrite as soon as I saw the announcement," Liisa explains. "I can cancel, but this way we're set."

Clearly I've been out of the loop on socials for a bombshell like this appearance to have escaped my notice.

"So we'll meet here and drive up together?" Liisa suggests.

Toni shakes her head. "I should drive separately in case I have to leave early."

"I'll take you," Mike offers. "I don't want you driving over an hour at night." Always gallant, always protective, always the upstanding citizen. Toni smiles at him gratefully.

"Well, why don't we get started?" Liisa suggests. "Mike, do you have anything new to show us?"

"Sure." Mike reads his newest page of prose. His snappy dialogue between the hard-boiled detective and the hardened criminal is laugh-aloud funny.

"That was wonderful," I praise him, which reminds me to pull up an email. "By the way," I tell everyone, "I got another rejection from an agent today. He says my work is not what he's looking for but feel free to query again with other projects. Maybe you guys want to try him?" Toni, Mike, and Liisa jot down the agency contact info, and then it's my turn to read.

I pull up the paragraphs I've labored over all week in the few spare minutes I had between moving Beatrice home from college, sorting the basement, and slaving over real estate. I enlarge the text to read aloud.

`Lady Lisbeth jumps from the saddle. Her nag snorts with exertion, puffing steam from his nostrils, and she leads him in circles around the muddy courtyard to cool down from their swift ride. Checking for signs of chafing, she loosens the cinch and removes the bridle and bit. She offers him some fresh water but knows it's too soon after the ride for grain.`

`"Lisbeth!" her stepmother yells, stomping nearer with her skirts swishing perilously close to the mud. "Turn the beast loose in the paddock and start cleaning the stable! Where is the wheelbarrow and` pitchfork? The other mounts need fresh hay. And don't forget to sweep the sawdust."

When I finish the rest, I look up. "That's it," I say expectantly. Toni, Liisa, and Mike are quiet.

"I like your use of the word *perilously*," Toni says at last, not meeting my eyes.

Mike scratches behind an ear. "Good word," he agrees.

"Thanks." I sink down an inch or two in my seat. "Um . . . Liisa? What did you think?"

"I think," she says slowly, "it sounds a little like *Black Beauty*. I think you could be more original. And a whole scene showing Lisbeth cleaning the stable doesn't make much sense character-wise since she's a lady and there are stable boys to do that in a castle. Unless you show her actively rejecting her privileged role? Just my opinion."

Back to the old writing board.

At home, I'm sprawled on my couch, taking a break from work to scroll through the thousands of photos and posts related to #FrancescaBarber and #JupiterBooks while plowing my way through a bag of cheese doodles.

The author is no youngster. In fact, she's about my age, maybe a year or two younger, but her shoulder-length dark hair, pale aquamarine eyes, and thick dark brows are timeless. She's got a killer body, too. I console myself with the thought that she's probably had lots of work done, and even if she hasn't had actual surgery, she can surely afford the best cosmetics and beauty treatments and personal fitness coaches available to humankind.

She's dabbled in directing, is the producer of the most recent film, and is reportedly collaborating on the screenplay for the third. She is so wealthy she definitely doesn't need the income from this latest project.

Regardless, the Jupiter series has left no doubt about her writing ability. I sigh. She has it all: beauty, fame, fortune. Her smile glows in pictures. She looks like she's on top of the world.

Francesca's daughter, Aspen Barber, is the current Hollywood "it" girl. As a child star she was the darling of the press in her role as Sadie in the old sitcom *Practice Makes Perfect*. Now, in the #JupiterMovies, she portrays the beautiful astronaut opposite Tabi Benlolo, the breakout star cast as her love interest. They were reported to butt heads on set, while gossip columns in supermarket checkout lines were rife with rumors about Aspen and the director's son. The shocking revelation of a secret romance between Aspen and Tabi rocked showbiz. Their brief affair culminated in a #fairytale wedding this past February. Memes featuring the sultry Brazilian actor and his starry-eyed and—**ahem**—scantily clad bride went viral on TikTok. I add #AspenBarber and #TabiBenlolo to my hashtag research and find about a million photos of the #AspenAndTabiWedding.

Enough. All the screen time is giving me a headache, it's late, and I have to be up early.

I haul myself to the bathroom to wash up. In the mirror, my bleary eyes stare back at me from a puffy face surrounded by brittle beige hair shot through with gray. I should pull myself together, I think.

Maybe tomorrow I'll have an inspiration for how to edit my stable scene, I think, and pop a handful of M&M's into my mouth on the way to bed.

CHAPTER FIVE

Here's a bit of good news: I may have snagged a new listing. For all the extra hours I put in at the office last week, it ends up happening organically.

My old Saab has been making a funny noise lately. It coughs hoarsely every time I accelerate. A smoker's cough. I drive it over to Garcia, who's been repairing our cars for years and whom Kevin trusts implicitly, and since I don't know anything about cars, I defer to Kevin on this one, too.

The shop is a few miles away in a district of dollar stores and fast-food joints, but every time I go, there are several luxury cars lined up to be serviced, so obviously people trust Garcia with their vehicles. I clamber out.

Garcia emerges from a garage and heads toward me, wiping his fingers on an oil-stained rag. "Long time, no see, Mrs. Codburn." He smiles. "Hey, are those for me?"

I'm holding out a platter of my special peanut butter cookies with a dollop of jam baked on top. I know they're good because I sampled several. "I remembered you love them."

"Don't tell my wife, she thinks I'm on a diet, but thank you." He winks, then looks over my shoulder to the car. "She acting up?"

"There's this sound when I drive." Garcia slides into the driver's seat and revs the engine. The car hacks and wheezes.

For the next hour I dab my face with tissue as I sit in the tiny, stuffy waiting area. My Saab is hoisted up onto the stirrups while Garcia pokes around between her wheels and does his thing. At last he assures me everything is fixed. He steps behind the cash register as I rummage through my purse.

While I insert my credit card, he makes conversation. "How are the houses selling?"

"Pretty good. I'm doing some residential, some commercial. This and that."

"Yeah?" Garcia looks up. "You know, we have a place, was my parents' when they were still with us, God rest their souls. A family restaurant out front, and we lived behind. My wife thinks we could sell it."

"Around here?"

"Nah, up in Back Bay. It's not in great shape but maybe somebody wants it."

"You never know."

"You have time to go see? I can give you the keys."

"I'd be happy to," I say. "Tell your wife I said hi."

The address Garcia gives me is off the highway on the outskirts of Back Bay, a place on a sea inlet, a little over an hour away from home, in woods so thick it feels as if civilization never made it this far. The town itself, if one could call it a town, consists of a single traffic light that swings desolately over an empty intersection, with an abandoned public school and a few boarded-up storefronts nearby. The only functioning business seems to be a country store, about a half mile down the street from the light, with one of those old-fashioned gas pumps out front. Its faded sign is supposed to say Back Bay Bait and Tackle but the *T* in "Tackle" has peeled off. It's all from another era.

I'm having trouble finding the location of Garcia's parents' place. I pass the gas pump a second and third time. I zigzag up and down the street, over and over, trying all the little dead-end side roads to no avail.

Eventually I spot a break in the trees that I'd overlooked. It's more of a laneway than a road, overgrown on the sides and thick above with a canopy of leaves so that not much sunlight filters in. I spot a roughly carved wooden sign nailed to a tree. My Saab bumps its way along the rocky path for several hundred yards until a tiny structure comes into view.

Gingerly, tripping over exposed roots and swatting at blackflies as I go, I make a loop around the cottage and come to a stop in front. It's run-down and old-fashioned and so dirty I can't tell what the original color was. It might have been a set for *Little House on the Prairie*, maybe an episode with an outbreak of tuberculosis; and what do you know, as if to confirm my thoughts, fifty feet away in a tiny clearing stands an outhouse.

Still, there's scalloped, peeling gingerbread around the rickety porch, and a front window stamped with the name Mom & Pop's, which lends a modicum of charm. I unlock the front door with its stained-glass insert and step inside.

Our unexpected heat wave has warmed the dank interior. I hold my breath as I walk through the dusty vestibule and into the area where Garcia's folks ran a little eatery that, according to a framed newspaper article on the wall, opened in 1977. A portly woman and thin man in aprons beam from the yellowing page, and in their laps are two small children, a boy and girl. Garcia of today looks just like his father. I imagine him as a little tyke, running around the place when it first opened, and later as a teenager, working on a Friday night, taking orders and serving meals to help his family and earn some tips for spending money.

I enter a large open space that I imagine served as the restaurant dining room. There's a big bay window with checkered curtains, a potbellied stove with piping up through the ceiling, and scuff marks all over the floor from what would have been the tables and chairs shown in the newspaper photo. Right now there's only one table left by the window, with four captain's chairs around it, and an old floral-printed sofa shoved against one wall.

Beyond the dining area, an archway leads to the kitchen at the rear of the house, from which emerged, I imagine, the traditional meals Garcia's parents cooked up. This place is the very definition of vintage. The decor hasn't changed since the seventies; I blink at the sight of fruit-patterned wallpaper, brown-checkered linoleum, and harvest-gold appliances. There's a rectangular turquoise table, the kind with metal legs and piping. A few pots and pans remain in the cabinets; there's mismatched cutlery in the drawer. I can just imagine Garcia's mother sitting here and peeling vegetables, red faced by the open window in summer, shivering despite the radiator in winter. I push open a creaky door that leads to a set of narrow stairs. The cellar. Not going down there, thanks.

There are three other doors, one leading to a carpeted bathroom sporting bubblegum-pink fixtures. Beyond it are two wallpapered bedrooms. Clearly the furnishings have been picked through, as there are clean square patches on the carpet where furniture once stood. But the beds are still here, even though they are devoid of bedding. One is clearly a child's room with two twin beds. In the other bedroom, which I suppose belonged to the mister and missus, judging by the family photos on the wall, there is garbage strewn on the floor and empty beer cans on the credenza. Garcia mentioned they'd had squatters in the past.

I return to the front restaurant area. Overall, the space is tiny, the finishes are ancient, and no doubt the plumbing and electrical need replacing. There's so much upgrading to be done, I doubt anyone would want to live here.

But the land, the land! According to Garcia it's over an acre, with what looks like empty lots all around it, so there's that.

I wonder what parcels of land are worth in Back Bay. I'll make some calls.

CHAPTER SIX

Mike and Toni join Liisa and me in the lobby of Hartford's historic Housatonic Hotel, and the four of us walk into the ballroom together for Francesca Barber's book talk. It's been set with theater-style seating and even though it's early, people are drifting in. Everyone seems to have dressed up for the occasion, and I, too, traded in my usual stretchy yoga pants for a pair of tailored black ones that are significantly tighter than the last time I wore them. I had the fly undone for the car ride over, but of course I can't do that in here, and I'm breathless as we squeeze into the middle of the second row. We have an obstructed view of a screen displaying a photo of the three book jackets in the Jupiter series: *Journey to Jupiter*, *Jovan of Jupiter*, and now *Jupiter in Jeopardy*.

Toni points out long tables bordering the wall at the back of the room. They're stacked with books, and there are more packed in boxes underneath. "Do you think all those books will sell tonight?"

"I bet they will," Liisa says, twisting around to see. "Look at the attendant. She's like a Brink's driver, guarding them. She's probably armed."

"Mike, maybe they should hire you part-time?" Toni suggests.

"I've done enough bodyguarding in my job, thanks," Mike says, puffing out his chest.

Liisa's index finger is moving in the air as she tries to count the boxes of books from where she sits. "Francesca will get carpal tunnel doing so much signing."

What I wouldn't give for carpal tunnel from signing books.

Before long, the room is packed. I'm sitting ramrod straight in my chair to lessen the strain on my zipper. At last the chandeliers dim, and a hush falls over the audience. We wait. In the dark, the image on the screen comes to life: We see that the books are actually floating in the Milky Way, alongside twinkling stars and swirling black holes. Comets streak past the striped billiard ball of Jupiter suspended in the corner. I hear Liisa and Toni draw in their breath. It's mesmerizing.

Halogen lights at the front of the ballroom illuminate a small stage set with a couch and chair, angled slightly to face each other like the set of a late-night talk show. A man steps up to the stage and crosses to stand in front. He's bald, with oversized black glasses, and I immediately recognize him as Donny Dingle, the entertainment reporter for the *Connecticut Constituent*, our state's major newspaper. Donny is famous for his outlandish getups; tonight he is wearing bell-bottoms with actual bells adorning the hems. As he moves, Donny Dingle jingles.

"Welcome, everyone, welcome," he says. "I am sure you are just as excited as I am to be here this evening. You came to see me, right?" He waits for us to finish laughing. "Right. Somehow, I suspect you didn't. Well, I don't know about you, but I am dying . . . simply dying . . . to have Francesca Barber come out and say hello." He claps. We clap, too.

A woman appears from the side of the room and waves at the audience as she ascends a few steps and crosses the stage. #FrancescaBarber in the flesh. Our applause loudens and we cheer. Gracefully, she heads toward Donny, shakes his hand. She's ever so elegant, wearing loose, flowy, cream-colored pants and a matching top with scattered sequins that catch and spray light. Half a dozen gold bangles on one slim wrist jangle as she continues to wave. The applause doesn't abate, so she throws a double-handed kiss to the room. Her bangles jangle. Finally, she turns and settles onto the sofa, crossing her legs in one fluid motion. Donny claps a few seconds longer before taking his seat. Between the two of them, there's a lot of jingling and jangling onstage.

"Francesca Barber," Donny says with an incredulous shake of his head. "Producer, director, screenwriter, and world-famous author of two award-winning books . . . and soon to be three, I'm sure. Is there anything you can't do phenomenally well?"

"I'm a terrible baker, Don. I've never made an edible cake. I'm famous for mixing up ingredients—baking soda for powder, salt for sugar—and for finding a way to burn the outside and leave the inside raw. Trust me, I'm no Martha Stewart . . . you don't want to be on the receiving end of my baked goods." She laughs her famous throaty chuckle.

I'm enthralled. Who cares about her culinary skills? She probably has no time to bake anyway. This woman is everything I aspire toward, and I hang on every word, every syllable, from which I can glean some insight into her success.

Donny asks Francesca several questions about her books. How did she come up with the idea? What is her favorite part? How did it feel to experience the antigravity chamber at Kennedy Space Center as part of the research for the story?

Francesca talks about her early love of science fiction, how she consumed the entire collection of Ray Bradbury's work. "I guess I loved sci-fi because it taught me what humans are capable of," she says softly, and just for the briefest moment, there is a crack in her veneer and we are allowed in. But then she hurriedly goes on to tell us about the extensive education she had to give herself in aeronautics and astronomy to make her written stories believable.

"For many years, scientists believed that the harsh conditions on Jupiter—the frozen temperature, the pressure, the gases that characterize the planet—cannot support life," Francesca explains. "There's this thing called the Great Red Spot on the planet's surface that has been visible to us since 1830. It's actually a storm system. Not long ago, in 2018, scientists made this incredible breakthrough discovery: They found water clouds in the Great Red Spot. And scientists believe that if there's water on the planet, there could very well be life. And that gave me the basis for the story." Her expression is one of wonder.

Donny's expression, meanwhile, is playfully skeptical. "Is that really true?"

"Absolutely true. Don't misunderstand—I'm pretty sure that by 'life,' the scientists mean microbes or something. That's where, as a novelist, I get to use a little literary license."

She goes on to tell us about Jupiter's role in literature. Jupiter was the king of the gods, sky, and thunder in Roman mythology. Did we know that another name for Jupiter is Jove, and that inhabitants of Jupiter—if there were such a thing—would be called Jovians?

"The fun part to imagine was what Jovan would look like," Francesca says, talking about her male character, the love interest. She's hilarious as she recounts the many different alien life-forms she considered for him.

"I couldn't conceive of Gemma's character falling in love with some sort of octopus creature." She chuckles. "Can you imagine the sex scenes? In the end, I knew Jovan would have to be humanoid . . . even though we all know there are parts of him that are, shall we say, superhuman." She winks, and we holler and hoot.

Donny Dingle turns to the audience and says, "I have a little surprise in store for you, folks. Let's bring out some people with firsthand insight into the Jupiter movies."

CHAPTER SEVEN

The lights dim, and murmurs ripple down the rows as we wait.

Then two people walk out on the stage: When the lights come back up, we see it's Aspen Barber and Tabi Benlolo. They're holding hands and, as we jump up and whoop, they indulge in a scorching kiss before turning to grin at us from the stage.

At that, three young women rush from their seats toward the front of the room, screaming Tabi's name. I think they are going to climb up onstage and cause a scene, but Tabi looks resigned. He squats down and fist-bumps the girls. They clamor to get photos.

"Okay, ladies, why don't you go back to your seats now," Donny suggests, and the girls reluctantly return to their row. He turns to Aspen. "Does that happen often?"

"Everywhere we go." She sighs. "It must be a pheromone, some scent he releases that we ordinary humans just find irresistible."

"And how does it feel to be married to the hottest sex symbol in Hollywood?"

"I thought *I* was the hottest sex symbol in Hollywood." Aspen pouts, then bursts out in laughter at her own joke. We laugh along with her.

Tabi chuckles as he guides Aspen to the couch. Francesca shifts over on the cushions to give them space.

"Hi, Mama." Aspen gives Francesca a kiss on the cheek.

"Hi, baby," Francesca responds. The audience coos.

Aspen sits in the middle and smiles at her mother. My heart.

Basically, Francesca's daughter is a younger version of her mother: the same dark hair, albeit down to her waist; thick brows above the same pale eyes that shine silver at certain angles. Tabi lets his fingers caress her bare shoulder. Aspen, in turn, can't keep her hands off her new husband. From one moment to the next she's rubbing his knee or pushing an errant black curl out of his eyes.

"Wow, the libido on that sofa," Toni says. "Aspen's all over him."

Liisa feigns fanning herself. "He is *ridiculously* hot."

Donny hitches a thumb at the couple. "Folks, do I need to introduce these two gorgeous people?"

We shout a resounding "No!"

He turns back to them and says, "Head over heels in love, on- and off-screen. Gemma and Jovan . . . am I pronouncing that right?"

"Yes, it's Gemma," Aspen jokes. She's clad in a cutaway pink dress that leaves little to the imagination. But the audience—which is 99 percent female—is focused on the man beside her.

With a lazy smile, Tabi stretches his arms along the back of the couch. He's over six feet tall and his legs are spread, which doesn't leave much room on the cushions. "That's right, Jo-vahn," he repeats in a deep, rich accent that draws out the vowels. "I'm sorry. I know it's a little hard to wrap your mouth around it." He touches a finger to the full lips pillowed atop a bed of perfect five-o'clock shadow, and I can practically hear the collective sigh.

It's easy to see why Tabi is a rising star. He is magnetic and darkly smoldering, and his new bride is clearly smitten.

"They make a pretty cute couple, don't they?" Francesca asks us, reading the room. We cheer enthusiastically, which leads to another kiss.

Donny waits for the embrace to finish. "Aspen, talk to me about how it is to collaborate with this brilliant mother of yours."

"She's the best," Aspen says, sliding her arm under Francesca's and laying her head on her mother's shoulder. "I couldn't ask for a better mom. I mean, she can be strict, but only because she wants me to try my hardest. She made me what I am today. Love you, Mama."

The audience lets out a singsong *"Aww."* I feel a prick of tears behind my eyelids—how it must feel for Francesca to hear this affirmation from her daughter! It's precisely what I long for from Bea.

"Tell us about traveling the cosmos," Donny continues to Aspen.

"I like to say that being an astronaut means you have to be high a lot of the time," Aspen says with a giggle as she sits up. "No, really, it was the most amazing experience. It felt so real, you know? We'd be filming inside the rocket ship, and I'd forget about the cameras. I was claustrophobic all the time. And the parts where I'm tethered to the rocket but floating in space? It felt so . . . so . . . *lonely* to think of being that far from Earth. I was pretty shook. The scene where we crash on Jupiter and I find out I'm the only survivor . . . it was truly terrifying."

"But then I save you," Tabi adds, crushing her to him. "And our first kiss is out of this world."

"I'm sorry, what page is that from?" Francesca asks. "I don't recall coming up with that line." Onstage they chortle, and we do, too.

Another question, from Donny Dingle:

"I'm sure readers are wondering: Biologically speaking, could Gemma and Jovan—a human and an alien—have a baby?"

It's certainly a possibility, hints Francesca. Maybe in book four.

Donny asks if the baby would be half and half.

"Yes." Tabi doesn't miss a beat. He tips his chin toward Aspen. "We would do Christmas with her family."

We laugh and laugh. Throughout the evening Francesca Barber is charming and warm. She's so accomplished . . . no wonder Aspen looks up to her so.

The banter continues until finally Donny stands up to say there is time for the audience to ask questions.

An older woman puts up her hand and Donny jogs, bells tinkling, down the aisle with the cordless microphone. A spotlight follows him and shines on the woman. "What books do you like to read?" she asks.

Francesca thinks. “Well, besides Ray Bradbury, as I mentioned, I’ve always loved Michael Crichton. And, of course, Isaac Asimov and H. G. Wells. I guess sci-fi has always been my thing.”

Donny turns and waits for Aspen and Tabi to answer, but they have the slightly blank faces of kids who have never read a physical book. Finally Aspen responds. “Um, *Twilight*?”

There is a light smattering of applause. Donny moves to the next person.

“This question is for Tabi,” a young lady says. She’s one of the three who rushed the stage. “How do you say ‘I love you’ in your language?”

Tabi winks and turns to Aspen. *“Eu te amo,”* he tells her in Portuguese, and smoothly dips her into his arms for another deep kiss. The audience loves it.

Toni has a question. “What advice would you give a struggling author?”

Francesca smiles in our direction. “Just stick with it,” she says, and it sounds ever so slightly rehearsed. She probably gets asked this all the time. “Succeeding in writing is all about tenacity. Keep writing, and reading, and don’t give up. You’ll find many supportive people in the writing community who are eager to help in any way they can. I know I am. We’re happy to take writers under our wings.”

More hands shoot up, until finally the questions seem exhausted. “Anyone else?” Donny prompts. “Anyone?” Finally, a woman raises her hand.

“I’m sure we’re all going to read *Jupiter in Jeopardy*, but can you give us a sneak peek into the story?”

Francesca answers, “I don’t want to spoil too much, but yes! My new favorite characters include a cruel warlord from a neighboring kingdom, a young soothsayer who can see the future, and an elderly chambermaid with a bawdy sense of humor.”

In my seat, I grow cold, then hot, then cold again. I don’t even realize what I’m doing when I find myself on my feet with words flying from my mouth.

"Oh my God!" I hear myself exclaim loudly.

The room goes still, except for the sound of bells as Donny Dingle homes in on me. The spotlight, when it finds us, is blistering, and I squint as Donny shoves the microphone in my face.

"What's that?" Donny asks me.

"I . . . well . . ." A huge, dopey grin spreads across my face as the fact of this new similarity between me and obvious literary royalty makes itself known, and I immediately dismiss the possibility that this is anything less than divine.

All eyes from the stage turn toward me expectantly. "It's just that I, um, wrote a book with the exact same characters, and they're my very favorites, too."

CHAPTER EIGHT

For a brief moment Francesca looks taken aback, but then she smiles and shrugs. "They are pretty common tropes, aren't they? I mean, I hope you didn't write about an astronaut and an alien, too, or we'll be in real trouble!"

Guffaws erupt, and I feel a twinge of disappointment. Are my characters tropes?

Donny Dingle waits until the laughter fades as he makes his way back to the stage. "Well, I think it's time to wrap this up, folks. Aspen and Tabi need their beauty sleep. And y'all need to buy some books."

He directs our attention to the back tables, where Francesca Barber will meet and greet us and where signed copies of her books will be available. He suggests that supplies are limited, and immediately people jump up and begin to form a single-file line that snakes around the perimeter of the ballroom.

"That's wild about your characters," Liisa says, flanking me with Mike and Toni.

Toni nods eagerly. "You're definitely doing something right if you come up with the same stuff as her!"

"Do you think so?" I ask. Over their shoulders I see handlers hustle Aspen and Tabi toward the door. The three young girls are there waiting for them. I watch as one lifts her arms to take a selfie with Tabi. She pushes her bouncy boobs against his side and cocks a hip for the camera. The fangirls do their flirtatious best, but I see Tabi fidget and tip his head in Aspen's direction with an apologetic look that says he's not even slightly tempted, because even though he is a mere mortal and these chicks are hot and seductive, he wants nothing more than to be alone with his new bride.

My thoughts are interrupted as Toni's cell phone rings and vibrates, and an expression of concern settles on her face. Mike, Liisa, and I wait to make sure everything is okay.

"I'm so sorry, I have to get going," she says. "Brady's not feeling well. You don't mind skipping the signing, Mike?"

Mike looks relieved. "Not at all. She's too rich for my blood—I can borrow her books from the library."

He and Toni leave, and I contemplate the signing table. It's thirty-seven dollars per hardcover, or all three for a hundred (and that includes a reusable #JupiterBooks tote.) Women are whipping out Benjamin Franklins in a frenzy. You'd think it was Chippendales.

Liisa and I jostle our way out of our row and into the aisle. Since we were so close to the stage and took so long to move, we find ourselves at the tail end of the queue.

At the back of the ballroom an assembly line is up and running: One attendant is taking payments; another is jotting down names on Post-its and sticking them on book jackets to hand to Francesca, who exchanges a few words with each reader as she personalizes their books and inserts a complimentary bookmark. A third attendant snaps photos.

My mind is spinning as we inch forward. There's too much happening for me to process the situation, but all I can think of is that I'm about to meet one of my icons, whose newest book features the very same characters I created for *my* book . . . the book that could very well propel me onto the *New York Times* bestseller list, just like her. Great minds think alike!

At long last it's Liisa's turn. She has to repeat the spelling of her name for the harried attendant, who scrunches up the Post-it and tries again. She gets it right the second time and passes it to Francesca. Francesca, however, is obviously exhausted and not paying close attention, and she inscribes the book "To Lisa."

Liisa chews her lip and points to the inscription. "It's actually double *i*, but don't worry about it."

Francesca stares at her handwriting blankly. She tries to insert the second *i* but there's no way to make it look presentable. She shakes her head. "I'm sorry. Just grab a fresh copy and I'll do it over."

"That's okay, it'll make a great story," Liisa says. She scoots around the edge of the table to pose beside Francesca for a photo, then walks off to wait for me.

As I step up to the table, I hear Francesca mutter to the attendant. "Jesus Christ, I thought this would never end."

"Just two more."

"I need a drink, and not the crap in the room. You guys better have a real bar."

The girl nods vigorously, eager to help. "We do. Sam Stone's, by the lobby. They named it after one of the founders of Hartford. It's really nice, you'll like it."

I buy all three books and move to the girl with the Post-its. My name is Marcy, I start to tell her, and then think better of it. "It's Summer," I say, and step to my right.

"Pretty name," comments Francesca as she scrawls it on the title pages.

"Thank you." Nervously I pull down the edges of my shirt to cover the bulges and flattened pleats of my tailored pants. Now's my big chance. "It's great to meet you. I'm a huge fan. I already own your first two books, but as you said, we authors should support one another, right?"

Francesca glances up. She's wearing shimmery bronzer artfully applied to enhance her smooth skin and dramatic cheekbones. Her eyes narrow in recognition. "I appreciate that," she says. "What do you write?"

"Historical romance. My book is called *A Knight to Remember*—that's *knight* with a *k*."

"Clever."

"My, um, storyline has a soothsayer, chambermaid, and warlord, too."

There's an awkward silence. Francesca's smile is frozen. "I guess we see eye to eye. It was lovely meeting you, Summer. I'll look for your title." She reaches for the next book, that of the last person in line.

Before I can respond, she's signing the name of the customer behind me, and there's a flurry of activity as the attendants begin packing up the Sharpies and Post-its and leftover Jupiter books (there are less than a dozen). Their night is over, and they can't get out fast enough.

I guess we're done talking. I step aside meekly.

"This was fun," Liisa says as we turn to exit the ballroom. "You didn't want a photo with Francesca?"

I slap my forehead. "Darn it!"

"Well, go catch up with her. I'm sure she won't mind."

But I waver, and then it's too late. I can see Francesca being escorted out the door near the stage, with several helpers following at her heels like eager puppies. Not that she needs assistance, they just want to be in her orbit. They are ignored.

I can't help but be reminded of my mom. How many times did I watch her trailing after Dad and my older brothers up the veranda steps, arms laden with dry cleaning or sports equipment—or me—while they all strode ahead and forgot her, eager to turn on the game or grab a snack?

Another of Candace's quotes jumps to mind.

A long time ago I'd been involved with a project: the sale of an exclusive, gated subdivision in Greenwich, still in development, that would be worth a *lot* of money in commissions. I was pregnant with Beatrice at the time, so another young agent and I agreed to share the listings fifty-fifty. I put in a ton of work during months of uncomfortable third-trimester pregnancy while my partner barely lifted a finger.

Yet, when it came time to wine and dine the developer, to discuss the project at swanky restaurants, I went home to put up my swollen ankles and fall asleep early; and, of course, I was avoiding alcohol. At least that's what I told myself as my partner sailed out of the office, leaving me bobbing alone in her wake.

When I told Candace the story years later, hoping for empathy, she looked at me sternly. "It's your own fault," she chided. "Opportunity knocks but once. Are you going to open the door?"

Candace has repeated the traditional proverb to me, in one form or another, half a dozen times since. I can just hear her now: *It's your own fault. You wanted to talk to Francesca but didn't have a chance? You wanted a picture but didn't have a chance? You've got to make things happen.*

I know she's right. And I know something else, something no one else knows: where Francesca is headed right now. So I'm finally going to take Candace's advice. I'm going to open a door.

"Let's grab a drink," I say to Liisa, as we leave the ballroom.

CHAPTER NINE

Sam Stone's, with its flickering candles in hurricane lanterns and heavy wooden decor, harkens back to Connecticut's early colonial history. Paintings of sailboats adorn the wall behind a long, dimly lit bar that crooks around a stack of wine barrels. Liisa and I order Long Island Iced Teas and sit on stools at the bar's joint, giving us a perfect view in each direction.

Sure enough, Francesca waltzes in a minute later. Liisa nudges me with an elbow, but I don't need to be alerted; I can feel the change in energy. I hear Francesca order a cognac, and a few seconds later I draw a shaky breath and turn to face her.

"Oh, hello," I say, aiming to hit the right note of pleasant surprise. "We just met at your book signing."

Francesca takes a long sip of her cognac and tips her head side to side, working out kinks. "You're the romance writer, aren't you?"

I'm thrilled that she remembers me. "Yes! Historical romance."

"And I'm Liisa, with the double *i*." Liisa leans in and holds up two fingers. "I'm a writer, too."

Francesca nods. She's not particularly interested. She takes another gulp of her drink and glances around. The bartender says, "Last call, ladies."

It's now or never. "Actually, we didn't get a photo taken together—do you mind?"

Francesca angles toward me ever so slightly as I hand Liisa my phone. I have to hunch down so we're on the same level even though she is sitting on a high stool. She's tiny. It always amazes me that people who are larger than life on a screen can be miniatures in stature. I gush over how photogenic she is, but she's clearly not listening. She's focused on the door.

Liisa sets my phone on the bar, and I stammer on. "I would be so honored if you'd consider reading my work. I mean, I know you're busy with your tour and everything, but someday. I would love your opinion, Francesca. You know, from one author to another."

Francesca looks past me as she says, "Mm-hmm. Well, I have a lot of books to blurb, as you can imagine, so please have your publisher reach out to mine."

"Oh, it's not . . . um . . . published yet. It's a manuscript." There's an uneasy silence. Francesca slips out her own phone and starts texting. Liisa and I glance at each other and stand reluctantly. Liisa offers effusive goodbyes, telling Francesca how excited she is to dive into her book and how much she enjoyed the evening, but the woman is barely listening.

Just then a commotion sounds from the lobby and a gaggle of teenage girls rushes past the door, screeching as if the Beatles had just stepped onto the tarmac.

Liisa and I hasten out of Sam Stone's to see, but whatever the excitement was, it has already passed, and the echoes of girlish voices fade away beyond the rows of potted palms. We head toward the exit, stopping in the ladies' room and browsing the windows of exclusive boutiques as we rehash the evening and the conversation with Francesca.

"She's pretty much like you'd expect," Liisa says. "Not exactly warm and fuzzy in person."

"Well, not to us plebs, anyway."

We make it all the way across the parking lot to the car, and I'm opening the passenger door when it hits me. "Ugh, I left my books at the bar. I have to run back."

Liisa situates herself behind the wheel and opens her purse. "No worries. I want to post my photo from tonight anyway."

I hurry back inside the hotel and across the lobby all the way to the potted palms at the entrance of Sam Stone's. The music has stopped, and the place looks deserted. The candles in the hurricane lanterns have been extinguished and it's even dimmer than before. It takes my eyes a moment to adjust before I can weave my way past the chairs stacked on top of tables to the stool where I'd been sitting.

I stop in my tracks. I blink.

At first, I don't quite understand what I'm seeing, but then the image coalesces in my brain: It's Francesca, standing in the shadows at the far end of the bar. Her back is to me, but I can make out her dark hair and the flowy cream-colored pants and cream-colored blouse. There are two large hands splayed across the spine of the cream-colored blouse, and her arms are raised and wrapped around someone's neck.

This is so embarrassing.

My #JupiterBooks tote is on the floor where I left it, several feet from where Francesca is . . . er . . . writhing. Briefly I consider turning around, but I sure as hell am not leaving a hundred bucks' worth of books behind. I have the wherewithal to pull my phone out of my pocket and silence it before I take another quiet step forward, as unobtrusively as humanly possible, praying I won't disturb an encounter worthy of Lady Lisbeth and Sir Devon. I cringe as I see one of the large hands drift downward to cup the cream-colored ass.

A floorboard creaks. Francesca pulls back from her companion; her lipstick is smeared and her hair is mussed, but it doesn't register because I'm no longer looking at her. No, I can't tear my eyes from the man whose hand is still firmly planted on her butt cheek.

Tabi Benlolo.

CHAPTER TEN

A gasp escapes my throat, and I clap a palm over my mouth. I see Tabi Benlolo wipe his lips with the back of his hand. He fixes his glare on me while Francesca fixes her glare on the phone I'm holding in my hand.

"I'm—I'm—I'm so sorry, I really didn't mean to . . . uh, interrupt . . . I—I forgot my . . ."

Quickly I step forward and bend over to retrieve the tote, dropping my phone inside and lifting the bag by its straps. "Uh, here it is, I'm—I'm going now—" I shuffle backward toward the door, bumping sharply against the edge of a wooden table as I do. *"Owww,"* I yelp, as pain radiates down my thigh. I turn and flee.

I run across the gleaming floor and almost crash headlong into the electronic lobby doors because they're no longer sliding open automatically at this hour. I'm stepping sideways to the regular door and my outstretched hand is reaching for its handle when I hear Francesca's unmistakable throaty voice.

"Summer!" she calls across the deserted lobby.

Even now, in this horribly awkward situation, I can't help feeling the tiniest scintilla of pleasure that she knows me by name. I brake to a halt.

She strides up to me and pauses to fix her hair, straighten her blouse, clear her throat. Collect her thoughts. "Listen, what you saw back there—"

"I didn't see anything, really," I assure her.

"But you did. You did see." Though she is so much shorter than me, her upturned crystal eyes bore into mine. "I need to know that you won't say anything or show anyone. A lot of people could get hurt if it got out that Tabi and I . . . well, it would be devastating, as you can probably guess. Can we keep this just between us, Summer, please?"

I look longingly at the parking lot. "I get it."

But she's taking no chances. She grasps my arm with her slender hand, and the gold bangles clink on her wrist. "Do you have children, Summer?"

"One. A daughter, Beatrice."

"Then you understand. As a mother, the last thing in the world we want is to hurt our daughters. Just imagine how this would affect Aspen if she were to learn of it. It would break her."

Truthfully, I hadn't thought about Aspen in any of this.

"You wouldn't want that"—Francesca leans in conspiratorially—"for anyone's daughter, would you?"

"Of course not."

"So I can count on you, mother to mother?" She looks hopeful, but she's no dummy. She's appealing to me on our most instinctive level.

My head bobs up and down. "You can count on me, Francesca."

Her whole body relaxes a notch. "Thank you. Thank you, Summer."

I push the door open and edge a toe over the threshold. "Good night, then." I'm almost outside. I take a gulp of fresh air.

"And . . ."

I turn.

She presses a card into my palm. "I'd be happy to look at that manuscript. You know . . . author to author."

I cross the parking lot in a daze. My head is spinning. When I reach the car, Liisa is so engrossed in the comments she's getting on her Instagram post, she barely notices as I slide in next to her. Finally, she puts down her phone and shifts into reverse.

"It's late, but I've already gotten thirty likes," she says gaily. "My caption is 'Brush with Stardom.'"

"Wow."

Liisa babbles on. "Elianna Abrams gave it a thumbs-up emoji. It's the first time she's commented on anything I've shared, isn't that great?"

"Huh?" I'm not really listening. "Oh, yeah. Amazing."

As Liisa merges onto the parkway, I decide not to divulge anything to her—for tonight, anyway. Not only because I feel obligated to honor the promise I just made, but because I need time to process everything that happened.

If I'm being honest, though, it's because a part of me is already protective of the unexpected connection I just formed with Francesca Barber . . . and I don't want Liisa to insinuate herself into our burgeoning relationship.

Not very best-friendsy of me, I know.

Liisa turns on SiriusXM and sets it to the eighties station. A one-hit wonder is playing, and I catch myself listening to the lyrics.

"Why would I try?" Liisa sings along, tapping the steering wheel as she drives. "Why would I try when it's easier to lie?"

I look sidelong at her. *Yes, I suppose it* is *easier to lie.* I feel another twinge of guilt . . . but not enough to confess anything.

"So, your characters . . . the soothsayer and chambermaid . . . what was the other one?" Liisa asks.

"Warlord."

"Right, warlord. Makes me wonder if I should do a glamorous, sophisticated double agent in a tuxedo, who gambles at a casino with a gorgeous woman, in my spy story? I mean, it sounds like everyone uses tropes, right?"

I frown. "I guess." We drive the rest of the way without conversation.

"Are we walking Sunday morning?" Liisa asks as she turns onto Alpine Lane.

"Sure. Thanks for the ride."

I'm halfway up my walkway when Liisa lowers her window. "Hey, you never told me—was Francesca still at the bar when you went back inside?" she asks.

"It was almost empty." This is true. "I guess Sam Stone's closes early during the week." Also true.

"Well, at least you got a photo with her."

"Right."

"See you Sunday."

I make a beeline for the kitchen and pour myself a glass of pinot grigio to steel myself. There's some leftover pizza in the fridge from a couple of days ago. I ordered pepperoni, but they sent plain cheese. I eat it cold.

Then, before I lose my nerve, I pull Francesca's card out of my pocket. All that's printed on it is her first name and a phone number. I gulp a bit more wine.

I can practically hear Candace quoting William Arthur Ward about opportunities and sunrises, chiding me for waiting too long to grab an opportunity. I don't want to miss this sunrise. I leave a voicemail.

"Hi, uh, this is Mar—Summer. Summer Branigan. I met you earlier this evening and you . . . uh, gave me this number after you"—*Stop stammering and get to the point,* I think—"and so I'm calling about my manuscript if you, you know, have time to talk."

I disconnect and drop my forehead on the counter. Well, that was embarrassing.

CHAPTER ELEVEN

Next morning I wake up with rubatosis. No, I don't mean halitosis, although I probably have that, too. What's rubatosis, you ask, dear reader? I'll tell you: Rubatosis is the unsettling awareness of one's own heartbeat.

And why, you ask, am I afflicted with this condition?

The memory of last night has come flooding back, especially of the moment that gutted me: when I realized what I was seeing in the shadowy corner of Sam Stone's—a steamy encounter between Francesca Barber and her *ewww*, son-in-law—and it's making me exceedingly uneasy. It's so taboo.

Mother to mother, is she kidding me? If she were so concerned about her daughter, how could she do something so awful? I can't think of anything more selfish.

And it sure didn't seem like an isolated incident. No, Francesca and Tabi looked like they were totally into each other. I suspect this wasn't the first time they've hooked up. They've been going at it for a while, I'm sure of it.

My phone is charging on my dresser, and I remember I haven't gotten around to posting my most recent pic—the one Liisa took of me and Francesca. She got so many likes on hers, I should do the same.

After all, how many opportunities do I get to rub shoulders with a famous person?

Francesca. I think about her aloof manner and how her demeanor shifted from arrogance when she first joined Liisa and me at the bar to . . . desperation. After I caught her with Tabi, she pleaded with me not to tell. No, *beseeched.* That's a good word to describe it. She beseeched me.

Because if word spread, the fallout would be catastrophic: Newlyweds Aspen and Tabi would surely split up. I saw how in love Aspen is . . . she'd be heartbroken to learn that Tabi isn't being faithful. And imagine her humiliation if news of the affair went public and people heard that the "other woman" isn't some Hollywood starlet or *Sports Illustrated* cover model or even some sweet young thing from Tabi's village back home, but Aspen's own *mother*!

Francesca Barber's career and reputation would be in shambles, as would Tabi's; still, it would be way worse for Francesca because, as we all know, philandering men are forgiven much faster than the women they cheat with. Maybe, with the negative press, she'd even lose her book deal or the movie studio would back out. What a disaster.

But the worst part would be the irreparable rift it would surely cause between Francesca and Aspen. It would be impossible to mend. I'd do anything to prevent a rift like that between me and Bea.

How could I have even considered taking her up on her offer to read my work? Do I really want a woman like her doing me any favors, no matter how well she writes?

I pull out her signed copy of *Jupiter in Jeopardy* and start reading, and before long, I'm completely immersed. I finish the first chapter. And I can't help but think, anyone who puts together words so beautifully must have a beautiful soul, no? Maybe Francesca Barber made a mistake. Maybe it was a one-off thing. Maybe Francesca Barber, for all her beauty and success, is a lonely, misunderstood woman. Who would never do anything to hurt her child. *That's* why she is so anxious to keep me from talking.

Really, I should give her the benefit of the doubt.

When I reframe the situation like that, it's easier to get excited about the fact that she has agreed to help me. I reach for my phone and open Facebook to post our photo, already imagining the happy face emojis that will caption it. *What's on your mind, Marcy?* asks Facebook.

And then something pops into my mind, something Francesca said. "I need to know you won't say anything," she'd begged. "Or show anyone." Show anyone what? I remember how she'd glared at the phone in my hand when she saw me at the bar. She must have thought I'd taken a picture of her and Tabi Benlolo as they were locked in their heated, suggestive embrace. Only, I didn't. It never even occurred to me to photograph them.

Later that morning I'm in Bob's office discussing details of the Back Bay listing. I describe the woodsy area of Back Bay and tell Bob that the house is likely a teardown but I'm curious to find out how much land is worth up there. Bob seems astonished that I'm on the way to securing what could be a solid listing, and he suggests I also look into ownership of the property adjacent to Garcia's to see if the owners are interested in selling, which makes sense. I'm on it.

It's all public record, so I log on to the local assessor's office to price out the most recent sales. Then it's on to the Public Use and Benefit Land Registry to research who owns the vacant lots surrounding Garcia's. It could be an individual, a corporation . . . who knows?

Turns out there are three plots of land owned by an LLC. Like Garcia's property, each one is about an acre and a quarter—almost a football field in all. If some developer came along, it could make a great subdivision. I'm getting excited; all I can think is that with a little luck (okay, a lot of luck) this could be a substantial sale that yields me some sorely needed revenue.

More digging, and I find out that the LLC is registered to an entity in New Canaan. Feeling like a regular Nancy Drew, I dig up a phone number and call.

A cultured voice answers. "Gil Carter."

"Hi, my name is Marcy Jo Codburn, and I'm with Robert Verney Realty," I tell him. He hasn't disconnected yet so I rush on. "I'm calling regarding your land in Back Bay?"

The man on the other end is polite but noncommittal. I'm not surprised, as real estate cold calls don't necessarily work out in my favor. But then he tells me he's open to discussion.

"How about we meet one day next week?" I suggest.

"I'll be tied up at a conference. If this is urgent, you can drop by my office this afternoon."

I'll be there in an hour, I tell him. I print out some paperwork, stuff it into the #JupiterBooks tote on my front seat, and off I go.

This May day feels like a hundred humid degrees and the walk from the parking lot to the building, which is maybe twenty feet, leaves me damp and frizzy. The last thing I want to see, when I ring the bell at the address in New Canaan, is the pencil-skirted, spike-heeled, sun-streaked young blonde who looks like a supermodel fresh off the runway. Without a word, she gives me a once-over before leading me to an interior office.

She knocks lightly before opening a set of double doors and standing aside as I enter. There's a fireplace and a floor-to-ceiling window and an ornate mahogany desk, behind which is a man with the most perfectly coiffed hair I've ever seen.

"Gil Carter," he says, coming around the desk and holding out a hand. "Can I get you anything? Coffee, tea?" he asks.

I want a bath, but I settle for a glass of ice water. "Thanks so much for seeing me," I begin. "As I mentioned on the phone, I'd like to discuss your property in Back Bay."

"Yes, my LLC holds the title," Mr. Carter confirms. "It's been undeveloped for generations, except for an old structure or two. Not much to see up there, I'm afraid. And the nearby area has really atrophied."

"You're right, and I'm wondering if you have considered selling? I ask because I'm currently listing the abutting corner lot"—here, I pull out a sheaf of papers to show him the plat map of the area, which shows where the original surveyors established property lines—"and together, my client's parcel, along with your three, could be quite valuable."

Gil Carter studies the map and nods vigorously. Not a single hair moves.

"Before I could go forward with listing it, I would have to discuss it with my partners, of course," he says. "But if a buyer came along, I think we would seriously entertain a decent offer. As I mentioned on the phone, I'm tied up at a conference next week, but I'll be seeing my partners there."

He escorts me to the door, and I thank him for his time.

CHAPTER TWELVE

I've been so absorbed with working on the Back Bay listing that when my phone rings in the evening I don't recognize the number on my screen.

"Hello, Summer," comes the distinctive throaty voice. "I received your message."

My heart stops in its tracks. "Oh, Francesca, thank you for calling me back!"

"I promised I would look at your work, and I will," she says. "A promise is a promise. Isn't that right, Summer?"

Talk about subtle. "Absolutely."

Francesca tells me to email the manuscript and she will get to it as soon as the hectic schedule of her book tour allows.

After I hang up, it occurs to me that the name she will see on the email is Marcy Codburn. I open my laptop and create a new Gmail address: Summer dot Branigan dot Author. I write a little note, attach *A Knight to Remember: A Novel*, and, with a deep breath, hit send.

I did it. I did it! I stand up and dance a little jig in my kitchen in celebration. I'm not a watcher, I'm a doer! For the first time in years I feel like I'm back in the game.

Bea is going to be so proud of me. I am breaking the cycle of inaction my mother passed down to me. My manuscript is *not* just sitting in storage—I *am* doing something with it, something transformative. For the manuscript . . . and for *me.* I can just imagine curling up on the couch with my daughter, reading aloud excerpts from Francesca's overview. Maybe we'll go out to celebrate—brunch at that fancy place with a pitcher of her favorite mimosas?

I won't tell her about what's happening just yet, at least not until Francesca gets back to me with her glowing critique, but then . . .

I jig again.

Beatrice begins her research program soon, so we go shopping for the close-toed shoes she'll need in her laboratory setting. I don't mean to boast about my daughter, but this program, offered through her grad school, is competitive. Only five students nationwide were selected, and believe me, it was a rigorous process! She was determined to snag a spot.

She chose to take two credits over again in her college freshman and sophomore summers to raise her already-exceptional grades. She tutored high school students in her spare time throughout her four years, and rarely complained about missing frat parties or tailgating. One of the requirements for the program was actual hands-on laboratory experience, and last summer she found it in Elizabeth, New Jersey. Every day for three weeks I drove her there and drove her home. I brought my laptop and passed the hours waiting for her in the cafeteria of the nearby IKEA, and by the end of her internship, I'd amassed two assembly-required bookcases, a pedestal table, a flat-woven rug, an outdoor plant stand, and a set of towel rods I don't know how to install. I also ate enough Swedish meatballs to last a lifetime and have about a thousand leftover screws.

Yes, those weeks were a pain, but I'm sure the glowing reference letter she received helped her into the current program, which includes seminars and a research symposium led by faculty she'll study under next fall.

I assumed she'd want sneakers, but she surprises me and tries on a loafer. I'm about to say: *Make sure they're comfortable because you'll be on your feet a lot,* but before I do, she stands and walks up and down the aisle. "I'd better get a half size bigger," she says, and I'm reminded she's not a kid anymore.

"Explain again what you'll be working on," I ask instead.

"Mom, I told you, the project is to develop a more effective fire-resistant paint." Bea turns her feet this way and that in the mirror. She's already explained several times, but I like sharing in the anticipation. "Right now the epoxy-based intumescent coatings only delay the spread of flames. Our team is developing a new formula that not only creates a fire barrier, it won't contain the dangerous vapors and aerosols that lead to respiratory problems when inhaled."

It certainly sounds impressive. *She* sounds impressive.

"Just think . . . one day I might have my name on a scientific paper published in an industry journal," Bea says dreamily as we stand in the long, snaking cashier's line. "My professors say getting published is unparalleled for personal growth and career advancement."

Don't I know it.

"I have no doubt it will happen," I tell her. "I'm so proud of you, sweetheart."

"Speaking of proud, did you hear that a gallery in the city is planning an exhibit of Dad's earlier works? It will feature sketches from his college days to now."

I didn't hear. I swallow.

We inch forward. Behind us is a young mother with two small children crammed into a shopping cart under a mountain of purchases. When one of them reaches for a toy, the harried mom swats his hand away, and he launches into a prolonged earsplitting shriek.

We're the very next ones in line, but I feel sorry for the woman. "Do you want to go ahead?" I ask her. She mutters something about spoiled brats as she wheels past, and we are forced to listen to the cacophony as she takes forever to pay.

"You're too nice for my own good," Bea says, covering her ears.

CHAPTER THIRTEEN

Someone might be interested in my listing. I can't believe it, but I actually receive an inquiry from a man in London regarding the lot.

We email back and forth. Victor Thane represents an investment group that buys property for a UK pharmaceutical giant that intends to open a distribution center in the tristate area—New York, New Jersey, or Connecticut—and my listing for "one-and-a-quarter flat acres with possible additional four acres, in undeveloped area with easy on-off access to highway and waterway" could be ideal. He wants well-situated East Coast land.

Mr. Thane will be in the US scouting locations in a few months. I'm pretty sure no one will want to acquire Garcia's place in the meantime.

Things have taken a (slight) turn for the better.

A respected (and connected) author is going to critique my manuscript.

I have a (potentially) lucrative new listing.

And Gil Carter has agreed to meet with me again in advance of Victor Thane's visit, which could mean an even more lucrative listing.

This time, I think, I'm not showing up at the elegant New Canaan office in yoga pants. I decide to take stock. My closet is full of stylish professional clothes—dresses and skirts and pantsuits—that I haven't been able to squeeze into since . . . I guess since before Kevin and I divorced. Many years before, actually. I pull out piece after piece I would happily wear if I could. The tight black trousers from the other night are in a heap on the floor, and I assess them balefully. Something in me snaps.

Before I can talk myself out of it, I put on Nikes and grab earphones and head for the trail. It's not a pretty sight, me part jogging, part waddling, and puffing with exertion, but I make it to the half-mile marker. That's a full mile round trip. I have to admit, I'm a little pleased with myself for actually doing it. Soon I'll push myself to do three-quarters of a mile each way.

After I shower, I jump in the car and head for the charming main street of our town. I pass Well Read, the secondhand bookshop; All Fired Up, the wood-oven pizza place; and Full of Hot Air, the new blow-dry bar. Beside the Sunny Side Up diner is the old-fashioned apothecary, where I buy a box of meal-replacement bars and a new mauve lipstick. My metamorphosis has begun.

CHAPTER FOURTEEN

A week has passed, and I've just come home from my weekly Espresso Yourself session with Liisa, where I forfeited my iced mochaccino in favor of regular iced coffee with a splash of cream and a sprinkle of Splenda. It tasted bitter after a habit of super-sweet drinks, but I'll adjust.

It's another sunny Sunday, and I bring my computer outside on the back patio.

'Tis a cold winter's night, and I see by glow of moonlight m'lord in his bed, and in his hand, his head," chuckles the maid to herself. "I've come to stoke his fire, as a good chambermaid should, but I see now that m'lord needs nought, for he's brought his own wood.

I'm staring into space, wondering whether my bawdy chambermaid should regularly speak in rhymes, when the sliding door slides open.

"Mom? *Mom.*"

I'm jolted from my reverie. "Oh, hi, Honey Bea."

"What are you doing? You're totally zoned out."

"I'm working. On a character." I turn my computer around so she can see what I've written just now. "Do you think it's funny?"

"I don't get it." She rolls her eyes. "Anyway, can I talk to you about something important? You know how I'm thinking of going down to Savannah before my internship starts."

No, I don't know. "Again?" I ask. "You were there last summer. Why the return trip so soon?"

"Patrick's parents live there."

Patrick is her boyfriend of the past year. I didn't know he hailed from Georgia. "You're visiting his family? For the second time? Dad and I haven't even met him yet."

"You will. You'll love him. Anyway, Dad is picking me up in a sec, and we're going back to his house. He's going to help me book a flight. He said he'd pay for it."

"I see."

"So I just wanted to let you know I won't be home till late. He and James are making dinner."

"Are they?"

"Yeah. They're into super-healthy cooking: whole grains, nuts and seeds, nothing processed. I love that."

There's a honk from out front and Bea lets the gate slam behind her. I turn back to my story and erase everything I wrote today. I thought it was good, but I guess not.

Before long the Sunday afternoon doldrums kick in and I move indoors. I start rifling through the cabinets and wrap my fingers around an open package of Oreos. I'm about to take a bite when Bea's voice comes to me and, before I have second thoughts, I grab a garbage bag and divest the shelves of all the cookies, crackers, candy. Anything processed. Out go the empty carbs from the fridge and freezer. There's a box of frozen waffles, but they're high fiber, so they survive the purge. I have a moment of sheer agony when I come upon an unopened tub of Häagen-Dazs, in my favorite white chocolate raspberry truffle flavor, but I force myself to throw it away, tie up the bag with a triple knot, and carry it outside. I even scatter some other trash over the bag once it's in the bin, just for good measure.

I'm taking out stuff for a salad when my laptop pings with a new email. It's from Francesca Barber! Sooner than expected. My hand shakes as I click my mouse.

> Hello Summer,
>
> I hope you are well. I've skimmed through the beginning of *A Knight to Remember*. You have a very good imagination and it's clear you've put a lot of work into this story. I like the character of Sir O'Keefe, and the king has some fun dialogue. My advice to you is:
>
> • Brush up on your grammar. I noticed quite a few split infinitives. Make sure you are consistent with pronouns and tense. *Grammar for Dummies*, or similar, might help.
> • Show, don't tell. Rather than you (as the author) explaining how a character feels, let the reader see it through the actions or expressions of the character.
> • Keep writing! Don't give up. The more you write, and the more you read, the better you'll get.
>
> Best of luck,
> Francesca Barber

Wait just a minute. This is it? This is the expert evaluation of my manuscript . . . a few generic paragraphs that could apply to anyone? She didn't even mention the coincidental overlap of our three characters. I scroll up and down in the email, but I've hit bottom. Maybe I overlooked an attachment, like a redlined version of the document? Nope. This is all she sent.

The big, bold headline I'd so hoped to share with my daughter—that I'd received a glowing, supportive, professional critique of my manuscript by a world-renowned author!—falls to the wayside like a newspaper discarded in the street and trampled by a thousand indifferent pedestrians. We won't be having mimosas anytime soon.

I drop my face into my hands. Here we go again. I know I shouldn't have gotten my hopes up, but secretly I thought this time my luck would change, that all my efforts would pay off, that something wonderful would happen. It's the story of my life, isn't it? Being thwarted and disappointed?

But then I pull myself up short. *Stop it,* I tell myself sternly. *Just stop feeling sorry for yourself. Stop rolling over like your mother.* That's what Candace would say, wouldn't she? I followed Candace's advice at the book signing—first I opened a door, walked through, and placed myself at Sam Stone's . . . and ended up meeting Francesca Barber. Then I grasped the next opportunity that presented itself . . . and emailed my manuscript off for Francesca's consideration. Well, it's true she didn't respond the way I hoped. But, as Candace would scold, why in the world would I stop now and squander what I had already accomplished? If I were writing my autobiography, I'd title it *Squandered Opportunities: The Marcy Jo Codburn Story* or *A Road Regretted: The Almost Successes of a Mostly Meh Life.*

Come on, Marcy. For Pete's sake, don't let this slip through your fingers.

I press reply and stare at the blank screen with a pounding heart. Finally, I type.

> Hi Francesca,
>
> Thank you for looking at the beginning of my book. I will definitely take the valuable advice you suggested. But I'm wondering if you might be able to read on in the manuscript so that you could give me more specific feedback? It would be very much appreciated.
>
> Sincerely,
> Summer

Send.

Just a few minutes go by and her reply hits my inbox.

> Summer, as you can imagine, I'm extremely busy these days with my book launch and other projects. I simply can't agree to an in-depth critique of your manuscript at this time. I hope you understand.
>
> Francesca

Her dismissive tone is one I know well.

I recognize that I have a choice here: to forget the whole thing, or not. I guess I can choose to be my mother, a puppy trailing after my father, awaiting validation; for that matter, choose to be what I'd always been as a wife to Kevin . . . the audience to his solo. I mean, that's how Beatrice has always known me.

I choose the "not." I think and think about how to respond to Francesca. I draft and delete several different responses. I decide to take a break and clear my thoughts before emailing again. As I pick at my salad, I think back to Francesca's proposal in the hotel lobby. I mean, she's the one who offered to read my manuscript, right?

I type,

> I'm a little disappointed, I thought we had a deal.

I hit send, but then I'm racked with regret. I shouldn't have phrased it that way, shouldn't have been so aggressive . . . it almost sounds like an ultimatum. She'll probably never speak to me again. Hours go by. Should I send another note to apologize? I walk around my neighborhood, force myself to do crunches on my living room carpet, take a shower, get ready for bed. When I'm done with all that, I refresh my inbox. There's a reply.

> Dear Summer: Let me see what I can do about reading the rest of *A Knight to Remember*. Please give me a little time to make my way through the manuscript as it is rather lengthy. Thank you so much and I'm looking forward to reading. Warmly, Francesca

Whoa. What just happened?

CHAPTER FIFTEEN

I'm back in one of Gil Carter's tufted leather chairs. His young assistant gave me another once-over at the door before showing me into his office, but this time I'm wearing discount store finds: a navy wrap dress with some jewelry and a bit of heel, and instead of carrying my paperwork in the #JupiterBooks tote like last time, I've switched to the Coach messenger bag I had tucked away in my closet. I speak with lips coated in Mulberry Mauve and tell her I'd love a coffee. Just a drop of milk, please.

"Sorry to keep you waiting," Mr. Carter says. He sits down across from me and steeples his fingers. "I did have a chance to speak with my partners. We're all in agreement about the property in Back Bay. Should an appropriate buyer come along, we'd be willing to sell."

"That's wonderful news, Mr. Carter." I imagine Garcia and his family jumping for joy if I can actually pull this off. "As a matter of fact, there is an interested party." I tell him about Victor Thane and the pharmaceutical group. I pull out my documents and show him the comps I ran. I explain how the location, with its close proximity to the freeway (the parcels of land are within sight of the overpass) and inlet would be ideal for a major trucking-and-distribution center. Such a project could signal the beginning of an entire revival of the town. It could herald promising new investment opportunities.

We chat about the real estate market in the nation and the changes since the pandemic. It's a lively conversation. I don't really know what Mr. Carter does for a living, and the brass plaque outside the front door for CARTER & ASSOCIATES is ambiguous, but he certainly understands the economy. He seems impressed with my expertise, too.

I ask him about his work.

"My grandfather and father amassed quite a bit of wealth in construction. Shopping malls, primarily, which are now defunct, of course, but it was profitable at the time. I invest the earnings. Dabble in hedge funds, VC, acquisitions."

"What sort of acquisitions?"

"On my trip to Asia last summer, I acquired a failing tech company in Japan. I'll do some stripping."

My eyes widen, and he chuckles softly.

"Remember Richard Gere's character in that movie, *Pretty Woman*? That's what he did. Asset stripping. I sometimes buy companies, then peel off the valuable assets bit by bit and sell them separately."

Vaguely, I recall something about a shipyard in the movie. "What sort of assets?" I ask.

"Subsidiaries. Equipment. Property. Wherever the value is."

"What happens to the employees?"

"Well," he explains, "the businesses I buy are going under. Either way, the employees would be out of a job."

I think for a moment. "But if the assets are so valuable, why wouldn't the current leadership of the failing companies sell off a few of the assets themselves to improve their financial situation? Reduce their debt burden?"

"Very astute observation. The answer is that when I get involved, it's usually a hostile takeover, which can get quite ruthless." He sees that I'm slightly taken aback. "Sometimes you have to be ruthless to get what you want. It doesn't make you a bad person, just one who does whatever it takes to reach a goal."

Kevin is coming by this afternoon. There are a bunch of tools in the garage he wants to take, along with his portfolio, which is fine by me; the less clutter I have to sort, the better.

When I open the door, still wearing my new navy outfit, he seems surprised.

"Look at you," he says, kissing my cheek. The kiss is new, too. I wouldn't say our divorce has been acrimonious, exactly, but neither have we been as amicable as Liisa and her ex. More accurately, we've been silent. What could I say to the fact that my husband wanted to trade in his wife for a husband? Clearly we'd drifted so far apart over the years that I didn't know him at all, and I guess he really didn't know me, either. We were a continental drift that turned into a permanent divide.

As with any couple splitting up, there is residual tension. Hence the novelty of cheek kissing.

"Thanks." The garage door is open, but I invite him inside. I set the portfolio by the basement door; then I pour us both a Diet 7UP.

Kevin looks around the house. He notices I've swapped out some of the decor since he left—the IKEA pedestal-base table to replace the heavy wooden one, a lighter-colored sectional, and the flat-woven rug—and painted everything alabaster white. It's much airier and fresher these days, especially since Kevin took away all his artwork that had crowded the walls. Mind you, he also took the good silver, the expensive bedding, and my favorite ice bucket.

"Nice job with the backsplash. Very Scandinavian." That, too, was a big project: subway tile to set off the white cabinetry. You have to look pretty closely to see where the tiles don't quite line up.

"I was surprised Bea is taking another trip to visit Patrick's parents in Savannah," I confess, perching on a stool at the butcher-block island.

"They're staying at his house, but with incidentals and meals out, I figured she'd need spending money, so I gave her some."

"That was generous of you." Correct response, I think. I'm proud of the fact that we aren't one of those couples who try to one-up the other when it comes to treating the kids, but still, I long for the day when my book starts selling so that for once *I* can be the parent to spoil my daughter.

One thing is for sure: Kevin and Bea have always been close, maybe even closer than Bea and me, and that's remained the case since the divorce. Being away at college spared Bea having to witness some of our drama.

We sip our drinks. I notice Kevin is wearing skinny jeans and a khaki army-style jacket loaded with decals, and has swapped his rimless glasses for a pair with wide, funky frames. He's also grown his hair into a short ponytail. He tells me about his recent exhibits—he's switched from oils to watercolors, which you'd think is earth-shattering to hear him talk about it—along with his subscription to a concert series in the city, his plans to go skiing next winter. When he asks as an afterthought whether I'm still pursuing writing, I tell him I am and veer into a recounting of the latest news from my writers' group.

"How's James?" I'm at the point where I can ask that easily. James and Kevin live several towns over in a beautifully restored historic saltbox.

"Good. He's visiting his sisters in California. He'll be gone for a week, so I thought I'd get a little yard work done."

Kevin thanks me for the soda, picks up the leather portfolio, and heads to the garage, where he finds the spreader and trowel and loads them into his Subaru. I'm impressed; I didn't think he knew what those tools were for.

After he leaves, it occurs to me how much he's changed. I don't mean his new outfit or new hairstyle or even his new medium—but rather a mental shift, expanded horizons, personal growth. Maybe it's high time I take a cue from my ex-husband.

A week and a half of radio silence from Francesca has gone by. It's a Thursday night, and my writers' group arrives at O'Keefe's. Even though it's only June, the air-conditioning at the public library is already on the fritz and the conference room upstairs is stifling, so we decide to hold our weekly session at the pub. Mike gets his usual craft beer, Toni and Liisa opt for cosmopolitans, and I order a plain, unsweetened iced tea.

Behind the bar, Brian lifts a brow. "What happened to your usual? You've never not asked for a Long Island Iced Tea."

"Trying something new," I say.

He peers at me and says, "You look nice." Mike, Toni, and Liisa turn to me and chime in with their own affirmations.

"Thank you." I feel a little flush of pleasure. I'm not used to being complimented or being the center of attention. I attribute it to my new eating program and exercise these past few weeks—the scale is inching, pound by excruciatingly slow pound, downward. My yoga pants and T-shirts aren't exactly baggy, but they are looser. Maybe I'll treat myself to something new to wear.

We get down to business. "I have news," Mike starts. His eyes shine with excitement. "It may be premature, but my short story 'A Middle of the Road Murder' has been accepted for publication in a literary magazine. It's slated to be printed in October. I guess we'll see if it gets cut or not." We applaud and give him a round of high fives.

Then Toni looks up with her usual shy expression. "I guess I have something to add. Now that the twins are starting daycare, I've accepted a job offer with *The Little Fork*, an online food-and-entertaining magazine. I'm going to write about New England cuisine." We applaud again and congratulate her.

Liisa grins. "Well, I'm not sure it's worth a round of applause, but I wrote a few more pages this week . . . that's about it." A few pages is fantastic, we agree.

"How 'bout you? What's doing?" Toni asks me.

Everyone turns to me. Of course, the last thing in the world I'm going to do is tell them about the circumstances with Francesca Barber that led to her critique of my manuscript.

"Nothing really new on my end," I say with a shrug. "But I'm so glad for you three."

The four of us clink glasses. “To bestsellers,” we toast. It’s our tradition.

Liisa and Toni take their leave early, and Mike raises his brows to me. “Up for one more round of tea?”

“I shouldn’t, I’m driving,” I joke, “but okay.” I sip my refill and smile at Mike.

We’ve never spent time alone together, and I don’t know much about his personal life, except that his wife died in a bicycle accident years earlier and he never remarried. But I’ve always liked him, always enjoyed a fun banter. He’s strong and decisive, perhaps as a function of his law enforcement job. It doesn’t hurt that he’s a nice-looking man, with his crinkly brown eyes and graying goatee. Understated, but with keen insight that comes through in his witty short stories.

I guess we’re on a similar get-to-know-you wavelength. He asks, “Coke or Pepsi?”

“Coke. You?”

“Pepsi. Pool or beach?”

“Beach.”

“Same. Early bird or night owl?”

“Neither,” I say with a grin. “I like to sleep. You?”

“Definitely early bird. Up at dawn every day. Boat or airplane?”

“I don’t really know. I hate flying, but I don’t have much experience with boats, although I like the idea of them.”

“I have one. She’s my baby.” The look on Mike’s face tells me this boat is his pride and joy. “You’ll have to meet her one day.”

The conversation returns to writing. Our chatter is comfortable and friendly, and before I know it, Brian is brandishing his broom . . . our cue to go home.

CHAPTER SIXTEEN

Mike's call comes out of the blue. He rings me at work as we're finishing our Monday afternoon meeting, so I excuse myself to see what he wants. What he wants is to have lunch. After our comfortable conversation at the bar the other night, I don't even think twice. We agree to meet in two days' time.

I'm under no illusions: He has no romantic interest, nor do I. But, thinking of the changes Kevin's made, back I go to my local pharmacy. This time I pick up a bottle of hair dye in my natural tone. I slip on the loose plastic gloves and start squirting. An hour later the gray has disappeared. It's a small improvement.

The restaurant, which I've never been to before, is located in a private yacht club, and its sliding glass front wall has been opened to take advantage of the unseasonable temps. When I arrive, the host leads me to a front table with an unobstructed view of the marina and, beyond it, a sandy-shored cove. Mike is already here, holding a coupe with a wedge of lime in it, which is strange since I've only ever seen him drink beer.

"Thanks for joining me," he says, rising as the host pulls out my chair.

As I sit down, a heavenly sea breeze wafts over me, stirred up by bamboo-bladed fans high above us. I haven't been to a place like this in forever. "What a lovely spot. Are you a member?"

"I am." He points out the window to a row of vessels moored several slips away from shore. They're rocking gently in the surf, and I can't make out any details except that they're huge, the kind I imagine Francesca and Aspen and their #celebrity ilk enjoying. "That's my girl right there."

For one brief second I imagine myself in a sailor cap, spinning one of those big wooden captain's wheels, and the fleeting thought makes me giddy. A waiter appears to take my drink order.

Mike says, "They make a mean gimlet."

"Well . . ." I look around the restaurant. Everyone seems to have a glass of something, and I don't want to be rude. I could have just one and get back on my sugar-free plan tomorrow. "Sure, maybe I'll join you."

"Two more, please." Mike lifts his glass.

The waiter sets two enormous gimlets in front of us. I sip, and it's delicious and so strong, I feel the buzz immediately. Whether it's the gin or the company, my tongue loosens, and our conversation flows like last time.

He tells me anecdotes about growing up in Worcester, Massachusetts, parts of which I recognize from his short stories. His siblings are a younger brother and an older, married sister, and while his brother lives in Austin and his sister with her husband and kids in Charleston, all three are still close. I tell him all about Beatrice and how I'm so proud of her life's trajectory, how she's the best thing I've ever done, how I'm sure she's destined for a Nobel.

"Thank you for inviting me here," I add. I'm a touch woozy from the gimlet. Wow, the detox must work—my body's really not used to alcohol. I give my head a little shake to clear it.

"You're welcome." Mike is smiling at me over the remains of his grilled salmon in dill sauce. He sees I've finished my drink and asks if I want another.

"I couldn't," I protest. "I'm already feeling the effects."

"If you aren't in a rush to get back to your office, we can walk a bit. I'd love to show you around."

After lunch that's what we do. Mike takes me on a tour of the club, making sure to grab me a large bottle of water as we go. The pickleball courts are full. Golf carts zip past. We head down to the marina, where he brings me to his boat. Up close, it's dwarfed by the neighboring craft, some of which look like they'd feature Doc, Gopher, and Julie Your Cruise Director. I can just imagine Isaac serving gimlets.

Mike's boat is sleek and shiny and looks fast. I read the metallic lettering aloud. "*Dahlia's Dream*. So pretty."

"Named for my wife." He holds out a hand. "Want to step aboard? You'll have to take off your shoes, though. Rubber soles only." He indicates his own Top-Siders.

Slipping out of my heels on the dock, I grasp his hand and step barefoot onto the hull. I'm unprepared for the motion underfoot, and whether it's the waves or the cocktail, I immediately lose my balance. Mike catches me before I fall, and I find my face about five inches from his amused smile. I'm not expecting the warm rush I feel, or the vague disappointment as he leads me to a cushioned fiberglass seat and plunks me down.

"Drink your water, lightweight," he says, mocking me mildly. I don't mind it one bit.

"We should have our next group meeting out on the ocean," I say.

He laughs. "We can write the next *Moby-Dick*."

We chat amiably as I sip from the bottle until it's empty, enjoying the scenery and rhythmic rocking. I almost don't want to leave except that I'm starting to feel ever so slightly queasy.

Suddenly my stomach roils in rebellion, and I clap a hand over my mouth. I lurch to the side of the boat and lean out, returning my salmon to the waters from whence it came. At last I catch my breath, thinking I'm done, but no—another wave doubles me over in a long retch so that the remainder of my meal, the crusty bread and asparagus and couscous, is deposited in Long Island Sound for the sea creatures to enjoy.

Mike guides me by my elbow to lay me down on the seat. "Mal de mer," he says, and busies himself below deck getting some ice and a washcloth to lay across my forehead until the dizziness passes. "Happens to the best of us."

I groan. My stomach feels like a tumble dryer, but the cool compress is definitely helping. Mike waits patiently as twenty minutes go by. "How are you feeling?"

Gingerly I pull myself up to sitting. "Mortified. I'm so sorry."

He laughs and holds out a hand to help me back onto the dock. "We'll have to work on your sea legs," he tells me, "but we'll make a mariner out of you yet."

I'm on the couch reading *Jupiter in Jeopardy* and shriveling inside because the prose is so eloquent and the story so engrossing. Why can't I write like this? When my iPhone buzzes with my daughter's signature bumblebee ringtone, I practically lift off the cushions, I'm so startled. I reach across the coffee table to answer.

"Hi! How are you, sweetheart?"

"Hey, Mom. I landed." I can hear tarmac noises in the background. "How's the hive?"

My heart melts. It always does when she kibitzes like this. She tells me Kevin is dropping her off, so I rush around and tidy up for her homecoming.

A little while later, I greet Bea with fresh-squeezed lemonade. "You look younger, Mom," she says. "Did you color your hair?"

"Do you like it?" I pour her a glass, pleased. "How's Patrick? Still writing song lyrics?"

"He's a *poet*, Mom. He's such a sensitive soul. He wrote me the most beautiful poem. Wanna hear it?" She opens her backpack and pulls out a piece of paper. "It's called 'Sun Love':

My love for you is not a rose
So fragile, small, and weak
Nor is it a birdsong, sweet but empty
Its sender meek
My love for you is like the sun
A candle in a world
Depressing and bleak
My love is nowhere of this earth
It knows not pain, cold, nor strife
My love for you is like the sun
Whose warmth and timeless beauty
Is the giver of all life.

"Isn't it great?" she gushes.

"It's something," I say.

Bea flops into a recliner and drapes her legs over the upholstered arm. She tells me all about her trip to Savannah: eating shrimp and grits, visiting the Bonaventure Cemetery, the Spanish moss dripping from the trees.

"What was the best part?" I ask.

"We did a paranormal mystery tour that was fun. Apparently Savannah is the most-haunted city in the US."

"And Patrick's parents were nice?"

"So nice!"

"Things must be getting serious if you've visited his family. Twice."

"Yeah, you know, I'd say things are pretty real."

I take a little breath. Bea had a boyfriend in high school and a couple in college, but nothing that lasted more than a few months.

She continues: "He wants to meet you and Dad."

"We would love that. Especially since we didn't get to meet him at graduation."

"Mom, we've been through this. Patrick really wanted us to go white water rafting with his buddies, and it was the only time they could do it. Being in nature is very inspiring for him."

I clamp my lips shut. I won't rehash it. Bea's skipping her college graduation weekend in favor of paddling some inflatable down a river with her boyfriend came as a shock. I hadn't wanted to make it about me or Kevin, though I couldn't help mentioning she was the only child we'd get to see in a cap and gown.

"On the mantel there's a big framed picture of me in a cap and gown from high school graduation," she'd pointed out at the time.

Now there's also a framed photo of her in a life jacket.

CHAPTER SEVENTEEN

Bob the Broker calls me into his office to discuss the Back Bay listing.

"Nicely done, getting that expanded property on the market," Bob says. His face is purple as ever despite his jovial tone. "I have some more commercial properties I think you're ready to handle."

I leave his office as the listing agent of a sprawling office park in Wilton as well as a factory in Wethersfield that produces roofing tiles. Moreover, Bob has asked me to tour two aerospace-manufacturing facilities near Hartford. They're part of Connecticut's so-called Aerospace Alley, a cluster of companies known as the world's premier aerospace manufacturers and known also for their highly skilled workforce. Both facilities make components for Lockheed Martin engines—nuts, bolts, assorted unrecognizable metal fittings—and while none of this sounds especially sexy to me, the plants turn a profit and sit on valuable land to boot.

Within just a few days of listing the Wethersfield factory, we have an offer, and it's a decent one. I'm amazed at how quickly and easily it happens, and when it goes through it will be the biggest commission I've earned in years.

Bob the Broker approves; his chins jiggle as he nods his head and taps a chubby finger on his desk blotter. "Primo job, Codburn, primo," he says, which is the highest praise he allots.

Buoyed and happy, I text Bea to see whether she wants to grab an early dinner, but she's not available. As a lark, I ask Mike; I'm not completely sure he'll want to after my maritime disaster, but to my pleasant surprise, he agrees. We meet at a halfway point.

"Nothing to drink?" Mike raises a brow as I push aside the cocktail menu.

"Absolutely not. I don't want to risk a repeat of my . . . er . . . incident at sea."

Mike lets out a hearty laugh. "But we're on dry land."

"Even so."

Later, over dessert, he asks me to go out with him on Saturday for a "sail" to celebrate the "sale."

I love a good homophone, I tell him, and accept the invitation.

In anticipation of the upcoming outing, I splurge on white capris and a pair of Sperry boat shoes. I don't typically spend much on clothes—you know, single homeowner budget with many a repair needed, plus a kid in school—but the Wethersfield check is practically in the mail.

In the days leading up to Saturday, I'm nervous. What if I get seasick again? As it turns out, without the alcohol my digestive system is one directional. The afternoon is glorious, warm and calm. It's not windy, which might be frustrating for Mike but is reassuring for a newbie like me.

"See?" he teases as we're docking. "Your first time, and you handled it like a pro."

Afterward, we go for another long stroll, this time around town. I suppose it's becoming our routine. It's effortless to be with him—his easy smile and charm and zero demands. I get the sense that Mike is perfectly happy to be spending time with a purely platonic friend.

Honestly, I don't question the arrangement much. It feels like the simplest part of my life right now.

On the trail the next day, Liisa is incredulous. "What do you mean, you went sailing with Mike? How do I not know this?"

"There's nothing between us," I say firmly, immediately regretting bringing up the topic. Then I hasten to add, in an attempt to distract from mentioning Mike: "I also have a new client, from New Canaan. You know the type: very well manicured, intelligent, successful."

"I want to hear more about you and Mike!"

"You know Mike . . . he's kind and considerate. And fun." My voice softens and Liisa notices.

She whistles. "You *like* him."

I examine my surroundings as we walk—ferns lining the rocky path, interlaced treetops. I'm super conscious of her gaze. I shrug. "You think he's cute, too. We discussed this."

"Uh-huh." She presses her lips together.

I want to tell her more, that he's attentive and courteous and makes me feel . . . heard. For the first time in a long time.

"So what prompted this pivot?" Liisa asks after a while. "You never mentioned being interested in Mike before. The new you?"

"We're just friends," I say firmly. "It's definitely the same old me."

Toward the end of the trail I beg off our social media session. I don't mention that Mike is taking me to the driving range since I've never tried golf before.

After a gazillion attempts to hit a ball, it hits me: I am *not* cut out for this sport. "Just believe in yourself, Marcy," Mike coaches, and whether it's his words or because I stop trying so hard, the club makes contact with the ball and sends it catapulting across the range in a gorgeous, straight arc. Mike whistles.

We're getting into his car, chuckling about my newfound golfing prowess, when my cell phone vibrates in my purse. It's a text from Bob: The buyers have pulled out of the Wethersfield deal, as they've decided to buy an alternative property—one of Candace's listings!

My heart sinks faster than a hole in one as I read the text a second and third time to make sure I haven't misunderstood.

Mike leans on my open car door. "You okay?"

I show him the bad news. "In my mind I was celebrating."

"I'm sorry, Marcy. I know it hasn't been easy for you since your divorce."

"I put in the work, and then get shafted. Every. Single. Time." Tears prick my lids, but I try to laugh it off. "It's just more of my characteristic failure. At least I'm consistent."

"Hey, hey. Don't do that. Don't beat yourself up. You deserve a win, and you'll get one soon, I'm sure of it."

A win would be sooo welcome. And more than anything—even more than a real estate deal—I want that win to come in the form of Francesca Barber taking me by the hand and leading me to the promised land of published authors.

My voice is small. "You really think so?"

"Absolutely. You've got what it takes. You just need to come out swinging and take no prisoners." He winks. "Pardon the mixed metaphor."

Mike is sitting across from me in the recliner while I'm on the couch. He didn't want to leave me when I was obviously upset, so we picked up takeout and brought it back to my place. Bea's out for a last hurrah before her internship starts, and we're watching reruns of *The Brady Bunch*. It's the pork chops and applesauce episode.

"Toni and her generation don't know what they're missing," Mike comments, plucking a shrimp with his chopsticks.

"Television gold," I agree.

"One thing I never understood is what Carol does all day. I mean, the six kids are at school, and Alice looks after all the housework. She doesn't even walk Tiger."

I don't answer, and Mike continues: "Her husband is a successful architect. She's like a groupie. Doesn't she want a career of her own?"

Hearing him put it that way makes me flinch. Is that what I did with Kevin?

"Her and Betty Draper." He laughs. "Good thing that era's over."

Later in the week, Bea and I are in the kitchen, she at the table tapping away on her phone and me standing at the sink, washing the dinner dishes. I'm trapped in my head, mulling over all the pieces of my life: the failed Wethersfield deal, my time with Mike, and the manuscript that sits in Francesca Barber's hands. What chapter is she reading now? Does she love it or hate it?

There's a lull in Bea's phone's continuous pinging and swooshing. I'm scrubbing a pot when Beatrice asks whether I could help find rental listings for the fall. I pounce on the invitation. I feel better already.

"What do you have in mind, a studio?" Mentally I sort through suitable neighborhoods: They have to sport trendy cafés and bars, lots of young professionals, and, of course, be near campus.

"Umm . . . actually, I think a one bedroom. So here's the thing: Patrick and I are talking about moving in together."

My daughter is twenty-two, an adult, and I certainly can't forbid her, not that I would anyway. But still. "That's a big step, hon," I say. "But I suppose if things don't work out, you'll be close to home."

There's a pause. "Actually, we won't. We'll be in Savannah." Another pause. "I really like it there, and Patrick wants to be close to his family."

The pot slips through my fingers and clatters into the sink.

Don't you want to be close to yours? I think frantically. My daughter is doing exactly what I regret doing—setting aside my own plans so Kevin could pursue his. None of which Bea knows about. "But you've already been accepted to grad school here!"

"They have lots of programs in the South."

"Bea, you've had a plan. For a very long time. That you've worked really hard to achieve. Why are you"—I want to say messing with it, or gambling with it, or ruining it, but I try to be diplomatic—"revising it?"

"I'll still become a chemist, Mom."

Okay. Okay, that's something. I take a little breath. It's not exactly the same thing I did, I reassure myself . . . my daughter will go to grad school as planned, just a different one. Where her *boyfriend* wants her to go.

"Anyway," she adds, "nothing is set in stone."

Slowly, I wipe my hands on a dish towel. "I'm sure Savannah is great, and I'm sure they have excellent schools down there." Slowly, I turn to face Beatrice. "You have the potential to be brilliant in your field. I don't want you to do anything to jeopardize that."

She doesn't answer, so I ramble on. "I want you to know something, honey. That bin you found of early chapters from my book? I've been writing it for years. *Years.*"

"Yup." She continues scrolling.

"It's just that when I married your dad . . ." I hear more swooshes of her outgoing texts. Should I be discussing any of this with her? I don't want to alienate my daughter by bad-mouthing her father. But on the other hand, I want Bea to learn from my mistakes so she doesn't repeat them. "When Dad and I got married, he was just starting to get traction with his artwork."

"I know. He worked super hard at it."

"He did, and he was confident he was going to be a success, and so . . . and so . . . my dream took a back seat to his. It's a, um, regret . . . I mean, selling houses instead of concentrating on getting published."

Bea finally looks up from her phone. "Yeah, Dad said you were a real go-getter when he met you, but then you gave up on it after you got married."

"What? No. I didn't give up." I frown. "He talked to you about me?"

"Sure." She reaches up to gather her thick sandy hair in a high pony. "He said you understood that his craft was very consuming. And that you were happy to support him in it."

"Yes, that's true, but looking back—" I want to explain further, but Bea's phone sings with an actual phone call. "Hiiiii," she says in the excited voice I've come to know means it's Patrick, and jogs upstairs for privacy before I have a chance to finish my sentence.

My first instinct is to call Kevin so we can commiserate on her sudden change of grad school plans for the fall. But now I'm not so sure he'd think it's a bad thing. Maybe he's all for her following in my footsteps, sacrificing her needs so her guy could fulfill his.

From the way she made it sound, Kevin practically characterized me as a 1960s suburban housewife, a Carol Brady, a Betty Draper.

Or my own mother.

When I think about it, I don't even know if my mother had any dreams of *her* own, except to orbit Dad. I didn't find her approach to life very admirable, and it's no wonder Beatrice doesn't admire that same behavior in me.

That night I read a few more chapters of *Jupiter in Jeopardy*, since I'm already miserable.

CHAPTER EIGHTEEN

With all the worrying about Beatrice and the Wethersfield factory and wondering if I'm turning into my mother, I am caught off guard when I get a notification for a new Gmail from Francesca Barber in my Summer dot Branigan dot Author inbox.

Dear Summer, she writes, Thank you for the pleasure of reading *A Knight to Remember* and I'm sorry it has taken me this long to read the entirety of the story. Please keep in mind that I'm still busy with my book tour, but I've done my best to provide helpful notes which you should, of course, take or leave as you see fit.

This time there's an attachment. It's two pages of commentary. I comb through it hungrily.

My heart sinks. I'm not really sure what I was expecting, but it wasn't this. Francesca provides a full page of empty praise—about how much stick-to-itiveness it takes to write a book, the effort and imagination I put in, and so on. On the second page she suggests edits. Lots of them. She says I should change the whole plot to make it less contrived. She thinks the relationship between Sir "Devin" (spelling!) and Lady Lisbeth is stilted and should be revised to make it more natural, more nuanced, more believable. She says she understands my "damsel in distress" trope but recommends modernizing it to something more female empowering. Then she says I should seriously trim down the word count, from 166,000 to 90,000, max. Everything she suggests is exactly what I could have found online in an article about editing a manuscript. In short, it sounds like a form letter, like there's really nothing about the book she finds redeeming; if there is, she hasn't mentioned it. What she is basically saying is I should rewrite the whole damn thing.

Maybe take the whole story out of the medieval era and bring it into the present? *Just a thought,* she ends with.

But it's historical romance, I want to shout. Bringing it into the present would even change the *genre.*

Okay, Marcy, I say to myself. *You've gotten this far. Now what?* I took the leap, and she gave me what I asked for: a full-on critique of my MS. Francesca is the expert here, not me. She's the bestselling author, not me. Am I going to squander this opportunity by ignoring her advice?

Down in the basement I wheel aside Bea's glittery bicycle with its swishy tassels and move her field hockey gear. I open the tub containing the ten extra printouts and carry one outside to my patio. I pull up Francesca's email on my computer. I fill my Novel Idea bottle and grab a pen and highlighter. Under my big striped umbrella, I prepare to buckle down to work.

I circle and highlight various parts of the story according to Francesca's critique in an attempt to correlate her notes with specific scenes. I cross out entire swaths of text, whole chapters. I'm at it for seven hours and forty minutes, and I am completely, utterly stumped.

It's not working. I don't know what I'm doing. I don't even know how to approach this rewrite because it's so overwhelming. The impulse to give up pokes sharply at my brain, but then I think of Francesca up on the stage, telling the audience how supportive the writing community is. I'm sure if I reached out to her and told her how I'm struggling, she'd help.

Her number is near the top of my call list, and I leave another voicemail. "Hi again, Francesca, it's Summer. I got your notes about my manuscript, which I really, really appreciate, but I'm having a lot of trouble making the actual changes you recommend. I was wondering if we could jump on a call, maybe tomorrow if you have time, and you could walk me through? Please let me know." I thank her and disconnect.

Before I even set the phone down, she calls back.

"Summer, it's Francesca," she says impatiently, "and no, I don't have time for a call tomorrow."

"But you told us—a whole ballroom full of people!—how supportive the author community is! You told my friend Antonia you would be eager to take people under your wing!" I'm speaking so fast I'm stumbling over my words. "And also, we have a *deal*!"

Damn . . . it slipped out. There's such a long silence, I'm sure she's disconnected.

"Fine," she mutters. "You get one hour. Tomorrow morning at nine."

Huh. It worked again.

It's 8:59 and I am trying Francesca's number, which goes unanswered. Same with the next try. Finally, fourteen attempts later, we connect.

"Thanks for taking my call," I begin.

"Let's make this quick."

I try not to be flustered by her brusque tone, but the questions I intend to ask fly out of my brain. Even though we've now spoken directly a few times, I still can't quite believe I'm talking to this woman. It's Francesca freaking Barber, about to help me realize my dream! My manuscript stares up at me from the butcher-block in front of me. "Um . . . first, I just want to say, I'm a few chapters into *Jupiter in Jeopardy*, and I'm loving it. Really, you are such a wonderful writer. An inspiration."

"Great to know, thanks."

I clear my throat. "I guess I'm wondering, overall, what were the parts of my book you actually liked? Because there seems to be a lot of . . . uh, flaws . . . you pointed out."

On the line I hear the rhythmic click of long fingernails drumming on a table. "I don't know, I suppose one thing I enjoyed was Sir Devon's friend, Sir Simon Segwin. He—" Her voice becomes garbled.

What? What did she enjoy about him? His heroic rescue of the little boy from the moat? The way he defends Sir Richard, Lady Lisbeth's father, from that pack of thieves? "Francesca, I have a bad connection in my house. Can we please switch to FaceTime so I can hear you better?" I press my video button and she accepts.

Suddenly I have a view of my literary icon standing in what appears to be the expansive living room of a high-rise apartment, judging from the view of the skyline out the floor-to-ceiling windows behind her. As she moves, I see green below and recognize the silhouette of Central Park, but even that's not the most impressive part, nor are the glimpses of plush furnishings, all white. It's not even the charcoal sketch of Marilyn Monroe nearly covering one wall that captures my attention. No, what I can't tear my eyes from is Francesca herself. Her lids are smoky and dramatic. Her hair is twisted at her nape in a chignon that showcases enormous diamonds dangling from her lobes, with a ridiculously large solitaire nestled at her throat. I can't help drawing in a breath at the sight of this glamorous creature.

"You look stunning, Francesca," I gush. "So you were saying you enjoyed something about Sir Simon Segwin?"

"Just the alliteration." She glances over her shoulder. "Summer, I have a magazine shoot, and I really should finish getting ready."

What happened to my hour? This was like five minutes. "Can we continue tomorrow?"

Francesca acquiesces grudgingly. As she disconnects, I catch the briefest glimpse of someone, a sleek, caramel-skinned someone, passing behind the white sofa. I'm pretty sure he's naked.

"In terms of my writing, what do you think needs improvement? I know you mentioned grammar?" Today I woke up early and prepped for our session with a list of written questions. I'm not wasting any time. My pen is poised above blank paper, and I'm ready to jot down her words of wisdom.

Francesca peers at me on FaceTime. "Move your camera," she says. "Don't you know that looking down like that gives you a double chin?"

"Sorry." I readjust my phone to lean against the fruit bowl on the kitchen counter. My half-eaten breakfast is now in the frame.

"Are those frozen waffles? I didn't think people actually ate those anymore."

I nudge the plate out of the frame. "About my writing?"

Francesca stands, and I am carried with her as she walks. I get glimpses of a staircase winding around a modern Sputnik chandelier with multiple branches extending outward in a starburst.

At last Francesca stops and focuses on me.

"One thing I noticed is the way you go on and on about things. You tend to bore the reader."

"Oh . . ." I chew my lip. "I'll make a note of it. Please go on."

"I don't know why you're writing a bodice ripper. If you want a bestseller, it should be a rom-com, not historical romance."

As that sinks in, I hear the rich toll of a doorbell, and Francesca moves to the entrance. A young woman enters. Wait, is that Aspen? I squint at the screen as the frame toggles, and yes, I can see over Francesca's shoulder, it *is* Aspen.

"I want to talk to you about what you're wearing to the LA event. It clashes with what I'm wearing, so I got you something else," I hear her say as she sets designer shopping bags on a chair. Aww, that's sweet . . . the daughter has gone shopping for her mother. How thoughtful. I tell myself to cut it out—subconsciously I am comparing them to Bea and me, and I shouldn't.

Francesca hurriedly tells me our call can be rescheduled. My screen goes blank.

CHAPTER NINETEEN

The *Jupiter in Jeopardy* book tour features back-to-back events in Los Angeles, where Francesca has a home. It's days before she answers my calls, and when I finally get her on FaceTime, she's lying beside an infinity pool beyond which is the most breathtaking view of the Hollywood Hills.

"Did you get the pages I emailed?" I ask. "I'm having a lot of trouble with the dungeon scene."

"I did." Francesca is dabbing sunscreen on her face as she talks. "One problem is you are using too many oxymorons. Didn't you pay attention in high school English class? Hang on." The picture blurs. I assume she is opening my document. "Here, in the second paragraph, you talk about Lady Lisbeth's 'terrible beauty' and her 'bittersweet' past. And then, when she is dragged to the dungeon where the prisoners are like the 'living dead,' she lets out a 'silent scream.'"

"Good point, I'll revise that."

I want to bring up the subject of our overlapping characters, but I don't want to sound whiny. I think carefully about how to phrase the point I want to make. "Anyway, this is also the scene where Sir Devon asks the bawdy old chambermaid to make a fire and she asks if she can touch his poker."

Francesca doesn't respond. I just want her to acknowledge that I am as good as she is at imagining characters, that she clearly is underestimating my talent if we both conceived of the exact same elements in our work. I add tentatively: "And coincidentally, I was just reading your chapter last night where *your* elderly chambermaid is introduced."

The FaceTime picture is still blurred out, but I hear a slight intake of breath.

"Did you notice any . . . similarity?" I prod.

No answer.

"Francesca?"

As I wait for her to respond, I hear the unmistakable slapping of flip-flops by the pool, followed by low conversation.

"So, our characters?"

It's that woman who saw us in the bar, I hear Francesca whisper.

What the hell does she want? Get rid of her, comes the deeply accented reply.

I clear my throat.

And then comes four distinctly angry words from the man, four words that render Francesca silent. *This has to end.*

There's a long pause, and at first I think Tabi means her phone call has to end, or her helping me has to end, but then I realize with a start that I may have misunderstood him. Maybe what Tabi *wants* is to end their relationship.

"It's just a coincidence," Francesca answers me at last. "Like I said, everyone uses tropes."

I spend the afternoon and evening sitting on the patio, trying to revise the dungeon scene. Even though it's the Fourth of July, I have no plans to barbecue or picnic or even light a sparkler, so I sit alone until dark, hearing the rat-a-tats of fireworks beyond the gloomy woods. The light from my computer screen is attracting giant moths that flit in front of my face, so close I feel the brush of their wings.

Finally I throw up my hands in dismay. I can't do this. I don't know what to make of Francesca's advice, and I'm ready to scrap the whole thing.

But then I think of Beatrice, and how it would affect her if she saw me giving up on myself yet again. All my life I swore I'd be a published author. Pushing yourself to realize your dreams no matter what—*this* is how you avoid having regrets, I imagine telling her. *This* is how you become fulfilled, proud. But she's already making a major life change—moving states—to please her boyfriend. What if she is subconsciously emulating me by putting aside her dream? I can't have her making the same mistakes. No. She *must* see me succeed. I need to be the role model she deserves.

Over the treetops I can see the heights of my town's yearly pyrotechnic display, the chrysanthemums and waterfalls and tourbillions. I give them a passing glance, then pack up and go inside.

I want a glass of chardonnay, but instead I grab an apple and take a frustrated bite. No matter what, I have to show my daughter that I am a driven, determined woman who will stop at nothing to succeed.

Come on, Marcy. Think of everything you've been told.

What would Ralph say?

Actively take a step toward the desired outcome.

What would Bea say?

You're too nice for my own good.

What would Candace say?

You've got to make things happen. Don't wait for opportunity to come knocking, kick down the door yourself.

What would Gil Carter say?

Do whatever it takes to succeed, even if you have to be ruthless.

What would Mike say?

Come out swinging and take no prisoners.

Between chomps on the apple I think, *Fine. I'll keep pushing ahead.* I try to concentrate, to drum up writing devices, but I find myself going over the past few weeks instead. What keeps coming back to me is the encounter at the bar with Francesca. Francesca Barber, writer of bestsellers. Francesca Barber, writer of my critique. Somehow, she is the key to this. I consider the circumstances—that is, me witnessing a tryst that was supposed to be a secret, leading to our deal; how, in the hotel lobby, she implored me not to say anything; and how she immediately changed her tune each time I reminded her of said deal.

Clearly I have information she wants concealed at any cost. At *any* cost.

I pause.

What would Summer Branigan say?

Be ruthless, kick down the door, do whatever it takes, and stop being so damn *nice*.

The possibilities flit in front of my eyes.

What I thought might be a moral dilemma no longer feels like one, not when I'm doing something for the good of my daughter. Certainly Francesca would agree with that sentiment, since she herself used love for her daughter to justify offering a deal in the first place. After all, she expressed the exact same thing in the hotel lobby that night. I remember her words verbatim: "As a mother, the last thing in the world we want is to hurt our daughters." So, really, I'm just taking a page out of Francesca's very own playbook.

Slowly, I put down the apple. I open a new email window and start typing.

> I'm going to need more than what you've provided so far, Francesca. That is, *if* you want me to keep quiet about TB.

Send.

CHAPTER TWENTY

The speed with which my cell phone rings is startling. Ah, the convenience of instant communication.

"Summer." She sounds breathless. "It's me. Of course I want you to uphold your end of the bargain. You can't let anyone know. Please, you can't."

"Okay."

"Exactly what do you mean by your email, then?"

This is it, my opportunity. I try to calm the tremor in my voice, choose my words carefully. "Just what I said. I need more than two pages of generalities or a couple of vague suggestions over FaceTime for how to fix my story. And you're . . . you're going to . . . help me do it."

There is a long moment of silence as Francesca digests my statement. Finally, she speaks. "What do you want me to do?" she asks flatly.

I take a deep breath. "Let's start with chapter one."

This is so not me, I keep telling myself, but at the same time I've never felt so empowered, so in charge. Gone are the days of sitting around morosely, at a loss as to how I will attain the life I want. The years of marriage I spent subjugating my needs so that I could fulfill Kevin's . . .

they're behind me. Kevin and I are done, and I no longer need to do backflips trying to be the wife he wanted—turns out he never wanted a wife in the first place, and nothing I could have done would have changed it. It's my time now, and I'm not wasting it.

And Bea needs to think that way, too.

Even back in the very early days of my real estate career, I had qualms about going after what I wanted. I spent eons agonizing over office politics and coveted from afar the juicy listings my colleagues snagged. My broker in the early days often told me he wished I had more of a killer instinct. And Bob, since I joined Robert Verney Realty, has known me only as a mediocre, not particularly ambitious—or productive—agent. Well, times change. People change.

Soon I'll turn fifty, which seems like a turning point. And Francesca? She has a deadline: a week to hand in the rewritten first chapter of my new book. I also realized last night, after we spoke, that I'll need a new synopsis if she's going to make substantial changes. I told her so in another email. So I guess now we have a pact.

You think I'm being manipulative, but Francesca is benefiting from this situation, too. She gets to keep her reputation and her relationship with her daughter intact. She gets to avoid the consequences of the situation *she* created in the first place, by fooling around with Tabi Benlolo.

Outside, the sun is definitely not jibing with my sunny state of mind; the freaky early heat wave has ended, and we're in the midst of raw rainstorms, one after the other. But that's Connecticut for you. The forecast for the weather is in transition, and so is the forecast for my life.

Francesca Barber submits the new chapter right on deadline. Good girl. I'm very pleased with her punctuality. I bring my computer to the couch and settle in to enjoy the experience. I can practically smell the bougainvillea!

There are two documents attached to Francesca's email. I open the one entitled "Synopsis" first. Francesca conceives of a completely different story from the one I wrote years ago. She has kept it medieval, at least, so my genre remains historical romance. Maybe she thought twice about setting it in the present, or maybe it was just too much work, but either way, I'm glad.

In her version of *A Knight to Remember*, Devon is apprenticed to his father, a metal forger who fashions chain mail to adorn knights. Devon is forced to pursue knighthood by his domineering mother, the metal forger's embittered wife. Though they are large, strong men, both Devon and his father are gentle and kind, beaten down by the controlling mother. Lady Lisbeth is secretly in love with Devon, but her parents will allow her to marry him only if he is knighted. Lady Lisbeth starts out in cahoots with Devon's mother but ends up leading her kingdom in battle against a warring faction.

I open the second Word doc, chapter one, and plunge in. The theme of metal forging—melting and beating metal to shape it to one's will—is introduced as a refrain in the story.

In this new beginning, Devon is introduced as a shy teenager, mocked for his sensitivity by the other village boys. The scene begins with the boys staging a jousting tournament. When a stick is shoved into his hands, young Devon drops it, refusing to fight. His mother sees and admonishes him to "be a man." By the end of the chapter, Devon has gained our sympathy and admiration.

And you know what? I don't mind Francesca's version at all. It's compelling and emotive. The writing is crisp and the dialogue pops from the first paragraph. There's action and forewarning off the bat. And I like where Francesca is going with Lady Lisbeth's character, who's all about female empowerment, which I must say I can totally identify with right now, as it's what *I'm* working toward.

I'm intrigued by this new direction. I am. Maybe it's just the thing I needed to kick-start my edits and guide my rewrite of the story; plus I'm gleaning valuable insights and techniques to improve my skills from Francesca's expressive writing. I print out the synopsis and save the chapter.

The rain is tapering off, but it's still chilly, so I decide against sitting out on the patio and settle in the kitchen instead. I have a pad of paper, my favorite pens, and the original bound manuscript I'd begun marking up. There's a bag of almonds in the pantry in case I need a snack, and my Novel Idea water bottle is at my elbow. Here we go.

And now I will write chapter two.

I try—oh, how I try—to make my words flow seamlessly from the three thousand Francesca provided. I can do this, I know I can. I stare at a blank page for thirty minutes.

My cell phone dings with a notification: the arrival of a photo. It's my daughter sitting on a stool in a laboratory, surrounded by Bunsen burners and beakers, holding an iPad and wearing a white lab coat over tailored pants and loafers. She's started her research program and my heart swells. Her frank gaze at the camera is the Bea I've always known—a person who knows what she wants, who has a clear vision of how her life will play out. Imagine her relief when she emerges from grad school without student debt, thanks to the sale of my breakout book!

As I turn back to my empty word document, with the mouse still pulsing alongside the *o* in "Chapter Two," I realize it's the same with Francesca. She has a clear vision for my story. I wonder if I will hamper it, get in her way. I decide the best course of action is to request a chapter-by-chapter outline that I can follow. I tell her so in an email.

It takes her two days to fulfill my request. Hallelujah! Back to the computer I go.

Summoning all my will, I squeeze out a couple of pages. It's slow going and the end result seems lifeless compared to what Francesca wrote. Even with the outline she provided, I'm having trouble connecting the plot dots in a meaningful way. I'm about to paste my pages in an email asking for her advice so I don't waste more time struggling.

Then it occurs to me: Why should I struggle at all?

Calm down. I can see you are getting all up in arms about this, but don't. Francesca Barber is writing two chapters. Maybe three, tops. Just to set me on the right path.

Authors are a supportive bunch, like she said, a community known for camaraderie and willingness to help each other. Think about how authors read and blurb each other's books. Everyone wins. Come on, if you were an established author, wouldn't you want to help a newbie realize *her* dream? Pay it forward?

It's the same with Francesca and me. We are both getting something we want. She has time to help me now that her book tour is winding down with only a few more events. There's still promotion, but her publisher's marketing team, along with the savvy PR professionals she no doubt hires privately, can handle it. They are flooding social media and broadcast and printed press with hype surrounding *Jupiter in Jeopardy*. Aspen and Tabi, as Gemma and Jovan, are plastered on subway ads and on the sides of buses, and their third movie is in production. There's already a teaser trailer. Francesca has endless resources, and doesn't have to do anything herself except take a few calls from reporters or show up at a literary luncheon or two.

Honestly, I bet Francesca Barber is enjoying my manuscript: It's her chance to explore historical romance, a genre very different from the science fiction she's been writing the past few years. And if she were to ask a favor of me in return—helping her with real estate, or parenting advice, or whatever—don't you think I'd be glad to reciprocate? Indeed I would.

So when a shiny new chapter three shows up in my inbox, and I reply by politely requesting she start on the fourth, I am quite astonished at her reaction.

My phone rings with a FaceTime call moments after I hit send. "Absolutely not," she huffs, without even greeting me. She's in a room I don't recognize, and she's clearly agitated. I hear another voice. Francesca's not looking into the phone, so I'm unsure whether she's speaking to me or someone else.

"I'm not your lackey," she's shrilling. "This is beyond ridiculous. I've given over and above what any rational person would agree to."

"Calm down," I say, which does nothing to help her calm down.

She turns back to the phone. "Frankly I have done more, far more, than I ever dreamed I would when this whole charade began." Francesca paces back and forth, back and forth. She carries me into a room and shuts the door. "You, Summer, you've wrung three entire chapters and an outline for a whole new book out of me. That's all you're getting. Do the rest yourself."

Being denied what is rightfully mine sends me back to the nasty situation with that young agent and her betrayal at the brokerage.

Together with our broker and the developer, we'd set a clear timeline for the subdivision project. Our first showings were scheduled for after my maternity leave.

What a backstabber that agent turned out to be! During the time I was giving birth at the hospital and then cocooned at home with a newborn, she moved up the showings and proceeded to handle them without me, and went ahead with a bulk sale as the sole listing agent.

How I wanted to throttle her. I fantasized about ways to get even, which I never acted on. Being a new mom—with all the accompanying fatigue and emotion—was tough enough, and the situation with the subdivision turned me inside out. But since there wasn't a thing I could do about it, and everyone around me, especially Kevin, told me to forget it and focus instead on our beautiful new baby, I had to let it go.

By the time I came back to work, the agent had moved on to an upscale firm in Manhattan. I never did confront her, and all these years later, that feeling of being powerless still rankles.

Now, with Francesca trying to thwart me, the feeling of powerlessness returns. Francesca thinks she holds all the cards. She's a superstar, and I'm a nobody. A middle-aged, middle-of-the-road real estate agent who puts everyone else's needs ahead of her own. How easy it is to trample all over Marcy Codburn, the Pushover.

Except now I'm not Marcy Codburn. I'm Summer Branigan, and I refuse to be ignored.

"Is that really how you want to play this?" I say.

"I'm not playing games."

"We have a *deal*."

"I know. I know! But I never said it would include all *this*. You want a new book? You'll have to write it."

I don't think so.

"Fine, I will," I sniff. And then I add, in a sinister tone, the morsel I know will seal the deal tighter than Tupperware: "Maybe I'll include some *photos*." I hear the sharp intake of breath. Message received.

CHAPTER TWENTY-ONE

Fun fact: It's surprisingly easy to get ahead if you have connections, and it's easy to find connections once you know where to look.

It's a pleasant Sunday in mid-July, and Liisa and I just finished a jog—well, I jogged in place as I waited for her to catch up every few minutes—and now we're sitting at Espresso Yourself.

"You're not even sweaty," Liisa says, pushing her damp hair back and taking a swallow of her mochaccino. "If I'd known you were going to get serious about this jogging thing, I wouldn't have agreed to come."

I scooch my chair up next to hers. Finish my ice water. Pull out my phone.

She's not taking the hint. "So, how's Mike?"

"Haven't seen him for a while," I answer lightly. I don't want to sound dismissive, but I'm on a mission here.

"And that new client?"

"Who? No idea." I have no time for idle chitchat, and anyway, I'm superstitious talking about my Back Bay listing because I'm afraid I'll jinx it. I start scrolling.

"Okay, Miss Secretive." Liisa frowns. "You missed Thursday at the library. Anything new with your writing?"

"Not really." I shrug.

"Cagey," Liisa mutters under her breath. At last she opens Facebook. I look over her shoulder; since her friends aren't all the same as mine, she sees different posts. "Oh, look. Yvonne Manning's new book won an award."

"Mm-hmm."

"And Sierra Eastman is releasing a biography of Cindy Crawford."

"Isn't there more than one already?"

"I guess there's always room for another." Liisa does a shrug-and-chug. "Hey, Elianna Abrams posted. *Jupiter in Jeopardy* is her Manhattan Book Club's next pick."

I stand up to go pee. "Of course it is."

"And look . . . Elianna gets to go to the studio's press party."

Press party? I sit back down. "Let me see that."

Blimey . . . the network is throwing a press party on July 17 to announce its release of the third Jupiter movie. It's going to be an evening event at a theater in the city, invitation only, to offer a glimpse of what scenes may look like in the new flick. There is no doubt, no doubt whatsoever, that the ladies Barber, and their shared South American boy toy, will be there. I mull it over. I wonder whether Francesca and Tabi will manage to steal a moment of alone time. Maybe I could wait in the wings to photograph the moment.

Did I mention that James, my husband's partner, owns a sporting goods store? Diamond Sports, right in the center of the town he grew up in. He's an avid runner, swimmer, and cyclist, with his own line of sportswear, and he's very fit. Kevin's gotten in better shape, too, ever since he started spending time with James. Which has nothing to do with anything, really, except that back when Kevin first sprang the news of his new relationship on me, of course I had to go scope out the competition.

I slunk into the shop one Saturday when I knew they were out of town, wearing dark sunglasses and a floppy hat so I wouldn't be recognized as the nosy ex. The young salesgirl at the register smiled but didn't approach me until I made the mistake of stopping in front of a display of exceptionally adorable children's beach apparel.

"Isn't it darling?" the girl asked, materializing at my side.

I thought of disguising my voice, but I just nodded enthusiastically.

"It's designed by Greta Diamond, one of the owner's sisters. They're all so talented: Greta designs kids' clothes, and her twin, Fiona, is a costume designer in Hollywood."

That tidbit springs to mind now. I know, the chances of Fiona Diamond being attached to the Jupiter productions, as a costume designer or in any other way, are minuscule. But if she lives in Hollywood, and is still in the industry, she might know someone who is.

I call Kevin and ask him to ask James to ask his sister if she knows anyone connected to the upcoming release. I don't hear anything for three days. While I'm waiting, I flog a bunch of other avenues to no avail.

Until James texts me to say Fiona herself isn't working on the project but as a matter of fact has friends in the "vanities," the hair and makeup departments on set, and by the way, why was I asking?

I can't tell him the whole truth, just that I'm absolutely dying to go to the press party next week in New York City. *Kevin probably told you how I am about writing and movies!* I text, inserting a smiley-face emoji, a popcorn in a red-and-white-striped bucket emoji, and a red heart emoji.

He types back, *I get it. I'll ask Fiona to see what she can do.* Sure enough, a few hours later he texts, *You're on the list.* And just like that, I fricking love my husband's lover.

CHAPTER TWENTY-TWO

Technically I could bring a guest to the press party, but I don't. I seriously consider inviting Mike, now that I'm Summer, a woman who actually takes initiative . . . but I decide against it because, after all, he is part of my writers' group, and I cannot come clean to any of them about attending this soiree. Mike, Liisa, and Toni would surely want to know why and how I came to be there, and that, I cannot disclose. But still, it's gratifying to know Summer *could* have invited a date. Between Marcy's lack of initiative and Kevin's lack of interest, it's a wonder they ended up with a daughter.

The day of the party, I'm at the ritziest salon in town. I'm sitting in the stylist's chair anticipating the process, and I suspect it's going to be an expensive one. Like I said before, I'm on a pretty tight budget, and whatever my next commission is will be slated for my hefty annual property tax bill. But this, too, is business. If I'm to accomplish what I want, don't I have to look the part?

"So, what are we thinking?" The stylist uses the royal "we" instead of "you," which makes her sound like the Queen of England. She runs her comb through my hair and looks at me from different angles.

"I really don't know." In the mirror, the split ends of my straight blah hair hang limply past my shoulders. "I've had it this way pretty much my whole life."

"We're ready for a change?"

"Yes," I say, "we are."

Two and a half hours later, my drab locks have been snipped and layered and foiled and lightened into a glossy, bouncy mane worthy of the most Claudia Schiffer–y of mere mortals. It's so flattering, I look decades younger.

The stylist adds a finishing spritz of hair spray, then grins at my reflection. "Do we like it?"

Admiringly, I turn my head this way and that. "We love it!"

I show up at the theater in a vintage black dress that works for this soiree—it's knee length and classic but with a few cleverly placed inserts of lace, just enough to make it chic. My lashes are coated with mascara and my painted lips are as coral as the Great Barrier Reef. And my hair: I glanced at it in the rearview mirror all the way here, just to make sure it wasn't a figment of my imagination. I cross my fingers and give my name at the door (*Did Fiona come through?* She did.) and make a beeline for the bar. I'll need to fortify myself for my mission to obtain an actual photo of Francesca Barber and Tabi Benlolo in some compromising position, thus spawning the evidence that Francesca already believes to exist, thus enabling me to increase pressure on her.

Catching sight of myself in the mirror behind the row of bartenders, I wonder whether it's really me. I pick up a glass of wine and sidle around the periphery of the crowd, phone at the ready.

The glitterati are out in full force: There are Hollywood types and reporters roaming around, and right in the middle there's Elianna Abrams talking with Sierra Eastman and Lilian Arnold. Elianna is beanpole-shaped and very tall, a full head taller than me, and Sierra looks even younger and fresher faced than in her pictures. I head over to them.

"Hello," I say, nodding at all three. They look curious. They must assume that I'm somebody since I am, in fact, here. I face Elianna. "I'm a huge fan of your book club." I smile at Sierra. "And congratulations on Cindy Crawford's biography! I'm so excited to read it." And to Lilian

I joke, "All my friends agree: Your mysteries make us want to visit Georgia. The tourist board should pay you."

All three smile broadly and thank me. They're engaged. Who doesn't love to be complimented? "And you are?" Lilian asks, tipping her head toward me. Her hair is pulled back in such a severe bun that her eyebrows slant upward.

"Summer Branigan. I have a new novel in the works." Over Lilian's shoulder I spy movement outside the grand double doors. The press is converging at the entrance. Flashes are going off, lighting up the dusk of the mid-July night. The crowd strains forward as Aspen Barber and Tabi Benlolo enter, followed by Francesca Barber and an entire entourage. For me, their timing couldn't be better: Everyone exclaims and applauds, and I turn away from Elianna, Lilian, and Sierra before I'm asked any further questions. I've made the perfect short impression.

I'm standing in the middle of it all so that when the crowd parts like the Red Sea to let the stars in, I'm front-row center.

Aspen and Tabi are holding hands and moving up the impromptu aisle, and Francesca is several steps behind them. She is gracious and magnanimous as she greets everyone.

I take a deep breath and lean forward. "Hello, Francesca." From the corner of my eye, I see Elianna, Sierra, and Lilian paying close attention.

Francesca dips her chin and looks away. I realize she doesn't recognize me. For a moment I panic; I certainly hadn't accounted for this. I don't look *that* different, do I? "It's so nice to see you in person rather than on FaceTime."

Her eyes widen with the realization. "Summer," she says, her smile fixed in place. "So nice that you came. How—?"

"I couldn't miss the opportunity to be here. And chat with Aspen, of course." I give her a confidential little wink.

Oh, if only I had a thermometer. I bet Francesca's internal temperature could freeze a lit match. The icy look in her crystal eyes gives me a fairly accurate reading.

Her bejeweled hand reaches out and clutches my arm. "Well, now that I have you here, I am not letting you out of my sight." To any onlookers, we must appear to be the best of friends, with her arm looped through mine, keeping me close. I know the truth; she's not going to take a chance on letting me anywhere near her daughter, or her son-in-law, or a reporter, for that matter. Who knows what I might blab? Inwardly I'm elated at how this is unfolding.

For the next hour, Francesca keeps my arm linked in hers as she works the crowd. I sip my wine with the other hand. It would be visibly rude for her not to acknowledge me, and as a result she's forced to introduce me to everyone she speaks to. I'm meeting movers and shakers I'd never dreamed of meeting, from her marketing team to Sally Janoff, her film agent, all the way up to the movie moguls and studio execs.

Francesca and the studio execs are deep in conversation when I am jostled from behind. My wine spills all over my hand and wrist, and while she's been clutching me the entire time, Francesca is forced to let go as I detach myself to use the ladies' room.

CHAPTER TWENTY-THREE

I enter the bathroom and stop in my tracks. I stare. I'm about to gush "Aren'tyouAspenBarberI'mahugefanofyourwork" because *the* Aspen Barber is indeed standing three feet in front of me, and the proximity to this mega celebrity is unsettling. I'm starstruck.

But then I remember that she's just an innocent girl, the same age as my daughter but unknowingly a hairbreadth away from being a victim of her mother's selfishness, and I feel my awe and admiration melt into pity.

I smile tenderly and lay my clean hand on her arm. "Hi, Aspen."

"Hi . . . ?"

"Summer. Summer Branigan." I pause for a second and add, "I'm a friend of your mother's."

She looks confused, so I take a step closer and elaborate. The lie rolls easily off my tongue.

"Yes, we've recently, um, connected. I just think the world of her."

"It's nice to meet you, Summer." She bestows on me the friendliest of smiles, and I'm immediately won over.

From the corner of my eye I notice that the beaded strap of her dress is twisted, and I point it out to her. She bends an arm up behind her shoulder blade to straighten it but can't quite reach.

"Here, let me help. I'm a girl mom, too." As I'm smoothing the fabric, I lean in and add conspiratorially, "Oh, and I'm also a writer colleague of your mother's."

I continue: "I'm forever fixing up my own daughter's wardrobe malfunctions. Her spaghetti straps always tangle like this. Now that I think of it, Beatrice must be exactly your age. She's going to grad school in the fall. Such a fun time of life." I smile warmly. "I love your relationship with your mom. It's obvious the two of you are so affectionate and close."

Aspen smiles back and thanks me for the help. With a pang, I find myself wishing Bea would be half as appreciative when I do things for her. The last time I tried to help her get dressed for an occasion, she brushed me off. Whereas Aspen seems grateful.

"You're a writer?" she confirms. And then, cautiously: "Not, like, a reporter, though? There's a ton of entertainment reporters here."

"God, no, I wouldn't know how to write about Hollywood gossip if you hit me over the head with a brick. No, I've been immersed in working on a novel, and actually Francesca has been giving me some valuable writing insights for it. She's been spending a ton of time with me to help me iron out some wrinkles."

Aspen nods and turns to the mirror to dab a bit of concealer under her eyes. As she's blending, I wash my hands and jabber on, happy to have an active listener.

"I'm certain my new book will be a bestseller. With your mother's help, no doubt it will be—and I'm sure it will be adapted for screen. In fact, I can imagine you playing the lead," I muse aloud. "It's a juicy role. Anyway, I should really send her something to thank her for all her help . . . it's the least I can do. But I wouldn't know where to send it."

"Mama spends most of the summer in the Hamptons. She says the solitude helps her think. She doesn't like people around when she's writing."

"The Hamptons! I'm sure it's glorious."

"It's open for the season. Her annual party is coming up. Every summer she hosts a party on the last Saturday of July."

"Oh, I bet she throws a fabulous party."

"You should come. Give me your address, and I'll make sure you get an invite. I love seeing my mom surrounded by friends."

My smile couldn't get wider. "Aren't you the sweetest! What a darling daughter you are." I can't believe my luck. We pull out our phones to exchange information. "This will be such a treat for me and Francesca."

Cue Francesca.

The bathroom door swings open so hard the knob hits the wall. She looks pissed as she strides around the corner, calling my name. "Summer?!" She stops in her tracks when she sees her daughter, a lot like I did. "Oh. Aspen, you're here."

"Mama? You okay?"

"Fine." She's looking back and forth between us, alarmed to see we have our phones in hand. "Have you . . . have you two met?"

We nod.

"We were just getting to know each other," I say. "I hope you know how lucky you are."

Francesca tries to control her annoyance. "Well, if you're finished in here . . ." She reaches out for my arm and pulls me none too gently out of the bathroom. I give Aspen a little wave as the door closes behind me.

CHAPTER TWENTY-FOUR

As we emerge from the alcove where the bathrooms are, Francesca's mouth is homing in on my ear, and I'm certain she's on the brink of lambasting me just as a Brooklyn type steps into our path. He leans down to kiss her cheeks.

Francesca exhales forcefully. "Please meet my friend, Summer Branigan. Summer, this is Ned Townsend, my publisher," she says through lips pursed so tight they're in danger of falling off. "Of the publishing house Temple-Townsend Books." Not that she needs to elaborate. I know exactly who he is.

"Very pleased to meet you, Summer," Ned says, raising his martini in greeting. He's young, painfully thin, an avant-garde Noel Airman type dressed head to toe in black, missing only a cigarette. "Are you in the movie biz?"

"Actually, I'm an author," I say, as Francesca's death grip tightens. "I write historical romance."

"And who's your publisher?"

"Oh, I'm not quite there yet," I murmur. "Putting the finishing touches on my debut novel."

Ned waves his martini. "Well, tell Francesca to make sure I get a first look at your manuscript. Temple-Townsend loves a debut." (Doesn't every publisher love a debut?)

"Thank you, Mr. Townsend, that would be wonderful! I'll make sure Frankie does that." I bet no one else dares to call her Frankie. How daring am I!

Francesca glares at me.

"Please, it's Ned. Anything for a friend of . . . Frankie's." He wanders off.

The moment he leaves, another fellow takes his place in front of Francesca. It's constant. She is bombarded by acquaintances and well-wishers, and I can feel her starting to tire, as her grip on my arm loosens. My attention is momentarily diverted: Across the lobby, I see people in costume, characters from the upcoming Jupiter movie, no doubt. A soothsayer. A chambermaid. A warlord. Figments of my imagination, and Francesca's I suppose, come to life. I'm gobsmacked.

When I turn back to Francesca, she touches her free wrist to her temple. "My head is throbbing," she says, and immediately members of the entourage who have been trailing after her all night offer to get her aspirin. "I need a drink," she mutters, ignoring them.

At the bar she tips back a cognac. She doesn't notice Aspen and Tabi converging on us until it's too late. The press follows. I am momentarily blinded by real flashes from real flashbulbs attached to real cameras.

"Hi, Mama," Aspen says affectionately.

"Hot Mama," Tabi Benlolo adds under his breath, before turning his simmering gaze to the reporters.

Tabi is standing right beside me, so close I can smell his spicy aftershave and see the definition of every bicep and pec and ab through his fitted shirt. His obsidian gaze is intense, and his magnetism is striking. It's what every Hollywood producer knows will transcend the screen.

Aspen wraps an arm around his waist and looks at him with adoration. I have a sour taste in my mouth; I'm so mad at him. How can he do this to her . . . hurt her with his infidelity? He glances my way and his eyes darken in recognition, but he doesn't even nod. I'm guessing his hostility stems from the fact I know his dirty little secret.

"Tabi, how about a pose with the Barber beauties?" calls out one of the photographers.

At that, Tabi reaches to extricate Francesca's arm looped through mine. "Would you mind if I stole her away?" He doesn't wait for an answer, just inserts himself between us with his brawn. I want to kick him. Yes, I'd mind if he stole Francesca away. And so would his *wife*.

Aspen chides him playfully. "Tabi! Where are your manners? This is your mother-in-law's friend Summer."

"You heard the man," Tabi says evenly. "Barber beauties only."

I scowl at him.

"Just ignore Tabi," Aspen tells me. "He's such a *guy*." She shines her radiant smile in my direction, and it's like a shower of twinkling stars. I can't help but smile back at this sweet, ethereal creature.

Standing off to the side, I watch as Francesca, Tabi, and Aspen step in front of the printed *Jupiter in Jeopardy* backdrop and grin for the cameras in various configurations.

A photographer gets up in their face at one point, says something, and I'm taken aback to see Tabi raise an arm as if he is about to hit the guy. Francesca jumps between them and says something to smooth things over. Fortunately, just then the lobby lights flicker on and off. Wow. Talk about a hot temper.

Tabi turns on his heel and disappears behind the backdrop. "Come sit," Aspen says urgently to her mother and me. "They're about to start the screening."

Oh! A darkened theater . . . perhaps Francesca and Tabi will try to escape for a brief interlude, especially if his blood is boiling right now? Could be my opportunity to snap a pic.

But Francesca shakes her head. "I'm leaving. I have a terrible headache. Summer, let's go."

"You'll miss everything," Aspen says sadly.

Rats!

"Get my car," Francesca barks to no one in particular, and immediately the members of her entourage pull out their phones.

I half jog to keep up with Francesca's pace as she drags me through the crowd and back to the entrance. Once we're outside, surrounded by her staff on the sidewalk, it's only a minute before a limo screeches to a stop and the uniformed driver jumps out to open the rear door for her. Francesca gestures for me to get in.

"I have my own car. It's parked two blocks over."

"Inside," Francesca hisses.

With everyone watching, there's no choice but to clamber onto the cool back seat. Francesca slides in after me, and the driver shuts the door on us. When he turns to look back at us expectantly, Francesca says, "Just drive," and slams shut the privacy screen.

New York City's traffic sounds—sirens, horns, back-up beeps—are muted as we pull away. In the confined, luxe interior, Francesca confronts me. "What the hell do you think you're doing, showing up tonight?"

The faces of Kevin, Candace, Elizabeth R., my colleagues, my father, and all the others in my life who underestimated me, who made me feel like a pushover, meld together into Francesca's.

"I just wanted you to know," I tell her slowly, "that two can play at this game."

"I told you before, there *is* no game. We're done."

"You think you're in charge." I shake my head in emphasis. "But really I hold all the cards."

Francesca's eyes narrow, glittering as they reflect passing streetlights. "What are you talking about?"

"Just that Aspen and I had quite a conversation in the bathroom before you came in." I pat my purse . . . a subtle gesture to remind Francesca of my phone and its de facto photo album, snug inside.

It must work, because her eyes widen and doubt creeps into her voice. "You're lying."

"She's a lovely, lovely girl." My words hang in front of us. "We had a long talk."

"God, no."

"She even invited me out to your beach house. For your annual party? Of course I said I'd be delighted to come."

"Like that would ever happen. She doesn't know anything about you."

I'm getting good at this. "I explained about our friendship. I told her I had some . . . fun pictures of you to show her sometime."

Francesca sags onto the leather, defeated. "I knew it."

"The beach sounds like a great place for you to write."

"It is." Her voice is thin. "It is."

"I'm so happy we understand each other."

"We do."

"So," I tell her, "you're going to finish *A Knight to Remember* this summer, and it's going to be a smash. Or else I sing like a canary."

As I speed up the Hutchinson River Parkway in my Saab, I've never felt so exhilarated. So triumphant. Tonight was incredible! I must admit, I was at my best. I rubbed shoulders with people I envy on social media. I met the likes of Elianna Abrams, Sierra Eastman, and Lilian Arnold. Sierra even said, "Nice to have met you, Summer," as Francesca pulled me out the door. Sierra Eastman remembered my name!

Just being at an event like that, among all those powerhouses? What a thrill. But to have everything fall into place the way it has . . . to have Francesca Barber eating out of my hand . . . to have the principal of the renowned publishing house Temple-Townsend waiting for a first look at my novel, which will no doubt be a work of art, now that Francesca is rewriting it . . . I am overjoyed. I can't wait for the successes to come, and to share them with Beatrice.

Is this me? I ask myself as I glance in the rearview. *Is this really my life?* The dramatic eyes looking back at me above the coral-colored lips are knowing, assertive. *No, this is not me,* I think. Or at least not the me I used to be.

I'm becoming someone else completely.

CHAPTER TWENTY-FIVE

Someone is shouting outside, and through the window I can see a finger jabbing at my doorbell.

"*The New York Times*? Are you kidding me?" Liisa stands on my porch and flattens the Arts & Entertainment page from the newspaper against the glass so it's the first thing I see when I answer the door. She's mad, of course; I committed two cardinal sins by not telling her I was going to the press party last night, and, worse, not inviting her to come along.

But my attention to Liisa is momentarily diverted by the paper she's flapping indignantly as she stomps into the kitchen. I don't know anything about the article that appeared today, and . . . *Holy cow!* It's all I can do to keep my hands steady as I set out cream and sugar and pour us cups of coffee, all the while keeping one eye trained on Liisa and her copy of the *Times*.

She stabs it with an index finger as I lower myself onto a stool. "An A-list crowd turned out to celebrate *Jupiter in Jeopardy*, the upcoming film based on bestselling author Francesca Barber's book by the same name," she reads aloud. She looks up at me ironically. "And look who's standing right beside Francesca Barber. Who knew Marcy Jo Codburn ran with an A-list crowd?" She splashes a torrent of cream into her coffee.

"Can I see?" My heart is pounding as I slide the newspaper closer. Liisa's right: There I am in the large photo. Above the fold, natch. The caption reads, "Francesca Barber; her daughter, actress Aspen Barber; Aspen's husband, actor Tabi Benlolo; and their guests were treated to a snapshot of the upcoming *Jupiter in Jeopardy* film . . ." I stop reading to stare at the picture. I can hardly believe it's me.

Liisa adds a few heaping spoons of sugar and stirs vigorously.

"I suppose you're wondering how I got to the party?" I venture.

"The thought crossed my mind. But I feel like you've been secretive—you haven't told me anything about your life lately, so . . ."

She's snippy, but she's right. I hadn't meant to say anything about the party, but now she's got me cornered. "It was very, uh, last minute and unplanned," I stammer. "It, uh, happened through"—I think fast—"Gil Carter. My client. One of his associates knows someone at the movie studio, and he was invited and so he invited me to come along at the last minute." It comes out as a rambling, repetitive mess, and I can feel my face getting hot with embarrassment.

"He's not in the picture."

"Right."

"You are beet red!" Liisa exclaims. "Wait a minute . . . you and this Gil guy . . . what exactly is going on with you two? Is that who you've been spending so much time with?"

Her question has me blushing even harder, since I've completely avoided telling her how much time I'm spending with Mike. Truth be told, I couldn't have orchestrated a more timely blush, because now Liisa has forgotten all about how I came to be at the party.

"Well . . ."

She's incredulous. "Oh my God. Are you sleeping with your client?!"

I grin like a dope and drop my face in my hands.

"I knew it! I'm so furious you didn't tell me."

My hands fall to the butcher block. "I'm sorry. It's just that this whole thing with him is kind of unexpected. I have these moments of panic when I'm afraid of doing something unethical." Which would be true, although I've never articulated it before; it's just that in reality the unethical thing is blackmailing Francesca, not sex with a client.

"Oh." Liisa's face softens. "You poor thing. I forgive you. Is that why you changed your hair and . . . everything?" She gestures over my body and the *Times* picture. "For him?"

I shift uncomfortably in my seat. "Maybe."

"Well, you look great," Liisa says, and adds grudgingly, "and it's a fabulous photo." She shovels in a little more sugar and takes a gulp. "Now tell me all about this relationship of yours. How's the sex?"

The train transporting Patrick is due shortly and a jubilant Bea drives the Saab to the station to bring him back to our house for a visit. He's in time for an early dinner. Kevin and James are coming (how's that for amicable?) and I invited Liisa, too, but she said no, I should enjoy my family time.

I'm waiting on the porch when Bea pulls in. The passenger door opens and The Boyfriend steps out into the driveway, takes a deep breath as if he hasn't breathed suburban air in decades, catches sight of me, and does a clumsy little bow. I'm not sure whether I should return the bow, but he saves me the trouble by hurrying over and launching into conversation.

"Very nice to meet you, Mrs. C.," he says, sticking out a hand.

Whatever I pictured Patrick to look like, this isn't it. He's basically a male version of Beatrice, whose children would undoubtedly continue the Codburn line of sandy-haired, hazel-eyed, medium-height folk. I expected ripped jeans and a Nickelback T-shirt à la starving artist, but he's more financial district: He's nicely dressed in a powder-blue polo and chinos. Missing is the ragged stubble and tattoo I anticipated; instead, he is smooth and baby faced. Moreover, he doesn't have the sulky and brooding persona I assumed I'd be dealing with, since sulky and brooding is my only frame of reference for *artist*. He is a chatterbox, talking a mile a minute.

"Many of my pieces can be adapted to song lyrics, as I'm sure Bea told you. Do you want to hear my latest?" He pulls a piece of crumpled paper from his pocket and starts to recite. Out of the corner of my eye I can see Beatrice straining to lift his bag from the car. "It's called 'Eyedrops':

> If salt and water came together
> In moments less than profound
> Why look for measures of love when there is
> An Index of Tears Shed around?"

"That's very nice, Patrick," I say, grabbing the duffel away from Bea and carrying it up the walkway. Once inside, she is so enthralled with her new beau she escorts him around to each room for a tour. In the kitchen I overhear her say something about "new tile." I wasn't aware she'd noticed.

We sit out on the patio and sip white wine and nibble from a charcuterie board of cheese, crackers, grapes, veggies, and a divine fig jam I picked up at the farmers' market outside of town.

"Tell her your idea," Bea prompts.

"I'm writing a whole series of poems about ants," Patrick tells me. "It's going to be an *ant*-thology."

When Kevin and James show up a little while later, I'm in the kitchen prepping Caesar salad.

"So what do you think of our resident poet?" Kevin asks after a while, finding a grater for the brick of Parmesan.

"I'm not sure yet. He seems polite enough, and according to Bea, he's very talented." We stand side by side at the window, looking out at our daughter. "But he's chosen a rather tough profession."

"She seems happy."

"She does." I hand Kevin the salad, and I carry a platter of fried chicken and a bowl of potatoes. There are also spicy chickpeas, broccoli, and two kinds of quiche from the market.

"Mom!" Bea's tone is so sharp and shrill, I almost drop the food. "Why is there chicken on the table? Patrick and I are vegetarian!"

"But Queen Bea, fried chicken has always been your absolute favorite!"

"I was younger then." She gives me a withering look.

Patrick puts his arm around her. "Don't worry, it takes longer for your mother's generation to learn new things. They didn't have all the information we do."

Grrr. "I made lots of veggies," I point out, as Beatrice serves him a massive portion of salad and a heaping scoop of broccoli. Patrick and Kevin launch into a discussion of grants for the arts.

"How was that party in the city?" James asks after a while, watching Patrick finish off the potatoes.

Kevin is deep into the chicken and doesn't seem to notice the disappearing side dishes. "What party?"

"Some movie studio thing," James says. "My sister Fiona got her in."

"Thanks again for that, James," I say. "Who wants chickpeas?" I brandish a serving spoon.

"I'll take some." Patrick holds up his plate. "Which flick?"

"The third Jupiter movie, based on the book."

James nods. "And how's your writing going?"

"Just trying to edit," I say. "Patrick, can I give you some quiche? There's some without the feta."

"Mrs. C.," he says patiently, "we're not vegan. We eat cheese. And, anyway, quiche has eggs." He winks at Bea, who looks mortified to have such an idiot mother.

"I love Francesca Barber's books. She's the author, right? Did you meet her at the party?" Kevin says, biting into a drumstick. Kevin apparently is trying to impress us with his literary knowledge.

"She is, and I did. I met the rest of the cast, too." I tell them about the venue, and the clothes, and the crowd, and the entourage. Of course, I don't breathe a word of what transpired privately between us. "Meeting famous authors like her is such an inspiration. That's why I went." Which is partly true; and while I didn't have a chance to get the photo I was after, I remind myself that in the end, my efforts will result in the new and improved version of *A Knight to Remember*.

When there's a lull in the conversation, I ask, "Anyone need butter?" and get a side-eye from Bea. Apparently another no-no.

"Who did you say you went with?" Kevin asks.

"I went alone."

He reaches for a wing. "Wow, that wasn't like you, Marcy, was it? To go to a swanky party in the city all by yourself?"

I shrug. "Anyone want dessert?"

I'm inside taking a fruit salad from the fridge, wondering whether strawberries and raspberries are objectionable to Bea and her boyfriend in some way. But then I pause and close my eyes for a moment, and smile.

Kevin's right, it wasn't like Marcy at all. But Marcy didn't go to the party. Summer did.

An hour later Kevin and James go home, and the kids leave to meet up with some of Bea's hometown friends. The house seems unexpectedly quiet with everyone gone. After I put away the leftovers, I make myself a cup of tea and stretch out on the couch for my Sunday social media spree. I open Instagram and see I have a notification: Apparently, I've appeared in a post.

Oh no. Liisa linked the *Times* article and added a caption about how "her writing buddy" is rubbing shoulders with literary royalty. She's added hashtags for the movies and books and tagged everyone in the photo. The likes are literally racking up as I refresh.

Should I be worried? Surely there are so many iterations of #Jupiter that Francesca couldn't possibly read them all. In fact, she probably has no interest. But she's tagged. The problem is so am I—as Marcy Jo Codburn, not Summer Branigan.

If I ask Liisa to take down the post, she'll be suspicious. Why would I do that when all I've ever wanted is to be a part of the literary world? It wouldn't make sense, so I resign myself to doing nothing, and hope that it all goes unnoticed by anyone who knows me as Summer: Francesca Barber and Aspen, Elianna Abrams, Sierra Eastman, Lilian Arnold, Ned Townsend . . . the list is growing.

CHAPTER TWENTY-SIX

Mike's teaching me golf and sailing. We like spending time with each other. When we're together, I feel like a confident, strong woman, which I haven't been for a while. I like the person I am when I'm with him.

Sometimes we eat dinners in charming little towns and we stroll around. Of course, we're careful to maintain distance between us, and our hands rarely brush as we walk side by side. Neither of us mentions wanting anything more, but this—this easy companionship—is so nice.

My office park in Wilton is under contract now, which I attribute to its being a valuable commodity, in a hot market; but also, the real estate agent I am these days has morphed. I guess Summer has seeped into that part of me, too. With a great deal of mental effort I managed to put the failed Wethersfield deal behind me. I thought and thought. On a trip into town, I looked around at all the shops—Well Read, All Fired Up, Full of Hot Air, and the others—and it occurred to me that a local landlord owns half the main street, along with the medical building where Bea's old pediatrician practices. I met with him, showed him the Wilton property . . . a property he didn't even know he wanted until I pitched it to him, and I negotiated hard until his offer went over asking. Now I'm thinking, Wouldn't it be great to sell him that mostly vacant strip mall? I'm becoming hungrier, and dare I say, developing a killer instinct!

It probably won't surprise you to learn that I'm playing hardball with Francesca, too. Days have passed since Liisa posted the *New York Times* article, and there hasn't been any blowback. I feel I'm in the clear. When Francesca finally sends me an email with two more rewritten chapters, I respond by calling her to say I need her to step up her timeline and write faster. Much faster. I remind her I need the completed manuscript by the season's end.

"I'm writing as fast as I can," she sighs. "I do have other obligations, you know."

Do I really have to threaten to spill the beans, again? "Shouldn't this be your priority?"

Francesca doesn't answer right away. When she finally does, it's to list her upcoming commitments, including a trip to NASA's Johnson Space Center in Houston for a Jupiter-related gig and an appearance at a Philly fundraiser for literacy. And it's time for her annual summer party, the one Aspen mentioned.

Now, you know as well as I do that when someone like Francesca says she is busy planning a party, it's not like you or me; she won't be polishing silverware, vacuuming carpets, or scrubbing toilets beforehand, or shopping for groceries, or preparing any of the food herself. All she'll have to do is delegate and show up. Maybe arrange some flowers. I'm not buying her "too busy" line, and I tell her so. Party, my ass.

But boy oh boy, when a large square envelope arrives by snail mail and I read the return address on the back flap, I can't resist letting out a squeal of excitement. My first thought is, she considers me a friend! I can't believe I am *actually* friends with Francesca Barber!

My second thought is: Here's another chance to get that photo I need.

Grabbing a letter opener, I lift the flap of the envelope, careful not to tear past the edges. And then I see the Post-it Note on the invitation from Aspen, inviting me . . . surely a result of our conversation in the theater bathroom. Aww, it came from Aspen! My heart grows a size, like the Grinch's. What a sweetheart. I'm delirious about going.

What to wear, what to wear? I try on myriad outfits and accessories and spend more time evaluating myself in the mirror than I have in years. I want to look *perfect*.

And the invitation? I leave it front and center on the kitchen counter so I can look at it all day. I can't wait to show Bea when she comes home in the evening. All the lettering is done by hand in professional calligraphy, in beautiful black swirls. Francesca's name at the top looks so elegant: *Francesca Barber*.

Sure enough, when Bea comes home and heads to the fridge for a snack, I hear her exclamation from upstairs and down the hall.

"Mom! Did you see this?" Bea's voice has risen an octave. "You are invited to a *party*. This Saturday. A party at *Francesca Barber's place!*"

I come downstairs carrying the empty laundry basket and grinning.

"But *why*?"

"Remember that event in the city I went to? Francesca and I are friendly . . . we got to talking about our writing over a glass of wine . . . and she . . . she agreed to mentor me!" *In a manner of speaking,* I add silently.

"She did? That's bizarre." Bea sounds skeptical. "Maybe you misunderstood her."

The day of the party arrives at last. On this gorgeous last Saturday of July, I'm on the scenic Montauk Highway headed to Sagaponack, one of the most expensive towns in Long Island and the third most expensive zip code in the country. I figured the traffic would be murder on a beautiful summer weekend like this, with nary a cloud in the forecast, and it is. It's taken me hours of driving to get this far, but even so, I'm early. So early that I'll have to find somewhere to stop along the way to pass a few hours.

My destination is Francesca Barber's beach house in the Hamptons. It's just one of her several estates—she has the home in the Hollywood Hills, obviously, as well as the Upper East Side penthouse, along with the chalet in Saint Moritz, Switzerland, where Aspen and Tabi were married in their fairy-tale #winterwedding.

My GPS says I'm only twenty minutes away. When I see the sign for STARFISH DINER, BEST FRIED CLAMS IN THE HAMPTONS, I pull into the gravel lot. The party starts at six o'clock and it's only ten past four, so I slide into a booth and order the first of what will be several cups of coffee.

I while away the hours scrolling social media. I text Bea, who is spending the weekend in Boston with friends now that Patrick left. She probably won't answer. I spend long minutes plotting how I will keep my hidden-camera gaze trained on Francesca and Tabi should they sneak off together.

The waitress who serves me keeps glancing at me, but I stick to my guns . . . I will not eat before Francesca's party, as I'm sure there will be plenty of delicious (free) food. Plus, the dress I'm wearing is very fitted.

A starfish-shaped clock over the door reads five forty-five. My eyes are blurry from staring at my phone for so long. I rise to use the restroom and touch up my dramatic makeup, ignoring the stares of the wait staff, who are probably irritated that I've taken up a booth all afternoon and spent a grand total of four dollars and twenty-five cents, including tip.

If I leave in fifteen minutes, I'll be fashionably late–slash–on time. I can't tell whether I'm jittery from all the coffee or from anticipation over what's to come.

CHAPTER TWENTY-SEVEN

Everything I've learned as a Realtor, everything I've read online, everything I've imagined, pales in comparison to what greets me as I pull into the drive and hand my keys to the valet. My jaw wants to drop open on its hinges, but I'm intent on playing it cool, and so I make a concerted effort to keep it clamped shut.

The front entrance is angled and cleverly hidden behind landscaped hedging for privacy. I enter the house and walk through, from the frosted glass doors of the front entrance to the wide-open back, trying to absorb every detail of design and furnishing. I do a full 360 to capture all the layered textures of metal and wood, the artfully placed splashes of color to the left and right that serve to enhance a minimalist vibe. Trying to be unobtrusive, I snap a couple of quick pics to show Bea. I'm walking so slowly I must look like a robot powering down. There don't appear to be any guests inside, just swarms of black-and-white-clad catering staff coming and going with trays and platters.

The party is outside in the backyard, the "backyard" being tiered lawns, manicured flower gardens (only pink blooms, mind you) surrounding the pool, statues and fountains, an expansive strip of sandy beach, and the unending Atlantic Ocean. I snap a few more pics.

As I look out to the patio, I congratulate myself: All the research I did, online and on TV, watching *Real Housewives*, has paid off.

The last time I went to a formal garden party was many years ago, harkening back to the days my worldview was informed largely by Judith Krantz novels of the eighties. I vividly recall what I wore at the time: a bright-turquoise taffeta floor-length number with contrasting sequins stitched in a seashell design that struck me as oh so beachy when I found it in a consignment shop, but felt tacky beyond words when I retrieved it from my closet a few days ago.

Hence the research, followed by a trip to the upscale mall several towns over. I spent a fortune, literally a good chunk of my Wilton office park commission, on today's outfit, but thankfully I fit right in. I'm wearing what all the other ladies are wearing, which seems to be white, pastel, or khaki cotton dresses or breezy blouses with capris. Their jewelry is a thin watch, dainty earrings. Somehow I have managed to look just like them . . . except for the makeup, I'm now realizing with alarm. Theirs is minimal, while mine is overdone, somewhat like the Real Housewives.

As I scan the crowd, I see a familiar figure, glorious waist-length waves cascading over tanned shoulders, brown legs flashing beneath a summery eyelet dress. She turns and sees me and raises her hand in a friendly wave.

Aspen Barber is smiling and heading over, with Tabi Benlolo trailing after her.

I raise a hand to wave just as a waiter passes at my elbow, and in my eagerness I tip his entire tray, dumping its contents—a platter of sushi and bowls of dipping sauce and wasabi—onto myself.

The young waiter freezes in confusion and disbelief. "I . . . I don't know . . . how . . ." he stammers, just as Aspen steps inside. She gasps at the brown soy rivulets running from my shoulder to my wrist, the clumps of rice caught on my bracelet, and the pieces of fragrant tuna and yellowtail that narrowly missed my dress and landed on the floor. I feel the heat of embarrassment creeping from my neck and up over my Maybelline Juicy Melon–infused cheeks.

"Oh no, Summer," she says, looking from me to the waiter.

"I'm . . . uh . . . so sorry, ma'am," the waiter says, looking from her to me. "I don't know what happened."

Tabi comes up behind Aspen, takes one look at me, and starts to laugh. "Nice going," he says to the waiter, who looks out to sea as if summoning a tidal wave to wash him away.

"It wasn't his fault," I say, glaring at Tabi. "I flailed."

"Never mind. Johanna, please look after this." Aspen signals to a woman to sop up some of the mess, then takes my hand and pulls me toward the stairs. "We'll get you fixed up in a jiffy. Be right back, bae."

Aspen leads me upstairs. On one entire wall, the length of the long hallway, is a museum-like display of framed photographs from the television set of *Practice Makes Perfect.* Signed cast photos documenting the years the show ran. The studio execs at galas and holiday dinners with Francesca and Aspen, the stars accepting awards, the stars interacting with fans. There's adorable Aspen from the time she was a little tot in overalls to pretty youngster with crossed ankles to blossoming preteen. Dozens of outtakes from scenes in the show, in the house that served as the primary set, in the park where Aspen's character played, and in the school Aspen's character attended. Candid shots of the cast: cast members hugging Francesca, Francesca hugging Aspen, Aspen hugging her sitcom dog with its signature underbite. There's Denise Dunne in a big gold Dolce & Gabbana gown, holding up a big gold Emmy. There's Denise Dunne in black Dior with her bare arm linked through Francesca's. There's Denise Dunne signing an autograph by a hospital bed. And there's a whole section of cast members with major movie stars from *other* Hollywood shows. I try to absorb it all, all the Tinseltown elegance, as I follow Aspen to what must be her and Tabi's suite of rooms, where their huge bed overlooks the ocean.

She slides open the bathroom's barn door. "Luckily it missed your dress for the most part, except for splashes near the bottom, but I think that will come out with soap. It'll dry quick," she tells me, looking me over. "But there's some on your cheek, so you'll have to redo your makeup. Go ahead and jump in my shower."

"Thank you so much. I can't tell you how much I appreciate this." I look down at my toes. "I guess I'm a little out of my element here, and I got a little overexcited."

"I should be apologizing to *you* for our clumsy cater waiter." She gestures toward a vanity table. "Feel free to use whatever you need. I'll see you outside at the party."

I'm taken aback by her generosity. After she leaves, I wash the hem of my dress, and thankfully she's right—the brown splotches disappear.

I towel off after a quick rinse and look around. Aspen's glamour lights illuminate an array of brands I've never heard of but I'm sure are imported and expensive. No Maybelline for this girl. I don't even know the functions of the various products: toners, serums, oils, primers, highlighters, and lip masks, along with a dizzying array of brushes and implements. I find a tinted moisturizer that glides on like silk, and dust on some tinted powder. A sweep of mascara and lipstick is enough . . . I've learned my lesson. I slip on my ensemble, fluff my hair, and whaddya know: I'm transformed from suburban wannabe to Hamptons socialite.

As I admire my reflection in the vanity mirror, I tell myself firmly, *Marcy is the one who gets overexcited and flails, but Marcy isn't going downstairs. Summer is.*

When I step into the hallway, Tabi is hovering right there. He looks around to make sure no one is in sight. "You shouldn't be here," he says to me in his deep voice. "You don't want to get mixed up with this family."

My mouth drops open, but before a single word emerges, he turns on his heel and walks away. *You'll do anything to protect your secret,* I accuse silently. I give myself a few seconds to shake off the indignation before heading down.

Outside, Aspen is by the door, waiting. She smiles and takes my hand. "You look perfect, Summer. C'mon, let's go find my mom . . . she's going to be so surprised to see you."

I want to hug the girl. "Thanks again. You're a real lifesaver."

We weave around guests and musicians and waiters, until we spot Francesca. For a second I thought maybe she'd disappeared into the house with Tabi, but no, there she is, down near the wooden gate that leads to the beach, greeting some neighbors who've come in the back way, near assorted watersport paraphernalia: paddleboards, paddles, lifejackets, buoys. Aspen taps her on the shoulder and she turns.

"Surprise," Aspen exclaims, stretching out her arms. "Look who came to celebrate!"

Surprise, indeed. Francesca's eyebrows shoot up so fast they almost fly off her forehead.

"Hi, Francesca," I say. "It's great to be here! It was so lovely of your daughter to invite me."

Francesca makes a little choking sound.

Aspen laughs. "Mom's overwhelmed. I'm just so glad you two can enjoy tonight." She plants a kiss on her mother's cheek and then, sweetly, adds one on mine. "Well, I'd better go find my husband before he gets up to some shenanigans. Love you, Mama. Have fun, Summer."

Francesca and I are side by side, watching her sashay away. Off to find her cheating husband, no doubt.

The sun is dimming behind us, and its early-evening rays illuminate Aspen in a golden glow as she disappears into the warm embrace of the crowd.

"She's wonderful." I sigh. "A truly kind, beautiful soul."

"I'd do anything for my girl." Francesca stares after her. "I'm sure your daughter is wonderful as well."

"She is."

We look sidelong at each other, and for a moment we have this powerful connection . . . two mothers who make mistakes, whose *own* mothers made mistakes, but who love their daughters and want to make them proud. I feel a bubble of regret ballooning between my ribs. What was I thinking? Maybe extorting the woman who shimmers beside me in palest pink is not the way to go.

"Listen, Francesca . . ."

"Come on, you're here now, might as well have a drink," she says, resigned. "You look very nice, by the way."

I follow Francesca back around the pool toward the nearest bar, where she hands me a flute of Prosecco. We clink, and I swallow a sip. "I've been thinking, and I just want to say—"

"Francesca, there you are! Oh, and Summer, hello!"

Interrupting us with a broad smile is Elianna Abrams. She looks me up and down and lets out a laugh. At first it stings because my instinct is to think I look out of place, but then I realize with a start that we are wearing the same dress; while mine is oyster colored, hers is a light sage. I give her what I hope is a friendly "what can you do, we clearly have the same taste and shop at the same stores" shrug.

Elianna is joined by Lilian Arnold and Sierra Eastman. As we five chat, I'm well aware, as if I were looking down at the scene from above, how surreal this is for me to be here with them, socializing. It's even more surreal when a photographer steps up in front of us and asks to take our picture, so we link arms behind one another's backs and smile for the camera. I feel like I'm in high school, posing with the popular girls for a yearbook photo.

After the photographer snaps a few shots, Francesca excuses herself to greet more arrivals, and I think the others are going to walk away, but they don't.

"I'm starved," says Lilian. "Anyone want to join me?"

We follow Lilian's lead and heap our plates, sit at a table for six where the other two people are Francesca's neighbors . . . a woman and her husband, the self-professed Birdseed King of the East. Who knew there was a fortune to be made in birdseed?

"Do you have children, Summer?" Sierra asks, and I tell everyone about Beatrice and then mention Patrick the Poet, and soon I'm talking about my divorce and everyone nods sympathetically as if they've heard it all before, which they probably have.

The Birdseed King's wife asks if I'm seeing anyone. I really want to impress them and think, *Why not? They'll never know* . . . I respond,

"Just casually. Gil Carter?" But my chutzpah seems ready to backfire, because not only do some of them know his name—Elianna knows him personally.

"We must do dinner next time you're in the city," she insists. "My husband went to school with Gil's brother."

I squirm in my chair. Damn. I've lied my way into a pickle. Should I confess to fibbing? Or, at the very least, hedge a bit? Marcy would. But when I see everyone looking at me admiringly, it's what I've thirsted for, a fountain after a drought. I push thoughts of Marcy, and her pathetic inclination to do the right thing, out of my mind.

Eventually, of course, conversation turns to books, and what we're reading and writing, and five faces face me when it's my turn to hold court, and so, after I note Francesca's location at a nearby table (don't worry, she isn't within earshot), I lean in and tell everyone about my new novel.

"It's historical romance, about a reluctant knight named Devon and the women plotting in his life," I say. "I picture Liam Hemsworth as the young male lead in the movie."

"Oh, has it been picked up?" asks Lilian, smoothing her tight bun. "My cozies were just optioned."

I shrug breezily. "Not yet, but a few producers have been sniffing around."

"Liam Hemsworth is fine," Sierra says, "but he's too old. You want someone *hot*. How about Tabi Benlolo?"

We turn to look across the crowd to where Tabi has an arm draped over Aspen and is scrolling on his phone with his free hand. He *would* make a phenomenal knight. As a group, we sigh. Even the Birdseed King.

I bring the conversation back around. "The scallops are delicious. Do I taste curry?"

Elianna chews and considers. "I think you're right."

"I may have to have seconds." I stand up to return to the buffet table, and Sierra, Lilian, and Elianna follow me. They follow me!

As we pass the bar, I point. "Look, there's a signature cocktail, the Franchini. It's a cucumber-and-elderflower martini. Ohhh, that sounds divine." Diet be damned! I ask the bartender to bring six of the drinks to our table.

As our drinks are served, I feel myself transforming into that strangely powerful persona again. When there's a pause in the music, I boldly raise a glass. "To our dear friend Francesca, queen of the cosmos," I call out. "May she enjoy a blissful summer and *stellar* success!"

Guests at nearby tables overhear, and before I know it, everyone seems to be toasting along with me and congratulating me on words well said; the Franchinis are flowing, hundreds of tiny votives are flickering. Francesca pulls up a chair beside her neighbors, and all of us are laughing and chatting like old friends.

All too soon, though, the crowd begins to thin as people drift to their cars. Francesca disappears into the house to oversee cleanup and Elianna, Sierra, and Lilian stand reluctantly.

"It's after eleven. We'd better get back to our inn," Lilian says. She's had a great time; tendrils have escaped her severe bun, and she looks uncharacteristically relaxed.

"Right, before they lock us out," Sierra agrees. "Where are you staying, Summer?"

"I . . . I'm just going home to Connecticut." As I rise, my head lolls slightly, and I realize how tipsy I am, several Franchinis in. I lean on the edge of the table.

"Oh, you shouldn't," Sierra says with concern. "Hang on." She vanishes and returns moments later with Aspen.

"Of course you're not driving back," Aspen says. "You'll stay here. We have plenty of space."

I can't argue. I may be lightheaded, but even I know it would be stupid of me to get behind the wheel.

I'm washing up for bed in the guest bath when I hear muted voices down the hall. They're getting louder, and I am able to catch snippets. It's Aspen and Tabi, arguing. I know I shouldn't eavesdrop, but I pad over to the door and open it a crack.

". . . overreacting," Aspen is saying.

"How many times do I have to tell you?" Tabi's voice is low but angry. "This isn't the way I thought it would be. There are constantly people around. Fans, studio execs, your staff. Now it's guests. We never have privacy."

Oh. A lover's quarrel.

"After the movie premieres," Aspen tells him, "things will be different. I'll figure it out, you'll see."

"That's what you said months ago," snaps Tabi. "I'm goddamn done with all your figuring." There's a crash of something falling to the floor.

Aspen! All my protective motherly instincts jerk into high gear, and I run to her suite. Aspen and Tabi are standing there, and when he sees me, Tabi glares at me darkly and then turns and stalks from the room. The bedroom door slams, there are determined footfalls down the stairs, and another door bangs in the distance.

"Are you all right? Did he hurt you?" I exclaim.

"Oh, Summer." Aspen curls onto the bed and sniffs. Just then Francesca rushes in behind me and slips her arms around Aspen.

"Thanks, Summer, I've got it from here," Francesca tells me curtly. "You can go."

Quietly I leave, straining toward the murmured conversation I can no longer hear.

Back in the guest room, I lean my head against my closed door. Francesca's words from the hotel lobby come back to me: "As a mother, the last thing in the world we want is to hurt our daughters."

I let out the breath I've been holding. Francesca's got her. Francesca will comfort her. Francesca will keep her safe.

I fall into a deep, dreamless sleep.

CHAPTER TWENTY-EIGHT

It's been ages since I slept so soundly, in one of the widest, most comfortable beds I've ever tried, with the windows thrown open to the pounding of the surf.

I stretch like a feline as the morning sun warms the sheets. Oh, the sheets! I roll over and turn the corner of the sheet inside out to read the label: SFERRA. It must have a thread count of a thousand. And the feather pillow, oh!

I'm still buoyed by the feelings of camaraderie and female friendship that spilled over from the heavenly party last night. How could I have misjudged Francesca so much? I finally met the real her: warm, funny, nurturing. So what if I didn't get an incriminating photo? Even if I had, I know now I couldn't bring myself to use it. Not against my new friend Francesca, and especially not if Aspen could become collateral damage.

And then I remember the quarrel I overheard last night. With Tabi. *Yech.*

—

As much as I'd love to laze away the morning under the covers, I don't want to be rude. I slip back into the linen dress, make the bed, descend to the kitchen. There's no one there. It's been completely scoured, and the only remnants of last night's party are the carboard boxes of dishware and glassware stacked against a wall. I'm parched, so I help myself to water from the dispenser on the fridge door before heading off. I just have to find Francesca and Aspen to thank them for their hospitality.

Cradling my glass and wandering out back in search, I see that the sheer scope of the property is even bigger now that the rented tables and chairs have been cleared away. I look toward the ocean. What a vista to wake up to every morning. Maybe I'll just dip a toe in the sand before I go?

As I step through the gate onto the beach, I spy a small figure crouched by the surf. I call out to her. As I near, I see her shoulders start to shake.

"Aspen?"

When she catches sight of me, she stands and quickly wipes her cheeks. "I'm sorry, I didn't know you were there."

"Honey." My maternal instincts start firing from all cylinders, and I step forward and fold her into an embrace. "What happened?"

"Oh, Summer." She allows herself to be held for a long minute before pulling back to press the heels of her hands to her eyes. We move to the lounge chairs and sink down as she speaks. "Tabi and I had a big fight last night, and he stormed out. You heard. When I woke up later, he was in bed beside me, texting someone, and when I asked who he was talking to so late, he was super vague. I think maybe . . . maybe he's . . . having an affair."

"Did you confront him?"

"Yes, but he denied it." A tear slips down her nose. "And now he's not speaking to me. We weren't supposed to leave until tomorrow, but he packed up and went back to the city early."

"I'm so sorry."

"Do you think I should go after him?"

"I always think it's a good idea to talk things out calmly rather than let things fester," I say carefully. "I'd be happy to drive you into the city."

"Oh, I have a car," Aspen says. "My mom gave Tabi a lift since she was going anyway, for a meeting with her agent. She'll be back tonight."

A meeting, on a Sunday? Ha! I bite my lip before I blurt it aloud. The last thing I want is Aspen going after him and finding the two of them—her mother and husband—in some compromising position. I backpedal.

"On the other hand, maybe you should take the day to relax here. Tabi probably needs some space to figure out an apology."

"That's true. Will you . . . will you stay with me, just for a little while?" Aspen sniffs. She looks like a lost little waif, and I want to bundle her up and take her home.

"Of course I will." We stand and slowly make our way back to the house. "Aspen, do you have any friends out here? Someone who can come keep you company after I leave, someone you can confide in?"

"No." She says it decisively. "When you're an actor, it's strange. There's people you go to parties with, and people you get photographed with, and people you work with or people you pay . . . and they all seem like they want to be your friends, but you can't trust them. You can't tell them *anything*, because they'll use the information against you one way or the other."

This little glimpse into Aspen's lonely world is heartbreaking. "Well, you can trust me." I tuck a loose lock of hair behind her ear, just as I would Bea's, and when I do, the gesture isn't rebuffed. "Hey, how about I whip up some breakfast? Pancakes tend to make things better." I think of the Pancakes Tropicana that went uneaten not long ago.

"My mom always burns them, or they turn out salty."

As we step onto the patio, all the conciliatory feelings I began to feel for Francesca start to evaporate, all the warmth of blossoming friendship cools, replaced by anger and outrage. How could Francesca betray Aspen like this? I ache, seeing how upset the girl is.

And Tabi. What a jerk. I want to tell Aspen that she is far too good for him, that he doesn't deserve her, that she'd be better off without him. But, of course, I don't say it.

"It's going to be fine, sweetheart." We pass the indigo pool. "Things will work themselves out, and you'll be okay. And if you ever need to talk, I'm only a phone call away. I think I mentioned I have a daughter exactly your age?"

"I remember you saying that."

"There's nothing like a mother-daughter bond. You know," I find myself confessing aloud, "I didn't have the kind of mom I wanted to confide in much, and I always swore I'd be different with Beatrice. And I try, I really do. Except that most of the time she's not interested in being with me. Which hurts a lot." My voice catches on that last part. I hadn't meant to reveal something so intimate.

Aspen slips her hand into mine. "You seem like a really good mom."

"And your mother is lucky to have you for a daughter."

"Thanks, Summer. You're so nice. I'm really glad you're here. I don't have anyone else to talk to." Aspen smiles at me gratefully, and my heart melts a bit. This poor girl! She's beautiful, famous, surrounded by adoration, but she's all alone. It's a good thing I'm here for her.

To be needed like this feels heavenly.

"Sometimes it's easier to talk to someone you don't know." I blink back a tear. "Now, how about you show me where you keep the frying pans?"

Aspen is devouring my chocolate chip pancakes, scrambled eggs, and sausage links, with sliced-up fruit from the bowl on the counter. It's so gratifying to see her appreciate my cooking. I'm tempted to pour her a glass of milk as she sits at the table with one foot up on her chair, hugging her knee, but I remind myself she is in fact a grown-up, no matter how young and sad and vulnerable she looks. She packs a surprising amount of food into her tiny frame, like it's been a while since anyone fed her a hearty, home-cooked breakfast.

"Your mom doesn't cook?"

"Johanna cleans and cooks dinners. She comes in later in the afternoons." Aspen helps herself to another sausage.

When she's done, she sits quietly for a while, as if she's deciding whether or not to speak. She looks up at last.

"Summer, can I tell you something personal?" We are sitting across from each other, the windows behind her are open, and her long, dark hair glistens as the sun climbs higher over the ocean. "But you have to promise not to say anything."

"Of course, honey. You can trust me." I wrap my hands around my water glass and smile reassuringly. This is just like it used to be with me and Bea, years ago at our own kitchen table, when she was much younger and talked to me about boys and school and parties and mean girls. In the days when she still needed me, confided in me. How I miss those days.

Aspen picks up her fork and smooshes a piece of egg as she gathers her thoughts. "I think you might be a little confused about my mother," she says, and her voice falters. "She's not who people think she is."

You could knock me over with a spoon. Of all the things I imagined Aspen wanting to discuss, *this* didn't even make the list. "What in the world do you mean?"

"Just that . . . I know you're friends with her, and I'm glad she's helping you with your writing. But she can be two-faced. And you're . . . you're . . . well, like you said, you're not really a Hollywood type."

I interpret her words to mean the popular refrain: *You're too nice*.

"Let's just say you seem very trusting, but Francesca always puts Francesca first. I mean, she was pretty nasty when I was growing up." Aspen shrugs, but then hastens to add, "Although she's much better now."

My emotions are everywhere. I'm shocked and befuddled that what I'd been witnessing all this time as the enviable relationship between a mother and daughter—one I aspired to!—could have such a deep foundational flaw. Although I'm relieved to hear that Francesca and Aspen have patched things up (maybe?) in the present, I am curious about the past. Very curious. And more than anything, I'm touched that Aspen trusts me so much she wants to divulge her unhappy history to me.

She said it herself . . . she has no one else to talk to. It's clear that she wants to unburden herself of past trauma. She senses how warm and loving a mom I am, so I will be the receptacle for her story. I will be the parent she so desperately needs.

I encourage her to think back, to describe the Francesca of her childhood. The secret Francesca, the story behind the story—that is, what the tabloids did not print.

The sound of the surf provides background music as Aspen pours her heart out.

CHAPTER TWENTY-NINE

"To this day Mama still talks about how I robbed her of her youth and ruined her dreams of stardom. She says I was a colicky baby and cried all day and night. Apparently I left perma-bags under her eyes and made her 'so bleary with exhaustion' she couldn't think straight, and any hot guys she brought home 'bolted at the sight of diapers stacked on the coffee table of our tiny apartment.'" Aspen parrots Francesca's voice. It sounds like this narrative has been drilled into her brain.

"She says that?"

"All the time. My earliest memory is being in the bathroom, crying whenever my mother took out a comb. I knew how hard she would yank at my tangles. I remember my chin quivering in the mirror and having to sit on my hands because when I tried to push the comb away, she'd smack my knuckles so hard they bled."

I flinch. "Francesca hit you with a comb?"

"Yeah. Then Mama would get exasperated and say to stop whining. She always told me, 'I'm not the one with the rat's nest on my head like your guappo father's.' I'd never met my dad at that point, but it was weird because my long dark hair was exactly like hers.

"The comb scared me, but so did the rough washcloth she used to scrub my skin red, and the snippers that trimmed my nails too short, and the black patent leather shoes that squished my toes together. She pinched my cheeks to make them rosy, or took away my ice cream cone before I was done. I'd get confused, because she'd say, 'Why can't you understand that everything I do is for your own good?' And I'd agree since she was the one who took me to the ice cream parlor in the first place and boosted me to the monkey bars at the playground and taped Tinker Bell Band-Aids on my knees after I fell."

Slowly I gather up the dishes as I listen. Aspen's still playing with her eggs as she talks.

"In the mirror she said I shouldn't be afraid of her, but then she'd smile this upside-down smile that signaled she was about to pull harder, and my head would snap sideways as she tugged. When she was done, she'd gaze at our reflection and say, 'What a beauty,' but I was never sure which one of us she was talking about."

I rise to bring her empty plates and cup to the sink. "Where were you living?"

"Hollywood, in a seedy neighborhood. Mom moved out there to be an actress. Then she got pregnant."

I'm silent for a while, thinking of everything the tabloids have written about the mother-daughter duo. I don't recall anything about Francesca being an actress. "How did you become a child star?"

Aspen sighs at the memory. She stands up to help, puts the maple syrup and ketchup back in the fridge. "We went to a casting call for the pilot of this show *Practice Makes Perfect*. I remember it like it was yesterday. It was at this place called Teddy's, which I took to mean teddy bears, but really it was this new nightclub off the lobby of the Roosevelt Hotel on Hollywood Boulevard. I remember sitting in the back seat, clutching a secondhand Cabbage Patch doll and staring at Mom's powder-blue eye shadow in the rearview mirror. She was gripping the wheel tight. She'd said hundreds of times how important the day was, but our dented old beater car didn't start right away; plus there was a huge snarl of traffic on the Ventura Freeway, and we were really late. I remember the corners of her mouth pointing downward, so much I could see a smudge of lipstick on her bottom teeth." As I squirt soap on a sponge, Aspen hoists herself up lightly and sits on the wide quartz counter beside me.

"I told her not to worry. I was sure they'd pick her. She said they'd better, or all the time and money she spent would be wasted. Her voice sounded like a fork swallowed by a garbage disposal. I didn't know what 'timeandmoney' meant, but I knew nothing made her madder than when I wasted it, like when I spilled grape juice on a clean dress or scuffed my preowned Mary Janes."

Preowned! I glance around the magnificent kitchen as I scrape the frying pan. They've come an awful long way.

"We got to the hotel just as the double doors of Teddy's opened, and out streamed mothers and fathers with their teenaged daughters. Most were crying. Some of the mothers were, too. Mom grabbed my hand and dragged me forward, and we got bumped and jostled in the crowd. I'm pretty sure, judging by a sudden yowl, she'd skewered someone's foot on her spike heel, but she pushed ahead.

"Inside, the room was empty except for two men and a woman at a long table, shuffling papers. We hesitated off to the side while Mom adjusted her tweed jacket over the safety pin fastening the matching skirt. Then she put on a smile and said, 'Good morning, I'm here to try out for—' but she didn't get to finish the sentence. The woman didn't even look up, just said, 'I'm sorry, auditions are closed.'

"Mom started to argue, 'We're only thirty minutes late—' but the lady told her they'd already made their selections. Mom's face started twitching like a pot of chicken noodle soup about to boil. She clenched her teeth and said to me, 'Do something.'"

I stack the dishes in the drainboard and wipe my hands. "What did she expect you to do?" I say it to myself as much as to Aspen. She shrugs.

"I could tell she was furious, probably because of all the timeandmoney, so I thought fast. I pulled my hand from hers and skipped over to the long table until I was standing right in front of it and said, 'What do you mean, no? How can you say no without even giving her a chance?'"

Aspen jumps to the floor and pantomimes herself as a little girl with her hands on her hips and her head tilted to one side.

My mouth is agape. "You didn't! Talk about guts. How old were you?"

"Six." Aspen chuckles. "Mom had rehearsed in front of me a million times. I understood that *Practice Makes Perfect* was a sitcom about a single mother trying to be a singer-slash-actress in Hollywood, whose precocious teenage daughter became her manager. Mom thought the show was practically written for her and said it would be unforgiveable if they didn't cast her."

I shake my head. *That's some ego,* I think, but I don't say it aloud.

Aspen continues: "The woman and the two men looked up in unison. I guess they were confused, so I just rambled on, something like, 'She is a crazy-talented individual. Just imagine her onstage, under the lights. And wait till you hear the sound she can belt out of those lungs!'

"I kept babbling, and at some point the casting team understood what I was doing: playing the part of Sadie, the Daughter, but changing the words of the audition piece so they applied to my mom. I just kept talking and wagging my index finger at the casting agents as if they were naughty children and I was the adult.

"Then one of the men jumped to his feet and yelled, 'That's her. That's Sadie.' He wasn't much taller than the others when he stood up. He waved his lit cigarette around. The man with the taxi driver hat and mustache nodded and said I was sensational."

I'm already emotionally invested in this audition, and at this praise for little Aspen, I clap my hands. I know I should probably dry and put away the dishes, but I'm hanging on every word of her story.

"But . . ." Aspen laughs ruefully and holds up her hand, as in, that wasn't the end of the audition. "But the woman picked up her clipboard and tapped it with her pen a few times. She said, 'I'll admit she's good. Really good. But the part calls for a thirteen- or fourteen-year-old, and this girl isn't even half that. What about the red-haired freckly one we agreed on?'"

"Uh-oh."

"They start arguing about the red-haired kid and the red-haired mother they'd already chosen. The taxi driver said something about them not going 'ethnic,' and finally the three of them huddled to discuss it, and meanwhile my mom was tapping her toe impatiently. Then the short guy said I'd have to meet the producers first, and the hair color might be an issue. He said, 'I think we've found our new Sadie.' The taxi driver asked my name, so I told him. Aspen Barbieri. Then I risked a little glance over my shoulder at my mom, and I saw her lips curl as if she'd eaten a sour lemon."

"Good Lord. Francesca was jealous of you?"

Aspen stops talking and bites nervously at a cuticle. I wonder whether she's afraid she divulged too much. Maybe I shouldn't have said that about Francesca being jealous.

"What do you think about going into town? You could show me around," I suggest. A change of scenery might be good for the girl.

Aspen and I drive to a neighboring village in my Saab. She's quiet during the ride, except to point out directions; me, I'm digesting everything she's told me so far, which is unsettling. The Francesca of her early childhood is not the one I have come to know . . . at least, it's not the public Francesca I've witnessed. Clearly she wasn't in a good place to raise a child back then.

When we arrive, there's nary a parking space on the whole main street. I cruise up and down, searching. It being a gorgeous Sunday morning, the patios are packed with breakfast-goers and the sidewalks bustle with families, tourists, and shopkeepers, and every other person has a dog.

Finally Aspen suggests I park at the public library, which feels apropos, as she is still in the middle of her story. It's a short walk to the main street to join the bustle.

"Do you, um, usually have an escort when you go out in public?" I ask.

Aspen is wearing huge dark sunglasses, and her long hair is piled into a baseball cap. She could be anyone—a stunning, sultry anyone. "I do in the city, but I should be okay out here. These people are used to celebrities, and they don't usually approach us." Still, to be safe, she asks me not to call her by name.

We stroll along and glance at window displays of jewelry and designer clothing and toys. I'm dying to hear more of her tale. "What happened after the audition?" I ask finally. "After the Roosevelt Hotel?"

"We went home."

I try to picture it. "What was it like?"

"A crammed apartment where the water ran yellowish brown and the door of the refrigerator hung halfway off its hinge. Mom kept it belted shut with a bungee cord around its waist. I mean, that's what it looked like to me." I follow Aspen's gaze to a window. She is staring at a mannequin in a gown with a cinched waist.

"Mama wouldn't talk to me for two whole days until it occurred to her she'd have more opportunities to impress the casting agents, since I'd gotten us a foot in the door. She must've realized the important thing would be to make sure I locked in the part of Daughter, so she did everything possible to make sure they hired me. I guess she figured they'd naturally cast her as Mother. A meeting with the producers was scheduled for the next afternoon."

We're in front of a trendy-looking hairstylist lit with industrial lighting reflected in all the mirrors. It seems to remind her of something. "Mama had this idea: She took me down a few blocks to a hair salon, where the owner, a fat man who styled my mother's hair, always called me Gumdrop. I didn't like him; he made me think of the oil that dripped from under our beater . . . especially when he lifted me up onto a stack of yellow pages and let his thumbs glide over my chest."

Inside the salon is a girl with tight blond curls, waiting to get a trim. Aspen shudders, and I put my hand over my mouth in distaste. She continues.

"He draped me in a plastic cape and snapped one of those tight rubber caps, the kind covered in holes like a colander, over my head, which hurt. Then he jabbed through the hole with a little crochet hook to pull out strands of my long black hair before smearing on some smelly, burning liquid. Tears streamed from my eyes. He said, 'Hop down, Gumdrop,' and led me to a new chair, where he did the thing with his thumbs again. This time he stuck my head under a church bell dryer. The third time I had to lie back for a shampoo, and the fourth time was the bell again. When my hair was finally dry, it had streaks the color of brown sugar. I looked up at my mother, and sure enough, she'd gotten the exact same thing done, so we matched."

"Did you like it?"

"Mama did. She was so happy, she bought us Popsicles from the convenience store on the way home. We even stopped at the playground, and for a little while we were just like all the other parents and kids."

We walk a little farther up the block, and Aspen pauses. She touches my shoulder. "Are you sure you're not bored, hearing this?"

I stop and lay a hand on Aspen's forearm, a lot like I did in the bathroom of the press party. "Aspen, I'm honored that you trust me with your story. Please continue."

We keep walking.

CHAPTER THIRTY

Aspen smiles at me gratefully, and I know I am doing the right thing by allowing her to unburden herself. Any mom would.

"The next day we had another appointment," she continues. "We drove to a nail salon, a place where a plastic cat waved from the cash register and the nice ladies in their matching smocks called out greetings. I liked that place; they painted little daisies on my nails while I waited for Mama. I didn't know why we were there so soon, since she'd just had her medi-pedi, as I called it, and when I glanced at her fingers curling around my shoulder, I didn't see any chips.

"The head lady smiled at me and said to us, 'Aspen, so pretty' and 'What you need today, missus?'

"Mama answered with a word I'd never heard, and we followed the lady as she shuffled to a back room, where she turned on a fluorescent light. Mama said, 'Arms and legs, Winnie, and upper lip and eyebrows.'

"She started stirring what I thought was a pot of honey, and then gestured for Mama to sit on the high bed that took up most of the room. Mama shook her head impatiently. 'Not mine. Hers.'"

I gape at Aspen. "No! She took a six-year-old to get waxed?!"

"Yup. Well, you can guess how it all went down. Winnie was horrified, but Mama was adamant. She said, 'It's better if we take care of the problem early. I know what's best for her.' I was shocked at the burning pain. Once I started screaming, Mama left the room to go wait up front. I just remember Winnie saying 'sorry, sorry, sorry,' over and over. By the time we were done, *she* was crying, too."

"I can imagine."

"As we drove away, Mama said, 'You'll thank me one day.' Then she said we had time for a stop at the local thrift store, where we were regulars, and maybe we'd find a new dress for me to wear to the meeting with the producers. But I guess I exhausted myself with crying in the car. I fell asleep, with my arms throbbing bright pink at my sides, and the backs of my skinned thighs sticking to the vinyl, and I didn't even notice when she went inside to shop without me."

"I don't know what to say." All of this was pretty stomach turning. "But . . . you got the part, at least. That much is clear."

"I did. Just before the pilot aired, the studio decided we should shorten my last name to Barber, saying our real one sounded too 'foreign.' After a few months, when it became apparent that the show was a hit, Mom changed both our surnames legally, so there was no question in anyone's mind that she'd birthed a star.

"My stint on *Practice Makes Perfect* lasted seven seasons, until I aged out of the premise of the precocious little kid—or, at least, that's what the entertainment columnists were told. By then I'd become a household name, with two Emmy Awards and a few Screen Actors Guild nominations under my belt. A limited-edition Sadie doll sold out at FAO Schwarz. I appeared on Hollywood gossip magazine covers, morning shows, musical specials at Christmas. A spin-off show was scorned by critics for"—here she makes air quotes with her fingers—"lacking the charm of the original cast."

"What happened to your mother during this time?"

"Good question." We turn a corner, and in front of us is a beautiful green space, with park benches and a gazebo. A large banner announces a jazz festival coming soon. "You sure you want me to continue this depressing drama?"

"Absolutely!" I nod as we walk through the park.

"Early on, she auditioned, then finagled, then *begged* for the role of Sadie's mom, the singer-actress. The part went to Denise Dunne, an up-and-coming ingenue, and Mom was beyond furious. You see, when she'd first arrived in Hollywood, she spent a fortune on formal acting training, only to find out she was pregnant. After that, everything—her paycheck, her energy—went to keeping us afloat.

"Ironically, Denise had dark hair with natural sugary highlights; she looked like she could be my mother every bit as much as Mom did. But that didn't stop Mom from believing she was *owed* the part.

"I suppose my earnings, which increased exponentially each year of the series, were an acceptable consolation prize. The lion's share automatically went into a trust for me that I could access when I turned eighteen. The studio insisted on setting it up, despite Mama's protests. We received a generous monthly allowance for our living expenses. She burned through it, renting a small house, then a bigger one, then a huge, fancy one; she went on luxury vacations, usually leaving me with a housekeeper; and she spent a fortune on what she called 'personal upgrades,' cosmetic procedures to beautify herself. Meanwhile, it was clearly spelled out in her contract she couldn't do anything to alter my appearance without the explicit approval of the studio."

We sit down on a bench facing a playground and watch a gaggle of kids playing in the splash zone. "That must've been a relief," I say.

"It was." Aspen arches a brow. She's quiet for a while as she watches a father lead his toddler to the sprinklers, and then comfort the child when he gets wet and starts to cry. "Guess who showed up halfway through season two?"

"Who?"

"Good ol' Dad." She grins wryly. "The deadbeat musician who'd sired me, Mama called him. 'Figures your good-for-nothing father's come back to snoop around,' Mama said to me. Even though he hadn't visited us in years, he said he wanted more Daddy-Daughter Time. 'Not gonna happen, shit for brains,' Mama said to him. And in season three he announced he wanted me to live with him and was moving from

Cincinnati back to California. 'He's getting a piece of the pie over my dead body,' Mama said to her new lawyer.

"Meanwhile, during all those years, she was a fixture on set. She thought of herself as part of the cast, buddy-buddies with the stars, with license to voice an opinion about everything from the script ('Sadie doesn't have much dialogue in this episode, does she?') to wardrobe ('Those overalls are not very flattering—how about putting her in those cute leggings?'). The director loved me and knew we were a package deal, even if *she* was a royal pain."

I listen to Aspen mimicking Francesca while I try to see it from her mother's point of view: Was she resentful because all the stardom, the fortune, the glamour was supposed to be hers, not her daughter's? She'd wanted to succeed so badly. How would it feel to be unbearably envious of your own child? I can't imagine ever feeling like that about Beatrice.

Aspen draws her knees up to her chin on the bench and laces her fingers around her ankles. "Each evening, as we left the lot after a day of shooting and said good night to the crew, her nice-nice facade dissolved faster than the Sanka in her hot water. In fact, the more famous I got, the nastier she got.

"Once, for Christmas, we went on a junket to the Caribbean. We arrived at the five-star hotel in sweltering heat. A bellboy recognized me and rushed over to take my suitcase, while Mama was left standing there with her luggage. After we checked in, she told me to stay indoors. 'We wouldn't want you to get a sunburn, would we?' she said. So I watched from the window the whole time. I could see her stretched out on a chaise lounge by the pool, drinking from a coconut, or walking on the sand. The price tag was still attached to my bathing suit when we got home.

"We stopped going to malls because shoppers rushed at me, clamoring for my autograph. At the nail salon, the hair salon, the bank, the grocery store . . . the stylists and clerks and cashiers fawned over me. More often than not, incidents like those got me locked in my room to 'learn my lines without distraction.' Which I didn't mind at all, since my room in our new house was pretty and comfortable. It was worse when she sent me to bed without dinner."

Aspen shrugs and swipes at a tear rolling down her cheek from under the sunglasses. I root through my purse for a tissue.

"Of course, there were the publicity department events where we *did* go to malls and amusement parks, appearances where crowds were intentionally encouraged. I would complain that my stomach hurt before those appearances because I was nervous, but once out there I was quite a natural, waving and smiling. Every year the crowds swelled, we were accosted by more and more paparazzi. It drove her crazy. Finally, the adulation became too much, and she couldn't help herself. She'd hiss, 'Get out of my sight, little attention whore,' and after that, she started using the nickname La-La, which sounded cute to the outside world, but she actually meant it as an acronym, LAW LAW, as in *little attention whore*. I quickly learned that the days she called me La-La were usually followed by nights I went to sleep hungry."

When I offer a tissue, this time she blots her wet eyes. She wads it up in her palm with another resigned shrug.

"I guess for her the last straw was Denise Dunne. She must have known by the way I stared wistfully at her that I wished Denise could be my real mother, not just my pretend one on the show. Denise was kind and loving, the type of woman you could picture kissing her children good morning and reading them bedtime stories at night. She cheered for me when I did a good job on set, and encouraged me if I flubbed my lines. She hugged me, made me laugh, brought me little gifts that I stuffed in my pockets or hid in my dressing room when I thought no one was looking. Mama was looking."

Aspen is quiet for a long time, remembering. The voices of the children drown out the sound of her softly blowing her nose.

CHAPTER THIRTY-ONE

The sun is beating down, and we stand up again. It's cooler on the shaded side of the street, under the awnings. I suggest a cold drink. Aspen leads me down a cute side street jumbled with flowers—petunias in pots, geraniums in baskets hung from light poles, lantana and marigolds adorning doorways. If she hadn't led me right to the door, I would've missed it: a bakery housed in a tumbled stone hut tucked behind the village post office, draped with so many vines and trellises it could easily be mistaken for a bush by someone not in the know.

We enter, and I'm hit with a heavenly aroma of baked goods fresh from the oven. As I drool in front of the display counter, I'm surprised to see Aspen lift her sunglasses to greet the stocky woman behind it.

"Look what the cat dragged in," the woman says, giving Aspen a little wink. "If I didn't know better, I'd say your mother sent you to complain about the cake, but I made it myself, so I know for a fact it was sensational."

"It was." Aspen laughs. "The best one yet."

"What can I get you? Coffee granita as usual?"

"Two, please."

The woman nods. "Grab a seat, and I'll bring them right over."

Aspen and I slip into seats at the back. She's obscured from the view of any other customers. For a second I see us as onlookers might, and I can't wait to tell Bea I had coffee with Aspen Barber.

"That's Millie," Aspen explains. "She made the cake for last night's party. She's been doing our desserts for years."

As I think back to the spread of confections by Francesca's pool, Aspen looks off toward the front window deep in thought. At last she speaks again.

It was funny, Aspen muses aloud, as if she is mulling it over . . . the more famous she got, and the more money she earned for her mother to spend, the more Francesca resented her, and despite Francesca's efforts to keep it contained, sometimes it trickled out.

"Speaking of cakes reminds me of the time the studio wanted to throw me a birthday party," she says. "I remember how much Mama resented it; she kept saying, 'Oh, La-La needs to be in the spotlight.' I was freaking out—the Backstreet Boys had been invited to play, and I wanted more than anything for her not to ruin it."

"Get out! The Backstreet Boys?"

Aspen grins. "Yeah, that was on brand. They held the party at a stunning home in Beverly Hills belonging to the head of programming for the network. As soon as we got there, the other kids my age whisked me out to the backyard. Inside, Mom spotted a bar cart. With every drink, and she drank several, she got angrier and angrier.

"Me and the network's other teenybopper stars were jumping around to the music. Mom lurched right up in front of the band and danced and gyrated. She didn't care who was watching."

Millie arrives then and serves tall parfait glasses of granitas tufted with whipped cream and garnished with orchid petals. We spoon into the icy granules.

"Eventually everyone started singing 'Happy Birthday,' and they brought out this gorgeous strawberry cream cake. I blew out the candles, and just as I was about to bite into a piece of the cake, Mom snatched the plate away and said really loud, 'You shouldn't eat dessert, your thighs are already starting to get fat.' I was *eleven*. Then later, when I opened Denise Dunne's present—a velvety soft white fur jacket with matching beret—she advised Denise to return it. Everyone heard her saying, 'By winter, it won't even fit her. They grow so fast. But you wouldn't know that since you're not a real mother.'"

"I'm sure Denise didn't take kindly to that."

"You're not kidding. She looked like she'd been slapped. She despised my mother so much and went out of her way to avoid her. But also the studio heads overheard, and the birthday party became a turning point, souring what little tolerance everyone had for my mother's attitude. Their disdain became more and more apparent. About a month later we showed up for work on a Monday morning to find a plexiglass partition had been erected to cordon off a corner of the set. Behind it was a chair for Mama. The producer said she was no longer permitted to roam freely on set. She was furious. She started yelling, 'I'm the mother of the *star*, you can't cage me like some animal!' and the producer told her, 'California labor law says a parent must be present until a child actor turns eighteen, and must be within sight and earshot of the child. We'll abide by the letter of the law, but I don't want you anywhere near my cast and crew.'

"Finally, just after I turned thirteen, the part of Sadie was written out of the storyline of *Practice Makes Perfect*, and my acting days were over."

"Everything good here?" Millie pops her head around the corner. "Can I get you anything else?"

"We'd love a couple of your Portuguese tarts." Aspen looks at me apologetically. "Tabi got me into them."

Tabi is a whole different discussion, and just hearing his name makes me mad. I crunch my ice. I'd much rather continue our current topic. "Your memory for detail is astonishing," I say, to keep us on track.

"Thanks. I think about my childhood a lot." Aspen stares at her granita. It's melty at the bottom, and she stirs thoughtfully.

I circle back to the last thing she said. "So you never acted after that?" I try to recall her playing roles after Sadie but before the role of Gemma the Astronaut came along.

"Well, I shouldn't say my acting days were *completely* over. Mom made me try out for parts in movies and TV shows, because we needed the income, but word in the industry spread like wildfire about the . . . uh, problems, and no one wanted to hire me. We had to move from the big, fancy house in Beverly Hills to the small one we rented back in season one. Oh—thank you, Millie."

Millie sets down two custard tarts, perfectly caramelized on top. Aspen lifts one to her mouth and groans with pleasure as she takes a bite. Pastry crumbs fall to her plate as she continues: "Mama got a part-time job at the local Toys "R" Us, which she felt was humiliating. While she was practically vibrating with rage over the fact I wasn't getting work, she also took a perverse pleasure in rubbing my face in it. 'Thirteen years old and already washed up, La-La,' she'd say sarcastically, when I was passed over for yet another part."

As I eat, I think about their dire financial situation, and something occurs to me. "What happened to the trust money?"

"So, my earnings were still growing exponentially in an invested trust, but that didn't help our situation, as I couldn't access it until I got older. One day Mama had an idea: a Broadway show based on *Practice Makes Perfect*. It would be a huge moneymaker, she reasoned. Granted, she didn't know much about Broadway, but she went ahead and contacted a well-known playwright to pen a script. What she neglected to consider was the funding involved. Not a single investor wanted to touch the project. The plan fizzled out before it even began, and she lost the money."

We stand up to leave, and on the way out, Aspen buys a box of four more tarts. When we get out to the sidewalk, she hands it to me.

"Oh, you didn't have to do that, Aspen!" I don't mean to exclaim it aloud and immediately regret it, because beside me, a group of young girls overhears. They can't be more than twelve years old. They surround Aspen without a trace of shyness, asking for photos.

She's so gracious, Aspen; she acquiesces as they take turns making duck lips beside her. Finally I step in. "Girls, Aspen has to get going now," I say, shooing them away like a professional handler.

"Thanks, Summer." She touches my shoulder again.

The girls leave, and we continue weaving our way around the charming side streets. Aspen spies a window display she likes and pulls me into the boutique. I trail after her as she wanders around, pulling items off racks and holding them in front of her. Every single thing would look glorious on her.

"Why don't you try something on?" she urges.

"Me? I'm too old for these designs, and besides, this stuff is way too pricey." I laugh. Not to mention what I spent on the dress and sandals for the party last night, which I am still wearing. I wish I could afford to shop for Bea in this place.

"Let me buy you a present!"

"Absolutely not. But that top you're holding is really cute for you."

Aspen buys it and a couple of other pieces. I don't think she even glances at the total when she taps her credit card. I'm wondering how I can nudge her to continue her story, but she does it on her own.

"God, we went through a few hard years back then, when I couldn't get work," she acknowledges, carting the large paper shopping bag as we leave. "All the nice things we'd acquired were sold off. Mama held on to the designer clothes and jewelry as long as possible until eventually she was forced to sell it all. The housekeepers were long gone. We were back to driving a beater. She wouldn't consider moving to a place with lower rent; she said she'd rather sell every stick of furniture and eat scraps off paper plates if it meant not giving up our 90210-adjacent zip code. Which basically left us back where we started, except we were struggling in a suburb instead of the crappy apartment in a seedy section of town."

"Did you go to school?"

"Yup. Since I no longer needed a tutor on set, I enrolled in the local middle school. I hadn't been to regular school since the beginning of first grade, and I loved it, loved my teacher, and loved having a desk of my own between my new best friends Katie and Mandy."

"Did you miss show business?"

"I did, but I also liked having a normal life."

"And Francesca? How long did she work at Toys "R" Us?"

"Not long. When she wasn't ringing up Rainbow Looms and Stomp Rockets, she spent hours sitting in a kitchen chair, downing cheap vodka and drumming her fingers on the table as she schemed to get our lifestyle back. When I caught the bus in the morning, she was sitting there, and when I got off the bus in the afternoon, I'd find her still there, drinking and drumming. One day she told me we were going to the studio in the morning. When we got to the producer's office, she made me go in alone and do the talking . . . to propose a reunion movie. The producer was looking at me skeptically and asked if it was Francesca's idea. I nodded. He said, 'It's actually not bad. Let me think it over.' Well, he decided to go ahead with the project, and Mama was delighted because for once they'd listened to her. We went roller skating and shopping to celebrate, and everything was peachy for a while."

I try to recall the movie. "Did Francesca play the part of Mother?"

Aspen lets out a short laugh.

"I'm sure she fully expected to. They wanted Denise Dunne, but by then she was a major player deep into her movie career. She opted out when she got an offer to film a bank heist flick in Barcelona. The studio went and found another actress to play Sadie's mother: Casey Wallace, a complete unknown, who Mama said was about as authentic as McDonald's caviar. She was livid."

"Yikes."

Aspen takes a breath like she isn't sure if she should tell me something. I wait patiently for her to continue as we walk to the Village Playhouse. Aspen pauses to look at the schedule of upcoming performances: *Pippin*, *Waiting for Godot*, *The Dollhouse*. When she speaks, it's to her reflection in the empty box office window.

"It was during that year and a half of production that Mama managed to befriend Casey, the mom of two very small children. Mama brought them all kinds of gifts from Toys "R" Us and babysat quite often while Casey was on set, and over those months, Casey had to interrupt filming several times to run home because one kid or the other got sick or hurt. I always wondered if Mama hoped they'd replace Casey, since she was causing so many delays. Anyway, filming wrapped up, and when it came time for the big Hollywood premiere of the movie, with Casey and me and the rest of the cast on the red carpet, somehow the children just . . . disappeared. They were there with a new sitter, but I always wondered if Mama lured them away. Everyone was frantic, the police were called, the press started reporting on the disappearance, and Casey was a complete mess . . ."

"Oh my God, how awful. What happened?"

"Well, wouldn't you know who found them in an equipment room. They were fine, unharmed, and Mama got her moment in the spotlight, and no one could prove they hadn't just wandered off on their own."

I have no words. Was Francesca really capable of that kind of subterfuge?

Through all of this story I've been trying to reconcile the Francesca of Aspen's childhood with the woman I've come to know. Yes, at first I was starstruck and wanted to be her protégé and friend. Yes, to the public eye she seems beautiful and successful and charming, but none of that excuses what she *is*.

I ruminate on everything I've experienced with Francesca since we met: her haughty dismissal of my requests, her diva-like behavior at the press party, her thinly veiled insults of my writing style, my eating habits.

Now I am beginning to realize that the way she treats people is despicable. And her treatment of Aspen was tantamount to child abuse.

There's so much I have to mull over, and my emotions are in such turmoil, I follow Aspen quietly as she leads us back to the library parking lot.

She shrugs as she opens the car door. "At the end, when it came out, our reunion movie was panned. And then my acting days were *really* over."

As we drive back to the beach house in my Saab, I can't help but think how unbelievable it is that Aspen Barber is sitting in the passenger seat instead of Bea. Would Bea have agreed to spend half a day with me like this, strolling around and shopping and drinking coffee . . . and baring her soul?

Aspen needs me in a way that Bea doesn't, because Aspen is lonely and has no one to confide in. And maybe she's a little bit scared? With every anecdote, every memory, Aspen makes it clearer that Francesca has a vicious streak. People don't change that drastically. If she was cruel then, she's cruel now.

I'm in a daze long after Aspen is done with the story, long after she hugged me goodbye and I drove off, leaving Long Island behind. One thing the revelation of this saga has made clear is that, as Aspen warned, Francesca is not who I thought she was. Not at all. I resolve to protect Aspen from her as I would my own daughter.

Any guilty feelings I had about the deal transpiring between Francesca and me evaporate. Because everything she told me so far—all the scary scenes of her childhood—it's nothing compared to what she told me when we got back to Sagaponack.

CHAPTER THIRTY-TWO

It took hours of battling late-Sunday Long Island traffic to get back to Connecticut. Guess who broke the cardinal rule about not shopping when you're starving? On the way home I stopped at a convenience store and, for the first time in months, loaded up on junk food. Now it's late, and, just like I used to, I'm sitting on the couch plowing my way through a party-sized bag of Doritos and a tub of dip. I'm determined to finish it and dispose of the wrappers before Bea gets home.

A Netflix movie is on, some thriller set in a dystopian society, and even though I'm a third of the way through, I have no idea what it's about because all I can think of are the horror stories Aspen told me, along with the infuriating images stuck in my brain of Francesca and Tabi together in her Manhattan penthouse, romping in bed, while poor Aspen cries her heart out in the Hamptons.

This is emotional eating at its finest, I know, and I'm trying to smother the feelings with food even though a voice is screaming from my frontal lobe to stop before I undo all the progress I've made. But my reptilian brain wins, and I continue on autopilot because I'm upset, digging into the bag, scooping up the onion dip, crunching while barely tasting, licking my salty fingers—digdipcrunchlick, digdipcrunchlick.

My anger at Francesca is a burning red flame. I may not be a perfect mother, but I would never, never hurt my daughter in the ways

Francesca has hers. While I've tried to support Bea in her aspirations, Francesca selfishly exploited Aspen's acting career.

Think of me as a fly caught in a spiderweb, comforting Aspen while I had to keep her mother's secret. You better believe I'm fuming. I crunch harder on my mouthful of Doritos. I can't believe I felt so warmly toward Francesca that we actually started to bond over shared affection for Aspen.

I'd been on the brink of telling Francesca to forget our arrangement and of reassuring her that I would never say anything to anyone, manuscript revisions or not. Well, I still won't reveal anything, because it would hurt Aspen even more, but Francesca doesn't need to know that. Let her continue to believe I'll spill what I saw at the bar. Should I feel guilty? Absolutely not. It's poetic justice: Francesca milked her own daughter so that *she* could live her dream life, and now she's getting a taste of her own medicine by facilitating *my* dream life of becoming a published author and role model for *my* daughter.

Ice cream! That's what I need. A scoop of ice cream with hot fudge sauce. Good thing I remembered to buy some. I'm spooning up the last of the Rocky Road when Bea calls to say her friend is dropping her off in a few minutes. I decide to check on Aspen.

Hi Aspen! How are you doing? I text. I crush the empty dip container and wad up the chip bag into the trash as I wait for a response.

She texts back almost immediately. hi Summer ok I guess I stayed n 2 watch a movie

Did you hear from Tabi?

yea hes comin back tmrw n we'll talk

Oh, I'm so glad to hear that. I hope you two are able to clear the air!

hey thks for evrythin I'll kyp gtg

Deciphering her punctuation-free shorthand is possible only because my kiddo communicates the same way; she taught me "keep you posted," "got to go," and other abbreviations, and uses the same spelling abominations. I'm just hitting send on LMK if you need anything! with a row of heart emojis when I hear a car pull up, some girlish voices, and then the scrape of a key in the lock. A moment later Bea drops her bag in the front hall and flops down on the couch beside me. She gathers her hair to one side and turns her back to me. She loves back tickles, and I oblige, drawing squiggles down her spine with my fingernail. "How was Boston?"

"Fun. We went to three different clubs. I didn't go to sleep until seven this morning."

"Sounds exhausting."

"It was. Patrick would've loved it."

"Did you eat?"

"We stopped for lobster rolls on the way. Speaking of which . . . ?"

I nod. "My purse is on the landing."

Bea heads for the stairs. "Thanks, Mom. I'm going to bed. I didn't nap in the car so Emma wouldn't get sleepy driving home."

"Good girl. Hey . . . don't you want to hear about the party in the Hamptons?"

"I do, I'm just really zonked. Tomorrow?"

"Oh . . . sure."

I'm loading the dishwasher when I get a call. It's Francesca. I slip outside into the dark for privacy.

"Stop communicating with Aspen," she snipes in place of a greeting. "I never would have let you stay over if I'd known you were pretending to be her parent. I'm warning you, keep away from her."

Well, I guess I'm no longer at the top of her friend list, either. "Because I kept her from jumping in the car and going after you and Tabi? Would you rather have had her walk in on you two going at it?"

"Who says we were together? He asked for a ride. I dropped him off and went to a meeting."

"Sure. On a Sunday morning, with your 'agent,' right?"

"Not that it's any business of yours."

"It became my business when we made a pact," I grate, making an effort to keep from raising my voice. I can't believe how self-centered this woman is. "And it became my business when Aspen cried in my arms and told me she was terrified her husband was having an affair. She told me everything!" I'm furious, and I really want to tell Francesca just how much I know, but I promised Aspen I wouldn't, so I swallow down the words and allow myself a small barb instead. "Say, why weren't the soothsayer, chambermaid, and warlord at your party, seeing as how you're such great friends? Not that I'm expecting you to tell me the truth about any of it. I'm not sure I'd believe you anyway." I breathe again. "But what I *do* expect is that you'll get back to work on my manuscript. You're only halfway through."

We disconnect and I'm still shaking my head. "Meeting her agent," I repeat to myself, using mental air quotes.

Which gives me an idea.

Now that my exceptional manuscript is well underway, and heading toward completion, it—and I—will need the top-notch representation I've been seeking. Right?

CHAPTER THIRTY-THREE

Mila Jorgenson is a powerhouse. From the outside you would think she is mousy, with her close-cropped brown hair and Coke-bottle glasses that magnify her eyes tenfold so that she looks a little buggish. But she's not. She's shrewd and assertive and a self-proclaimed beast when it comes to negotiating contracts for her clients, among whom are iconic authors across every genre, memoir to cookbook.

The literary representation firm she founded, the Jorgenson Agency, is housed in a historic skyscraper off Avenue of the Americas, with fat gold-flaked pillars, travertine floors that gleam under antique chandeliers, and crown molding that can make you weep. Inside the offices, there's a low hum of activity: A cadre of assistants tote armloads of ARCs while agents take phone calls and tap away at keyboards. The Jorgenson Agency wouldn't be what it is if Mila weren't a tigress, so I believe her self-assessment, especially as I look at the framed images of bestselling authors, the awards they've won, and the books they've written plastering the walls of the reception area. The three oversized Jupiter book covers hang front and center. I've been staring at them for the past forty minutes.

A receptionist, who looks young enough to be celebrating her bat mitzvah, finally leads me down the hall to Mila's office and lets me in.

"Summer Branigan. As you doubtlessly know, Francesca Barber suggested we speak. Nice to meet you," Mila says, stretching a hand from behind an L-shaped desk. "I'm sorry to have kept you waiting this long, but three of my authors chose to miss their editors' deadlines yesterday."

"Thank you for seeing me. I . . . er, respect deadlines. I'm a stickler for them." I let out a nervous titter. Francesca requested this meeting (rather, I demanded she request this meeting . . . which is the only reason someone like me is now sitting in front of someone like Mila Jorgenson, especially on such short notice), but there's no guarantee the agency will sign me, pressured or not.

Mila doesn't smile. "Good to hear. So you and Francesca are close, I take it?"

"We've become much closer in recent months. And she's been very helpful with my writing. She's giving me suggestions." I clear my throat.

"Mm. I'm sure she has some insight into the inner workings of the industry. Well, I've had a chance to read through *A Knight to Remember*, and even though I rarely look at unfinished manuscripts, I must say, I'm impressed so far," she says, pulling up the file on her tablet. "I would prefer a rom-com. And yet . . . it's compelling. In my experience, it's rare to find a debut fiction as well structured, or characters as well developed. In parts, it actually reminds me of Francesca's work." She peers at me through her glasses. "When do you expect to be done?"

"Oh, within the next few months, I'm sure." (I'm not sure, but I hope.)

"Obviously I'd like to see the completed manuscript as soon as possible. Judging from the word count, you are more than halfway through." She leafs through a planner on her desk. "It's the beginning of August now. A draft by end of month would be ideal. Doable?"

I shift in my seat. That's just four weeks. "I'll make sure of it."

"Good. Now, Summer, tell me about your platform." She turns away to face her computer screen and types a couple of words.

Um, nonexistent? Summer Branigan does not have a presence, social media or otherwise. "I'll work on it."

"Please do. It helps when we start shopping for a publisher."

We? I can't believe what I'm hearing. "Actually, Ned Townsend said he wanted to have a first look. Francesca introduced us."

Mila swivels back to face me and for the first time has the hint of a smile on her coppery lips. "Well, that is good news! Temple-Townsend would certainly be tremendous. In fact, I'm meeting Ned and Barry this week to go over several projects. I may even bring this." She pats the printout. "But not to worry. If Temple-Townsend doesn't work out, we'll find another, even better, home for your novel."

My novel. My heart beats faster. Is this really happening?

CHAPTER THIRTY-FOUR

Saturday night, Mike, Liisa, and Toni take me out to celebrate. We drive to a small hamlet, where we sit outside on the veranda of a rustic bistro overlooking a river.

After we order, they raise their wineglasses and smile broadly. "A toast," Liisa says. "Here's to the first one of us becoming a published author."

We clink, and Mike winks playfully. "And here I thought you were just a poser, like Liisa, Toni, and me."

They're looking at me expectantly, as if I have sudden new insight into what it takes. "It all happened fast. I didn't want to say anything in case it didn't lead anywhere. And if it did, I . . . I . . . didn't want you guys to feel bad that my dream is coming true."

"Do you think so little of us?" Liisa asks. She punches my arm, just hard enough so I'll know she's not entirely kidding.

"You help us celebrate our wins every week. Every time we reach a goal," Toni adds.

Mike says pointedly, "Don't you know how excited we are to celebrate *you*?"

"I didn't mean . . ." Hurriedly I sip my wine. "I'm sorry, I love you guys, really."

"We couldn't understand why you'd gone dark, and we're not jealous, we're thrilled for you!" Toni exclaims. "This could be life-changing."

"Who knows how far she'll go?" Liisa says to the others incredulously. "To sign with a top agent . . . it's an amazing step."

It's hard to contain the grin spreading all over my face . . . although, one tiny brain cell of mine objects to Liisa's characterization of my accomplishment as a "step," because I feel it's a much bigger victory than that.

Mike turns from her. "What did you say her name is?"

"Mila Jorgenson."

"Cheers to Mila Jorgenson." We clink again.

"I'll be sure to tell her about all of you," I promise them.

After we order, Mike circles back. "Tell us about the contract. And did the agent suggest any edits to your work? Does she have publishers in mind?"

I laugh and hold up a hand. "Slow down! What is this, *Meet the Press*?" Until our food comes, they continue to pepper me with questions; as soon as I answer one, they're on to the next. I bask in the attention, surely a portent of things to come.

Finally, Mike sits back in his chair. "Well, I'm going to be the first one to buy it. *A Knight to Remember*, by Marcy J. Codburn. Heck, the three of us will buy out the bookstore."

I take another sip. I don't tell them about my pen name. I want to keep my two identities separate for now. I had to disclose my legal name on the contract with the Jorgenson Agency, but Summer Branigan will appear on my book jacket, and so far no one else knows we are one and the same. Eventually, I suppose, I'll have to tell.

My phone dings with a notification. "Oh, guys. I just received an email from Victor Thane, an investor I'm working with."

"More good news, I hope?" Mike asks.

I nod as I scan the email. "He's letting me know he is coming to scout my listing next month. He says he has narrowed it down to a few properties he wants to see, in Jersey and Connecticut. He says my Back Bay listing is a top contender."

Mike chuckles. "When it rains, it pours. Now we'll have two of your successes to toast."

"Let's not get ahead of ourselves. Victor Thane is interested, but it's far from a done deal, Mike."

"You're on a roll. I have absolutely no doubt that you will be as successful with selling the Back Bay property as you were with landing Mira Jorgenson."

"Mila Jorgenson."

"Right." Mike chuckles again.

"It's lovely to see you like this," Toni says. "Happy and succeeding."

Liisa sips her wine. "Do you have time for our walk tomorrow? Or do you have to work on your manuscript? Now that you have a deadline, I mean."

A deadline. Right. I almost forgot.

My friends are absolutely correct. I do have a deadline, and one I can't afford to miss. Liisa and I compromise with a walk on the trail, but afterward I excuse myself to go home and "work on my manuscript," and by that I mean demand that Francesca work on my manuscript.

I text her. It's Summer. We need to talk. Just in case she misses the text, I also send an email. She's not responding to either, so I leave a voicemail. "Francesca, I know you're receiving my messages. This is important. Please answer me."

The rest of Sunday drains away in slow motion, as if there were a clump of hair clogging the pipes. I do a little gardening, water the potted plants, sweep the patio. I throw in a load of laundry for Bea and make her sandwiches to take for lunch. I shower, then text, email, call again. No word from Francesca.

In a rare occurrence, Bea has no plans for the evening. She and I go out for dinner, to her favorite Mexican place in town. We decide to walk to the restaurant, and immediately I'm reminded of strolling around in the Hamptons with Aspen.

Over chips and guac, I ask about Patrick and his progress finding an apartment in faraway Savannah, their mutual friends, her progress at the lab. As our steak fajitas are served (I guess my "vegetarian" daughter is flexible with her eating habits), Bea asks, "What's going on with you?"

I'm bursting—but I ease into it by telling her I have a potential buyer for a piece of land. Bea gives me a thumbs-up.

Then I go on to tell her all about signing with Mila, and she looks a little skeptical, but when I've sufficiently convinced her it's true, she squeaks and says, "Hooray, I'm so proud of you!"

"Thank you."

"Mom, why didn't you start with that? That's great!"

"It is pretty great, if she can get me a book deal! It's what I've always wanted, as you know." For a millisecond I consider returning to our conversation about my putting aside my dream for Kevin's, but I stop myself. At this point, I think, actions will be more effective than words. With Francesca working on my MS, I'll be a model of success in no time, and that will go further than anything I could possibly say.

Bea fills her fajita and takes a bite. "Maybe you can introduce Patrick to your agent! How amazing would that be?"

"And also," I add, glossing over her suggestion, "I have a new friend I've been spending time with."

She swallows and puts her fork down. "You do?"

"Mike from my writers' group. We're just friends, but I don't want you to be surprised if he drops by."

"Oh."

"He's really nice, Honey Bea. I think you'll like him."

"Okay."

"I'm allowed," I say, frowning. "Sometimes it's nice to have male companionship. Until I meet someone special one day."

Is that my imagination or did her chin just pucker in that unmistakable way it does when she's about to cry? She rarely cries. I cover her hand with mine.

"You weren't thinking that Daddy and I would get back together, were you? I think you know as well as I do, that ship has sailed."

"I realize that." She picks up her fork, plays with the rice and beans on her plate. "It's just really hard to imagine you with another man."

"That's exactly what I said to Dad."

CHAPTER THIRTY-FIVE

Monday, I'm back in the office, working on a packet to give to Victor Thane. It's basically a "why do business in Connecticut" sales pitch about everything the state has to offer a prospective company. I'm busy researching and downloading, printing and stapling, and in between all that I'm obsessively checking my phone for a response from Francesca, but there is none. With each passing hour I get more anxious.

Tuesday, I send her a long text. I tell her I've signed with the Jorgenson Agency, and I beg her to stick to her end of our bargain.

No reaction.

I follow up with a row of question marks.

Hours later, she finally, finally responds. I'm sorry, I'd like to but I can't.

I repeat my note, in all caps this time, and again hours go by.

She answers, I'm busy with Aspen.

I start formulating a reply, and I guess she must see the three dots that indicate I'm typing, because she says again: No, Summer.

I continue typing.

She adds, Whatever you are about to say, the answer is no. Not now.

Erasing everything I've written, I type instead, I'm calling you.

Her response: I won't answer. I'm going for a walk on the beach to see the sunset and de-stress. I'm not bringing my phone.

I didn't think my inner turmoil could get any more moiled (it's a word, look it up), but it does.

That evening I'm dressing a salad for Bea and me when she comes downstairs. "Mom, can I talk to you for a sec?" She sits on a stool, rotating side to side.

"What's up, honey?" I reach for a pair of tongs and start tossing.

"I've been giving this a lot of thought." Bea picks up the stump of a celery stalk and peels off thin fibrous strands. "You know that things with Patrick are pretty serious, right? Well, when we get to Savannah, I'm going to look for a job."

I drop the tongs. I feel like I've been punched in the stomach, making the words coming out of my mouth as sour as throw-up.

"Beatrice. Tell me I heard wrong. I really, really hope you mean a job *while you're in grad school.*"

"You didn't hear wrong, Mom. I've decided to postpone going back to school for now."

I don't know what to say.

"Before you get the wrong idea, Patrick didn't ask me to. I just want to give him a chance to concentrate on his poetry. Down the road I can always pick up where I left off."

It's morning. Bea was fast asleep when I left before six for the Hamptons. I'm so distraught and distracted, it's a wonder the car is going in the right direction.

I keep picturing Bea in a town house in Savannah, watering the flowers in her garden and *not* going to grad school. Or doing laundry in the laundromat across from her new apartment, *not* studying. Or swinging on the cute porch swing of her duplex, *not* being a chemist.

Everything I've engineered to this point, the entire deal between Francesca and me, that finally seemed like it's going to pay off, is balanced on the edge of a knife, about to topple over at any moment. Everything our daughter's built . . . everything Kevin and I *helped* her build . . . could collapse. All the clichés for impending disaster run through my mind. Beatrice is following in my terrible footsteps. And I'm so close to succeeding! I have an agent and everything! I can't lose it all now. Bea can't see me fail. It's imperative.

Francesca simply wrote "no" about ten more times in answer to my texts. She's holding her ground. Just like she warned me, she didn't answer any of the two dozen calls I placed to her number last night.

Now I'm frantic.

It's cloudy and the forecast calls for heavy rain. On an overcast weekday like today, the traffic traversing Long Island is a fraction of what it would normally be on a sunny summer weekend, like the weekend of the party. Even so, it feels like it's taking me forever to get there.

Should I tell Francesca what I know? I want to keep my promise to Aspen. Francesca will think I'm extending an olive branch to her, even though right now I feel like the only thing an olive branch would be good for is to whack her over the head with it. She doesn't deserve my compassion.

I step on the gas. My tires spray up loose gravel as the sign for STARFISH DINER, BEST FRIED CLAMS IN THE HAMPTONS passes by in a blur on my right, and in another fifteen minutes I'm screeching to a halt in front of the tall wrought-iron gates guarding her circular drive. I hop out of the car just as the first fat raindrops start to fall. The gate is closed, and there are huge NO TRESPASSING, NO PHOTOGRAPHY signs hung on it. It wasn't closed last time I was here. Now what? Even if I press the buzzer for entry, there's no way she'll let me in.

I drive a little farther before pulling off the side of the road where the shrubbery is thick with overhang, so thick the rain isn't even wetting the windshield. Stuffing my phone and keys into my pockets, I walk along the perimeter of her estate. Down the laneway past the gate there's a break in the shrubbery. There I can see that the stone wall separating her property from the road really isn't very high; it's an ornamental fence more than anything, and all along it are the signs, warning off paparazzi, I suppose. I'm not paparazzi. I part the branches and leaves and start to shimmy over. The wall may not be high, but my shimmying days are long past, and I scratch myself—my hands, my elbows, my cheeks—on the brambles.

It's raining harder and the temperature is dropping. My shoes are slick with dew and rain as I run diagonally across the grass, and the moist air is steamy, but I don't even take notice. Last time I was here, I ogled the manicured gardens with corkscrew-shaped plantings and the hedging that looks like it's precision trimmed with cuticle scissors. But I don't pay any attention this time. I set my sights on the frosted double doors.

Just as I near, one of the twin doors opens a few inches. I understand now the curious angle of the home's entrance: Its construction, along with the hedging, protects Francesca from the wide-angle lenses of paparazzi who are within their rights to shoot from the road. But here, by the garden, I'm so close I can see into the house. I scooch down behind some euonymus.

There's Francesca in the front hall, in a little tank top and thong, and Tabi Benlolo, smartly dressed in jeans and a pressed shirt with a leather duffel slung over his shoulder. No walk of shame for him.

When Tabi told Francesa "This has to end," I thought he meant their affair. But clearly the manipulative Francesca had convinced him to stick around.

Francesca looks at the wall just inside the door, then peeks out over the lawn. I follow her gaze and see the iron gates swinging open. Argh . . . *now* she opens them? When I look back inside, Francesca and Tabi are kissing. I push my dripping hair off my face and blink the rainwater off my lashes before looking again. And . . . still kissing. Without even realizing what I'm doing, I've got my phone in my hand and I'm zooming in to snap a few frames. Ha! Who says this isn't a game? It's fifteen–love, Marcy. I got photos after all! I have the advantage!

I pocket the phone before it gets too wet. Even after all that, they haven't parted. It's like Tabi can't tear himself away, and when he manages to take a step toward the door, Francesca clutches his shoulders and pulls him back for another smooch. They murmur and smile against each other's mouths.

Their embrace becomes more passionate, and Tabi lets the duffel slide to the floor. His hands are sliding up under Francesca's tank top, and her head falls back on her neck. He trails kisses across her collarbone while using a heel to shut the door.

Seriously? I wriggle closer to the house and crouch behind a barberry to shelter from the rain. I wonder how long I'll have to wait.

By the time the door opens again, I'm a pathetic, dripping lump, which reminds me of pathetic fallacy (that's when the weather mirrors—oh, never mind).

I wait through another round of goodbyes until at last Tabi picks up the bag and sprints out to his car. He speeds down the driveway and hangs a sharp left out the gate.

At last, I straighten. My knees are aching as I ring the bell and rap on the door with the knocker. I don't have to wait long before Francesca opens it, a dreamy smile parting her soft, just-kissed lips.

"What did you forget . . ." Her face blanches. *"You!"*

For a moment we just stare at each other. I can easily guess what she's thinking: Did I see him before he drove off? Did anyone else see? And how on earth did I get here?

Without a word, she shuts the door in my face.

CHAPTER THIRTY-SIX

My palm shoots out to brace open the door.

"You can't be here," Francesca hisses.

"Please, let me in. I'm soaking wet and cold."

She looks over my shoulder toward the road, then grabs my arm and yanks me into the house so hard I stumble over the threshold. She pulls a towel from the powder room and tosses it to me, then steers me to the kitchen and into a chair.

My teeth are chattering as I speak. "I just want to t-talk for a minute, then I'll go away, I p-p-promise."

"I need coffee. And where did Johanna put my pills?" Francesca lifts the door of an appliance garage and slides out what I assume is a coffee maker. It looks space-age. As she putters, I slowly warm up.

"Thank you for letting me in." There's so much new information I now know, and so much I have to say, and also I'm trying to keep my emotions in check. I start neutral. "How's Aspen?"

Francesca glances up sharply. "She's fine. Why do you ask?" Her hands shake as she fills the reservoir with water.

"No reason." *Except that she needs protection from you,* I think. I choose my next words carefully. "Look, I know this hasn't been easy for you, Francesca, and despite what you think, it hasn't been easy for me. This is not an alliance either of us ever expected. But please hear what I've been trying to tell you: I have a *contract* with the Jorgenson Agency. Mila *signed* me. She expects the finished manuscript by the end of the month."

Francesca is scooping coffee. She doesn't answer.

"And my daughter . . ."

"What about your daughter?"

Briefly I wonder if telling Francesca about the situation with Bea would help persuade her, but then I remember she's not exactly the caring motherly type.

"It's complicated." I wrap the towel tighter around my shoulders and make an effort to stay calm, but it's hard, knowing what I know about her. "Francesca, I don't want to sound blunt, but I have to remind you of our . . . deal . . . which was *your* idea, if you recall . . . your help in exchange for my silence. Remember?"

"Of course I remember."

"Well?"

"Well, I already told you, Summer." Francesca presses a few buttons, and the coffee maker glows blue. I can see her fingers shaking. "I'd like to help, but it's just not a good time."

"What do you mean, not a good time?" I throw my hands in the air with exasperation. "I'm the one who's on a deadline!"

She ignores me.

"You can't just refuse. Or I swear, I'll . . ." My words taper off. I clamp my lips together so I don't say something rash.

Francesca turns slowly. "You'll what? What will you do?"

I can't help it; I explode. "I'll make you regret it!" My hot thoughts flow out like word lava. "I'll tell! I'll tell everyone what I saw! I saw him leave just now. You and Tabi Benlolo, making out, hooking up again. Your son-in-law, for Chrissake. I have *pictures*. I'll put them on social media. Tweets, posts, the works. I'll go to the press. I'll tell the whole world. And then your daughter will know! She'll know. You. Are. Having. An. Affair. With *her husband*." Spit flies from my mouth, I'm so agitated. There's so much more I want to say, but I promised Aspen I wouldn't.

Francesca looks stricken. Her words, when she finds her voice, come out weak as a kitten's. "I think if you really had pictures, you would have used them by now."

"The truth is I didn't before, but I do now. Look!" I pull out my phone and click on the recent photos. Francesca leans in close to peer at them. Tabi is completely recognizable as Tabi, but from my low-down angle, his wide shoulders obscure most of the face of the woman in his arms. All you can see is dark brows and dark hair . . . a lot like Aspen's.

I can feel the color drain from my cheeks. Our heads are almost touching, and Francesca closes her eyes briefly.

"You can go ahead and post those, Summer. Be my guest." She isn't wearing any makeup, but she still looks beautiful, with her flashing crystalline irises set off by olive skin tanned deep bronze from time at the beach. What she no longer looks is threatened.

"About our deal," I say.

Francesca smiles. "What deal? Seems to me anyone can say anything they want online, but without proof to back it up . . ." She shrugs. "So. I guess we're done."

I'm so angry I'm seeing little bursts of red. This woman is ruining everything. I think of my half-finished manuscript sitting on Mila Jorgenson's desk. Mila is itching to see the full. To send it out to publishers. To get a contract signed. To get it on bookshelves. How can Francesca do this to me? And then I remember her history of meanness. Of *course* she would double-cross me.

"I'm going to take a quick shower while the coffee brews," Francesca says. "Aspen said she might visit. She could arrive anytime. Help yourself to coffee when it's ready, and then please leave." She says it cool and casual, as if I came over to borrow a magazine.

"No doubt you need caffeine . . . you probably got no sleep last night. You and your *son-in-law*."

"I don't see how my private life is your concern."

"It's not. I really couldn't care less. What I care about is that you finish my book, because you said you would!"

"I actually never promised that. I only agreed to help you—not do it all myself—because I thought you had photos." She smiles again. "But you don't, now, do you?"

Francesca reaches for a basket on the island. It contains all kinds of vitamins and supplements: collagen, biotin, omega-3 fatty acids, antioxidant blends, adaptogenic herbs, and more. I see a label reading Moon Juice Sex Dust. She takes a bottle of distilled water from the fridge. She busies herself with dispensing her daily servings. I'm immediately reminded of Bea as a child with her chemistry set, measuring from this jar and that.

The anger ratchets up. This is the story of my life—the good girl, the naive girl. The Pushover. I play by the rules, I keep my word. I try to be helpful. And then, every time, I get screwed, bullied, or trampled on.

With Francesca, I kept my part of the agreement to the letter: I didn't breathe a word to anyone of what I saw at the hotel bar. I can feel myself growing more desperate. The little red bursts become full-fledged Fourth of July fireworks.

Think, Marcy. *Think.* I have to find the right words, the right sentences that will convince her to get back to work on my manuscript. What can I possibly use for leverage? I kick myself for not taking better photographs.

Outside, a fierce wind is blowing up the surf into frothy waves that crash on the sand, but I don't hear the wind or the crashing waves. No, what I hear instead are voices talking about me. Toni's: "This could be life-changing." Liisa's: "Who knows how far she'll go?" Mike's: "The three of us will buy out the bookstore." Mila's: "We'll find the perfect home for your novel." And, of course, Bea's: "Hooray . . . that's great!" I think of the expression on her face when I told her about signing with the Jorgenson Agency, how happy she was that my dream, my lifelong, cherished dream, is finally coming true. I think of her postponing grad school instead of chasing her *own* dream. I have to find a way to make my book happen.

What if I simply tell Francesca I won't leave until she does the work? Can I stand over her while she sits at a keyboard and force her to type? Force her how? It's not like I can point a gun at her head. And anyway, it would be too risky with Aspen appearing, as she might find out what we're up to vis-à-vis my manuscript. No, there's just no way Francesca would ever do what I want her to do while she's in her own home.

But maybe . . .

Maybe . . .

Maybe she would do what I want in *my* own home.

I muster a deep breath and try to sound reasonable, as much as I can. "You're right," I say. "I don't have photos. But we did have a deal. We're almost done. Just give me a week, Francesca. Can you do that? Come to my house for a week. No Aspen, no Tabi. No distractions. You can finish the book, and then I'll be out of your hair forever."

Francesca laughs merrily. "Believe it or not, I'd love to get away . . . just disappear for a while and leave all the Barber–Benlolo drama here behind. But I can't. Aspen wouldn't like it. And trust me, the last thing I want to do is trade one complicated situation for another. Me waltzing out of here isn't an option, so unless you want to kidnap me, I'm staying put." Shaking her head, she pads out of the kitchen and toward the stairs.

I blink. Did I just hear her correctly? "You . . . you want me to kidnap you?"

Francesca snorts. "Please. Like you're creative enough to do that. You'd need me to write you a step-by-step outline to pull it off. One: Tie her hands and feet. Two: Gag and blindfold her. Three: Sneak her out the back door. You don't have the guts." She laughs again and disappears up the stairs.

I pace back and forth across the kitchen. Clearly she's challenging me. But *kidnap* her? What does that even mean? And why would she want me to? Don't get me wrong—it's all I can do to keep from jumping up and down that there might actually be a way to get her to comply, which is what I've wanted all along—but I just don't understand why she would even suggest something so drastic.

I grow cold, then hot, then cold again. The sudden realization hits me in the face. Oh my God. She literally wants me to take her away *from Aspen*! I think—and the more I chew on it, the more I recognize I'm correct—Francesca is sick! She knows she can't stop herself from hurting her daughter. She needs *me* to stop her. It's a cry for help!

Yes. Yes. My footsteps quicken as all the pieces slide into place. I need to take Francesca away from here to get my book written . . . which will lead to its being published, and becoming a bestseller . . . which will set a good example for Beatrice to realize *her* own dream. And at the same time I will be protecting Aspen, keeping her safe from her mother's cruelty. So in reality I am being an exemplary mom to two daughters.

I can't think of anything more virtuous.

Which just leaves the mechanics of how to accomplish a kidnapping. It's not like I can say, "Francesca, I cordially invite you to follow me outside so that I can kidnap you." Obviously if I *said* I was doing it, she'd laugh in my face again.

Well, she's wrong. I am creative and gutsy enough to accomplish this alone. I just need to figure out a way to make her comply without her knowing she's complying.

But how? Am I supposed to clobber her over the head and knock her out? I catch myself looking wildly around the familiar kitchen, at the waterfall quartz with gold fixtures that sparkle under the island lights, as if the decor could spur an idea. For something. Anything.

It's all normal kitchen stuff (well, if you don't factor in how crazy upscale it is). A six-slice toaster. Gold-handled kitchen knives in a wood block. A pink cake box from Millie's. Absolutely nothing helpful.

Then I think of that heavy cast-iron frying pan I used to make pancakes last time I was here. It's stored right in the lower cabinet against which I'm now leaning. But it's a ridiculous thought, because obviously I'm not going to *hit* her. I'm not the monster in this story.

CHAPTER THIRTY-SEVEN

A series of otherworldly chimes announces the pot is done brewing. My eyes flit over to the coffee maker and then land on another object in the corner of the counter. It's a pill bottle. Left there by Johanna. Francesca *wanted* me to find it. Such a small, unobtrusive little thing, but I reach over to examine it. I turn it around so I can read the label. I draw in a sharp breath.

It's a prescription for sedatives. And it's almost full.

No. No, I can't. *I can't.*

Can I?

Before I have a chance to talk myself out of it, I'm throwing open the cabinets. I grab two mugs—a cobalt blue and a seafoam green. I shake out a handful of pills and, using the heel of the blue cup, grind them into tiny particles at the edge of the counter. With my finger I sweep the powder into the green cup.

Francesca comes back downstairs daisy fresh in white capris, a cropped yellow T-shirt, and silver sandals. I'm sitting quietly at the kitchen table, sipping coffee.

"I poured for you," I say calmly.

She nods and perches across from me. We take our time sipping our coffees, right down to the dregs.

Oh my God.

Oh my God.

Oh my God.

Francesca is out cold, slumped over with her head on the table.

It's interesting the things that occur to you when you are immersed in some really absorbing activity, like kidnapping.

Fragments of information materialize, maybe from all the made-for-TV movies I've seen, all the discussions of plotting between my writing buddies. I'll spirit her to my house. Should I wear a mask? Probably not necessary. I should pack her some clothes, as I want her to be comfortable, although she's welcome to borrow whatever she wants from me. My mother always taught me to be a gracious host. I'll have to find her house keys to lock the door behind me. Oh, and also—didn't Liisa always tell us you have to take the battery out of a phone so it can't be traced?

These bullets remind me I should add laundry detergent to my shopping list at home. But not the expensive pods, the store-brand powder works just as well. Concentrate, Marcy. I mean *Summer*. Successfully pulling off a caper like this is something Summer would do, not Marcy.

I jog up the stairs. Past the tribute wall to *Practice Makes Perfect* is the door to the guest room I slept in after the party. Across the hall is Aspen and Tabi's suite, where I showered. I give cursory glances to the cast photos as I pass a few more bedrooms in search of the more-spacious primary suite.

Around the corner is a sitting area, and then I open double doors. The rooms I passed along the way are breathtaking, but no doubt *this* one is Francesca's bedroom.

The Realtor in me is going gaga. What a listing this home would be: *Escape to your private paradise with this coveted waterfront property. Sprawling estate boasts six beautifully appointed bedrooms, seven and a half baths, including two main en suites with soaking tubs. Modern, luminous kitchen featuring Sub-Zero fridge. Panoramic water views. Elegant open floor plan. The home also offers a meditation room, infinity pool with walkout to beach, outdoor fireplace, outdoor shower. Exceptional living, all amenities for the discerning homeowner. Listed for* . . . hmmm, I would say about twelve million. Maybe twelve point five?

Stop it. Stay on track, Marcy . . . Summer.

As I suspected, inside Francesca's room there's an opulent walk-in closet behind French doors, *Sex and the City*–style. I'm totally taken aback by the racks and racks of designer dresses and shoes and handbags, all softly backlit by recessed lighting, and I have to force myself to stop gawking. And this is just her Hamptons closet; I can't even imagine her wardrobe in New York or Los Angeles.

There's a square island in the middle of the space, and I start opening drawers. On one side there's only lingerie, delicate, frilly, lacy lingerie, not the stretchy cotton muffin-top control kind. I scoot around to the other side, where the first two drawers contain jewelry in separate velvet compartments and *holy cow look how gorgeous this ruby-studded bracelet is as I slide it onto my wrist and it fits perfec*—No, you are not here to try on her things, I chide myself. Then I think, *Would she even notice if I took something? Just one thing, like a ruby-studded bracelet?* I return the bracelet to its velvet bed. For Pete's sake, I'm not a criminal.

I grab sets of matching underwear. What else, what else? Onto the bed I throw gorgeous clothes—shirts, jeans, dresses—and flats and sneakers, and even a pair of heels. (You never know.)

I look around the bedroom. In a different closet (she has more than one! The sheer amount of storage space is killing me) I find what I need: luggage. From the row of options, I roll out a small suitcase. It leaves behind a marginally lighter square of carpet, which makes me think Francesca's cleaning staff should really be vacuuming more thoroughly.

Neatly I pack the items inside. I even remember to grab sunglasses and a hat in case she wants to sit out on my patio. From the bathroom I grab her toothbrush and a bunch of skin care—sure, she could use mine, but I'd rather try hers! See, I think of everything!

There's her phone, charging on the nightstand, beside her Prada. I grab the purse and slip the phone inside my back pocket. I am truly quite adept at this.

The suitcase is zipped. I know I really shouldn't leave Francesca alone in the kitchen, just in case she wakes up. But before I go, I want to take one more peek in her closet. For fun.

As I'm standing there ogling, I realize that our circumstances—Francesca's and mine—are about to change, and everything will fall into place.

CHAPTER THIRTY-EIGHT

Back down the stairs I go, carrying the suitcase to the front hall. This is turning out to be good exercise.

Francesca is exactly how I left her. Clearly she swallowed enough tranquilizers to take down an elephant. Wait. What if she's not breathing? I crouch down to her chest. It's rising and falling rhythmically. She's probably getting some much-needed rest after a strenuous night. Ha.

Gently I lift her head off the table so that I can wrangle her arms around my neck. But as I tip her backward, her bottom slides off the chair, and she slips from my grasp and onto the floor. Her head bounces on the Italian marble.

Oops.

She's still breathing. We're good. But now she's lying down, and it'll be harder to lift her.

I try to pick her up. Holy moly, the woman is solid. Even though I'm only average height for a woman, I'm still a few inches taller than her, and even then I can barely get her tiny torso in the air. She looks so petite, but man, it's not easy to carry an adult human! I really should start weight lifting. At my age I have to protect against osteoporosis. I should add calcium supplements to my shopping list, after laundry detergent.

I hook my fingers under Francesca's armpits and drag her to the front door. Her sandals are coming off her heels, and I push them back on. I check to see whether there are drag marks, and there aren't. Thank you, *CSI: Crime Scene Investigation*. Wait, *should* I leave drag marks, to make this seem more authentic? I could really use Francesca's input, but she's incommunicado.

Panting, I have to stop to rest. And then I remember what she said when she asked me to kidnap her, about tying her up and gagging and blindfolding her. It seems a little extreme, but clearly that's the way she wants it.

I go back to the kitchen and open drawers, but I don't find any of those plastic thingies they use for handcuffs. What I do find is a whole roll of pink-and-black leopard-spotted duct tape. Pretty!

A piece around her wrists, a piece around her ankles, a piece over her mouth (don't worry, she can breathe quite easily from her nose), and a piece as a blindfold, and we're ready to go.

There's just no way I can lift her to the car like this. I open the front door. It's pouring buckets. How am I supposed to carry her and her stuff all the way to my car down at the road? Duh . . . I'm not. Right beside the door is a large keypad. I take a closer look; it operates the alarm system and, yup, the iron gates. In fact, there are two buttons clearly labeled "Open Gate" and "Close Gate." I press "Open Gate." Through the downpour I can make out the gates at the end of the driveway, and if I'm not mistaken, they're slowly swinging open.

Making sure to stay on the flagstone (because I don't want to leave my footprints in the mushy grass—or do I?), I hurry around the circular drive and back to my Saab. By the time I sit in it, I'm drenched again. I pull the car up to the house and as close to the front door as possible, and hop out.

I need something to carry her on. I pop the trunk. Inside are For Sale and Open House signs, a rubber mallet and tent spikes for hammering posts into the ground, and other assorted tools of my trade: screwdrivers, measuring tape, paper booties to protect my clients' floors.

I thought I had a . . . yup, there's a blanket, one of those giant heavy scratchy ones, which I keep handy to cover the floor of a construction site. And which I guess I should've washed because, oh man, now I remember: A couple of days ago I cracked a jar of pickles in a grocery bag, and the whole trunk reeked of pickle juice. Oh well, there's nothing to be done about it now. At least the blanket's dry as I lay it out in the front hall and roll Francesca over and over, until Francesca becomes a French crepe.

Grasping the brain end of the crepe, I slide the whole bundle out the door. This time I'm careful not to let her head hit the edges of the steps, but the process is exhausting. Even though she's much easier to handle with her arms and legs swaddled, I can't believe how unwieldy she is.

Finally, I get her onto the back seat and buckle the seat belt around the vicinity of her waist. I lay her luggage in the trunk. We're almost good to go.

Except, I realize, there's one more thing I need to do. How could I forget?

I race around the first floor until I find beveled glass doors leading to an office. Her *stunning* office. I try not to gape at the floor-to-ceiling bookcases along one wall, with her Jupiter books displayed prominently on acrylic stands on the desk, and across from it a walkout to the patio with an incredibly wide view of a deserted stretch of rain-pelted coastline and the gloomy gray Atlantic beyond.

This is what I came back for. I sink into the buttery leather chair, and for a few glorious minutes, I visualize, in full sensory detail, how it would be to live the life of Francesca Barber, my writing icon. I close my eyes and feel how it feels to be the woman who sits at this desk in front of the ocean and writes the ingenious novels that dominate the in-your-face display of popular new releases.

On her desk is her laptop. The temptation is just too powerful. Maybe I'll peek at my manuscript? I power it on.

The lock screen is up. *Think.* What the heck could her password be? If she were me, it would be "Aspen." But Francesca isn't me. I try her name. I try "Sagaponack" and "Hamptons" and "Atlantic." Nope. Then I have an inspiration: I type J-U-P-I-T-E-R and voilà, her desktop appears.

There's no document or folder marked "Summer" or "Branigan" or "*A Knight to Remember*" or anything else I can find connected to me. Sadly, I close the lid and leave the office. I retrace my steps to the kitchen, where I turn off the coffee maker, rinse the pot and leave it in the drainboard, and wash our mugs and put them back in the cabinet. After all, I'm not one to leave a mess.

And then I remember I was supposed to take the battery out of her phone. I slip it from my back pocket. But first . . . in my best throaty Francesca voice I tell Siri to text Tabi Benlolo, and Siri responds with What do you want to say to Tabi? It takes me a few tries, but I get it right in the end: a vague message about rethinking our relationship because it's just not fair to Aspen. There . . . that's for you, Aspen sweetheart!

Now I can take out the battery. It should be easy. I stare at her phone. I have no idea how. I open YouTube on my phone. I search for "How to remove the battery from a cell phone" and click on the first video.

The narrator says I will need a P2 Pentalobe driver, a Phillips driver, an iOpener, a suction handle or iSclack, iFixit Opening Picks, a spudger, and a pair of tweezers.

What the . . . is this even English? The only item I recognize is the tweezers. Forget it. I don't have time for this. I'll deal with her phone later. I shove it into my back pocket.

Anything else? Yes, I have to pee. The last thing I want is to pull into a rest stop with Francesca Barber draped across the back seat. I use her powder room and gosh, it's nice! The toilet is a Bluetooth-connected, self-cleaning, self-flushing masterpiece, surrounded by pretty wainscoting and tasteful wallpaper. I wonder how much it all cost. God knows I begged Kevin a hundred times to refinish our bathroom, and wall coverings are so fashionable now.

I wash my hands, take the bunch of house keys off the key ring (I assume they're Francesca's, as there is a fancy gold *F* on the ring), and, just before I leave, I run back to the kitchen and grab the pill bottle, because you never know. Then I lock the door behind me, climb into the car and slide behind the wheel, open my GPS app, and take a deep breath. Here we go. I circle back down the driveway and use the remote on the key chain to close the gate behind me.

I'm feeling pretty confident as I navigate to the highway. Everything, literally everything, has occurred to me, and I am convinced my (our) plan is going to go off without a hitch. When Francesca wakes up, she'll be so pleased to have that "time away" she wanted (read: distance that prevents her from abusing her daughter).

In a few minutes, I'm heading west on Long Island and back toward Connecticut.

I know, I know, you probably think I'm nuts. But I'm just doing everything Francesca asked. Seriously, wouldn't you have done the exact same thing?

CHAPTER THIRTY-NINE

I'm still congratulating myself on having thought of absolutely everything and reveling in how this arrangement will benefit me and the girls. What *doesn't* occur to me until I'm minutes from home, because I'm so immersed in thoughts of the successes to come, is that I can't actually go home . . . because guess who's there? *One* of those girls. Beatrice, my daughter, who I completely forgot is still staying with me. She may be at the lab right now, in the middle of her workday, but she'll be home in a couple of hours. When I realize this, I get so panicked I careen onto the shoulder and send up a rooster tail of spray as I plunge through a deep puddle. What in tarnation am I supposed to tell her? *Hey, Bea. Oh, you mean this unconscious celebrity author? My mentor, Francesca Barber? She'll be our guest for a while, as she wanted to be kidnapped so she wouldn't hurt her daughter.* And who knows what Francesca might say?

I pull into a gas station. I have to close my eyes and catch my breath. Should I just turn around and take Francesca home? She hasn't come to yet. Maybe I can reverse direction, drive back to the Hamptons, drag her inside, put away all her stuff, and slink off before she even wakes up.

No! We've come too far to turn around now. We're invested in this. The whole thing was her idea; she's all about cooperating, it just can't be at my house. There must be a way.

A brilliant idea worms its way into my brain. Funny how that happens, right? Just when you need a good idea, one appears in your head. And this one's a doozy.

After filling up with gas (jeez, prices have gone up, so unfair), I finish the last leg of the drive home. I wind through the wet streets until I arrive at Alpine Lane and pull into my driveway with my precious cargo still snoring away behind me. I have a new strategy. Just going to do a quick in-and-out of the house for supplies; then I'll be on my way. Luckily, I won't have to answer any questions as I won't run into Bea.

Bea pokes her head out from the kitchen as I shut the door.

"Hi, Mom, you're just in time," she says. She turns down the music pulsing from her phone.

I stop in my tracks. "Why aren't you at the lab?"

"I'm making Dad's famous chili, remember? I'm glad you're here. I don't know how much spice to put in."

The kitchen looks like a tornado tore through. The counters are heaped with open bean cans, discarded onion skins, empty ground beef packages. A soup pot is bubbling on the stove and splattering everything within range. I don't have time to deal with this now . . . Francesca could wake up at any moment, if she hasn't already. For all I know she is running down the street, gaining the attention of my neighbors.

"Um . . . I'll show you. I put in this much salt and this much chili powder. I usually add some cumin and paprika, too." I spy a six-pack. "Are you having someone over?"

"Mom." Bea laughs. "Very funny. We talked about this? Since we all had the day off, I'm making dinner for my new friends, the four other kids in the research program. We get along great, we have so much in common."

A vague recollection of this conversation strikes me as I'm backing out of the kitchen, and I feel a stab of hope. "Are you . . . are you rethinking going back to grad school in the fall?"

"Nope." Then Bea adds a zinger. "Cooking is a good life skill, and I should practice."

Which is terrific, but the only life skill Bea was ever interested in was chemistry.

"Well, enjoy. I'm actually headed out of town. It's a . . . a writing retreat thing."

"Sounds fun, Mom."

I nod weakly. It's a half truth, isn't it?

I give Bea a hug and rush around the house to gather what I need and stuff it into reusable bags and totes. I also pack an overnighter for myself. Now, where did I put that key?

I return to the kitchen to grab a box of protein bars from the pantry, and give one last goodbye to Bea.

But she's already turned the music high and is happily sprinkling more paprika into the chili. She doesn't look up, just says, "Make it a bestseller!"

Oh, I intend to.

The radio is playing "A Hard Day's Night" as I drive, and I think, how apropos . . . I *have* been working doggedly. Blackmailing Francesca is arduous business.

I'm tired but pleased. Staging a kidnapping was an imaginative idea on her part, and it's all going according to plan. Actually, it couldn't be going much better. For novices, we really did everything right: the prep work, the location, the myriad supplies I remembered to bring . . . all of it. And soon, very soon I hope, all this work will pay off—Francesca will get out of her own way and finish the manuscript, I'll turn it in to Mila Jorgenson, and before I know it, I'll be a published author . . . etcetera. I can just picture Lilian Arnold and Sierra Eastman coming to the book club event Elianna Abrams will host. Maybe Julian Segal and Yvonne Manning will come, too!

Several Beatles songs later, I turn off the radio. The hours of highway driving, rhythmic metronome of the wipers, and drumming rain lull me so that when there's a loud musical vibrating from my back pocket, I jump. Francesca's phone. I forgot all about it. I fish it out of my jeans and see Tabi's name on the display. Maybe he got "her" message.

The infernal buzzing and ringing continue, and I'm trying to silence it with my thumbnail as I drive left-handed. Why, oh why, didn't I remove the battery? I should have just smashed the thing with a rock. Without thinking, my body goes on autopilot. In two swift motions I roll down the passenger window with my left hand and fling Francesca's phone as far as I can onto the grassy shoulder. There, untraceable.

Then I realize I didn't have to worry much about waking her. It could have been a ten-piece brass band parading through the car, trumpets blaring, saxophones wailing, for all the effect it had on her. I glance again in the rearview mirror to see she's dead to the world.

At last I exit the highway and find myself in the familiar nowheresville, passing under the eerily swinging traffic light that looks as if it hasn't directed traffic in eons. There's the bait shop in the distance, so this time I know when to expect the turnoff onto the hidden lane, followed by the faded wooden sign nailed to a tree.

I pull up. I'm pretty sure I'm hidden from any street view by the dense foliage, but you can't be too careful, so I loop around the far side of the house, where the car is all but hidden in the bush, and cut the motor. I think Liisa would've plotted it this way for a spy thriller.

I unlock the stained-glass door with the key Garcia gave me and start carrying in the provisions from the trunk. I make several trips with bags, totes, suitcases. I even remembered to bring a package of toilet paper (the one-ply was on sale—a bargain!).

In the bathroom I put our toothbrushes, soap, and hand towel on the edge of the sink, and the toilet paper beside the toilet. I remembered toothpaste, the expensive whitening kind, which I think Francesca will appreciate. I also brought some bath towels, lemon-scented hand soap, and a sweet little washcloth with satin piping and embroidered tulips. What a nice touch of home. It'll go perfectly with the bathroom's bubblegum pink.

For a second I hesitate in front of the bedrooms, but then I place my overnighter in the larger room and wheel Francesca's carry-on into the kids' room. I'm the mastermind here. I'm sure she'll be just as well rested in a smaller bed.

Unfortunately, the place is incredibly dusty. In the trunk I have some rags and Windex, which I grab, and yet it takes hours of spritzing to make a dent, and I'm slowed down further as every few minutes I'm running out to the car to check on my passenger.

Fortunately, there's a broom in the closet; I sweep up the garbage strewn on the floors and the spiderwebs in the corners. I gather up the empty beer cans, just like my mom used to do after my dad and brothers watched a game, and open the windows a crack to let in fresh air. I make our beds, hers with a pretty floral blanket and mine with my grandmother's sewing circle quilt. I set lined paper and pens and pencils on a table by the bay window in the dining room. I'm feeling my lower back, but at least everything is starting to look clean and nice. I hope Francesca will appreciate the hard work I've put in. I hope she'll like what I've done for her. I scarf down a protein bar as I lug in a case of water bottles, heave it up onto the kitchen counter, and chug a bottle dry.

Maybe for dinner we'll order a pizza. It's just like when we moved Bea into college!

And now for the tricky part. I'll have to do this fast, as it's still raining, not to mention getting dark. I run back to the car and open the rear door. Sleeping Beauty is still snoozing. I unfasten her seat belt and attempt, to the very best of my ability, to lift her up over my shoulder in a firefighter carry. But I can't get the leverage, and I don't have the muscle, and I'm soaked, and soon she's halfway out of the car and I'm practically on my knees trying to arrange her weight across my back, but alas, I lack the strength. I have to take a break for a sec. I close my eyes and picture myself as a soldier saving a wounded comrade on the battlefield and try again. And again. But despite my best mental effort, it's not gonna happen.

Instead, I grab a handful of blanket to slide her the rest of the way out of the car and onto the ground. There's no help for it. The ground is full of muddy puddles, but I drag her through them, up the porch steps, and into the old-fashioned vestibule to rest again. Rainwater and puddles have soaked the thick blanket, and not only is it substantially heavier than before, it seems as if the odor has been reactivated. My nostrils are assaulted by pickle juice.

Now there's another problem: The vestibule's door is set on a ninety-degree angle from the front door. Locking it behind me, I push and pull and bend the bundle to get it around the tight corner. I have to wonder, as I'm struggling, if my own passive mother ever would have gone to such extremes to set an example for *me*.

At last, we're inside. I'm sweating and panting as I drag Francesca to the back bedroom. Argh, my back . . . I straighten to stretch out the ache. It persists. Francesca's lying at my feet, sleeping so soundly, so comfortably. I just don't have the strength to lift her up on a bed. Maybe I'll let her sleep in her cozy cocoon for a few minutes while I rest. Then I'll order our pizza.

I go next door and ease my aching spine onto the bed I've made up. I have about three seconds of consciousness before my eyes close and I'm fast asleep.

CHAPTER FORTY

I awake to the regular drumbeat of rain on the roof. The low barometric pressure is making my head pound. I glance at the light filtering through the dirty window. It's morning! I slept through the whole night in my exhaustion. That means Francesca's been out for twenty-four hours.

I stumble into the next room to find Francesca on the carpet, exactly where I left her, except this time there are savage growls coming from under the rancid blanket. I reach over at arm's length to start unwrapping her. As soon as I touch her, she goes wild, struggling against her restraints, flopping like a fish on a dock. A very enraged fish. A very enraged fish that smells like it's been marinating in brine.

I wait a few seconds for her to stop. I kneel down on the carpet. It's like unrolling a burrito across the floor to reveal the filling. As soon as she's lying face up, she begins writhing again.

Gingerly I reach for a corner of the duct tape over her mouth, and slowly pull it. Her skin is lifting up with the adhesive, and she bucks in protest. I get the tape halfway off, exposing her mouth, and she lets out a bloodcurdling shriek.

"HELP! HELP! SOMEONE HELP ME!"

I realize she doesn't know who I am. "Francesca, calm down, it's me, Summer. No one's going to hurt you. I'm trying to take your gag off."

"Summer? It's *you*? You fucking idiot, just rip this thing off fast, like a Band-Aid. Don't you know anything? Haven't you ever gotten a bikini wax? You're supposed to do it quickly. The glue is goddamn killing me." I tear off the rest of the tape fast. It leaves a bright-red rectangle around her mouth.

"What the fuck are you doing!" Her voice is hoarse, as if she's used it up behind the gag. "Where am I? And what the hell is this putrid stench? Get this shit off me and let me out of here right fucking now!"

"Shh." I hold a hand over her mouth. "I have a headache. Stop shouting or I'll gag you again." I lift my hand an inch to see if she obeys.

"Untie me! Untie me right now!"

"How are you not woozy from the pills?"

"What *pills*? Hurry the fuck up and get me out of this!"

I'm having a hard time grasping the edge of the blindfold because her teeth are gnashing and I'm afraid she's going to bite me. "Calm down, please."

"Calm down? Calm *down*? You bitch, you need to explain what's happening, right fucking *now*!"

Hello . . . here's the woman Aspen warned me about. "Francesca, you need to relax, please. I can't deal with you like this. Stop moving so I can take your blindfold off."

"Fine," she says. "I'm calm. But this time rip it off fast."

"Okay." I grab a corner of the tape and take a breath. Then, with a swift swipe of my arm, I tear the tape off, really fast like she said. *Fffftttt.*

I look at her.

I look down at the piece of duct tape.

I look back at her.

Oh shit.

Her eyebrows are resting in my lap, stuck on the adhesive in two perfect arches of silky hairs.

"What?" She's stares up at me as I'm staring down at her.

"Nothing." I glance over at the mirror above the dresser.

I wonder whether she's in shock, and she doesn't feel anything? The blindfold was her idea, not mine. As soon as she realizes what has happened, I'll remind her of that. "Francesca. I really need you to stay calm. I'm going to take off the rest of the tape, okay?" I roll her away from me onto her side so I can reach down and pick apart the tape at her ankles. I used several layers and it's taking a while.

"Hurry up, and then start explaining what it is you think you're fucking doing."

"Francesca. I'm doing exactly what you said. Anyway, it's morning, and we can discuss it over coffee."

"Why is my skull throbbing? It feels like someone thwacked me with a crowbar."

"I may have bumped your head—slightly—during transport. I apologize for that. But everything else went smoothly, and now we're here! We can get to work on my manuscript!"

"Your manuscript? You're fucking crazy, you fucking lunatic!"

"That's not very nice. Please don't speak to me like that."

You wouldn't believe the stream of curse words she lets loose. I stand up and slam the bedroom door. I can still hear her bellowing, but now it's muffled. This is just like when toddlers throw tantrums. Best to let them wear themselves out.

It occurs to me how badly I need to use the bathroom, and when I'm finished, I push the handle on the bubblegum-pink toilet. But the thing doesn't flush. And there's no water coming from the sink, either. Uh-oh. Well, I'll have to deal with the plumbing later. Good thing there's an outhouse. For now I wash my hands with a bottle of water before returning to the bedroom.

Francesca hisses up at me like a viper about to strike.

At last I succeed in ripping open the tape at her ankles, and then her wrists. I hoist her up by her armpits. She's unsteady on her feet—from the sedation, I guess—but at least she's vertical.

Immediately she turns and slaps me across the face.

"Ouch!" I back away, holding a palm over my smarting cheek. "Darn it, Francesca, that hurt!"

She's massaging her shoulders and upper arms, which I imagine are pretty stiff from being swaddled. "Is this where you *live*? It's stomach turning. Even uglier than I imagined."

"Can you please stop with the insults? I couldn't take you home because my daughter is there."

"What the fuck do you mean, take me home? I was home!"

I try not to do a double take at her new appearance. I have to force my gaze away from her naked brow. "I mean when I kidnapped you."

"What?"

"I kidnapped you, like you asked. You said you needed a break, and I went to a lot of trouble to do everything you wanted and to bring you somewhere appropriate."

"What are you talking about? I didn't ask to come here. And appropriate would be a nice hotel—"

"Where you'd be recognized?" I don't add that I can't afford a nice hotel at the moment.

"You can't possibly expect us to stay here." She looks around, both rabid and repulsed.

"I think it's charming." I back out to the hallway, and she stalks me to the kitchen. "Once we . . . er, once I . . . get it cleaned up a bit more—and, um, figure out the running water situation—it'll actually be quite homey. At least there's an outhouse."

"I'm calling the police. Where's my phone?"

"Francesca, do you have amnesia or something? This whole thing was your idea, remember. You asked me to kidnap you. In fact you challenged me to do it. You said I'd need a step-by-step outline to pull it off. You even specified about tying you up, gagging and blindfolding you. But guess what? I didn't need your help, and I did an excellent job, if I do say so myself." I smile. "Now you can have that getaway you wanted." *And Aspen will be safe,* I add silently.

"You moron." Francesca slumps against a wall. I think she might faint. "I didn't mean it literally."

"Stop calling me names. Maybe you should drink some water." I point. "Behind you."

Francesca fishes a bottle out of the plastic casing. She unscrews the cap, slumps against the counter, and gulps down several swallows.

"Sorry about the blanket," I offer. "I spilled pickle juice on it."

"It was vile." She takes in the details of the kitchen—the fruit-patterned wallpaper, the brown-checkered linoleum, the harvest-gold appliances—and grimaces. "On top of everything else, I'm getting a throwback headache."

"I know it's not exactly the Mandarin Oriental. But it's quiet and there won't be any distractions. And no one will be the wiser."

"I can't deal with this until I've had coffee."

"Don't worry, I brought everything we need." Except, I'm just realizing, coffee.

Francesca walks out into the dining area, takes in the furnishings, and stops in front of the bay window. She looks up to read the inverse lettering.

"Where are we? What the hell is Mom & Pop's?"

"We're in Connecticut. I'm a Realtor at Robert Verney Realty, and I'm the listing agent for this property."

"Good luck selling it."

I ignore the sarcasm. "I'm just going to do a little more cleaning while you get comfortable." I return to the kitchen and try the tap, but again, there's moaning in the pipes, and no water. Okay, this is a problem.

"Summer," Francesca calls, "you didn't answer me. Where's my phone?"

I peek past the archway. "It's gone. I threw it away on the highway."

Francesca stares at me open-mouthed. ". . . you . . . what?"

I grin. Either she's going to be so impressed with how I thought of everything, or—

She screams. "Get in the fucking car right now! Drive back and get it!"

My grin disappears. "What? No. If you're going to be kidnapped, you can't be traced. Someone might come for you. That defeats the purpose."

Her face turns white, then splotchy blue. With the red rectangles, she's looking quite patriotic. Quickly I duck back into the kitchen before she can scream some more. She's quiet for a while, and then she hollers again.

"Summer! Where's my laptop?"

I shake my head.

"I have to send an email. Is there Wi-Fi here?"

I didn't bring her computer, I start to tell her, but before I can get the sentence out, Francesca screeches for me again, several octaves higher. This time it sounds as if she's in pain.

"Summer!"

I rush out to the dining area. "What?"

Francesca is frantically flicking a light switch up and down. "Where's the goddamn electricity?" She runs around trying to turn on lights, but none seem to work. It's okay, I'm a Realtor, I tell her; I know what to do. I just have to find the fuse box, but it's not by the front door, and it's not in the kitchen, and there's no garage. Therefore, it must be in the basement. I open the door to go downstairs, but it's pitch black. I grope on the wall until I find a light switch—but of course the light doesn't work, since there's no electricity.

"You imbecile, use your flashlight on your phone, unless you threw yours on the highway, too," Francesca snaps. "Did you?"

"Of course not." If only I knew where I left it; I hurry to the bedrooms and the kitchen. Nope. I run out to the car. It's raining steadily, and the mushy ground sucks my shoes in as I squelch through the mud. There's my phone, in the cup holder. I bring it inside.

With the flashlight flicked on I descend the dark, creepy stairs of the basement. I shine the light around the walls until I find the fuse box way at the back. I flick the breakers and rush back up the steps to try the switch.

Nothing.

"It's okay," I say. I pocket my phone in case she's thinking of trying to grab it. "We can use candles at night."

Francesca's puffing out air as if she were in a Lamaze class.

"You think I'm staying here in the dark?" she sputters. "You lost my phone. You didn't bring my laptop. And now you're telling me there's no electricity? What could possibly make you think I'd agree to stay?" The fury on her face is dragging the corners of her mouth down so far I can see her gumline. I'm reminded of Aspen's childhood story: seeing a smudge of lipstick on her mother's bottom teeth in the rearview mirror.

"You'll be able to write my book in peace."

"Idiot." Francesca is livid. "There are about a million reasons why that won't happen. Here's just one: It's all on my computer."

"The good news is I brought paper, so you can work on my manuscript the old-fashioned way, like authors have done for centuries."

"I don't even remember where the story left off."

I want to answer by reminding her it's a good bet that whatever the soothsayer, warlord, and chambermaid were doing in *her* book, they were also doing in mine. But I don't, thinking snarky isn't a flattering look. "Lady Lisbeth and Sir Devon are making love in the woods, remember? She's dressed as a peasant? And her father, Sir Richard, is riding toward them on horseback with the Duke and his hunting party?"

"I don't give a flying fuck what they were doing. I'm not staying. I cannot and will not remain anywhere under these conditions."

"For God's sake, Francesca, can you drop the diva act for a minute? I went to a lot of trouble to get you here, and if you could just be honorable, have some integrity, in a few days we could put this whole thing behind us! Just . . . just stop being so *selfish*!"

I can practically see the cartoon steam coming out of her ears. "How dare you. This whole thing is ridiculous. Our deal, you bringing me to this dump, you giving me an ultimatum I can't meet."

"Can't? Or won't?!" Anger is creeping up from my diaphragm and filling my already-bursting head like an overinflated tire.

"Does it matter? Whatever the reason, your book is not getting written, unless you write it yourself."

"You're rotten," I spew. "You're like a caricature of an entitled celebrity—you're rich and you're in the spotlight and you think you have no responsibilities. No accountability."

She laughs bitterly. "Okay."

"And the minute you're out of your comfort zone, away from your assistants and assistants to assistants you pay to coddle and serve you, you shut down!"

"Whatever you say."

"It's true! We had a deal, and I've kept my end! I have not told a single, solitary soul about your relationship with Tabi Benlolo, or the way you betrayed your own daughter. And what's more . . . I've done everything I can think of to make you as comfortable as possible, but no, you just want to be back in the lap of luxury in your Hamptons palace!" I pace back and forth. My head is going to explode. I'm so close, so incredibly close to getting what I want. I let out a little scream of frustration.

"See? You're unhinged."

I boil over. "Francesca, I could throttle you!"

"Believe me . . . same here!" Francesca clenches her hands into fists and shakes them in my face. It's such an aggressive stance that even knowing what kind of person she is, I'm taken aback. I stare at her in disbelief.

"You would rather have an actual *fight* than finish my manuscript?" I'm so incensed, I can't see straight. How can anyone be this stubborn? "I've never heard anything so stupid in my life. Why can't you stop resisting and just write the damn book!"

"You *dunce*. Don't you understand? I'm telling you. I. Can't. Write. It."

"What are you talking about?"

She opens her mouth, then shuts it again. "I don't write historical romance," she says finally.

"So what? The chapters I read were great. I loved them."

"I need a computer!"

"You're just spoiled. Write it all down by hand and we can type it into Word later . . ."

"Get out of my way." She makes a break for the door, but I block her path.

"No."

"Move."

"No!"

We stare at each other in a showdown, until she caves in exasperation.

"Don't you understand? Do I have to spell it out for you, numbskull? I need a computer with *internet*." Francesca lets out a howl of frustration, a piercing, purely animalistic sound that wouldn't have been out of place in the rainforests of Borneo. "So I can use AI."

"What?"

"Artificial intelligence."

"I know what AI is. What are you saying?"

"I wrote your dopey princess story using AI. A computer program." Her shoulders slump.

My jaw drops. I can't even begin to digest what she is saying. "Let me get this straight. The chapters you gave me were generated by artificial intelligence? Not your imagination? And without citation?"

Francesca closes her browless lids.

"So . . . so . . . the beautifully written, perfectly structured manuscript I submitted to Mila Jorgenson, which she is *pitching to publishers* as we speak, was written by a computer program, not a human?" My mouth continues to hang open as I process. "But that's cheating!"

Francesca starts to laugh. At first it's just a chuckle, and then it blooms into mirth, and before long it's bordering on hysteria. "Are you . . . are you joking?" She clutches her ribs and doubles over, gasping. "Really? Oh my God, you are something else. Your hypocrisy is beyond! You think using AI is cheating, but blackmailing someone . . . kidnapping someone . . . so they can write your book *isn't*? A book that will have your name on it?"

No, no. This can't be happening. I cover my ears to block the cackling. My dream is dissolving like a mouthful of cotton candy . . . all the promise of sweetness is melting away into nothingness.

I try to comprehend the enormity of what this means. I can't breathe. I need to get out of here. Peals of laughter accompany me as I bolt through the front door.

CHAPTER FORTY-ONE

I make it as far as the rickety porch. And then I stop. I turn.

I retrace my steps, back through the vestibule, back to where Francesca is still standing by the table and chortling and holding her water bottle.

"You used AI to write the chapters of *A Knight to Remember*, because you don't do historical romance, you said." I move closer. "But how is it that a professional writer like you couldn't come up with something, anything, even if it wasn't your best work? Because you're a *science fiction author* is what I thought you meant. But you admitted it yourself. You said, 'I can't write it.' And it just dawned on me that you actually meant you can't write *anything*."

Francesca's grin fades.

Now it makes sense—the "coincidental" overlap of "character tropes" after I posted my excerpt on #LitAgentSeeker. The useless "critique" that sounded like a form letter. The even more useless phone "tutoring" sessions.

I move closer still until I've breached her personal space and we are mere inches apart.

"And Mila Jorgenson and Ned Townsend don't suspect a thing! Francesca, you used AI to generate your Jupiter books, didn't you?"

She swallows.

"Francesca Barber, you are a phony, and a thief. A complete fraud."

"ME?" Her eyes blaze with indignation. She stares at me defiantly and reaches up, and I flinch because I think she's going to hit me again, but then her hand falls limply to her side and her chin drops to her chest in defeat.

When she finally speaks, her words are almost inaudible. "Summer . . ." she begs. "Please don't tell."

Do you remember way back when I first gleaned that tidbit of information during Francesca's book signing—that she was headed to Sam Stone's, the bar at the Housatonic Hotel in Hartford—and used it to my advantage, to meet her? And then I managed to get myself invited to her press event, and then to her Hamptons party, where her daughter confided in me about who Francesca really is? And do you recall how, all along the way, she's been difficult and obstinate, reluctant to give me what I want? Change is in the air. I smile.

"It seems to me that if I tell the whole world how you've used artificial intelligence to generate your beloved, bestselling novels, you will be finished. Publicly humiliated. And ostracized," I muse aloud. "No more celebrity status. No more movies. No more Jupiter income."

I walk the length of the room as I think, to the archway and back repeatedly, taking in the paintings of donkeys pulling wooden carts of colorful clay urns on cobblestone streets. Francesca's crystalline eyes are huge as they track my movements. At last I come to a standstill to stare out the bay window into the woods. I don't even bother to face Francesca, because I know that every fiber of her attention is laser focused on the back of my head.

"So," I say, "here's what's going to happen. Today is Thursday, August 7. You're going to finish my book. It will be completed by the end of this month to my, and Mila's, satisfaction. And if—"

"Do it yourself. You can use a computer, right?"

"Not as well as you, it seems." I know I sound a little snippy, but I don't appreciate Francesca's interruption. I take a breath and regain my composure. "As I was saying, if you agree, if you finish my book on time and to our satisfaction, I will keep all your secrets, about your use of artificial intelligence, and your cheating with Tabi Benlolo. All of it."

The water bottle she's been holding slips from her grasp and rolls away on the linoleum floor. There's a long silence, until at last she utters the words that are music to my ears.

It's a deal.

"There's a store down the road," I say after a while. "Do you want to come with me and get some coffee and breakfast?"

"No."

"All right then. Why don't you get started on the manuscript, and I'll just be a few minutes."

"How exactly do you think this will work? Now you know I can't write without AI."

"You've pumped out three books. I'm sure some of it is original, no? Just start writing and we'll figure it out when I come back."

Before I leave, I turn.

"And, Francesca? I'm, uh, really sorry about . . ." I point vaguely at my eyebrows.

She looks at me, confused and unfocused, before touching a finger to her face. She goes down the hall to find a mirror.

I rush out to my car accompanied by the sound of her shrieking.

A tiny pang of guilt pokes me, but quickly I remind myself of who will benefit in the long run: me, of course, with my bestseller, and my daughter, who, I believe with my whole heart, will change her mind about going to grad school and chasing her dream once she sees I've achieved mine. And I remind myself of who *else* will benefit: Aspen, who is, temporarily at least, safe from her abusive mother.

And in case you think I don't feel sufficiently bad about what I've done, let me tell you: You don't know everything Francesca put Aspen through as a child, how she exploited her. How she exploited other people. In fact, you don't know the half of it. Because there's a whole second part to the saga Aspen told me that day when we returned to Sagaponack.

Want to hear what else Aspen told me?

CHAPTER FORTY-TWO

So we'd just arrived back from town. Aspen didn't say anything during the drive. I kept glancing over at her, saw her biting her lip and glancing at *me* like she really wanted to tell me something more, but it wasn't until we'd gone inside the house and I emerged from the bathroom, startled to see her standing outside the door, waiting for me, that she broke. She didn't want me to leave until I'd heard the full extent of the horror. I knew it was going to be bad from her pained expression.

She and her mother were back to shopping at Goodwill, she stammered, rummaging through the racks of donations because Francesca had been fired from Toys "R" Us. They'd sold their car. Aspen knew they didn't have money for clothes, but she couldn't help it; she was getting teased at school for outgrowing her T-shirts, and no amount of starving herself seemed to have any effect on her round bottom, while her tiny waist couldn't get narrower or she'd snap in half.

"Make sure you're only looking at the orange tags," Francesca called from the other end of the aisle. "Orange is half price this week, Aspen."

Aspen cringed every time her mother did that, even though she realized the chances of bumping into someone from the industry, or even from school, were practically nil. Her friends wouldn't be caught dead there. But one day a man approached her in the aisle and said, "Hellooo, gorgeous," and waggled his eyebrows suggestively. And later, as Aspen and Francesca were heading down the sidewalk, some older boys started to hoot . . . fell into step alongside Aspen, asking how old she was, if she had a boyfriend, if they could get her number. She hunched her shoulders around her ears and stared at the concrete as she walked.

Then, at the bus stop, a group of hard-hatted workers leaning against the chain-link fence of their construction project let out lewd catcalls. I can just imagine how uncomfortable this made the girl—I mean, it's one thing from brainless teenagers, but another thing altogether to have full-grown men react to you hungrily.

Aspen worried that Francesca would resent her for taking the male attention she herself used to bask in. Aspen was sure Francesca would make some La-La comment on the bus. But she didn't. She was formulating an idea.

Fast-forward a week, and Aspen was upset because she had an English quiz to study for on *Of Mice and Men*, but Francesca ignored her protests. Instead, she put the finishing touches on Aspen's makeup: Her lips shone with a layer of pink gloss, and her pale eyes were huge, ringed in liner, lashes spidery with mascara. Her thick hair was loose and tousled. It wasn't at all her normal, innocent schoolgirl style.

They were in an old warehouse, empty inside with concrete floors and a webbing of exposed pipes. A photographer waited, a shady guy with slicked-back hair, whom Aspen wondered how in the world they would pay. He whistled when he saw her.

"We only need one good shot, and even if a monkey takes enough pictures, we're bound to get it," Francesca said, plunking Aspen in front of him.

Well, I won't go into the details of the photo shoot, or of what Aspen was forced to wear (or not wear), but you can imagine Francesca's intent. And you can imagine the slimy photographer's comments as he brought the camera to his face and snapped shots of Aspen, making a 180-degree arc around her.

Poor Aspen. She said she tried to block it all out and concentrate on her test. *The animal Lennie clutches too tightly is a mouse* and *Slim drowns four puppies. He says the mother can't feed them.*

The shutter on the camera clicked until Francesca was satisfied at last and said, "Let's wrap this up." Afterward, she went home with the guy to "develop the film." It was the middle of the night when she returned.

The next day, Francesca was in a good mood. When Aspen came downstairs, she found her mother at the kitchen counter, looking at glossy photos. Aspen hardly recognized herself: The woman-child in the pictures radiated scintillating heat, tousled like she'd just gotten out of bed after a sensual night of sex. There were three blowups, the middle photo being objectively the most artistic, and the one where Aspen looked prettiest. But it was also the most suggestive, in a way that made you want to stare at it for hours. Can you imagine Aspen's dread? "You can't . . . you won't . . . you're not going to show these to anyone, are you?" she asked.

Francesca snorted. "Well, why do you think I went and arranged a whole photo shoot? We're not exactly using these for holiday cards. We're going to sell them, baby girl. *Sell.*" Apparently, Aspen used to get a ton of fan mail when she starred in *Practice Makes Perfect* . . . thousands and thousands of letters from devoted fans. The studio used to send out cast pictures in return. Well, Francesca figured fans would pay through the nose for these new ones. She thought they'd become collectibles.

Every day, Aspen said, when she came home there would be something new: sometimes something big, like a piece of furniture where before there was an empty space on the carpet; sometimes small, like an electronic gizmo. The refrigerator bulged at the waist. Francesca went back to wearing chic outfits and getting drunk on more expensive vodka. There even stood a used compact car in the driveway—a far cry from the convertible they'd once leased, but worlds better than the crowded city bus.

Francesca spent her days working on her new fan-mail business, and when Aspen came home from school, she had to help. Her job was to sign the photos with a neon-pink Magic Marker—"XOXO, Sadie"—and when they were dry, slide them into manila envelopes alongside a piece of thick cardboard to keep them from creasing. Francesca addressed the envelopes, dated and filed the orders alphabetically in a cabinet, and kept a balance sheet of all the transactions in a book. In a separate section of the book, she tracked expenses, such as rented post office boxes (jumbo size), gas and postage, and developing the pictures; plus sundry supplies, like the envelopes and markers.

Business was booming. Mail orders came from all over. Several of the customers ordered additional photos and asked whether more would be available in the future. Many wanted to meet Aspen in person. She got marriage proposals. And other proposals. She tried not to see the photos as she signed them. It made her sick to look at them.

—

Even though Francesca said she took precautions—like having the mail orders go to a post office box rather than home—a stranger, a man from Nevada who bought all three photographs, figured out where they lived.

At first, the man started calling their house phone. When Aspen answered, there was only heavy breathing, which probably freaked her out, poor girl. Francesca shrugged it off and joked it was a sign their customers were engaged.

But after a few weeks he started talking. He wanted to meet Aspen. Would she visit him in Carson City? He had his own place, and they wouldn't be bothered by anyone, he said. Aspen started leaving the phone off the hook, but Francesca kept putting it back on the cradle in case, she said, the studio reached out with a new project, which Aspen knew was never going to happen.

The calls stopped for a week. When they started again, the nature of the calls had changed. Suddenly it became apparent that the man from Nevada knew what the house looked like, and then after a while they realized he knew what it looked like *inside*. He even knew the color of hair band Aspen wore each day. She thought he must be spying somehow, with binoculars, from *nearby*. They closed the blinds, parked the car in the garage, and went in and out the back door.

Flowers started appearing on the stoop: bunches of carnations and baby's breath. Plush Care Bears with rainbows and hearts on the tummy. Cards for "my beautiful Aspen" that rambled on about how much he loved her and wanted to spend his life with her. Aspen must have gone berserk; I can just imagine how afraid she'd be, how she'd feel hunted like prey. She said she begged to call the police, but Francesca refused.

What kind of mother refuses to protect her own daughter?

It wasn't until he started writing things like "we'll be together forever" and "I can't live in this world without you, and I don't want you to live in it without me" that Francesca finally took action: She called a locksmith to install new dead bolts. She said they'd be perfectly safe.

Well, let me tell you, they were *not* safe. Aspen cried hysterically when she recounted this last part of her story.

On a Friday night, Aspen huddled in her room with her driver's handbook open in her lap, trying to distract herself from thoughts of the man from Nevada. She'd just turned sixteen; Francesca finally agreed to let her get her learner's permit. She studied the diagram of an intersection.

After a while, she went downstairs in search of a snack. Francesca had fallen asleep under a knitted blanket in front of the TV, with a sitcom playing and a half-empty vodka bottle and glass on the table.

Aspen munched on a pretzel when movement outside the kitchen window caught her eye; she noticed a beam of light briefly illuminate the needles of the nutmeg tree.

She raced over to the couch and shook Francesca's shoulder. "Someone's in the back. With a flashlight," she said, but only got a mumbled "Pro'ly a cat" in return.

Aspen was terrified. She crept back to the kitchen and by the flickering light of the television pulled open the cutlery drawer and groped around for the biggest knife she could find, a chopping knife with a thick blade that weighed heavy in her hand. She grabbed the phone and sank down against the wall, squatting over her ankles, and called 911.

"There's a man outside my window," she told the emergency operator in a panic. "He's been watching our house for a few weeks, and I'm afraid he's trying to break in."

The operator promised to send a patrol car and kept Aspen on the phone while she waited.

"What did you mean, he's been watching your house?"

In a frantic whisper, Aspen told her about the calls and flowers and cards. About how he could see what she was wearing.

Two minutes went by, two minutes in which she said she could barely breathe, as if air couldn't get past her throat and into her chest. You know how it is to hear nothing but the sound of blood rushing past your ears?

Suddenly she heard a quiet click. He must have gotten into the garage from the yard, and there were muffled footsteps on the wooden stairs leading to the house. Aspen scooched around to face the back hall, pointed the knife toward the door to the garage, and let out a whimper. She saw the outline of the door in the dim light, slowly opening.

"He's here," Aspen choked. "He's inside."

"The police are on the way, honey," the operator said, trying to reassure her. "They'll be there any second."

Like a shadow monster from a nightmare, Aspen told me with a stutter, a huge man stood in the arched doorway of the living room, taking up all the space. She stopped breathing.

"I see you there," he said in an unnerving, thin voice. "My Aspen, my beauty. We're finally together."

He moved toward her in a blur, and somehow the knife clattered to the floor. Everything happened at once: the sirens wailing, the pounding on the front door, Francesca waking up with a start and tripping over the coffee table . . . and the stranger kneeling in front of Aspen and wrapping his hands around her throat, squeezing.

And then the policemen pulled him off her and oxygen rushed back into her lungs and somehow she was screaming, screaming, screaming.

She thought she would never stop screaming.

"You're okay," a policeman told her, gripping her shoulders, sitting her down on a kitchen chair. "Aspen, you're safe. I'm Officer Dave, I'm here to help. An ambulance is on the way."

I want to cry thinking of how terrified she must have been, of how she thought she was going to die!

Aspen said she blinked fast to clear her sight. Officer Dave's partner had the man from Nevada in cuffs, but the guy was still crying out to her in that creepy high voice as he was dragged outside. "I love you, Aspen Barber, you'll always be mine . . ."

Red lights pulsed rhythmically through the open front door and around the curtains on the front windows. Officer Dave grabbed the blanket from Francesca and draped it over Aspen's shoulders. Despite its warmth, she couldn't stop trembling.

After the paramedics checked her over and left, Officer Dave sat down beside Aspen and taught her the calming technique used by the police force: slow deep breaths through the nose, out through the lips, until her dizziness receded and her limbs relaxed.

A deep voice called out. "Hey, Dave, you gotta come see this."

"Keep doing the breathing. I'll be right back," Officer Dave said, and jogged over to join his partner in the dining room.

They'd found the bins of photographs. Francesca went in, too, and Aspen could hear the conversation.

"Did you know it is a criminal offense to produce, distribute, receive, or possess, with intent to distribute, any obscene—"

She interrupted in a slurry voice: "Aspen's autographed photos are not *obscene*. They're art. For her fans."

"—obscene visual depiction—"

"Don't you know what a pinup girl is? Haven't you ever seen a picture of Marilyn Monroe or Brigitte Bardot?"

"—obscene visual depiction of a minor engaged in sexually explicit conduct?"

"Raquel Welch? Jayne Mansfield?"

"They were adults. Your daughter is a *minor*. It's exploitation."

"Says who?"

"Federal law."

When the studio found out about the mail-order business, and it was inevitable they would, they shut it down via court order. Of course, they owned the rights to any and all images associated with the hit show *Practice Makes Perfect* . . . including all likenesses of the character, Sadie.

"Mama was slapped with a massive fine. She was lucky she didn't go to jail," Aspen told me in conclusion to her story as she wiped tears from her eyes.

After hearing all that . . . everything Francesca Barber did so many years ago . . . it's a wonder I didn't crash my car as I left Sagaponack and drove home to Connecticut. And, honestly, it's a wonder I managed to be as gentle and considerate as I was in bringing Francesca to Garcia's place. Believe you me, there were moments—many moments!—I would've liked to make her suffer a lot worse.

Now do you grasp the extent of how diabolical this woman is?

CHAPTER FORTY-THREE

Thinking about how terrible a person Francesca is helps keep me focused. It also reminds me to text Beatrice. Maybe I can suggest a girls' trip to the mall followed by shakes and burgers (or veggie burgers, depending on Bea's shifting dietary status), although it's doubtful she'll agree to spend that much time with me.

I pull up at BACK BAY BAIT AND ACKLE into a weed-filled lot bordered by the rusted-out husks of old dinghies and outboard motors. The screen door creaks when I pull it open and slams shut behind me. Gingerly, trying not to trip over the crumbling threshold as I swat at horseflies, I enter. I find myself in a dim, cramped store with shelves in disarray: a small display of comic books, heavy-duty protective gloves, a bottle of Tabasco sauce here, a can of bug spray there. I find a packet of birthday candles and some matches. There's a mostly empty freezer chest with some Klondike bars and a couple of bags of ice at the bottom. Along the back wall is a small refrigerated section with beer and milk, and right beside the milk, the clear tubs of wriggling creatures for which the store is named: worms and shiners, minnows, leeches, live and cut saltwater lures.

I was hoping for freshly baked goods, or fresh fried-egg sandwiches, or fresh fruit, but I have a feeling that there's nothing fresh in this store except the bait.

"Hello?" I call out.

". . . 'Lo," comes an answer from over my shoulder, and I spin around to realize there's an old man staring at me from a chair almost hidden from view behind a wooden rack of rods, tackle boxes, waders, and fishing line in different weights. On the wall above him is a fading sign showing a cartoon bullfrog and, printed underneath, WOTTA FROGS SOLD HERE.

I step closer. "Good morning." I cough from the cigarette smoke curling from his mouth, a mouth which, curiously, looks a lot like that of the frog in the drawing above his head. "By any chance do you have coffee?"

"Yep." He tips his chin and I look to the corner, where there's a half-filled pot and a stack of Styrofoam cups. "Two bucks. Help yerself."

I pour coffee into two cups that may or may not have already been used. The coffee is thick and sludgy, and it's doubtful we can drink it, but I slap on lids. My back is turned to the proprietor. I can feel his eyes on me, and I try not to cringe as I turn around.

"Um, do you have any portable water containers here? Like the five-gallon kind?"

"Yep." He tips his chin toward a large white Igloo. "Fifteen bucks."

"Can I fill it?"

The man responds, but, honestly, his backwater accent is so thick, I have no idea what he's saying. After three repeats, I finally understand that there's a well out back and I can help myself. For ten bucks.

Dreary, monotonous rain on the return trip makes Back Bay seem even more depressing. The traffic light sways in the wind, and large dirty puddles border the broken curbs. I park behind the house, and after lugging the Igloo up to the porch, I come inside with the coffees and a plastic bag over my wrist.

Francesca is sitting at the table by the window. I take a tentative step forward. She doesn't look at me. "How's it going?"

"How's it *going*?"

"I mean the writing." I scan the lined paper on which there are some hastily scrawled notes in blue ink—some nonsensical points about Devon and Lisbeth. Nothing of value, and certainly nothing resembling a page of usable text. "Francesca, this is garbage. Why aren't you trying harder?"

Francesca's jaw drops. "Um, because I don't want to be here, and because I wanted a bath and there's no water! And because I had to use an *outhouse*!" While I've been gone, Francesca has worked herself into a frenzy. Her hair is frazzled, and her eyes look drawn. "And because I need coffee, and I'm starving, and I smell like full sours!"

At least you got plenty of rest yesterday, I think, but I don't say it out loud. I set her coffee on the table.

She takes a sip and gags. "And what the hell is that stuff?" She's glaring angrily at the colorful boxes I'm placing on the table.

"There weren't a lot of options at the store, but I did get us some snacks. You're welcome." Who doesn't like Pringles and Slo Pokes?

"I'm supposed to thank you for this crap? I haven't eaten carbs since I was twelve."

I let her rant. I know she's just being a grouch. So don't eat, I want to say, but I bite my tongue and tear open a packet of Mallomars. I'm starving, too.

"You're asking me to eat garbage, in addition to hiding me in this shithole!" If her voice went any higher, dogs could go deaf.

I'm losing my patience. "There are protein bars in the kitchen. If you don't want to eat, don't. I'll warm up water for your bath."

"How? There's no water."

"I bought some. I'm going to make a fire in the stove and heat it up, and fill the tub for you."

"What do you think we are, pioneers?"

If only I'd been a Girl Scout, making a fire might be easier. The only reason I even remotely know how to do it is because Mike once wrote a short story about an ex-con on the run who camped outdoors while evading police. I can't believe how long it takes to find dry wood from the bottom of a wet woodpile outside, gather dry kindling from under the porch and under thick bushes, carry it all into the house and stack it, tear strips of paper, set up a teepee. Thank goodness I bought matches at the store or I'd be spending the rest of the week rubbing two sticks together.

At last I get the woodstove crackling, fill an old pot with water from the Igloo, and set it on top to warm. It's a long, slow process, the afternoon drifts by, and Francesca has eaten all the Pringles, half the Slo Pokes, and is on her third protein bar by the time the first potful comes to a boil. She complains the whole time.

She sits there at the table as I slave, and ever so slowly cranks out a few paragraphs.

Sir Devon stared down at Lady Lisbeth as she lay on the mossy ground, her hair aflame around her shoulders, her fingers shaking as she unbuttoned her ragged peasant garb. His lips were fire as they touched hers.

Suddenly there came the thundering of hoofs through the forest. Lisbeth and Devon sat up in fear and peered through the leaves. Could it be? Someone on horseback, galloping toward their idyllic spot?

"By God's bones," Sir Devon whispered, "'tis your father, Sir Richard, with the Duke and his hunting party!"

Frantically Lady Lisbeth pulled the rough cloth over her heaving, alabaster bosoms, and Devon wrapped his arms around her protectively. Sir Richard came upon them and roughly reined in his steed. The horse reared up on its hind legs and whinnied.

"Whoreson," spat Sir Richard at poor Devon. "Unhand my daughter."

"This is pretty terrible." I sigh, reading over her page of handwriting. "No publisher would print this garbage."

"Our deal was for me to write *something*, and I did!"

"It's rubbish!"

"I'm trying," she whines. Her demeanor has shifted. She seems shriveled. "Let's get out of here. I'll do better. Anywhere but this place." Her voice has a hint of a quiver.

"Maybe . . . maybe we should go back to Sagaponack after all," Francesca suggests in the hopeful tone of a child asking for an early birthday present. "I could finish your book in no time. It will be my number one priority. I will cancel every other engagement until your book is done to your satisfaction. And—and hey, you could stay with me. I have lots of guest rooms. Yes! We'll stop off at your place and pack you clothes for the rest of the summer. Or you could borrow outfits from me, anything you need. Anything. And you could live there with me on the beach until I write your manuscript just the way you want it. I'll bring in a chef to make us delicious meals, and we can eat outside by the pool. We could take long walks together by the ocean at sunset . . . just imagine how nice it would be! And you know how pleasant it is to fall asleep to the sound of the waves crashing . . . it's so soothing . . . you'd be so well rested. And then before you know it, I'll have your book finished and you can give it to Mila Jorgenson or Ned Townsend, and off you go!"

I don't say anything as I study Francesca. I've never seen her like this: She's deflating faster than a helium balloon three days post-birthday. Even in the hotel lobby in Hartford, on that fateful night after I caught her making out with Tabi Benlolo and she beseeched me not to tell, she didn't seem to be as unwound as she is now. I am taken aback by this raw, unfiltered version of Francesca.

She clasps her hands in front of her chest imploringly. Her pale, hairless face looks racked as she stares at me from large crystal eyes that, without the dark brows framing them, are ghostly. "Or . . . or . . . if you'd rather, we could go to my penthouse in New York. It has the most spectacular views of Central Park and the Empire State Building. At night we could order in whatever you feel like—lobster or goulash or pho, any food you can think of, it can be delivered—and we could relax up on the private rooftop terrace. During the daytime you could sightsee. Visit the Statue of Liberty, go on a double-decker bus ride or take in a Broadway show. Have you seen *Hamilton*? I will get you front-row seats! Or you could go shopping. I have an account at Bloomingdale's, you just buy whatever you want, on me! And I'll stay in the apartment and write!"

When I don't answer, she cries out desperately, "California? How about California? The Hollywood Hills! *Please?!*"

There is silence as I think about it. Finally, I give my head a little shake. The old me, the Marcy I used to be, would have caved, would have trusted Francesca to keep her word. But Summer is proving to be ruthless.

"No dice," I say as I stand up to carry another pot of steaming water into the bathroom. The sound of her sobbing is drowned out as I fill the tub.

CHAPTER FORTY-FOUR

While Francesca is soaking in the bath, I make a mental list of things to do. First, I should touch base with Bob the Broker and let him know I'll be tied up for a while. I haven't talked to Liisa in ages. And I'm going to have to figure out meals for Francesca and me.

I check my phone for voicemails from yesterday. Bob called to say we have interest in one of the aerospace plants, and he needs me on it. He leaves a number.

The signal is a little better on the porch. "It's Marcy Codburn," I say, when they pick up. It feels strange using that name; Marcy is the person I *used* to be.

I connect with a large aerospace manufacturer who wants to acquire our facility. Like with the Wethersfield deal, the team wants to expedite this one, which means giving them a tour ASAP. Problem is, I have no idea how long I'll be tied up with Francesca, so I hem and haw and tell them I'll get back to them at my earliest. Damn. I could really use a sale right now.

Next, I send Aspen a sweet, motherly little note with emojis of hearts shot through with arrows, checking in on how she is doing and whether she and Tabi have cleared the air. I'm careful not to mention anything about her mother.

She texts back immediately. O hi summer we r all good thx 4 asking

Are you in the Hamptons? I write.

Ended up staying in the city, on set + studio meeting tmrw

I can't wait to see your movie! I'm sure it's going to be just fantastic. In the meantime, I'm here if you need me FWIW.

She sends me back a heart and flower and my heart warms. I can't help but compare how quickly Aspen answered compared to Bea's usual crickets. I smile at Aspen's emojis.

Back to my voicemails. There's one from Mike, so I call him next.

"Hi there," he says. "Long time no speak."

"Hi, yourself."

"Lucky for us the rain is supposed to stop tonight and we're to get beautiful weather through the weekend."

I strain my brain, trying to recall what he's referring to. I completely forgot . . . he's invited our writers' group out on the boat Saturday, the day after tomorrow, and to Port Jeff for dinner.

"I have good news and bad news. The good news is that I have an inquiry regarding one of my properties. The bad news is I have a ton to do for it . . . and . . . and also for my deadline." My half-truth comes easily.

"That is good news! Well, you're right, I certainly wouldn't want to jeopardize a possible sale or your deadline. You'll join us another time. Even though we do have lots to talk about with our friend, the Novelist."

The Novelist! I feel a flush of pleasure. "Well . . . I really don't want to miss the outing. Let me try to switch things around."

After I disconnect, I find the number for the country store. Honestly, I'm surprised they have a phone. The line rings and rings until at last the old man answers. "Yep."

"Hi," I say, "I was in this morning . . . I bought a cooler and some water . . . er, anyway, I was wondering if you knew where I could order a pizza around here?"

"Nah."

I knock on the bathroom door to tell Francesca I'm going out for food. The trip ends up taking me far longer than I expect, and as I drive, the chilling thought occurs to me that, despite her promise, and even though it's raining and she doesn't have a phone or car or even a compass to navigate her way out of the woods, Francesca won't be there when I return.

"I'm famished." Francesca's sitting at the table with arms folded when I return.

So am I. "Mayor McCheese and the Hamburglar send their regards," I tell her, coming in with a grease-stained bag. An expression of distaste settles over her face. "I'm sorry, it's the best I could do. I had to drive forever down the highway to get it."

"You expect me to eat this?"

"I don't care if you eat, but I do expect you to write. Did you get any work done while I was gone?"

Defiantly, she holds up a sheet of paper covered with doodles. Upon closer inspection, the illustrations look a lot like me, but with horns, a tail, and a pointy beard.

"I'd keep my eyes on my fries, if I were you. Which is a metaphor for *get to work*." (Well, it's not really a metaphor for "get to work," but I'm too hungry to think of something more literary.)

I open the bag and lay out our dinners in their boxes. The aroma blasts my olfactory receptors. Francesca looks like she's wrestling with inner demons, not unlike the ones she drew, as she eyes her double cheeseburger, her extra-large pile of golden french fries, her chocolate shake, and the order of chicken nuggets I bought for us to share. Delicately she picks up the burger and nibbles the edge of a patty, then takes a small bite, then an *enormous* bite. I do too. She leans back in her chair and chews and moans, with the exact same expression her daughter wore when she bit into the Portuguese tart at Millie's. We chew and swallow and slurp in unison until every last morsel of food has disappeared.

Francesca lets out an inadvertent burp, and then we both burst out laughing.

At dusk, when the room is becoming too dim to see our own handwriting, I pull out the birthday candles and matches. But it's not like we have tiny candlesticks, or even a cake, to set them in. I think and think and finally fish the Styrofoam coffee cups from the garbage, turn them upside down, and stick a candle in each bottom. It'll do for now.

The way I see it, I'm going to have to bring us some supplies, not to mention take care of a few things at home.

"Francesca," I say, as we sit side by side on the sofa watching the tiny flickering flames set on the iron top of the woodstove, "I'm sorry about dinner. I'm going to leave you here for the night, but I'll be back as soon as I can with supplies."

She stands up and leaves, passing through the archway and shaking her head as if she can't believe the situation she finds herself in.

"Oh, and Francesca?"

She turns.

"I'll see you tomorrow."

The country roads and highway are all but deserted as I speed through the dusk. It's quicker without traffic, of course, but the carb-fat-sugar overload is making it hard to keep my eyes open.

When I get home, Bea is watching TV on the couch. I flop down beside her sleepily and tell her I'm taking a break from the writing retreat. She turns her back to me for a tickle, but I'm too tired. How did the chili turn out? Did her friends like it? I yawn through her answers.

"Do you need me to give you cash for food?" I ask.

"I'm good. Daddy and James loaded up the fridge when you weren't here."

"That was nice of them."

"Hey, I got your text. I can go to the mall Saturday," she says. Then she asks whether I want to see an apartment in Savannah they're looking at. I nod yes, even though I ache to lie down.

She opens her laptop and excitedly clicks on the rental video of a first-floor unit in a clapboard house with a gorgeous weeping willow out front. She's jabbering on—it's furnished, it has a dishwasher, and so close to Patrick's parents—when I receive a text notification.

My heart flutters. It's from Aspen! And she's taken the initiative to reach out to me first! That means she's thinking of me, maybe wistfully remembering our connection in the Hamptons. A second wind energizes me, and I snatch up the phone and bolt from the room.

"Hey, I thought you wanted to see this." Behind me, Bea's voice sounds disappointed.

"Just have to touch base with someone," I say over my shoulder. "Start without me."

Out on the patio, I read the message. hey summer by any chance have you heard from my mom recently Aspen asks.

My heart starts to pound. I type and retype five responses before settling on a simple reply. No, why?

no reason shes not ansrng my calls

She's probably busy? Book event stuff, I'm guessing.

thats what I thought, Aspen writes. i was just starting 2 wonder

I'm sure she'll reach out soon! 🙂🙂🙂!

After we say good night, I open Francesca's text stream and delete everything I sent her so there will be no evidence of our conversations. Then I send her a new text telling her how nice it was to reconnect this summer, how much I enjoyed her Hamptons party, and how it would be great to grab dinner in the city. Maybe tomorrow?

By the time I let myself in from the patio, Bea has gone upstairs. I tidy up the kitchen, glance at the mail, and plug in my phone to charge, all before I remember we were in the middle of something.

"Don't you want to look at apartments?" I call up to Bea. "Don't you want the opinion of a Realtor?"

"Never mind, you're busy. Patrick and I will figure it out," she replies. "Good night."

My priority the next day is meeting the aerospace buyers. I reach them first thing in the morning and am fortunate to set it up for early afternoon. There's no point coming home afterward, I'll just head to Back Bay from there, so I set about packing more provisions to take with me.

The showing doesn't go well. It's not that they don't like the facility—it's impressive—and they already know it's a profitable business. It's just that, even though I'd studied the specs way back when, I never got around to doing the necessary prep, and I cannot answer their questions adequately about the land value, the terms of the sale, and so on.

"I'm sorry. I'll get you the information as soon as possible," I tell the team as we're heading back to the sticky parking lot, where a hot sun is melting the asphalt. "I've been a bit overwhelmed with a big project. It's kept me very busy. I've practically been locked in the office."

The buyers don't seem very empathetic, and I think to myself I probably shouldn't mention this meeting to Bob.

My car practically knows how to drive itself to Back Bay, as I've been back and forth so often these past few weeks. And now, here I go again, straight from the showing.

Last night after texting with Aspen I felt a few misgivings, so this morning I cooked up some carb-free pasta made from lentils with tomato sauce, cheese, and lean ground beef, which I have in a cooler, along with some fruit, rice cakes, almond butter, and a salad. And I'm bringing more water, a couple of bottles of wine, and fat scented candles in glass holders, the popular New England kind.

On this day it's so hot outside, the air conditioner in the car is on full blast. On a whim, I stop along the way and pick up a couple of large iced coffees, one for me and one for Francesca. How nice am I?

I unlock the door while balancing everything. Inside, the windows are open, but the place is sweltering. Francesca is sitting on the sofa in her underwear, leaning her head against the wall. Flies are buzzing around her like miniature assault helicopters.

"Whew, it's hot in here," I exclaim. "It feels like the inside of a furnace."

Francesca is rising off the sofa. As she nears, I see there is sweat trickling down her face, down her neck, down her sides.

I wrinkle my nose. "Oh, someone needs a shower. How about I run out and buy a fan? Oh . . . right. No electricity." I press my lips together.

"I hate you," Francesca hisses. She is creeping toward me like a furious, sweaty spider.

"I thought we were friends."

She laughs balefully. "I wish you were dead."

I ignore that. "I cooked us healthy food and brought some lovely scented candles. And iced coffee." I set it all down gingerly, careful to stay at arm's length.

Francesca snatches up the coffee and takes frenzied slurps through the straw. She's muttering to herself between gulps. "It's all Tabi's fault. If it weren't for him, I wouldn't be in this mess."

Is she going to tell me about her intoxication for her son-in-law? "Good to know." From my peripheral vision, I see that the paper and pens are still untouched.

"You know, I realize you're used to AI, but this is starting to get old. I'm bringing you everything I can think of to make you comfortable. I even brought water for another bath. And in return you could at least *try* to write something. Or I'll have to take a different approach."

Francesca wipes her lips with the back of her hand. "What are you talking about?"

"You want to go home, I understand that."

She narrows her eyes suspiciously.

"We can switch to a reward system. Maybe you did this with your daughter when she was young? I did it with mine, starting at potty training. Good behavior earned stickers. When she brushed her teeth without being reminded, or finished her dinner without complaining, or got ready for school without dragging her feet . . . she received a sticker. She accumulated stickers until she got a bigger prize."

"You think I want stickers?"

"From now on, you will be on a reward system. You want a nice, home-cooked dinner? Fine. You want coffee? Fine. But you'd better get going on the manuscript, Francesca, or you are not getting any of those things."

"You're going to leave me here alone to starve?"

"Don't be silly. I'll bring food, but it might not be the kind you prefer. After all, it's a lot easier and cheaper for me to pick up a loaf of Wonder Bread and some grape jelly than to cook you healthy, low-carb meals."

"You *wouldn't*."

"You're starting to understand! You'll be rewarded, and your ultimate prize will be putting this whole thing behind us. Or you can choose to leave without doing the work . . . but then no deal, I squeal."

"You can't do that!" Francesca is practically screaming. "Summer, get back here!"

As I carry the cooler into the kitchen, Francesca's empty plastic coffee cup hits me in the side of my head.

—

We heat the food in a pot on the woodstove over a fire I taught Francesca to make. Lentil pasta makes it an odd juxtaposition of primitive and modern.

"There's plenty left over for another meal, not to mention the other food in the cooler," I tell Francesca when we're done.

I leave after dinner. I tell Francesca I'll be back soon. "Just a few things I have to take care of," I say.

On the highway, I call Mike. "Turns out I can join you on the boat tomorrow," I say happily.

And then I remember about my plans for shopping with Bea. But "the Novelist" really wants to go on the boat! I'm sure she'll understand. Our mother-daughter outing can be pushed back.

CHAPTER FORTY-FIVE

Toni, Liisa, Mike, and I returned from a gorgeous day on the water and dinner in Port Jeff too late for me to think about driving up to Garcia's, so I'm heading back there now, early Sunday morning.

I thought about staying home another day—it's been too long since I jogged with Liisa and I'm running out of excuses—but last night I had an epiphany. It was right after I opened an email from Mila Jorgenson—she wrote to ask how the final chapters were coming along. I thought, maybe Francesca is just not used to writing with pen and paper. It is tiring, after all, when you're accustomed to a keyboard. A completely different set of muscles, isn't that so? But since there's no Wi-Fi for her computer, and anyway, there's no electricity to charge it, I'm lending her the next best thing.

I work up a sweat as I lug the heavy Olivetti and a ream of blank paper through the vestibule and set it on the table. It's a vintage manual model I've had forever. I only keep it for show, but it works perfectly.

"Ta-da!" I say with a flourish as I straighten, blowing strands of hair off my damp forehead.

Francesca stands in front of it, regarding me. "How exactly do you see this ending, Summer?"

"What do you mean? We both get what we want. I get my bestseller; you get my silence about . . . everything. Then we go our separate ways." I roll a piece of paper into the carriage.

"But you do realize that kidnapping is a felony."

"Come on, this isn't real kidnapping. It was all your idea for me to take you somewhere away from all your distractions, so you could focus on my manuscript."

"I was *drugged* and you brought me here unknowingly *in your car*. You literally left me here with no means to leave. I believe that's the very definition of kidnapping?"

Dang. I hadn't quite considered it from that angle.

We fall into an uneasy truce, and I make an effort to forget what Francesca said. She's obviously trying to scare me into dropping the deal, but despite my efforts, it niggles at me.

Francesca finally produces a page of typed prose. Aha! So the typewriter idea was genius after all. I was correct in assuming Francesca can't write with a pen . . . she does her best work on a keyboard. I start reading over the paragraphs excitedly. But as I read, my excitement fades.

"Francesca, this sucks."

"It's just really hard to concentrate in here. It's so dusty, and airless, but when I go outside, there's mosquitoes." Francesca shows me bites all over her arms and neck. "Not that I don't appreciate everything you are doing for me . . . your cooking is delicious and the candles smell so pretty and the bed"—she pauses to swallow—"the bed is quite comfortable."

I look at her suspiciously. I can't tell whether she is being sincere.

Francesca clasps her hands. "Aspen won't like me being gone so long."

I have to hand it to Francesca, she's trying everything.

She sits on the chair, closes her eyes, and chants, "Breathe in through your nose on a slow count of four, expanding your belly like a balloon. Hold for four. Slowly exhale through your lips on another slow count of four. Repeat. In through the nose, three, two, one. Hold, three, two, one. Out through the lips, three, two, one. Repeat."

"What are you doing?"

"Deep-breathing exercises I learned. It gets so dark at night in the forest," she says, "and I'm . . . I'm afraid. Summer, I'm terrified that someone will . . . will break in." I can hear her quickened breaths. "My breathing technique isn't working anymore. I'm going crazy in here!"

I sit down beside her at the table. "No one is going to hurt you." I sigh. My phone dings with a notification. I pull it from my pocket: Liisa wants to know if we're going on the trail.

"Wait, is that your phone?" Francesca exclaims, sitting up straight.

I shrug. "I got a text."

"Don't you know what that means? You have data! There's a cell tower somewhere around here! We can run an AI program through your phone and transcribe the content onto the paper. And you can charge your phone in your car."

"You mean write my book using artificial intelligence?"

"Well, why not, for heaven's sake? Three-quarters of it already *is*."

I'm silent as I think about it. She's right, actually . . . what's the point of stopping now? I can't argue with her logic. Besides, if I object, nothing's getting finished. Turns out the one thing Francesca has been honest about is that she really *can't* write. "Okay," I say slowly. "Show me what to do."

Monday through Saturday that week, Francesca and I sit side by side, taking turns: one of us using my phone to prompt the AI generator and reading the results aloud, the other typing on the typewriter.

Some of it flows, but there are hours of frustration where we try to connect the dots from previous chapters to make the story of Lisbeth and Devon unfold to its logical conclusion.

On Monday, I get a text from Bea asking why I didn't answer her about rescheduling the Saturday mall day to Sunday; on Tuesday, she messages me to ask whether I want to take her to get a haircut; and on Friday she says she's available, if I am, for burgers and shakes. But at this point my priority has to be Francesca.

"Can't you type faster?" Francesca gripes at one point, eyeing me as I return the carriage on the Olivetti. "It's like watching a preschooler use one finger."

"At least my fingers aren't orange."

"What?"

I chuckle to myself, remembering. "When Beatrice was little, I caught her at my desktop. Her fingers were covered in the orange cheese dust from a bag of Cheetos. She thought if she typed in orange on the keyboard, the print on the screen would be orange, too. She was really angry that it wasn't working."

Francesca laughs with me. "That's cute."

"The funniest part is that it didn't take long for her to figure out how to make different colors of ink using foods. We always knew she'd grow up to be a scientist."

"Really, is that what she is? A scientist? She must be very smart."

"She is."

"I guess for single moms, we've done okay."

"I wasn't a single mom, I'm recently divorced." I clear my throat. "My husband left me."

"I'm sorry."

She doesn't ask, but I continue . . . I haven't had an interested listener in so long. "We, um, weren't right for each other, but he was—is—a good father. You know, supportive, caring. We both were. I thought we did everything right to get Beatrice on her way. In fact, she was supposed to go to grad school for chemistry next month, but she decided to postpone it. For a *boy*."

Francesca nods sympathetically at my aggrieved tone. "If only we could force them to stick to *our* outlines for how we want things in their lives to go. But these daughters of ours certainly have a mind of their own, don't they?"

"I happen to think Aspen's is perfect." *Despite her many challenges with her mother,* I think to myself.

"Believe it or not, it can be hard to reason with Aspen, too. She's in such a rush to have it all right away. Instead of enjoying the milestones in their right time, as they come. She just wants the big Hollywood ending."

Is Francesca confessing something about herself, with that little regretful shrug? Is she admitting she had a baby too young, or didn't want or was plain ill equipped for motherhood? Is she saying she regrets having Aspen at all? I look at her questioningly.

"If I had a do-over, I'd handle things a little differently. I just don't want Aspen to make the same mistakes."

"I'm sure Aspen will be just fine. She's a bright and sensitive young woman."

"I know you're very fond of her, Summer. And . . . in case I didn't mention it . . . I really appreciate that you came into her room to check on her the night of the party, when you thought she might be in trouble."

"I heard Tabi getting angry. I was afraid he'd do something to her."

"Tabi can be temperamental." Abruptly, Francesca stands up to go to the kitchen. She's gone for a while. I can hear her opening a bottle of wine and pouring, and she comes back with two chipped cups full. I lift mine.

"To our daughters."

"May they learn from their mothers' mistakes."

For a split second I forget to whom I'm speaking. I lean forward to confide, and as I do, I feel a little bubble of emotion catch in my throat. "If Bea would just listen to me, without being dismissive, I would tell her how much she's going to regret putting aside her dreams. Like I put aside *my* dream of being a published author when I was young. Now, here I am, heading toward fifty, and nothing to show for it."

"You're almost there." Is that a note of actual warmth in Francesca's voice? "With a little help from technology, we'll get you there. Together."

I let out a little laugh and swipe at my wet eyes. "Thanks. And together we'll *keep* you where you are, too."

"May our daughters never find out how we did it."

We both burst out laughing and clink our cups again.

CHAPTER FORTY-SIX

Liisa is sitting across from me under one of the lime-green umbrellas at Espresso Yourself. Honestly, I would've happily skipped our former ritual, especially since Francesca and I have started making progress during the time we've been in Back Bay, but I needed supplies anyway, and had to come home to check in with everyone. Had I bailed again, Liisa would've been even more vexed than she already is. I sense the resentment brewing under the surface.

"You're looking great," she says, eyeing me up and down over the lid of her mochaccino. "Did you lose more weight?"

A little, actually. My clothes are getting baggier since my diet has been somewhat limited of late. "I've dropped a few. So much stuff going on."

Liisa looks at me expectantly.

"I'm, uh, consulting on a complicated project."

She purses her lips. Clearly she wants more detail, but I don't offer any. "Are you still hanging out with Mike?"

I shrug, even though it feels forced to talk about him with her, since she's so out of the loop. I guess she's out of the loop on everything. "We're seeing a matinee this afternoon."

She asks about Beatrice, and I have to look away. After I bailed on her for the mall last Saturday, she asked to go Sunday, but I forgot to answer, as I was in a rush to get back to Francesca. And, honestly, I forgot to text her back during the week, even though I really meant to. Rather than stay in an empty house, she accepted Kevin's offer to live with him and James for the last weeks of her research program.

Soon she'll be packing to move down south with Patrick, in an apartment he found that I haven't even seen pictures of. And now she's not returning *my* texts. I guess she's busy, but deep down I'm pretty sure she's hurt.

Soon we'll patch things up and she'll understand that everything I'm doing is for her. "Mom, that's fantastic. I'm so proud of you!" she'll exclaim when my book is a hit, just like she did that time at the Mexican restaurant. And Aspen? Aspen will be so grateful for how I protected her, and we'll be in each other's lives forevermore.

"Bea's moving in with her boyfriend," I say carefully, and sip my plain iced coffee.

We sit in silence for a few moments. "Sounds like you've had quite a summer," says Liisa. "You haven't made it to the library in weeks. Are you still part of our group?"

"Oh, sure I am. But like you said, it's been hectic."

More awkward silence. I can feel Liisa's eyes glued to me. "Well, I don't know if you're interested, but . . ." She trails off.

Another of Liisa's big announcements. I can practically hear the drumroll. "Shoot."

"I got a kitten."

"But you always said you're a dog person?"

"I've been thinking about it for a long time, and I've decided to transition."

I didn't know such a thing was possible. "What did you name it?"

"Lassie."

"For a cat? That's funny," I say. "It's also an anagram of your name, sort of."

"I never thought of that!" Liisa looks at me admiringly.

The ice between us melts a few degrees, and we reach for our phones and open our feeds in tandem. The posts start loading in sync. Liisa gasps aloud as she takes in the headlines.

"Are you seeing this?" she asks.

Me, I'm so shocked I can't utter a word.

Francesca Barber has been reported missing.

I stand from the table so abruptly I spill my coffee and our lime-green umbrella rocks precariously in its stand. People look over curiously, and I hear Liisa exclaiming aloud as I dash toward the alley and the wooded entrance to the trail. She hastens to gather our stuff and scurry after me.

My thoughts leapfrog one atop the other as I sprint over the dirt path toward home, hopping over rocks and roots and ducking the low-hanging branches heavy with August leaves. I must get in front of my computer, understand what's happening, sort out my next steps. Then I realize how guilty this must look to Liisa, who is probably a hundred yards behind me and breathlessly shouting my name. I skid to a stop and wait for her to catch up.

"Christ Almighty," she pants, pressing her hands against the stitch in her side as she limps up beside me. There's a wheeze in her airway from the sudden onslaught of exercise. "What are you doing, Marcy? Why did you freak out like that?"

"No, no—I just, um, remembered I had an appointment today. But now I realize it's not until later." I knock my knuckles against my skull. "A moment of senioritis, I guess."

Liisa glares at me, chest heaving. "Stop it. Just stop bullshitting, Marcy. I'm not stupid. You've been acting evasive all morning. In fact, you've been acting evasive all summer. If you don't want to tell me what's really going on, fine."

"I'm sorry. You're right, Liisa, I haven't been myself. I just can't discuss it right now."

We walk in silence in the dappled light of the trail as Liisa's panting subsides. Try as I might, I can't think of a plausible excuse for my behavior, but after a while, Liisa relents and resumes her normal babbling. "Can you believe it . . . Francesca Barber? We just met her! And you know her better than me."

My head snaps up. "What do you mean?"

"You know, when you went to that party in New York City? I assume you spoke with her there. You're in the newspaper photo with her, after all."

I'd completely forgotten about that.

Liisa adds, "Aspen must be beside herself."

"How do you know Aspen?" It slips out before I can think it through.

Liisa looks at me strangely. "I don't *know her* know her. But I know who she is from the Housatonic Hotel event, same as you." She adds ironically, "Wow, your 'senioritis' *is* bad today."

I clamp my mouth shut before I can bury myself any deeper.

—

Liisa comes inside to use my bathroom before she drives home, which means several more minutes of idle chitchat. At last she arranges herself behind the wheel of WAS HIS and backs out of the driveway.

The millisecond she disappears around the corner, I'm on my computer, frantically consuming the headlines. California Woman Disappears from Hamptons Estate, Bestselling Author Reported Missing, and Where's Francesca?

> **New York, NY. (Reuters)**—A missing person report has been filed for Francesca Barber, a California native and author of the bestselling science fiction series "Journey to Jupiter," "Jovan of Jupiter," and most recently "Jupiter in Jeopardy."

> Barber's son-in-law, Brazilian actor Tabi Benlolo, filed the missing person report. Benlolo stars alongside Barber's daughter, actress Aspen Barber, in the film adaptations of the Jupiter books.
>
> Last seen at her summer home in Sagaponack, an oceanside town on Long Island, NY, Barber was initially thought to be on vacation. However, her prolonged absence and lack of contact with family, friends, and business associates has sparked concern.
>
> The circumstances of her disappearance are unclear. Authorities say they are treating the disappearance as suspicious and are not divulging all the details at this time. The case is under investigation.
>
> Anyone with information as to the whereabouts of Ms. Barber is asked to contact the police.

I whip out my phone to text Aspen.

I just read the news, I type. My panic might be mistaken for deep concern. What's happening???

She responds immediately. Idk im at the beach house and im rly worried. Tabi thinks we should hire a private investigator cuz the police r stretched thin

Dear Lord! Sweetie, I'm sure she's just fine. And the police know what they're doing.

As I hit send another text comes in, this time from Mike. Meet in theater lobby at two? he asks. It takes me a second to remember our plans. How am I going to concentrate on a movie when all I can think about is that the authorities are now looking into Francesca's disappearance?

A reply from Aspen: summer i know its askin a lot but do u think u could come out here and stay with me

Now what do I do? I've told Aspen several times she can count on me for help. But I can't possibly go out to the Hamptons and leave

Francesca locked away alone in Back Bay . . . how would she eat? I can't even order a pizza. This is a fine mess. I put my phone down and pace the kitchen floor until finally I think of something.

> Honey, I'm so sorry, but I'm sick and I'm probably contagious.

You are? Mike asks. Why didn't you say something earlier? I'll bring chicken soup. See you in a little while. 💋 🙂

Bugger all! Wrong text stream. Quickly I copy and send the note to Aspen. But now what do I say to Mike? I can't tell him the text was meant for someone else—he'd ask who. And I don't want him to think I'm a liar.

Aspen says, no worries hope u feel better.

Weakly, I type Okay to Mike and Thank you to Aspen. I unlock the front door and, despite it being a hot afternoon, change into flannel pajamas. I grab a bottle of aspirin, a thermometer, and a water bottle and set up shop on the coffee table.

Mike arrives with a bulky brown paper bag. "Ding dong," he says, taking out three quarts of broth and putting them on the kitchen island. He busies himself with fixing a tray and comes into the living room, where I'm curled up on the couch, sweating under a thick fleece blanket. He lays a palm against my forehead. "You do feel hot," he says, sitting down across from me.

I cough a few times. "Thank you for the soup. It will soothe my sore throat," I say hoarsely.

"You sound terrible."

"I feel terrible." Cough, cough. "But hopefully it's just a twenty-four-hour thing. Can I get a rain check on the movie?"

"You bet." Mike smiles.

After he leaves, I type Thanks again for the chicken soup. I receive a question mark in return. And then I see I've texted Aspen.

CHAPTER FORTY-SEVEN

One thing's for sure: Now that people have caught on to Francesca's disappearance, she and I must complete my manuscript with gusto. I'm not sure what else I can do to speed things along, but I'll think of something before I see her next, which won't be until after my meeting this afternoon at the aerospace facility—the investors have asked to see the space again, which is great news, albeit bad timing in terms of the Back Bay Situation.

I'm exhausted. I was so nervous about the headlines, I tossed and turned all night, only falling asleep toward dawn, and then I slept right through my alarm. In my mind I skimmed through every scenario: Did they dust for fingerprints and find mine? Traces of sedatives in a cup? Footprints in the grass?

I'm listening to a Long Island news outlet report on the case right now. "Concerns are mounting in the mysterious disappearance of renowned author Francesca Barber from her Hamptons beach house," the reporter is saying, "and according to sources, local authorities may suspect foul play."

Stop worrying, I tell myself forcefully. *We did such a good job covering our tracks. Moreover, everyone in Francesca's world knows you as Summer.* I compose a mantra and repeat it over and over:

They don't know it's you. They'll never find you.

They don't know it's you. They'll never find you.

They don't know it's you. They'll never find you.

In a bid for good karma, I pack up the contents of the fridge. Thank you, Kevin and James, for stocking it for Bea, who didn't eat half of it. I scoop quinoa salad and diced watermelon into containers; I slice carrots and celery into sticks. I take out some vitamin water from the beverage fridge and even grab a couple more bottles of white wine. I'll bring it all to Francesca in the cooler. Maybe I'll boil water again for her to have another bath!

I'm sliding turkey-and-Swiss sandwiches into baggies when the doorbell startles me, and I drop a dollop of mayonnaise onto my blouse, leaving a big, oily stain front and center. Dammit. I grab a dishrag to swipe at the stain, and only succeed in spreading it.

There are two strange men on the stoop. They're wearing suits, they're not smiling, and, when I open the door, they flash badges. My stomach plummets like someone cut the cables.

"Can I help you?"

"Marcy Jo Codburn?" the older one asks, glancing at my shirt.

"Yes."

"We are investigating the disappearance of Francesca Barber, and we'd like to ask you some questions."

The younger man says, "Can we come in?"

As if I have a choice. I glance over my shoulder toward the kitchen. Behind me, I can hear the newscast about Francesca's disappearance still playing on my computer, which I was watching while I prepared her meal. My breath catches in my throat and my mouth goes dry as I realize there are probably a dozen open pages of articles about her up on the screen.

"Sure . . . of course." As the men step inside, the narrative moves on to the next news story, about global warming. The reporter starts talking about cows. I let out the breath I've been holding.

"Going on a picnic?" the younger one asks, spying the cooler and sandwiches.

"A picnic? Yes. Yes, I am." I casually shut the lid of my laptop as I pass the island and indicate the chairs at the glass table. "Please, have a seat. Can I offer you some coffee?"

They thank me. As I set out mugs and milk and sugar, I try to keep my breathing even and my hands from vibrating. I can't help but wonder whether they purposefully gave me this task to see if my hands *would* shake? I slide onto a chair and pour. It's almost impossible to keep the hot liquid from sloshing into the saucers.

From the corner of my eye, I can see that the older one, a middle-aged Black man with close-cut graying hair, has taken out a pad and pencil and flipped to a blank page. He jots something down while his young partner looks around my kitchen from small blue eyes set so close together they are practically joined at the bridge of his sharp, beaky nose. Neither is wearing a uniform, so I assume they are detectives; both are big and broad and take up too much air. I feel strangled.

"I'm Detective Waite, and this is Detective Novogrodski," the older one says. "As I mentioned, we are looking into what may have happened to Ms. Barber."

"I'm not sure how helpful I can be."

"You're a friend of hers, am I right?"

"Um, yes." I lodge my hands between my knees. "But not for all that long."

"Understood. As far as you know, has she had any mental health issues?"

"I don't think so."

"Drug or alcohol addiction?"

"None that I've seen."

"We're contacting her friends and relatives to piece together a timeline of her last few weeks. Mrs. Codburn, when was the last time you saw her?"

I swallow. "Several weeks ago, at her end-of-July party in the Hamptons."

Waite and Novogrodski exchange a glance. "And when you spoke to her, did she mention anything out of the ordinary . . . ?"

"Well . . . she was feeling stressed. I think she may have said she was thinking about going to a spa, you know, to relax." I can hear myself rambling. *Stop rambling, Summer.*

Waite jots something on his pad. "Did she say where?"

"No, nothing specific."

"And have you heard from Ms. Barber since the party?"

"No, no, I haven't, actually. What do you think happened to her?"

"We don't know yet," Novogrodski says. "Can you think of anyone who might want to harm her? Have a grudge against her?"

Um, her daughter? I shake my head.

Novogrodski's beady blue eyes, which have been flitting around my house, alight on me. "There was no ransom note, no phone call with demands. Ms. Barber doesn't have a criminal past. Her family is pressuring us to investigate, but the truth is, these celebrity types disappear for vacations all the time, and there's nothing unlawful about it."

I sigh. "Poor Aspen."

Waite taps his pencil on his pad. "You've spoken to Aspen Barber?"

"Yes. I'm very fond of her. She's worried sick."

"I'm sure she is," Novogrodski says. "Because if her mother *was* kidnapped, that would be very serious indeed."

"Right, well, I'm sure we'll get to the bottom of this," Waite says, and then something seems to occur to him. "Oh, and congratulations. I understand you've written a book? Ms. Jorgenson, your agent—who is also Ms. Barber's agent, am I right?—mentioned you when we interviewed her yesterday."

Now I understand.

"You were quite the mystery until then," Waite continues. "Aside from a seven-year-old in Arkansas, we couldn't find any record of a Summer Branigan. She almost doesn't exist."

"It's my pen name. I . . . um . . . want to be known as Summer Branigan in the publishing world."

"I see." Waite takes a last gulp of his coffee and stands up, and his partner does the same. I'm ushering the detectives to the door when Waite turns around, looking at his notes. "Just to make sure I have this down correctly . . . you said you haven't seen Ms. Barber since her party."

"Uh-huh."

He nods. His partner is following him out the door and stops to hold up a finger, as if he just thought of something. He scratches his temple. "Where did you say you were heading?"

"Pardon?"

"For your picnic." Novogrodski tips his beak toward the fixings on the cutting board.

"Oh. Probably a park, or maybe down to the beach. I haven't decided."

Novogrodski smiles. "Thank you for your time. Here's my card in case you think of anything else. Oh, and just don't go far . . . we may have another question or two."

As I watch them walk to the road where they parked their boxy black SUV, I realize that the sky is gray and thick with storm clouds. It looks like it will start pouring any minute.

—

Once the detectives are gone, it takes some doing to pull myself together. If I still smoked, now would be a great time for a cigarette, but I quit ages ago. And I don't keep a single piece of chocolate in the house anymore, not even for emotional emergencies. Like this.

Am I suspected of something?

CHAPTER FORTY-EIGHT

Brian approaches the table with a craft beer in one hand and an old-fashioned in the other. He serves us, exchanges some pleasantries, then goes back to unpacking bottles of wine behind the bar. Mike is sitting across from me. We're in a quiet corner of O'Keefe's in the afternoon, too early for the regular crowd to shuffle in.

I wrestle with how to broach the subject to Mike. It's so messy I don't know where to begin. Nor do I know how much of these past two weeks I'll have to account for.

But Mike has kindly interrupted his afternoon of short story revisions, and I owe him some sort of explanation for my urgent request to meet. I'm mulling over what to say. I certainly can't tell him how this morning's visit by the detectives has me rattled.

"Cheers," he says, popping open his can, pouring frothy beer into a glass, and taking a sip. He peers at me. "How's your cold?"

"All better." I take a big gulp of my drink, and then another. We chat idly for a few minutes, until finally Mike says, "How can I help?"

Another swallow. "Well, um, I thought I'd dabble in crime . . . crime writing, that is . . . for my next project. I need law enforcement expertise."

"You've come to the right person." Mike puffs out his chest with a wink. Always gallant, always protective.

Here goes. "When a person does something questionable but maybe not exactly illegal, say making a deal with someone to get what she wants, but no one is supposed to get hurt, in fact the deal is supposed to protect people, but then things sort of spiral out of control . . ." I stop abruptly. Yes, I realize I sound like a blithering idiot.

Mike waits as I swallow more of my drink and try again.

"Say she is blackmailing someone, but for very good reasons, and in fact the person being blackmailed is pretty much okay with it. Because both parties benefit. So it's more like a mutual deal than blackmail, I suppose. But then things escalate. Is that bad?"

He raises a brow. "Blackmail and extortion are illegal, yes, but you haven't given me much to go on here. Care to expand?"

I signal for another round.

I'm quiet for a beat as I look around and wait to be served. Besides us, the only other patrons are three men in baseball caps, pregaming before heading to the stadium, and two college-aged kids, a guy and a girl, by the jukebox. Supertramp starts to play. Do I really have to hear about schemes and adventures? I have my own crime of the century in the works. I take a breath.

"Say the person doing the blackmailing takes the person being blackmailed and hides them somewhere, like sort of kidnapping, but they're in on it together . . . is that a crime?"

Across from me, Mike looks confused. "Kidnaps are very serious crimes. What do you mean in on it together? Was a person confined without consent, by physical force, intimidation, or deception?"

"No, no, nothing like that."

"Was the victim a child under sixteen?"

"No!"

"Was the intent to compel a third person to pay ransom?"

"Not at all."

"Was the person being kidnapped somehow injured or drugged?"

I don't answer.

"New York elevates the commission of the crime if the kidnap was with the intent to compel the person to engage in particular conduct, or refrain from engaging in particular conduct. This elevates it to kidnap in the first degree with an aggravated charge. This is the most serious level of the crime, a class A-I felony. Such felonies are punishable by a minimum sentence of fifteen to twenty-five years and a maximum term of life imprisonment. Whereas kidnaps in the second degree are a class B violent felony. Persons convicted of a class B violent felony offense are subject to a sentence of five to twenty-five years in prison."

Twenty-five years! Under the table, my foot gets the jitters, and when I kick the table leg, our full glasses of liquid slosh around. I grab the edges of the tabletop to steady them.

"Hang on . . . what if the kidnapping was staged, and it was actually the idea of the person being kidnapped. And no money was involved."

Mike leans back in his chair and scratches his goatee. Then he smiles. "Very creative, Marcy. I love the idea of your characters staging a kidnapping."

"So there's no crime if there's consent?"

"Right." Mike raises his beer with a grin. At least he's enjoying this. "However, there are implications when the disappearance involves a lie and results in harm or unnecessary public costs, like for an investigation. And," he goes on, looking quite proud of his expertise, "in most states, lying to law enforcement is called filing a false report, which is a misdemeanor, and can result in penalties of up to a year in jail for a conviction and fines of up to a thousand dollars.

"There have been some interesting cases of people staging their own kidnappings," he continues. "Sherri Papini was a notable case, you might recall: She staged her own kidnapping in order to receive disability benefits. Then there was a soccer player who fabricated this elaborate tale of being kidnapped and robbed at gunpoint because he was late for practice. In Alabama, a young woman claimed she'd been kidnapped to get the attention of her ex-boyfriend. And in one famous case in England, a woman staged her own kidnapping just before Christmas. She was bulimic, and believe it or not, she wanted to avoid overeating at holiday parties."

He sits back and spreads his arms wide. Ta-da.

I try to digest it all, and force myself to ask: "In the case of a kidnapping, would there be . . . you know . . . a police car parked outside the house of the person kidnapped? Like, all day and night?"

"Police surveillance isn't as common as people think. Most police departments are stretched too thin for round-the-clock surveillance. It's much more likely that officers will check in with the family at regular intervals throughout the day, three, four times. Unless"—Mike holds up a finger in warning—"the case is a child kidnapping where the FBI is involved. In that case, there very well might be a cruiser stationed outside overnight." He chuckles. "But even then, there's such a thing as eyelids closing. They're only human."

My voice comes out in a squeak. "So from what I've described, it's hard for you to know if there might, um, be legal ramifications?"

"As you've written it, it could go either way." As he's leaving a tip for Brian, Mike adds, "But here's the thing: You might want to check your character. Even if there are no legal consequences, the behavior is immoral. Make sure that's clear to the reader."

Always has to be the upstanding citizen, doesn't he?

—

It's raining hard as I pull into the entrance of the aerospace factory, and there's the investment team opening their umbrellas and walking in a cluster toward the parking lot. Damn. I'm so late, I've missed the meeting.

I pull in, step out into the storm, and hurry toward them with my tail between my legs, ready to beg forgiveness.

"I'm sorry to keep you wai—" I start to say. One of the VPs holds up a hand as he walks.

"Please, no more apologies," he says without breaking stride. "I don't think this deal is going to work for us."

I hurry to keep up with him as the wind whips my hair into my face. "If you could just give me a few minutes, I could show you the data I put together . . . ?"

"Thanks, but *this*"—here, he turns and palms a circle in the air to include the building and, along with it, me—"is not the right fit."

Another buyer nods agreement and adds, "We've decided against moving forward at this time."

Just great, I think. I wonder what excuse I can make up this time to tell Bob.

The unexpected appearance of the detectives had me so overwrought, I forgot the cooler at home, so I drive back to get it. I brake to a stop fifty feet from home. There's a boxy black SUV parked on the road in front of my house, and Detectives Waite and Novogrodski are standing on my porch. Waite's finger is on the doorbell.

Quickly, before they see me coming, I shift into reverse and back the car into the driveway two doors down. It's well hidden behind a row of arborvitae. If anyone asks why I'm here, it's to check on my elderly neighbor, whom I haven't seen in months. If anyone asks why I needed to drive my car, I'll blame it on the rain.

Normally I'd be congratulating myself on the cunning ruse, except that this whole escapade has become very, very real.

Fifteen minutes later the detectives are sitting in their car. I can see them from my vantage point; they must be hanging around, waiting for me to arrive. Finally they give up and drive away. Even long after the SUV has disappeared from sight, I'm still not sure it's safe to go home. Are Waite and Novogrodski surveilling me from afar, like I've just been surveilling them? I think of all the bad things I've done. I ache to curl up with my computer and figure out why they returned after this morning's visit. My computer. I recall that my computer is on the island where I left it, which reminds me that three-quarters of the rewritten manuscript for *A Knight to Remember* is saved on my desktop. The thought opens a valve and a stream of fresh tears fills my eyes. Now I'm in trouble and I don't even have anything to show for it.

I glance up. My neighbor, Mrs. Nagy, is peeking through the living room curtains. I can see her thick glasses under a tuft of white curls as she waves at me. Drat. I rummage through the stuffed glove box for a tissue, then clamber out of the car and hurry to her front door.

"Hi, Mrs. Nagy," I say. She tried to teach me how to say it years ago, but the best I can do is pronounce it "nudge."

"Marcy, my dear!" Her Hungarian accent is thick. "What are you doing here on this rainy Monday? What a nice surprise."

"I wanted to drop by and see how you were doing."

Her gnarled hand reaches for my elbow and draws me in. Mrs. Nagy looks grateful for the company, and I follow her into the crowded kitchen and watch as she sets a pot on to boil. It's a wonder she can find the stove burner under the mess: It's hoarder-level cluttered in here.

"I made cabbage soup," she says and reaches for a bowl.

The last thing I'm in the mood for is cabbage and chitchat. I'm saved by my phone; it dings with a text notification from Victor Thane.

I stutter out an apology before I even finish reading. "Oh dear, I'm so sorry, Mrs. Nudge," I say. "I have a work emergency. I'll have to try the soup another day." I hurry out to my car to reread Victor's message.

Greetings, he writes, although I arrived in New York just yesterday, I am under a great deal of pressure from London to inspect the sites and make a recommendation. I hope my timing is not inconvenient for you, but I would like to see the Back Bay property. I can head over now. Please do advise your availability. And please pardon the last-minute request.

I have to get Francesca out of there and back home. Who knows if the detectives are on to us. Who knows if Victor Thane will recognize her, or what she might say.

This changes everything.

CHAPTER FORTY-NINE

Within seconds I'm flooring the gas on the slick interstate as pitchforks of lightning pierce the sky. I keep glancing in the rearview mirror, expecting at any moment to see a boxy black SUV chasing me. But I arrive in Back Bay without a tail, as far as I can tell.

I directed Victor Thane to meet me at the intersection of the main road and the laneway, to keep him away from the house. I'm praying that he'll have trouble finding the place like I did, giving me extra time to prepare.

When I burst back into the cottage and shake off the rain, I'm hit with air so warm the windows are steamy. There's a fire smoldering in the stove. I find Francesca lying on her bed, dozing in the warmth. "You're back so soon," she mumbles when I enter.

"Get up," I snap. "We need to get out of here." I rush around while she's draped across the bed, lazily watching me. I collect items I'd brought and bring armfuls to the car while balancing my umbrella: the luggage, the paper and pens, the toiletries. I return for the typewriter and awkwardly lug it onto my front seat. I pull the quilt and sheets off my bed and stuff the whole bundle into the trunk.

"Where we goin'?" she slurs as I run around cleaning up.

"Home. I'm taking you home."

The last thing to get in the car is Francesca herself, but she's woozy and sluggish. I pull off her blanket, and as I do, I see the empty wine bottle beside her.

"Oh no, Francesca, you didn't!"

I get a giggle for an answer. Then my phone dings with a text from Victor Thane, saying he's almost here.

There's no time to hide her. And who knows what she might blurt in her current state? I open my purse and pull out the little bottle of sedatives I've been carrying around, shake two pills onto the table, grind them with a spoon, and mix the powder into a bottle of water.

I prop up her shoulders and hold the plastic bottle to her lips. "Drink," I command, and she does. I close her door.

—

Victor Thane bumps along the road as I'm rushing outside with the last of our things. I drop everything beside the soiled sheets and hurriedly slam shut my trunk. I don't think he can see me as I scramble up the lane to where he's parked in his rental.

When I emerge into the clearing, he rotates on the driver's seat, opens an umbrella, and steps onto the wet, pebbly ground.

"Pleasure to meet you," he says, shaking my hand and thanking me profusely for meeting him on such short notice. Victor Thane has the biggest, shiniest balding head I've ever seen, with a fringe of white around the sides. As he nods under the umbrella, I see a flurry of flakes landing on the shoulders of his expensive trench coat. I'm immediately reminded of a snow globe.

The rain is letting up, and we walk back toward the main road, and down the shoulder under the swaying traffic light, toward the bait and tackle. He wants to walk so he can see the outermost boundary of the property, a crest that plummets down a steep embankment toward a stream feeding the bay. The viewing goes well, despite the gray skies and soggy ground; not that he gushes about the woods or the town or anything, because he seems to be a very self-contained, dignified gentleman who strides with one arm bent behind his back, except for when he reaches into the breast pocket of his suit jacket for his phone so that he can snap a photo or two. But I can tell when he approves of what I'm showing him by his subtle signature gesture: a thoughtful chin dip with raised eyebrows.

"I'm impressed," he says, as we're back at his rental car at last. "I like the highway access and the location, and the road is in fairly good condition. And I must confide, the places in Jersey weren't as promising as I'd hoped."

"Oh?"

"I toured a defunct textile plant and a tannery. Doubtless, the ground below them both is contaminated . . . what you'd call an EPA nightmare. They would certainly be red-flagged for soil testing, which would cost us hundreds of thousands, and perhaps another hundred thousand to cap the ground per your environmental protocol. And dumping contaminated soil would be another major expense."

"I have to admit, I'm happy to hear that," I answer. "This land is nothing if not pristine. How about we meet back at my office to discuss further? My broker, Robert Verney, is eager to meet you. I'll let him know we're on the way."

He's looking over my shoulder toward the woods. "Where is that coming from?" he asks.

I look over the treetops. There's a thick plume of smoke curling into the sky.

"Oh, there's just an old, abandoned building in the woods." My heart is jackhammering in my chest. I'm praying Victor Thane won't ask to see it.

"May I see it?" he asks, heading down the lane and swatting at the mosquitoes I've learned to ignore.

"I . . . um . . ." I stammer. "I assumed it would be demolished if your company acquired it."

"Perhaps not. Depending on its footprint, it could be repurposed during the construction phase."

"Right." I pretend to fumble with my keys at the front entrance. My hands are so sweaty and shaky, it's hardly an act.

Victor Thane steps inside, and I follow as he wades deeper into the warm room.

"Well . . ." I say. "Not much to see in here."

"Someone made a fire. I thought you said it was abandoned?" I tag along behind him as he checks out the kitchen, bathroom, and main bedroom. "I believe we could make it work."

"Great! Let's head back outside."

But Victor Thane is eyeing the closed door. I'm praying he won't ask to see what's inside there.

"What's inside there?" he asks.

"Oh, that? It's just another bedroom, and there's no electricity and anyway it's probably locked—" And just as the jumbled words are tripping over each other as they exit my mouth, Victor Thane reaches out to try the doorknob. Of course it turns.

In the short time I was in here earlier, I'd managed to remove Francesca's designer suitcase and expensive belongings scattered about, but, of course, there's the matter of Francesca herself, splayed on the bed with the empty wine bottle at her side.

"My word," Victor Thane exclaims. "There's a woman in here!"

An explanation leaps from my lips as I try to block the doorway. "She—she must be homeless. The current owner, Garcia, told me they'd had a problem with squatters in the past."

"Is she all right?" Concerned, he brushes past me and takes a few steps toward the prone figure. As he leans down to look at her, a low moan issues from beneath the veil of hair.

"Drunk," I tell him desperately. "I wouldn't get too close. You never know."

"Indeed." He straightens and faces me. "Shall we ring for help?"

"You go ahead to my office and meet with Robert. I'll call the police and see that she gets to . . . to . . . a shelter."

"You're sure you'll be safe?"

"Oh yes. Don't give it another thought. I'll let Robert know you're on the way, and I'll be there as soon as I can. I just hope this unexpected situation"—I glance toward the bed—"doesn't change your mind about the property."

"This unfortunate woman's circumstances certainly aren't your fault." He hesitates before leaving the room. "Perhaps I should wait with you until the authorities arrive."

"No, no, you go ahead and meet with Mr. Verney. There, uh, might be another interested party, and I want to make sure you are prioritized."

"Ah. I quite appreciate that," Victor Thane says, nodding. "Quite."

I walk him back to his rental. As soon as he pulls away, I am racing to the house and trying to hoist a familiarly comatose Francesca from the bed. It's not like I ever got the hang of the fireman's carry thing, so once again I am pulling her along the floor. I haul her out of the house, lock the door behind me, drag her along the mud-soaked ground into the twilight, and fold her onto the back seat of my car. I grab my quilt from the trunk, the one my grandmother and her sewing circle stitched together, and cover Francesca with it.

CHAPTER FIFTY

Bob the Broker sounds aggrieved when he calls to ask what's taking me so long, but that's just Bob. In truth I'm flooring it, and I arrive at the office a short while after Victor Thane does. I apologize profusely for keeping them waiting.

The meeting with Victor Thane goes "swimmingly." (His word, not mine.) He is very pleased with the Back Bay property and with all the information Bob and I provided, and tells us he plans to return to his hotel and call his London headquarters with a solid recommendation to make an offer.

After Bob and I walk Victor Thane out of our office, I return to my car. Francesca is snoring comfortably in the back seat, hidden from view, tucked under Grandma's quilt. I bet Grandma and her sewing circle cohort never would've imagined their quilt would be used in the staged kidnapping of a bestselling author–cum–fraudster.

I'll just close my eyes for a minute, I think, before setting out on the long drive to the Hamptons. When my eyelids snap open again, though, it's two o'clock in the morning. I shake myself awake and speed away, desperate to arrive before dawn.

My plan is to arrive in the dark just in case any reporters or nosy neighbors are lurking nearby. As Mike said, chances are low that police are surveilling the place in the dark.

So that's what I'm banking on. With a little luck, I'll get Francesca inside without anyone being the wiser. And if there is anyone watching, well, she and I will come up with something, since we're in this together.

Now I notice my gas tank indicator flashing near empty. I pull into the nearest service center to fill up. As I'm standing at the pump, swiping my debit card, a patrol car pulls in right behind me, and two uniformed officers get out. My heart stutters to a complete standstill. Are they after me? No. They disappear into the all-night convenience store.

As I pump gas, I'm hyperaware of Francesca asleep on the back seat, just inches from where I stand. I imagine her running across the concrete (although she's barefoot) or screaming bloody murder (although she's out cold). Theoretically, all she has to do is hop out of the car and race the few yards toward the glass doors of the store. But of course she doesn't. She doesn't budge.

Don't scoff. I'm very well aware that I might be in deep trouble; my whole plan was foiled; I've wasted a ton of time and energy, not to mention money, and more miles on my odometer than I care to count; and in the end my computer-generated historical romance is far from done. The historical romance that my enviably high-powered agent is waiting for so she can get me an epic publishing deal.

How was I to know?

I'm sure it's over with Francesca. Even if I threaten to expose her—which I'm sure by now she doesn't believe I'll do thanks to the dirt she has on me—there's no way she'll agree to help once she's back in the comfort of her own home. She's snoozing behind me. Nice for her—I'd love to be snoozing, too, seeing as it's now three o'clock in the morning, but of course I don't have the luxury of being chauffeured back and forth like she does.

All the way through Connecticut and across that dark, deserted highway spanning Long Island, I think about Lady Lisbeth and Sir Devon. What will happen to them? I have no idea how Francesca . . . or rather, the algorithm posing as Francesca . . . intended to tell the story. And even with the use of AI, I'm afraid there's an infinitesimal chance I can make the prose flow seamlessly the way she can.

My phone pings with the delivery of an email. There's no one on the road, so I tap on my inbox as I drive. Mila Jorgenson. I don't question why she's working in the middle of the night, and I don't have to read the message to know what she's asking: When will I have the completed manuscript? It echoes the two other reminders she's sent in the past week. My deadline is looming. So much for what I told her about being a stickler for them.

I stare out at the highway, imagining Francesca slipping back into her glittery celebrity life, while I barrel toward my fifties with no book of my own to display on a shelf, nothing to keep Aspen bound to me, nothing to make Beatrice proud of me.

I suppose I'll drop Francesca off at her estate, fortify myself with some strong coffee, and never see her again.

Thanks for nothing, I think.

CHAPTER FIFTY-ONE

My heart is pounding as I switch off my headlights and turn onto Francesca's road. The velvety black curtain of night sky is lifting to reveal the next act: a faint gray dawn. Fortunately, I look up and down but don't see any other cars lying in wait, so I use Francesca's remote to open the iron gates and pull the car up front. I grab her keys and peer at the quilt in the back seat. There she is, snug as a bug, still sleeping. I jump out to open the rear door. "Hey," I say. "Hey!" I repeat louder in her ear. "Wake up, we're here." I shake her shoulders none too gently.

Her puffy eyelids open a crack.

"Let's go," I urge, wrapping the quilt snugly around her. It takes a bit of doing to get her up on her feet; she sags like a soufflé. At last she's standing, though more like a boneless invertebrate, so once again I hook my arm around her waist and maneuver her toward the house. In the dark she seems disoriented, as if she doesn't recognize her surroundings. She pauses on the doorstep and takes several deep breaths of salted air.

"Hurry up," I say. I want to get her inside and out of view. It's getting lighter out.

"Is the nightmare over?" she whines as we enter the living room. She's only been gone two weeks, but she looks around with a bewildered expression, as if it's been two decades.

I purse my lips. "You can drop the act. Show's over."

Francesca draws herself up an inch or two. She shakes her head, tightens her slack mouth, blinks her cloudy eyes, folds her arms.

"Did you drug me again?"

"Just a little. You couldn't have been comfier. And see? You're home."

She fans her face delicately, like a Southern belle. "I need a shower and coconut water spritz."

"I don't know about coconut water, but I'll make coffee while you shower."

Francesca disappears upstairs as I putter in the kitchen, trying to figure out how to use her space-age machine. In a drawer I find the instruction manual and finally manage to get it brewing. It chimes in completion just as the doorbell rings. My throat closes. I sneak along the wall and peep out the margins of the frosted glass.

It's Detective Waite and Detective Novogrodski.

I lean against the wall and force myself to breathe. My car, with its Connecticut plates, is parked right out front, so they know I'm here. They walked right by it when they got out of their black SUV.

All night long I'd hoped to avoid the police, and here they are on the doorstep. My heart jackhammers as I open the door. "Good morning, Detectives."

They're grim as they step over the threshold.

"We're a little surprised to see you out here, Mrs. Codburn," Waite says. He and his partner hover in the entrance hall.

"Yes . . . I . . . I just got here." It takes a considerable effort not to (A) faint, (B) vomit, (C) wet my pants, or (D) all of the above.

Waite flips open his pad and jots something on it. "I have quite a few follow-up questions for you, Mrs. Codburn."

"Let's start with this one: Why are you here?" Novogrodski asks.

"Actually, I—"

"Gentlemen?" Our heads—Detective Waite's, Detective Novogrodski's, and mine—swivel in unison toward the voice.

It's Francesca.

She has appeared at the top of the stairs on the landing, centered against the tribute wall of *Practice Makes Perfect* photographs. She's wearing a fluffy bathrobe, and a large towel, twisted like a turban, covers her damp hair. She pauses for a theatrical moment before doing a graceful Norma Desmond descent down the stairs. "May I help you?"

The detectives are floored. "Ms. Barber," Novogrodski says, "you're home?"

"That's stating the obvious," Waite mutters to his partner.

"I am." Francesca glides closer. The scent of soap and shampoo precedes her . . . an enormously welcome improvement over earlier. She's ready for her close-up, it appears.

"Care to tell us where you were?"

I hold my breath. Time stands still.

Here's Francesca's big chance to get revenge and tell the cops every terrible thing I did: how I blackmailed her; dragged her—while she was drugged—and rolled her into a pickle juice–soaked blanket; basically held her prisoner in a musty, dusty, isolated cabin; fed her carbs and junk food; and tried to force her into finishing my book . . . not to mention her regrettable loss of facial hair as a result. When I put it in those terms, I wouldn't blame her for having me arrested on the spot.

For a moment Francesca doesn't respond. Then a weak sigh escapes her. "Gentlemen, I'm not well. I've been undergoing . . . *treatment*." Francesca's voice is frail, like she's wasting away.

I gape. In truth, she really does look sick . . . with no eyebrows, and the way the towel covers all her hair . . . for a minute I'm convinced she might be dying.

Novogrodski clears his throat. "We're . . . uh . . . very sorry to hear that."

Waite's pencil is poised. "May I ask, what is the nature of your illness, ma'am?"

"The Long Island kind."

Waite and Novogrodski exchange horrified glances. "Since you are safe and sound, we'll be on our way. We'll just need the name of the hospital, if you don't mind. For the record."

"It was a private facility, very discreet," Francesca says, looking him straight in the eye. "I won't divulge details, as you can imagine what would happen if the public or the press were to find out. Very detrimental to my career, you see."

Waite and Novogrodski shift uncomfortably.

Francesca continues: "This is my personal battle to endure, Detectives. I'm sure you understand."

Waite considers her for a minute, then turns to me. "You knew about this, I'm assuming?"

"I . . . I . . ." I'm floundering.

"I didn't disclose anything to her, but she may have recently begun to suspect," Francesca offers on my behalf. "My dear friend here would never pry, because she knows how much I value my privacy."

Novogrodski strokes his chin. "Ms. Barber, you didn't even tell your daughter?"

"If she thought I was terminal, she would have been too upset to do her job for *Jupiter in Jeopardy*. She and her husband, Tabi Benlolo, are newlyweds. They're trying for a baby. I didn't want anxiety over my health to mar their happiness." Francesca shakes her head sadly. "I didn't know everyone would worry so over my absence."

Waite writes a few notes before looking up toward the staircase. "Can we have a word with them?"

"Aspen is sleeping," Francesca says, "and Tabi has probably gone for his usual morning jog." She peers out the sliding doors. "I see his towel on a chair, and his sneakers aren't there."

Waite flips his notebook shut. He and his partner turn to leave. "All right, then. We'll need a sign-off from Mr. Benlolo, since he filed the original missing person report, but seeing as you're home, he can just drop by the station at his convenience, am I right?"

"Good luck with everything." Novogrodski tips his chin to us.

"You take care now, gentlemen."

Francesca shuts the door after them.

"Thank you," I say, "for not saying anything about, you know, everything."

"You're welcome."

"Mama?" Our heads—Francesca's and mine—swivel in unison toward the voice.

It's Aspen.

She's streaking down the stairs, bare legged and barefoot in a babydoll nightie, long sleek hair streaming behind her, radiating dewiness and adorableness.

"Mama, you're home?" She sprints to Francesca and stops just short of flinging herself into her mother's arms. "Oh my God, oh my God, what happened to you!" She recoils ever so slightly at the sight.

"I'm sorry, darling. I know you were worried."

"I have so many questions!"

"I'm home . . . I'm safe . . . but I'm feeling a little lightheaded. Can someone please cut up fruit and squeeze fresh orange juice? Where's Johanna?"

"Coming later this afternoon."

"I'll do it." On the quartz island, there's a bowl filled with oranges, grapefruits, pomegranates, and lemons, chosen, I suppose, because their colors complement the sparkling gold fixtures. I take a couple of gold-handled knives from the wood block and look for a cutting board as Francesca wilts onto a stool. Aspen peppers her with questions. Where was she? Why didn't she call? What happened to her face? Francesca says she was stressed and needed a getaway because she felt ill. She says her eyebrows fell out "as a result of medication" and "it's just temporary" and "there's nothing to worry about." She improvised so adroitly with the detectives, and now she's doing it again. I'm impressed at her cleverness, considering she didn't have much of a chance to put any thought into this reunion. As far as I know.

"Well, I'm just so relieved you're home, Mama," Aspen says.

My hand is getting tired as I cut navel oranges into quarters and squeeze their juice into a cup. I pass Aspen a knife so she can help. She's slicing into a pomegranate just as the sliding glass door to the pool opens.

"Francesca?" Our heads—Francesca's, Aspen's, and mine—swivel in unison toward the voice.

It's Tabi Benlolo.

He's standing there in a pair of shorts, kicking sand from his sneakers, with a towel draped over his bare bronzed shoulders. His appearance is one of a Greek god, or perhaps a Brazilian one, all chiseled lines and rippling angles. He's obviously back from an early-morning run on the beach.

"Tabi," Francesca exclaims softly. She's rooted to her seat, with an eye toward me, but it looks like it's all she can do to keep from flinging herself at him.

He pulls the earbuds from his ears as he crosses the floor in a single stride, and before any of us has time to blink, he lifts Francesca into his arms.

Between you and me, Francesca doesn't look so great. She's waxy and pasty from being in the airless cottage so long, she's bloated from too much sugar and fat, and her unexpected eyebrow removal has transformed her into something of an alien.

Which makes this reunion all the more poignant. I am melting into the floor with a lump in my throat the size of a navel orange as I witness Tabi's reaction to Francesca's homecoming. Are those actual tears streaming down his cheeks?

Francesca and Tabi don't look like a couple sharing a torrid affair. They look like a couple in love.

Beside me, I hear Aspen clear her throat. I glance sidelong at her as she stands motionless, caught in the act of slicing through a pomegranate. She is staring at her husband and mother in an embrace just inches away. "Tabi?" she whispers.

Tabi sets Francesca back on her feet, pulls the towel off her head, and frantically covers her, her face, her wet hair, her hands, with kisses.

"Tabi?" Louder now, but there is a small quiver to Aspen's voice.

Tabi presses his forehead to Francesca's and says "I was so worried" and "your text broke my heart" and other things we cannot quite decipher. Between murmurs he cradles and rocks her.

"Tabi, what are you saying?" Now the quiver is gone, ice creeping into its place.

Tabi ignores her. "I love you so much," he says to the woman in his arms. He crushes her against his chest. "You're the only woman I've ever loved. I can't live without you."

Francesca gasps. Aspen gasps. I gasp.

Not in front of Aspen, I think, but I'm not sure if I say it out loud.

Aspen stamps her foot. "Tabi, I'm talking to you!" she yells at the top of her lungs.

And then it happens fast, so fast, in the time it takes me to blink:

"WHAT?!" Tabi roars in exasperation. Incensed, he spins around to face Aspen with his arm raised, just like that other time . . .

Not realizing his wife is standing directly behind him . . .

The next thing I know, the gap between them is closed . . .

And the long, sharp blade of the knife Aspen is clutching has sunk up to the hilt, right between those sculpted bronze pecs.

Aspen gasps. Francesca gasps. I gasp.

And Tabi Benlolo gasps and buckles to his knees, and blood that looks just like pomegranate juice burbles from his beautiful mouth.

CHAPTER FIFTY-TWO

Francesca, Aspen, and I are too shocked to move. We stand frozen over Tabi's lifeless form, mesmerized by the widening pool of blood seeping outward on the floor like a macabre Rorschach inkblot. I think someone screams. It's several seconds before one of us speaks, I can't be sure who.

"Oh God."

"Should we call an ambulance?"

"I think it may be too late for that."

Francesca crumples, and a few seconds later Aspen crumples, and before I know it, the two of them have fallen to their knees and are sobbing their hearts out over Tabi's body.

I think back to the fight between him and Aspen the night of the party. When he angrily said, "This isn't the way I thought it would be" and "there are constantly people around" and "we never have privacy," he didn't mean privacy for him and Aspen. He meant for him and *Francesca*.

And how about his heated response to the photographer? Maybe he was protecting her.

I think even further back, back to that FaceTime call with Francesca in California, when I overheard Tabi say "this has to end." At the time I thought he meant his relationship with Francesca had to end. But maybe he meant the pretense, the facade, that he was in love with anyone *other than* Francesca?

And then the magnitude of it all hits me, and I have trouble breathing. My lungs don't seem to be inflating. I rock back on my heels and sink down the wall to the floor beside them.

It could be a minute or an hour later, I have no idea. Aspen draws shaky breaths and wipes her tears. Her eyes are huge and terrified.

"Will I go to jail?"

Yes, I think.

"No," Francesca says.

There's another silence that seems to stretch into eternity, and then Aspen turns to me. She touches my shoulder softly, the way she did when we were walking and talking together, in that familiar friendly gesture. "He was attacking me. You saw that, right, Summer?"

"What?"

"You saw him come at me, didn't you?" she says. "He was going to punch me, and then Mama pushed him, thinking she could move him away from me and keep me safe, but instead he fell on the knife. Isn't that so?"

Suddenly I'm bewildered. Is that what happened?

Aspen shifts her grief-stricken gaze to her mother. "You tried to protect me, Mama, so I forgive you. I forgive you for killing my husband. I won't tell anyone about your affair with him because in the end, you did everything you could to save me, didn't you?"

Aspen's voice is barely audible as she searches her mother's face for confirmation. "You saved my life. It's just like you always say, 'There's nothing a mother won't do for her daughter.' Isn't that so, Mama?"

Francesca lowers her face into her hands and starts to weep.

"I'm so confused," I say, trying to sort it out, trying to discern in my mind the reality of what I did or didn't see. Aspen's words twist around in my skull this way and that, a Rubik's Cube of interpretations. Did Francesca push Tabi out of the way so he couldn't hurt his wife?

Or . . . my God . . . did Francesca *deliberately* push him into the knife to his death?

But as I sit there, shaking my head, my thoughts arrange themselves into uniform grids. "That's not . . . no . . . I was right beside you, I was *right there*, and I saw you . . . I *saw* you stab him, Aspen."

Aspen's face darkens. "No," she says, rising to her feet. "No, that's not at all what you saw, Summer."

I stagger up to standing also. "I didn't see Francesca move. Not even an inch. When Tabi turned around, I saw you reach out with the knife and stab him—"

"NO!" Aspen screams, reaching her arms toward me, and just as I feel the shocking sensation of her fingers brushing the skin of my throat, at first gently but then gripping so tight I can't breathe, Francesca springs up between us to shield me with her body. She grabs hold of Aspen's shoulders and gives her a firm shake.

"Stop! Aspen, stop, I'll handle this. You are going to go upstairs right now and wash the blood off your hands and put on clean clothes. Then you are going to get in your car and drive away. And I will clean up this mess. I'll clean up your mess, like always."

Aspen's fingers fall away as her face transitions from stone hardened back to humanoid form. And then she turns and bolts up the stairs. I suck in air as I watch her run past the tribute wall, hair streaming behind her, until she disappears from view.

I grow cold, then hot, then cold again.

Understanding blooms in my consciousness from dreary shades of Kansas gray into vibrant Technicolor Oz. I teeter farther into the living room so I have a better view of the landing upstairs. I don't know why it took me so long to realize: the photographs. All those photographs up there, lining the upstairs hallway like a museum. So many candid shots from the years of *Practice Makes Perfect* on display, of Denise Dunne and the rest of the cast and all the studio execs. Them and Francesca Barber. Chatting together, dining together, hugging each other. All of them together, the best of friends.

How could it be? In the story of Aspen's childhood, her evil mother—the conniving, jealous, overbearing Francesca—was despised by one and all, Aspen said. She was the real reason they cut the role of Sadie, Aspen suggested, as opposed to what the press reported about her aging out of her role. But the pictures told a different story, of camaraderie and genuine affection. And pictures don't lie.

Which could only mean one thing: Aspen lied.

I'm such a fool.

—

"I thought we were . . . I thought she cared about me. I thought Aspen needed my help, wanted me to be there for her. As a mother, as a friend. But why?" I ask Francesca. "Why would a loving girl like her lie like that?"

"She's good, isn't she?"

At first I don't understand what she means. And then it hits me: Aspen is an *actress*. The sweet, affectionate daughter I came to know, the smitten newlywed the *world* came to know, was just her portrayal of a character. "She lied to me about her childhood, didn't she?" I say. "She made *you* out to be the villain."

I see it now. She reversed the roles in the story. It was *Aspen* who schemed, *Aspen* whom people detested. Maybe for Francesca, living with *Aspen* was hell.

With that insight comes a cascade of new realizations: Were the difficulties managing her daughter the reason Francesca needed sedatives in the first place? Is that why she was eager to leave the beach house but worried about Aspen's reaction if she stayed away? Was that why it was her son-in-law, not her own daughter, who filed a police report when she went missing?

Now I am a firsthand witness to what Aspen is capable of: deception. Rage. Violence. Maybe Francesca tried so hard to keep her relationship with Tabi Benlolo a secret not because she feared hurting Aspen, but simply because she feared what Aspen might do if she found out.

"The story Aspen told me was a fantasy, wasn't it?" I say slowly.

"You aren't the first person she's told it to."

"Taking her to be waxed when she was little, the medi-pedi, leaving her in the hotel room on vacation, ruining her birthday party?"

"None of that happened."

"You didn't call her La-La?"

"Please."

"And the photos? The stalker . . . the man from Nevada?"

"Modeling for those photos was her idea. I was horrified when I caught on, but by then she'd sold hundreds online. There was a stalker, Simeon Dale Stanton from Carson City, Nevada, and he did show up at our house one night. He tried to strangle me when I blocked him from going up to Aspen's room."

I shake my head, overcome by the truth of the narrative. "But why would she tell me that story?"

"Don't you see, Summer?" Francesca is incredulous at my naivete. "She wanted to bring me down, and she needed an ally. That's what prompted her to invite you to the party here . . . she must've had a gut feeling she could manipulate you. And I saw it all happening, how fond you were becoming of her, and I tried to warn you on the phone, but in the end I let it play out because I needed you to keep your word about not going to the press with the story of me and Tabi. I knew you wouldn't want to hurt Aspen by going public.

"It all worked out so damn well for her, didn't it?" Francesca continues. "You had no idea, absolutely no idea, how she played you that party weekend. She wanted to cultivate your sympathy. She strung you along by making you think she was some abused little girl. It was so easy for her to paint the story of her childhood the way she'd been rehearsing in front of the mirror for years."

"Are you saying none of it was real?"

"'Medi-pedi' is a little too cutesy to be real."

"So . . ." My brain is furiously working to realign everything I'd thought to be true. "You weren't jealous of her . . ."

"Me, jealous? That couldn't have been further from the truth . . . nothing made me happier than her success. Isn't that all we mothers want for our children? I worked my fingers to the bone to support us, get us to Hollywood so she could be a star. I believed in her all those years after *Practice Makes Perfect*, when she couldn't get work. I even figured out a way to get her *back* into the limelight by writing a role just for her, even if I did resort to cheating."

"You did everything you could to support her, and despite it all, she's . . . she's horrible."

"No! No, you're wrong, Summer. Aspen acts this way because she doesn't know what's good for her. It's all my fault. I never should've pushed my dreams of stardom onto her. I never should've taken her to California and gotten her involved in Hollywood. That lifestyle, of being a child star, it destroys kids. I tried my best to protect her, because it was all my fault she needed protecting in the first place."

"I don't understand. Then, why? Why would she be so spiteful toward you?"

"Because the one thing she really, really wants is the one thing I refuse to do."

"Which is?"

"Well, of course she wouldn't have mentioned this part." Francesca laughs mirthlessly. "She wants me to release her trust fund. Under the original terms she was supposed to access it when she turned eighteen. But even as a teenager she was so selfish, so vindictive, so impulsive, I couldn't in good conscience let her near that much money. I had the studio lawyers change the terms to age thirty-five. She's been threatening and demanding I give in and allow her to access the money, but that's the thing I won't budge on. For that, she'll never forgive me."

I look around the kitchen, everything top of the line and beautiful, save the body bleeding out on the gorgeous imported Italian marble floor. "Why does she need her trust? You're not exactly roughing it out here."

"Because it's there." Francesca shrugs. "Because she does. Because nothing is ever enough."

"And yet despite her vindictiveness, you are willing to clean up her mess, as you said. Like you always do, you said."

"I'm her mom. Nothing changes that."

We stare at each other. I'm making a concerted effort to keep from seeing Tabi's blood on the floor in my peripheral vision. "Aspen knew about you and Tabi all along, didn't she? Whose idea was it for them to get married when he was so clearly in love with you?"

"Mine." Francesca smiles softly. Tears roll down her face and drip onto her collarbone. "The #AspenAndTabiWedding went completely viral, and there was an avalanche of media coverage. It was good for both of them, for their careers."

"But it wasn't good for *you*."

"Sometimes we women sacrifice it all for those we love, don't we?"

I'm frozen to the spot. I allow my eyes to wander toward the floor but focus only on the edge of Tabi Benlolo's lifeless hand. "So you loved him, too. You never hated him, never wanted him gone. You didn't deliberately push him. Are you going to take the blame for an actual murder? You didn't even touch him."

"You can't prove I didn't."

There's a long silence. Then Francesca takes a deep breath to steady herself and, to my shock, reaches over to pull the knife from Tabi's dead flesh. I want to avert my eyes, but I can't. The blade comes out wet and red, with what I think are either pomegranate seeds or bits of tissue stuck to it. She drops it in the sink.

I'm sent stumbling to the bathroom near the front entrance to bend over and retch into the Bluetooth-connected, self-cleaning, self-flushing masterpiece of a modern toilet, surrounded by pretty wainscoting and tasteful wallpaper. Just as I am splashing cold water on my face, I hear footsteps and Aspen's and Francesca's voices and then the front door slamming shut. The sudden crack of sound jars me into action, and I return to the kitchen, my eyes glued to the gore Francesca is now sopping up with Tabi's towel.

"The police," I stammer. I close my eyes. It's all I can do not to buckle at the sight. "We have to call the police."

"Summer." Francesca's voice is suddenly hard.

My eyelids open, but the rest of me seems paralyzed.

"We are not calling the police. No one is to know about this. You are not telling anyone about Aspen."

"You can't keep this a secret!"

"It seems to me," she says coldly, rising toward me menacingly, "you have many secrets of your own, haven't you? You've been hiding a *lot*. And you are every bit as involved in this situation as we are."

My mouth falls open.

Francesca's eyes narrow into slits. "Do you really want your daughter to discover what you've been up to? You're a blackmailer and a kidnapper. And you're a witness to Tabi's death. I'd be happy to tell her—Beatrice, isn't it?—all about it. Don't think I'd hesitate for a moment! Thing is, it might be hard for Bea to get through life—let alone grad school—with that kind of baggage. Knowing all the terrible things her mother has done. Knowing what kind of person she is.

"Or," Francesca says, her voice softening, "I can finish your book like we agreed, and you'll get your bestseller on time for Mila's deadline . . . and your daughter will be so proud. Think how proud she'll be, Summer."

I'm rooted to the spot.

"Are we in agreement?"

Not again . . . I don't want to be back there, I think blankly. That's how all this started. I want to protest and say it aloud, but I'm spent. Nothing more comes out of my mouth.

Instead, I back up, and back up, until I'm halfway to the front door, and then I'm outside, tossing Francesca's carry-on from my trunk so I can peel away.

It was one thing to dream of writing a great manuscript, signing a book deal, and becoming a published author. It was one thing to take advantage of an opportunity, to make a pact with a celebrity, even to resort to blackmail, when no one would be the wiser and both of us would benefit. Faking a kidnapping was just part of the plot to make it all happen, and it was a harmless part, a joke even, certainly not a *crime*. Sure, I wanted something at any cost: a bestseller. And I wanted to protect my daughter from repeating the same mistake that thwarted my success. To make sure that someway, somehow, Beatrice would be so inspired she'd never give up on *her* dreams. No one was supposed to get hurt.

But now someone did get hurt.

An innocent man is dead. Aspen killed him. She killed her own husband. The girl I felt so protective about, so affectionate toward, so responsible for. The girl I thought of as a second daughter is not who I thought she was.

She's a *murderer*.

CHAPTER FIFTY-THREE

As I leave Sagaponack, my thoughts are going a million miles an hour. Starting with: What in the actual fuck just happened? Someone died in front of me—and that someone is a major Hollywood celebrity, whose wife killed him, whose family the police are already investigating, whose mother-in-law I drugged and practically held captive at a property I am selling, and whom everyone on the Eastern Seaboard will probably be looking for within twenty-four hours.

Images of Francesca's wrecked face haunt me as I drive, but my mind veers to darker ground.

I can't imagine how she is planning to dispose of the body. My thoughts spin out of control, and in my head I tick off authorly disposal methods. The most obvious way is to bury it, and Francesca certainly has lots of space on her property, but it would be very strenuous for her to dig six feet down in solid ground, alone. Not to mention she'd have to avoid drawing the attention of her nearest neighbors, the Birdseed King of the East and his wife. What choice does she have? Launch it into space? Disperse it in a woodchipper? Of course, there's always Davy Jones's locker.

Or she could dissolve it in hydrofluoric acid à la *Breaking Bad*, but where would she get hydrofluoric acid? It's not like the chichi organic Sagaponack market stocks it, and she sure as shit won't be doing a Google search: "Where to buy acid to dissolve a body near me." Francesca does have a fireplace, so theoretically she could throw it in, but everyone knows human bodies don't burn all that well, being made up of mostly water; they leave behind a charred husk that's easily identifiable as, in fact, a human body. And even in an incinerator at one thousand degrees, there are chunks of bone left behind that need to be ground up, and the teeth, which seem to withstand every possible assault (except from Coca-Cola, if I remember correctly from Bea's seventh-grade science fair). I wonder whether there's a pig farm nearby.

Cut it out, I tell myself. Concentrate on driving. In the cup holder at my elbow, my phone beeps with a notification, but I wait for a red light before picking it up. When I touch my home screen, the text notifications and missed calls load fast and furious. They're all from Bob the Broker.

Victor Thane has advised the pharmaceutical company to move ahead with the Back Bay property. An offer needs to be typed up. Why aren't I at the office?

I can't believe this. On top of everything else, I have to worry about my day job? Now?

I dial Bob's cell with shaky fingers. "I'm so sorry," I tell him when he answers. "Something urgent came up, and it'll be a few hours before I can get there."

"Marcy," he shouts, "this is not the time to drop the ball! This could be the biggest deal you've had all year, and I *need you on your game*."

"Bob, it's an emergency." Which it certainly is.

On the other end of the line, there is a long, low growl and some huffing . . . the distinctive sounds of Bob the Broker getting ready to blow. "If you don't finalize this deal, you'll regret—" he shouts at the top of his lungs. But instead of finishing the sentence at full power, his voice dwindles down to a series of little bleats. There's a crash and muffled exclamations in the background.

"Bob? Bob, hello?" He doesn't respond. I dial the office landline. Our receptionist picks up, distraught. "It's Bob! We think he's having a heart attack. We're calling 911 now."

Good grief, did I just give Bob a coronary? How can this be happening? I ask the receptionist to call Victor Thane and let him know that Bob has collapsed and I will meet with him as soon as I'm able. I beg her to keep me posted on Bob's condition.

As the miles pass, I keep an eye out the passenger side for the low brick building I've noticed on my trips back and forth to Sagaponack. It's the regional police station. I imagine Detectives Waite and Novogrodski inside, eating doughnuts while filing away the notes on Francesca Barber's disappearance, unaware that shortly they will be investigating a new missing person case.

I wonder how long and how many chocolate frosteds it will be before they realize that Tabi Benlolo is not only missing . . . he's dead.

How did he die? Was it homicide or manslaughter or random bad luck? And what will it all mean for Aspen, Francesca, and me? I need to figure it out, to talk to someone, to confess what I know.

And I will confess, I promise I will. I'll do the right thing. Let me just deal with Bob the Broker first. One crisis at a time.

I'm pulling up to the hospital's emergency entrance as "Bohemian Rhapsody" starts to play, and Mama, you know *that* verse. I snap it off and park.

My colleagues and support staff from Robert Verney Realty are gathered in the waiting room of the emergency department. Through the glass I can see Candace, flanked by the prepubescent in horn-rimmed glasses and the gangly young man in a bow tie. When the double doors slide open and I rush in, Candace jumps up to embrace me.

"I came as fast as I could. How is he?"

"It's serious. The family is in with the doctors now. But Bob is a real fighter. Like I told him as they were putting him into the ambulance, it's important to keep in mind what Theodore Roosevelt said: 'When you're at the end of your rope—'"

"I get it." My attention is diverted to a group of people entering the waiting room, accompanied by white-coated physicians. The family members. They're not crying, which seems to me a good sign. I beg Candace to let me know if there's any news whatsoever, and then I'm gone again.

Our office is deserted with everyone at the hospital, but Bob would want me to close this sale. I start work on the offer.

Victor Thane arrives later, and it's emotional with Bob in the hospital, but I try to be stoic and professional. The offer is ready for him to sign. Once he does, I will present it to Garcia and then Gil Carter, who will sign on behalf of his LLC. It's almost a done deal.

Victor signs.

With several back-and-forths, the offer ends up taking until late at night to finalize. Both Garcia and Gil Carter sign. Now, at last, it's wrapped up: one of the biggest deals I've ever closed. I can't wait to tell Bob; he'll be elated. *This one's for you,* I tell him silently.

I go home to a dark and silent house. Briefly I consider texting Liisa or Mike to see whether they want to go out for dinner to celebrate the sale, but, of course, I don't. It would be inappropriate to celebrate anything with Bob in the hospital. I debate going back there to check on him; however, I know visiting hours are long over, and anyway, I'm physically and emotionally depleted. I turn in early. But even though the day was intense—not to mention incredibly terrifying and taxing—and I've been functioning on a sleep deficit, sleep is slow to come that night, what with everything crowding my head.

I've just dozed off when my phone rings. Bob the Broker has passed away.

A day later, there's news.

> **New York, NY. (Reuters)**—In a peculiar twist in the case of Francesca Barber, who went missing and who some assumed had been kidnapped, the California native and author of the bestselling science fiction series "Journey to Jupiter," "Jovan of Jupiter," and "Jupiter in Jeopardy" has reportedly returned home. Barber's family filed a missing person report after they lost all contact with the woman for several days.
>
> Now a strange development has added to the drama: Barber's son-in-law, Brazilian actor Tabi Benlolo, has disappeared, sources revealed.
>
> Earlier today the family filed another missing person report: this time by Aspen Barber for her husband. The two star together in the film adaptations of the Jupiter books.
>
> Once again, authorities are investigating a suspicious disappearance within the tight-knit family amid speculation that a second missing person case cannot be coincidental.
>
> In a statement, Police Chief Mark Minzer said, "The community is relieved to welcome home Francesca safe and sound, but the subsequent disappearance of her son-in-law is cause for concern."
>
> From her summer home in Sagaponack, NY, Francesca Barber is declining to account publicly for her unexplained departure, prolonged absence, and sudden return.

You know what they say about truth being stranger than science fiction.

CHAPTER FIFTY-FOUR

The funeral of Robert Verney is a somber affair. I can't say I'm particularly surprised to be here, since I've observed Bob's excessive tension for years. The service is long and tedious with lots of formal prayers and psalms that drone on and fail to distract me from the spiraling thoughts that have occupied the entirety of my brain for the last forty-eight hours: Do the police suspect anything? Where is Aspen? What has Francesca done with the man I knew as her son-in-law and lover, who fans knew as Jovan of Jupiter, whose corpse may or may not still be somewhere in the Hamptons?

Bea is sitting beside me on one side, and Kevin, who knew Bob for years, is sitting beside me on the other, and James beside him. It's odd to have them all here. It feels like ages since I've been with my family, and I guess I should be grateful they showed up; but I feel oddly distant, what with all I've been keeping from them and how secretive I've been. At least no one asks about the progress of my manuscript, which is nil; if I could just get through these two calamities—that is, Bob's passing and the situation with Tabi Benlolo—maybe I could concentrate on my book.

My phone vibrates. The ringer is off, but I tap it on the pew next to me and discreetly read a new message. It's from Francesca.

She says she's been trying to call. She updates me in a text: When Tabi didn't show up on set, the studio heads started calling. Aspen reminded them she wasn't scheduled to film this week, and said she'd assumed Tabi left the Hamptons for the city after his usual early-morning jog.

By late afternoon, when no one had heard from him, Aspen began to panic. Maybe it was the stress of her mother's health concerns, but her imagination was getting the best of her. At least that's what she told police when she filed the missing person report.

I just wanted to remind you of our deal. Where are you? Francesca types at the end.

At a funeral, I respond.

And maybe it's seeing those words in print, or the fact that Bob's two young stepsons are now tearfully climbing up to the pulpit to eulogize the only father they've ever known, but for the first time in days I stop thinking about Francesca and Tabi and Aspen and me and my book, and focus on the present moment, which is mourning the untimely death of a friend and colleague.

"He was big and loud and sometimes he got impatient," one of the boys reads from his phone. His voice is adolescent, hinting at a more masculine timbre to come, and thick with unshed tears. "But he was the best dad. He came to all my wrestling matches"—he jerks a thumb at his brother—"and his robotics competitions. Even when he was tired after work, he helped us with our homework. He packed us the best lunches, and in the summers he always let us plan our family vacation, wherever we wanted to go, even if it was, like, someplace he'd be bored. We were supposed to go to the Wrestling Hall of Fame in Albany next weekend, but now . . ." His face scrunches and he steps back. Pretty much everyone in the chapel, including me, has tears in their eyes.

His brother steps to the mic. "He said all the time how he won the lottery with us, how he couldn't have gotten luckier with his family. He said it wasn't because of our trophies or belts." His thin shoulders quake, and he covers his face with a bony hand and turns away, embarrassed, sobbing. It's all he can do to return to the mic and get his last sentences out with a broken voice. "He just said he was proud of the men we were growing up to be. I'm going to miss him so much."

It's like someone throws a bucket of ice water in my face, and I realize with a start, for the first time during this service, maybe the first time this summer, how I've lost sight of everything that means anything because my girl is here beside me and I only have her for a little while longer and I love her so much it hurts and it's never been about grad school or her becoming a chemist and it's not because she makes me feel needed or because I want her to be proud of something I've done so that I can feel validated and be proud of something I've done. Which is a good thing, because right now, I'm not proud of *anything* I've done.

My role in life, I realize belatedly, is not to make her proud of what I'm accomplishing, but to make her proud of who I am . . . and if that's the case, I've got some work to do.

All the ugliness of these last days and months churns around in my gullet until it rises up in a series of guttural sobs, which startles everyone in the pews around me but which they attribute to understandable grief for Bob. I can't meet Bea's questioning gaze or I'll crack, but instead I reach for her hand and weave my fingers through hers, and she doesn't pull away but in fact squeezes me back, and my throat aches and my tears are flowing and I'm swept back to that transcendent sweetness of picking her up out of her crib and kissing her warm feathery hair and feeling her fall asleep with the downy softness of her cheek on my shoulder. She didn't always fuss, I remember clearly now; there were so many nights and months of oneness before, somehow, she grew up without my permission. I'm desperately groping for the years that have escaped my grasp, and I just want to stay in this moment, this sacred, simple moment, connected to her, and her to me, forever. I don't ever want it to end. I don't want to lose her.

Gravity seems to have intensified its downward pull as I drag myself around the house under a heavy, crushing weight whose origin I can't really pinpoint and can't really define except to say that shame and fear and loss weigh heavily in the mix. Every time I pass Bea I reach out to hug her, to clutch her in my arms lest gravity has the opposite effect on her and she floats away, untethered.

After three or four of these encounters, Bea extracts herself from my orbit and escapes to say goodbye to her lab friends, and then my arms are empty once again.

In the quiet house, the sadness becomes an echoing, monotonous throb in my head. Thud. Thud. It began at the funeral, I realize, when the chapel service ended and I joined Bob's family and friends to gather graveside, where the heels of my black pumps sank into the soft soil as if to pull me out of the earthly life I'd created for myself.

I'd teared up behind my sunglasses as cemetery workers lowered the coffin containing Bob into the freshly dug ground, and a line of family and friends formed to deposit shovelfuls of loose dirt into the trench.

The sound of earth hitting the casket became a reprise of dull, painful thuds, each one an ending, each one more final than the last.

"Hey, stranger." Brian smiles behind his beard and leans his elbows on his polished bar. His tousled hair falls over his eyes.

I climb onto a barstool. For the first time since I started coming to O'Keefe's, I don't even register how adorable he is. "Hey."

"What can I get ya? Long Island, old-fashioned, or are you back to unsweetened iced tea again?"

"Anything you have that's super strong."

"Uh-oh. Trouble in writerland?" Grinning broadly, Brian takes a tumbler off a shelf and examines it for spots, adds a few ice cubes and some sprigs of mint. He pours bourbon and a splash of simple syrup, squeezes in a wedge of lime, muddles it, and slides it across to me.

I take a long sip and feel the burn in my throat. "You have no idea."

"I've got time." Brian looks around pointedly. It's Saturday afternoon, and I'm the only customer in the place, but it sure beats hanging around the empty house while Bea spends a last few hours with Kevin.

Brian sets out a bowl of mixed nuts, the expensive kind he reserves for his regulars. It occurs to me that he looks like an AI-generated image of a handsome bartender as he pulls a white towel from his apron and starts drying wineglasses. A character trope of a barkeep.

How I wish I could tell him everything, but of course I can't. A lump forms in my throat, and I try to force it down with another mouthful of alcohol; I find myself blurting, "My broker, Robert Verney, passed away suddenly, and the funeral was yesterday." It hadn't even occurred to me to mention Bob, and upon hearing the words spoken aloud, I start to cry. I grab for napkins to stanch the unexpected flow of tears.

"That's terrible, Marcy. My condolences."

"Thanks." I take a shaky breath. "Wow, sorry. That took me by surprise. But, you know, it's all the rest, too. Like you said, about the writing."

Brian waits quietly.

"It's just . . . it's just, I wanted so badly to do something worthwhile, something my daughter would admire. Something life-changing that could transform me from this"—I glance down at myself, meaning failed wife, unpublished author, uninspiring mother, mediocre Realtor, and all-around mundane *meh*—"to someone special. I was making progress! I visualized the whole thing! I was on the brink! But in the end I did the exact opposite. I transformed myself into someone I didn't even recognize, and not in a good way."

Brian nods and reaches for another wineglass. "I know you've had this dream for a while," he says slowly. "I guess you just have to be clear in your mind about the difference between dreams and goals."

Sullenly I swirl the ice around my drink. "I'm listening."

"Dreams are just wishes and thoughts in your head. Goals, you can achieve. They're step-by-step points on a plan of action. Like I've always wanted to own a bar, right? So I went to business school. Drew up a marketing plan. Borrowed money from my dad and uncles. Took out a line of credit from the bank. Bought this place."

"Then you've realized your dream."

He shrugs. "Not exactly. The *dream* is the chain of profitable bars that makes me a rich entrepreneur. With this place, I'm just treading water. I'm in debt up to my eyeballs."

I didn't know that.

"Don't get me wrong, I love it here. But I also understand that the *dream* may never happen, and that's okay, too. Doesn't mean I'm not worthy. Just means I have to create a different set of goals. It's all about achieving the goals and celebrating them along the way."

There's a long silence. The lump is back in my throat. "It's just really hard to think I failed again."

"You didn't fail, Marcy." Brian hangs the last of the stemware upside down on the track over his head. He takes out a tumbler and pours himself a splash of bourbon, clinks his glass against mine. "You can still achieve your dream. Just don't lose yourself in all this dreaming."

CHAPTER FIFTY-FIVE

Bea is leaving tonight. Her luggage is zipped and standing in the front hall, and in the garage she has left several boxes that I will ship down to Savannah. She's in her room, packing her backpack for the plane and doing a last rifle through her desk drawers when I knock. I'm holding a present: two of my mother's long-stemmed crystal flutes packed in Bubble Wrap. I already gave her a bottle of champagne to squeeze into her suitcase. I thought she and Patrick could pop it open later tonight to christen their new place, their new life.

"Can we talk?"

"Whassup."

I sit on the edge of her bed and look around. Her room is barren without her binders and myriad stacks of papers and chemistry books. Only a few framed photos remain: Kevin, Bea, and me at an agricultural fair; Kevin and Bea decorating a snowman; Bea learning to skate; Bea building a sandcastle. She's even made her bed, with her bedspread no less, and the finality of it is unmistakable.

"Can I help with anything?"

"It's all good."

"Did you remember to bring the extra towels and bedding from school?"

"Yup. I went through all my dorm stuff. I finished organizing the basement last week."

She did? I haven't been down there in months. "Thank you, Honey Bea." I stare down at the gift bag in my lap. "I just want to say I'm sorry I haven't been around these last few weeks, what with . . . with my writing retreat."

The weight I've been feeling becomes inexplicably heavier, and at the exact same moment Beatrice is telling me not to worry about it, I find myself blurting, "That's a lie."

She looks up. "What?"

"I lied just now." I press my lips together as if that would keep another lie from emerging. "I wasn't on a writing retreat. I was with Francesca Barber."

"Your mentor? That's great." She frowns. "So why do you have that look on your face?"

"She was never my mentor. I lied about that, too. Oh, Bea, I'm sorry, I don't know what happened to me, but I've done terrible things this summer, really terrible."

Bea does that half laugh like she's not sure it's funny. "What are you talking about?"

How far back do I go? To what transpired just the other day in the Hamptons, or before that in Back Bay, or the weekend of the party in July, or the screening in New York City? How about when Francesca first started critiquing my manuscript and the idea of blackmail sprang to mind? Or all the way back to when my writing group decided to go to Hartford?

Do I have to go back even further to explain how it is I ended up at this stage of my pathetic life, so desperate to have something to show for myself?

In the end I reiterate what I said to her the night she announced she was moving in with her boyfriend. "When Dad and I first got married, my dream took a back seat to his, and I was afraid you'd make the same mistake with Patrick." And that becomes my starting point for telling her the whole sordid tale, in dribs and drabs, all the events that happened since she came home from college three months ago.

Bea's expression, as I recount the tale, alternates between disbelief and dismay. Rarely before has she ever paid such close attention to anything I've said, and it hurts to think that now, when she finally does, it's with such disgust. She clambers up to the bed to listen cross-legged, her desk and backpack abandoned.

I'm up to the part where I smuggled Francesca home from Back Bay. It's excruciating to say aloud. My voice wavers. Just thinking about the scene, the aftermath, all the blood, has me so shocked, still, that it's hard to convey plain facts. "In my mind it wasn't so bad, everything that had happened until then," I stutter. "In a way none of it felt real, because it wasn't really *me* doing any of it." I try to preface the next part, but I know my words fall short. "I never thought it would lead to . . . violence."

"*Violence?* Mom, what happened? What did you do?"

"I didn't . . . it wasn't . . ."

I start shaking so hard, I'm on the verge of dropping the bag holding the champagne flutes. Bea takes it from my lap impatiently. "Just say it," she demands.

"Tabi was so very relieved and elated to see Francesca when he came in, but it made Aspen angry. Really, really angry. And she . . . she was holding a . . . a . . . knife . . ."

"Oh my God." Bea claps her hands to her mouth in horror. "You're not saying what I think you're saying? She stabbed him? Did he die? *Mom!* Did he? Is he dead?"

I'm crying too hard to answer.

"What happened? Did the police come? Was Aspen arrested? What did they say to you? Do you have to testify at her trial or something?"

I reach for tissues at her bedside and blow my nose. "No," I tell her. "No one came."

"Why? Why *not*?"

"When I wanted to call the police, Francesca forbade it. She threatened me. She said if I did, she would . . . tell you everything. I wanted to protect you. I knew that if you found out how awful I really am, all the bad things I've done, you'd hate me. Beatrice, I was so scared of . . . this. Exactly this."

Bea jumps off the bed. "Mom, this is crazy. This isn't you. You would've freaked out if I kept a secret like this for someone! And it doesn't matter what *I* think. You have to tell. You have to go to the authorities. Like right now! You have to tell them what Aspen Barber did and how her mother tried to cover it all up!"

"I know I do." It's just that I've been paralyzed, I want to tell her.

"I'll come with you. I'm canceling my flight."

"Absolutely not. You're going to Savannah."

"Mom. How can I leave you here to deal with all this alone?"

I laugh through a fresh set of tears. "I'm the grown-up here, kiddo, even if I haven't been acting like one lately. I'll be fine. And if there's one thing I know from my friend Mike, police investigations take time. Nothing will happen today, or even tomorrow. Not for a long while. I will keep you updated on everything. And if for any reason you have to come home, I'll let you know."

"You have to promise me you're going to tell me every single thing they say to you."

"I'll call you after I file a report." I swallow. It sounds very official, and scary.

She nods. And then she pauses, choosing her words, and speaks again. "You know, that thing you keep saying about Dad, it's not true. It's not like he ever asked you to be a real estate agent. You didn't make a mistake. You made a choice."

Bea and I stare at each other for a long minute. After a while I drop my eyes. And then I feel a soft touch on my shoulder, a lot like the ones from Aspen.

"Mom. I don't hate you."

It's okay if you do, I think to myself, and I go downstairs to find the little card with the phone number left by the detectives. I deserve it.

That night, after Bea departs, I dream about Lady Lisbeth. She is on horseback, galloping down a path cut through a mossy forest, wearing a billowing white dress and cinched bodice with her fiery red hair flying unpinned. Someone is chasing her, and she keeps looking back over her shoulder, fearful. Faster and faster she rides; when she comes upon a fallen log, her horse rears up and bucks her off. Lisbeth goes tumbling down a steep embankment, leaves and twigs embedded in her hair, until at last she slips over the crest of a cliff, a crest just like the one in Back Bay. As she plummets downward, the red hair turns to beige, the white dress to black, and it is me falling through the air toward a dark, deep pit, falling, falling.

It's dawn and my eyes pop open like champagne corks. It doesn't take a genius to figure out the symbolism of the dream. But it gets me thinking again about Lady Lisbeth, how her story has just dropped off precipitously and disappeared into an abyss. So much went into the making of this manuscript. I don't want to lay her to rest forever.

Draping myself in my quilt, I sit down at my computer and start typing. The chapters flow through me; I am an emptied vessel that the cosmos now fills with words, which I in turn pour onto page after page.

All the despair and regret I am feeling about my actions become Sir Devon's despair and regret for not being true to himself. My guilt and self-loathing belong to Devon's embittered mother. Sorrow over Bob's passing turns into a poignant scene where the elderly chambermaid dies with one last witty remark on her lips. I channel the horror of Tabi Benlolo's death into a savage swordfight and the gruesome murder of the warlord, which was all predicted by the handsome, wise, bearded soothsayer in his early vision of the future. My heartbreak over Bea's moving is mirrored in Lady Lisbeth's when she realizes she must leave her beloved Sir Devon to do the courageous thing: lead her kingdom.

My writing has never been so authentic and raw. And the startling part of it is that I accomplish it by myself. My historical romance is finally complete. There is deceit and retribution, greed and cunning, and, finally, redemption.

When I type the words *THE END* and close the document, it feels like a beginning.

CHAPTER FIFTY-SIX

Once again I'm wide eyed as I enter the skyscraper off Avenue of the Americas and confront the opulence of the lobby, with its fat pillars and antique chandeliers reflected on glistening floors. I'm a few minutes early. I allow myself a beat to swoon at the crown molding before stepping into an elevator that deposits me at the Jorgenson Agency.

This time the receptionist (the one who looks as if she should be studying for a midterm) doesn't even give me a chance to sit down before escorting me to Mila's office. As I follow her, other agents smile at me over their monitors and from their slush piles.

Mila jumps up from her swivel chair and strides over to me in greeting. Her close-cropped brown hair and Coke-bottle glasses are unchanged, but this time her coppery lips are stretched into an enormous smile. It's quite a different demeanor from last time.

"Thank you for coming, Summer," she exclaims. "Sit, sit. So, I reread *A Knight to Remember*, and I loved it. Loved it! If anything your voice is even stronger in the second half of the book than the first. There's an intensity to those last few chapters, a ferocity that is just gripping, evocative. And the way you end it, leaving it open to interpretation . . . and perhaps a sequel . . . is simply inspired. Perhaps *A Knight to Recall*? Just a thought." She splays her fingers in jazz hands.

I'm agog.

"Now, you were a day late with handing in your manuscript," she chides playfully, clucking her tongue, "and I need my authors to respect deadlines. But this was worth waiting for."

I still haven't spoken a word. I'm not sure I can.

"In any case," she continues, "I have plans for this story. I would suggest we explore film rights immediately. Getting it optioned now would mean a tremendous bump in sales at launch. In fact, I can picture the leads playing Sir Devon and Lady Lisbeth. I'd like to announce that soonest."

Can this be happening?

"But back to the book. Here's where we stand. Ned Townsend expressed early interest with a perfectly respectable offer. But after receiving your completed manuscript, I thought it would be wise to cast a broader net. Three additional solid offers, all of them from leading houses, have come in in the past twenty-four hours." Mila reaches for some documents and spreads them out facing me on the desk. I am utterly, utterly floored when I read the names of the publishing houses on the letterhead. Am I dreaming?

"Of course, I will go over all of them with you. They all have their strong points. But I suggest we circle back to Temple-Townsend and give Ned a chance to rethink his original bid, both in terms of advance and royalties. Do you agree?"

I can only nod.

"Good. Remind me to send Francesca some flowers to thank her for sending you my way." Mila smiles. "Let's get that book cover of yours up on our wall, shall we?"

Liisa licks mochaccino foam off her upper lip as she scrolls through Facebook and stops on my latest post. "Here it is," she breathes. Her expression as she studies the red, white, and blue announcement of my book deal is as rapt as mine. When she finishes reading, she sits back and exhales contentedly, as if she's just eaten a grand meal. "I can just picture the cover: a woman descending the stairs of a turret, red hair blowing behind her. It's flowery and feminine, yet Lady Lisbeth will look fierce with her torn leather vest and spear."

"Thank you. I'm in love with the idea of Lisbeth becoming a warrior in the end." The genesis of which came from Francesca, if I recollect: She suggested the whole female empowerment theme. How ironic.

"You've gotten over five hundred likes and tens of shares."

I grin at my phone. "I pinch myself every morning."

Liisa sighs. "You are one hundred percent living the dream," she says. Do I detect the slightest hint of envy? I can't blame her.

"What's going on with your spy thriller?" I ask.

"I wrote another page."

"Excellent, Liisa! Keep it going!" My eyes shift back to my screen, reading the newest comments as they post in real time.

"I guess you're getting an advance soon?"

I can't help myself, I'm so excited. "Yes! Enough to help Bea and Patrick with rent and things."

Liisa sighs again. She takes a big bite of her blueberry cheesecake and licks her lips with a purple tongue. "It's unbelievable. You actually did it. Before you know it, you'll have a movie deal, I bet, now that you're signed with Francesca's agent and publisher. It feels like just yesterday we met her on the *Jupiter in Jeopardy* book tour. And look where *that* got you!"

Talk about bursting my bubble. I squirm uncomfortably in my chair; I'm trying *not* to look where that got me.

Abruptly Liisa rises from the table. "I'm having another slice of cheesecake," she says. "Need anything?"

She doesn't wait for an answer.

Two things happen almost simultaneously. The first thing is that I have just gotten home when I see the news drop.

> **New York, NY. (Reuters)**—An arrest has been made in the disappearance and subsequent death of Brazilian national Tabi Benlolo.
>
> Family members became concerned when Benlolo, a popular Hollywood actor, failed to return from an early-morning jog near his family's oceanside estate in Sagaponack, Long Island, NY, nor did he show up for filming on set as scheduled.
>
> Benlolo's wife and costar in the Jupiter movies, Aspen Barber, filed a missing person report the next day.
>
> In a startling turn of events, police took Francesca Barber, Benlolo's mother-in-law, into custody for questioning and later placed her under arrest after she confessed to a number of charges relating to the case.
>
> Barber, the well-known science fiction author of "Journey to Jupiter," "Jovan of Jupiter," and "Jupiter in Jeopardy," was at the center of an earlier investigation after being reported missing by Benlolo.
>
> A second suspect, Marcy Jo Codburn, who uses the alias Summer Branigan, is being questioned as an accessory.
>
> Authorities have not yet released the cause of death and are still actively investigating.

The second thing is that my doorbell rings before I'm finished reading.

CHAPTER FIFTY-SEVEN

It feels as if it's taken forever to get here, but at long last I am in the Hamptons, standing in front of the guest room mirror, admiring myself as I sweep the bangs of my new hairdo across my forehead. I slip into a rose-colored dress in a swishy, silky fabric that picks up the exact color of the strawberry-blond streaks in my hair. Simple rose gold hoops and a matching choker, plus the ruby-studded bracelet Francesca loans me for the day, are the only accessories I need.

I don't look or feel much like I did at the outset of this journey, not back when I was stuffing Pepperidge Farm cake into my mouth, or chugging mochaccinos at Espresso Yourself, or morosely swigging a Long Island Iced Tea at Sam Stone's bar . . . which, really, is the night it all began.

Next week is the beginning of my book tour, and I'm hitting famous bookstores from coast to coast. Additionally, the Temple-Townsend PR department has scheduled me for appearances on national morning shows (*eek!*) and syndicated radio programs and podcasts.

The London Book Fair is coming up, and so is Buchmesse in Frankfurt. While in Europe I hope to stop in Tuscany to scout villas (not that I'm buying one right away, but soon!). It's more than I ever imagined.

Actually, it's not. It's *exactly* what I imagined.

"Oh, Summer, you look amazing," Aspen gushes as we meet on the upstairs landing of the beach house.

"Thank you, love." I reach out affectionately and smooth her long, glossy hair. This exquisite creature is like a daughter to me. "So do you. Is the photographer here yet?"

"Setting up."

"Marvelous."

We link arms and descend the stairs to the main floor. The kitchen is a hub of activity. They've outdone themselves with the food. On a draped cart ready to be wheeled outside is a sumptuous cake in the shape of a warrior's breastplate, ringed with roses the color of my dress and the book title written in calligraphy.

In fact, everything for this glorious launch party is flowery, feminine, and medieval themed, and Francesca has executed all of it flawlessly. And there she is coming toward the house, smiling. As she opens the sliding doors from the patio to step inside, I pause.

"What's that?" I ask, tipping my head toward the faint sound so I can hear better.

"A little surprise. Come." Francesca crooks a finger and leads me back the way she came. Seated at one end of the pool, under strings of hanging lanterns, a trio of musicians is tuning up.

"Oh my God, are those lutes?" I clasp my hands with glee and then fold Francesca into the umpteenth hug of the day. "You are incredible. Have I thanked you yet?"

"About a million times." Under her thick, dark brows, her aquamarine eyes are merry. She steers me past blazing torches, a tower of cupcakes stuck with little gold spears, and a calligraphy-inked sign for the signature drink of the evening, "Summer's Ale," which is served in a keepsake metal goblet.

"No way," I breathe.

Guests begin arriving: Bea and Patrick, with Kevin and James right behind; following soon after are Liisa, Mike, Toni, and Brian. Just shy of fashionably late are Elianna Abrams, Sierra Eastman, and Lilian Arnold, accompanied by Julian Segal and Yvonne Manning. Mila Jorgenson arrives with Ned Townsend, who's holding a giant bouquet of flowers and is flanked by Barry Temple and their team of managers from the publishing house. More people stream out, many I don't know.

The party kicks off. Francesca, Aspen, and I greet guests, make introductions. Tables fill up and the Summer's Ale flows. When the musicians play, the ocean breeze carries the strains of magical, medieval melodies. It couldn't possibly be a more perfect evening, and it's all set like a precious gem against the vast backdrop of the glittering silver sea.

An hour into the party, Ned Townsend taps a microphone for our attention. He's at the far end of the infinity pool beside a table stacked with signed copies of my book. Everyone applauds as I stand there smiling beside him.

"We're here tonight not only to celebrate the launch of a debut novel, but to mark what is sure to be the launch of a new author's incredible career," Ned says. He brandishes a copy of my book. "When I first read *A Knight to Remember*, I was struck by the beauty of a story told in haunting prose." He holds out a hand to me. "I am honored to welcome Summer Branigan to the Temple-Townsend family of talented writers."

My dress swishes as I move to stand in front of the mic and clasp my hands together. For a second I'm so overwhelmed, it's hard to speak.

"Thank you. Thank you. This is a moment I've waited for my whole life. I can't tell you how it feels to finally hold my book! I must acknowledge some special people who made this night a reality. First, my outstanding agent, Mila Jorgenson, who fell in love with Sir Devon and Lady Lisbeth from page one; and Ned Townsend and Barry Temple at Temple-Townsend for believing in me; and all the incredible people in the art department and copy and editing and marketing and PR . . . and Sally Janoff, who optioned the film rights."

I stop for a breath. "To my dear friends and writers—Liisa, Toni, and Mike, and Brian O'Keefe, the best listener ever . . . thank you." Liisa, Toni, Mike, and Brian hoot on cue.

"And a special shout-out to Aspen Barber, who, I am thrilled to announce, has agreed to play the role of Lady Lisbeth!"

Exclamations fill the air. The reporters and bloggers in the crowd turn toward Aspen, thirsty for content. Aspen raises her goblet in a silent toast.

"I can't wait to see Aspen's portrayal of Lisbeth," I continue. "I can't think of a more talented young actress."

And then my eyes alight on Bea. "Tonight and every night, I have to thank my incredible daughter, Beatrice, who I love more than *anything*, and who is a constant source of inspiration to me." Her face is radiant as she blows me a kiss. "I hope I made you proud, Honey Bea. Because nothing in the world makes me prouder than being your mom. I can't wait to see how the next chapter of your life unfolds."

On cue, bartenders pop open bottles of champagne. I hold up a flute.

"Finally, my gratitude goes to Francesca Barber, who not only mentored me during the writing of *A Knight to Remember*, but has been so generous in throwing this gorgeous party. Thank you, Francesca. Everything is just *perfect*."

"Glad you approve." The woman holding the ladle smirks.

I get a shove from behind: Go, already. I'm jarred from my fantasy, and in its place, reality quickly sets in. I am not in the Hamptons—far from it. There will be no party with cupcakes, no lanterns, no keepsake goblet, no lutes. No bubbly. There will be no book launch party for my bestseller, because there will be no book. Once the whole sordid story came out, Temple-Townsend rescinded its offer. Not so much because of the notoriety I'd achieved after the saga went public—that would've helped sales tremendously—but because of our use of artificial intelligence. Mine and Francesca's. What with the traditional publishing world cracking down, we are being made an example to others.

In front of me Francesca picks up her tray and carries it to our table. I follow. For a minute we stare at our lunches, which are the same lunches we get almost every day: two slices of white bread, a piece of unidentifiable processed luncheon meat, some watery gelatin or pudding, and a piece of fruit. Today's meat appears to be bologna, and the fruit is an apple. At least, I think it's an apple; it's so bruised, it's hard to tell. I wonder whether they bring in rotten apples on purpose with the hope they contain worms: extra protein, after all. Generally, the protein we are served comes in the form of beans, which are barely edible. Honestly, I might prefer the worms.

If it's not Meat Sandwich Day, it's likely Cheese Sandwich Day, which comes with the same two slices of white bread but features a square of waxy prewrapped cheese that's shiny enough to see your reflection in.

Today the chefs have opted to forgo the beans and replace them with a scoop of last night's mashed potatoes. They're the powdered kind from a box, and so dried out there's practically dust on them. Francesca is listlessly tracking her fork through the hardened white paste, and I have to laugh.

"What?" she looks up, frowning.

"Remember how much you complained about eating McDonald's? I bet you'd give anything to trade now."

"Don't kid yourself. Anything in the world is better than this slop. Every meal here takes a week off my life. And you might want to ease up on the salt . . . you're not looking so svelte yourself."

Don't I know it. My baggy orange pants aren't nearly as baggy as they were when I came in. And my hair, which was once so artfully layered and highlighted, has all grown out and is pretty much back to what it used to be.

At least it's not just me. The midday light from the caged window is hitting Francesca's crown of gray roots dead-on.

Clearly she can read my mind by now, and dips an index finger into her mashed potatoes and smears it on top of my head. "Huh."

She sniffs. "A perfect match. I think L'Oréal makes this color: Dirty Dishwater Beige."

"You didn't." It's all I can do to hold back from letting fly with a spoonful of JELL-O that would land right in her face, to wiggle and jiggle on her nose before sliding off and landing on her orange sweatshirt. "You get your AARP card yet, Granny?" I joke instead.

Francesca sucks in her breath sharply. For a moment she is frozen. And then she lets out a shriek.

One of these days she'll spring into action. She'll stand up and reach across the table with both hands, and before you know it, we'll be pulling each other's hair and clawing each other's faces. The other inmates will circle around to goad us on. Our world will be reduced to the gnashing of teeth and the ripping of skin. We'll grunt and hiss, wild animals who want our pound of flesh.

But before any of it can happen, the surly guard steps over to our table with a warning and sends us back to our cells.

"Way to go, *Marcy*," Francesca mutters as she flops onto her bed. Her tone is derisive. Sometimes she still forgets and calls me Summer, but I correct her. I'm Marcy.

I hear the springs protest under her thin mattress from the other side of the wall that separates our cells. "Wasn't my fault."

"This whole thing is your fault. How far back are we going? I seem to remember it's *all* your fault."

"I can go *way* back, actually. First you copied my characters. And I was a complete stranger when you made me witness that disgusting scene of you hooking up with your son-in-law."

"No one invited you to watch. But you sure as hell could've shut your mouth about it."

"I never said anything to anyone, because you *begged* me not to tell . . . and then sealed the deal by offering to help me with my manuscript."

"You call that thing a manuscript? I thought you fished it out of the hotel garbage bin. It wasn't even recognizable English until I fixed it."

"You mean your *computer program* fixed it."

"Whatever. You didn't object too hard when it came to using AI at the cabin."

"I just wanted it done so I could wash my hands of *you*."

"Oh, *puh-leez*. You wanted fame and fortune and you were willing to do anything to get it. Including blackmail, kidnapping, hmm, what was the other charge?"

I purse my lips. "You know damn well what it was." Forcible confinement.

"Too bad we're not living in medieval days. I would've cut off your tongue for blabbing to the authorities."

"I had to confess what happened. It was the right thing to do." I glare at the wall that separates our cells. "Anyway, with or without me, the police would've pieced it all together. I mean, who wraps a body in a shower curtain and garment bag and weighs it down with hardback copies of her own books? No wonder he washed up on shore."

"You're such a bi-otch."

Our lobbing of grenades, back and forth from opposite sides of the wall, goes on and on like always. As the other women file back from lunch, the groans of "Not again!" and "Shut up already!" can be heard up and down the corridor.

Then Aspen appears in front of our cells, and we shut up.

"Guess what I heard." She smiles sweetly at me. It's ridiculous how she can manage to look so pretty in an orange jumpsuit. "Margot Robbie's been cast as the lead in that new spy thriller they're filming. I hear she has a great Russian accent and she does her own stunts. That's the script based on the bestselling book by Liisa Oja, isn't it? I would've been perfect for that part, don't you think? I would've won an Academy Award for sure."

I'm trying to tune her out, as she's already rubbed it in three or four times.

She examines her long nails as she turns toward Francesca and continues: "Although, if you ask me, playing the part of Mrs. Tabi Benlolo should've won me Best Actress. The way I gazed up at him, all starry-eyed, and pawed him every chance I could? No one could've guessed how nauseous I felt every time I kissed him. He was so *hairy*. All that time I stayed in character, when no one else—not Shailene or Saoirse or Zendaya, not Millie Bobby Brown, no one—could have. The problem was Tabi wouldn't stay in character, would he? No . . . he didn't care if the world found out he was in love with *you*. But then, when they found his body? And I played the part of the grieving widow? IMHO I was absolutely sensational. My fans just ate it up.

"Anyway, my lawyer says he's making real headway with an appeal. I really thought that his temporary insanity defense based on—how did he put it?—'mental defect as a result of years of abuse' was brilliant. I can't believe the jury didn't go for it, even when you admitted to all the years you abused me as a child, Mama. Anyway, if we win the appeal, I'll need you to sign over the title to the Hamptons house, the Upper East Side penthouse, the place in the Hollywood Hills, the chalet in Saint Moritz . . . whatever Tabi's family doesn't get in the civil suit. You would do that for me, wouldn't you, Mama? It would make me a very happy girlie."

She's jostled by other prisoners returning from lunch. The surly guard, the one from the cafeteria, appears in the corridor and tells her to move along, back to her cell.

I'm told I have a visitor. I'm escorted to the designated visiting room, where husbands, boyfriends, girlfriends, and children come to spend a few hours with us inmates.

My gaze immediately settles on a young woman with a high, thick ponytail, and bright hazel eyes. My girl. My Bumble Bea. I want to wrap her in an endless embrace, but we're allowed only the briefest hug before we sit down across from each other.

"Sweetheart, what are you doing here? Is everything all right?"

"Everything's fine."

"You look beautiful."

"Thanks. You look great, too."

I know it's not true, but I don't waste time arguing. It's been months since I've laid eyes on her face. I can't stop beaming.

She leans forward. "I wanted to tell you in person instead of on the phone. I moved back from Savannah."

"You *did*? With Patrick?"

She shrugs lightly. "Nope. Things didn't work out. We broke up."

"I'm sorry," I say, and I am.

"It's okay. It wasn't meant to be. I guess you could say we were bleach and ammonia. We didn't belong together. Or maybe I like steak fajitas too much? Either way, he was a little too pretentious for me. But . . . I think you'll be relieved to hear I'm starting grad school next semester. And before you say anything, don't worry about the tuition. I can take out loans like everyone else."

"There's a little left from the sale of the house." Which I sold to pay for my legal bills.

"I'll figure it out."

"I'm sorry," I say again, and this time I mean it in a much, much broader sense. She understands.

"Maybe you'll be free by the time I graduate, in a cap and gown."

"Maybe."

"Are you okay? Like, safe and . . . okay?"

"I'm fine. And I just want you to know that whatever you decided—whether you stayed down south with Patrick, went back to school or not, whatever—it would've been the right decision for you. And I'm so proud."

Beatrice looks around at the other tables of us orange-clad women, the wives and mothers, sisters and daughters, all of us living with the choices we made.

"I know you are, Mom."

Yes, we women go to the ends of the earth for our loved ones. We sacrifice our youth, our bodies, our dreams.

And sometimes, as in the case of Francesca Barber, we sacrifice our freedom. Because, as I saw with my very own eyes, Aspen didn't need any help to kill Tabi Benlolo. She just expected Francesca to tie up the loose ends and take the blame. And Francesca tried. She really tried. And I think she'll keep trying forever.

EPILOGUE

Francesca and I have an unexpected visitor this morning.

A guard buzzes us into the visiting room. We stand at the doorway and exchange confused glances. We have our own attorneys handling separate legal cases. The media attention on us faded away a long time ago, and the reporters who used to come sniffing around have long since lost interest. Besides my daughter, who sees me alone, and Kevin, who showed up once, no one else ever comes. Who would want to meet us both, together?

We glance around the crowded, noisy room and spot her at the same moment . . . a mousy woman with close-cropped hair and Coke-bottle glasses, waiting patiently at a table, alone.

Mila Jorgenson.

"There's no law against it," Francesca says from her mattress on the other side of the wall.

"You're absolutely right about that."

"And we have lots of time on our hands."

"So true."

"It would be a nice distraction."

"Definitely."

"Can you imagine if we succeeded . . . ?"

"Oh, I can imagine."

We're on the same page (pardon my literary pun). Francesca and I fall into companiable silence while all around us convicts clang on their bars, call out to the guards, clamor for attention. We're lost in our own thoughts, in our little bubble.

Mila Jorgenson has a proposition. She wants us to coauthor a book, if you will, about our joint experience (another pun). She thinks we should ride the true crime wave, that readers worldwide will devour the story behind the headlines: of the sordid affair between Francesca Barber and her son-in-law; the chance encounter between Francesca and me; our agreement to exchange my silence for her help with my historical romance; my scheme to blackmail and then kidnap her; and, ultimately, the death and disappearance of Tabi Benlolo.

Of course, there's a caveat: We're absolutely forbidden from using AI. Even if our written word turns out to be less than optimal, Mila can assign heavy editing afterward.

She already has a working title in mind for the story of our pact: She wants to call it *A Novel Crime*.

She thinks it could be a blockbuster.

We're already visualizing it. The acclaim, the movie rights, the fortune to be made.

All we have to do is write the manuscript . . . assuming we don't kill each other in the process.

Acknowledgments

The first iteration of this book wrote itself quickly (quickly for me, anyway). In just a few months, back in 2023, I churned out 90 percent of the manuscript; then, suddenly, I found it tough to write in general, and *this* story especially hard to navigate.

It wouldn't be in your hands today were it not for an army of supporters.

To Sarah Bedingfield, the most spectacular agent, thank you for inviting me into your home at Levine Greenberg Rostan Literary Agency. So much gratitude to you and Rebecca Rodd for shepherding my words into print.

To Megha Parekh at Thomas & Mercer, who is simply magnificent, and the whole Amazon Publishing family, including my keenly insightful editors Selina McLemore and James Gallagher, proofreader Sarah Engel, cold reader Jessica Poore, production manager Miranda Gardner, cover designer Kimberly Glyder (such gorgeous artwork!), and Andrew George in marketing. I am beyond thrilled to work with you. What a privilege! Thank you all.

Author friends, you are a fantastic part of this gig! For all your early reading and advice along the way, my heartfelt thanks to Gregg Hurwitz, May Cobb, Samantha M. Bailey, James L'Etoile, Luca DiMatteo, Elise Hart Kipness, Tessa Wegert, Greg Wands, Elizabeth McCullough Keenan, Des Ryan, Charles S. Weinblatt, Ox Devere, all my sisters (and brothers) at the Connecticut chapter of Sisters in Crime, and my old and new buddies from ThrillerFest and Bouchercon. Love and gratitude to my dear friends and the better "thirds" of our Crime Trio, Wendy Whitman and T. M. Dunn.

To Patrick O'Donnell, thank you for sharing your wealth of law enforcement experience. To Marlene Fischer at William Raveis Real Estate, and to Ray Martin of the Martin Agency, thanks for your real estate savvy. To Atty. Adam Federer, another thanks for your help with criminal law. (Next time I reach out to you for legal advice, don't worry . . . it's for a character, not me. Hopefully.)

Many thanks also to Harold Rosnick, president of Chick Rosnick Boxing Club, Inc., and Dr. Jim White, chairman, president, and CEO of Post Harvest Technologies, Inc., for your patience during the writing and releasing of this novel.

To my family: Mama Vera, the best one in the world; hubby Craigie and my favorite children in all the universe, Jordyn, Jake, and Coby (and now, of course, Adam), who inspire me more each day; Peter and the Vadas gang; Bubbelainey, Benny, and the whole Levison clan; and everyone at Federitaville, I love you *so* much. (And special thanks to my fam for brainstorming titles, and to Coby, whose idea hit!) I would be remiss if I didn't acknowledge Moose and Gigi for keeping me company as I tapped away on the computer for endless hours.

To my beautiful community of lions and lionesses, everyone from R4TL and TGIS1 to MyLadies, MyGreeks, MarLiRoDe, The Mish Mish, EJT, WW, and Choir Girl: Here, in Toronto, and abroad, both IRL (in real life) and online, you have helped keep me sane in a world turned upside down. May we go from strength to strength.

And to all the incredible bookish folk—booksellers, librarians, bookstagrammers, reviewers, podcasters, bloggers, and, of course, readers wherever you are, whoever you are, whenever you are—thank you for sharing this story.

About the Author

Photo © Regina Madwed, Capitol Photo

Deborah Levison is the award-winning author of the novel *A Nest of Snakes* and the true crime book *The Crate*. Her life has two parts: the first in Canada, where she attended the Royal Conservatory of Music and the University of Toronto, and the second in Connecticut with three children, two doodles, and one husband. Her love of storytelling began one summer night by a camp bonfire, listening to the ghost story "The Monkey's Paw." The memory still makes her shiver. Visit her at www.debbielevison.com. She loves connecting with readers!